P9-BYR-552

Acclaim for David Guterson's

ED KING

"Compulsively readable and witheringly funny. Guterson's narrative voice—by turns savage and sad, amused and outraged—becomes a kind of Greek chorus of one.... [Will] keep even the most ardent classicist entertained."
—*The Seattle Times*

"Guterson succeeds in recasting one of literature's most haunted and vaunted tales as a plausible page-turner.... Compelling."
—*USA Today*

"Old stories survived millennia because they tell us about the human condition. Brave writers like Guterson can renew them."
—*The Oregonian*

"Daring.... Guterson keeps [*Ed King*] winningly good-natured and almost farcical, all the better to teach timeless lessons about hubris, ambition, and the consequences of long-ago sins."
—*O, The Oprah Magazine*

"Guterson takes the reader through a rollicking half-century of American hubris and gluttony."
—*The New York Times*

"A tragic and darkly funny modern myth in an omnipotent, wry voice reminiscent of Philip Roth.... The Greeks weren't afraid to take on God, and neither is Guterson.... A master storyteller."
—*Bookreporter*

"Guterson has managed to infuse this novel with feelings of freshness, relevance and even believability that are sure to delight twenty-first-century readers. A special pleasure will be experienced by those who can appreciate how the old elements have been modernized. Oedipus may not have been Guterson's to begin with, but by the end, readers will have no doubts that *Ed King* is a creation entirely his own."
—*BookPage*

"[Guterson's] portraits of humanity are real, and exceedingly enjoyable to read."   —*San Francisco Chronicle*

"A great story and a riveting read."   —*Daily Mail* (London)

"Sharply written."   —*The Guardian* (London)

"David Guterson . . . retells one of the oldest stories we know in a way that makes you hang on every twist and turn. . . . A largely entertaining book that should add to Guterson's already glittering reputation."
                              —*The Free Lance-Star* (Fredericksburg, VA)

"[*Ed King*] has original characters, a race to discover the truth as gripping as the denouement of Daphne Du Maurier's *Rebecca*, and some insights into human relationships so sharp that they make a reader cringe."   —*The New York Journal of Books*

DAVID GUTERSON

ED KING

David Guterson is the author of the novels *East of the Mountains, The Other, Our Lady of the Forest,* and *Snow Falling on Cedars,* which won the PEN/Faulkner Award, as well as a story collection, *The Country Ahead of Us, the Country Behind,* and *Family Matters: Why Homeschooling Makes Sense.* He lives in Washington State.

ED KING

ED KING

A novel

DAVID GUTERSON

Vintage Contemporaries
Vintage Books
A Division of Random House, Inc.
New York

FIRST VINTAGE CONTEMPORARIES EDITION, JULY 2012

Copyright © 2011 by David Guterson

All rights reserved. Published in the United States by Vintage Books, a division of Random House, Inc., New York, and in Canada by Random House of Canada, Limited, Toronto. Originally published in hardcover in the United States by Alfred A. Knopf, a division of Random House, Inc., New York, in 2011.

Vintage is a registered trademark and Vintage Contemporaries and colophon are trademarks of Random House, Inc.

This is a work of fiction. Names, characters, places, and incidents either are the product of the author's imagination or are used fictitiously. Any resemblance to actual persons, living or dead, events, or locales is entirely coincidental.

Grateful acknowledgment is made to the following for permission to reprint previously published material:

Alfred Music Publishing Co. Inc.: Excerpt from "Do You Remember Walter?" words and music by Raymond Douglas Davies, copyright © 1969, copyright renewed by Davray Music Ltd. and ABKCO Music Inc., 85 Fifth Avenue, New York, NY 10003. All rights on behalf of Davray Music Ltd. administered by Unichappell Music Inc. All rights reserved. Reprinted by permission of Alfred Music Publishing Co. Inc.
Hal Leonard Corporation: Excerpt from "Killer Queen," words and music by Freddie Mercury, copyright © 1974, copyright renewed 2002 by Queen Music Ltd. All rights for the United States and Canada controlled and administered by Glenwood Music Corp. All rights for the world excluding the United States and Canada controlled and administered by EMI Music Publishing Ltd. All rights reserved. International copyright secured. Reprinted by permission of Hal Leonard Corporation.

The math problems referred to in Chapter 6 have been culled from Gordon Raisbeck's *Information Theory* and from David Harel's *Algorithmics: The Spirit of Computing*.

The Library of Congress has cataloged the Knopf edition as follows:
Guterson, David.
Ed King : a novel / David Guterson.
p. cm.
1. Orphans—Fiction. 2. Free will and determination—Fiction. 3. Fate and fatalism—Fiction. 4. Millionaires—Fiction. 5. Psychological fiction. I. Title.
PS3557.U846E33 2011
813'.54—dc22   2011010255

Vintage ISBN: 978-0-307-45590-1

Book design by Virginia Tan

www.vintagebooks.com

Printed in the United States
10 9 8 7 6 5 4 3 2 1

ED KING

A novel

DAVID GUTERSON

Vintage Contemporaries
Vintage Books
A Division of Random House, Inc.
New York

FIRST VINTAGE CONTEMPORARIES EDITION, JULY 2012

Copyright © 2011 by David Guterson

All rights reserved. Published in the United States by Vintage Books, a division of
Random House, Inc., New York, and in Canada by Random House of Canada, Limited,
Toronto. Originally published in hardcover in the United States by Alfred A. Knopf,
a division of Random House, Inc., New York, in 2011.

Vintage is a registered trademark and Vintage Contemporaries and colophon are
trademarks of Random House, Inc.

This is a work of fiction. Names, characters, places, and incidents either are the product of
the author's imagination or are used fictitiously. Any resemblance to actual persons, living
or dead, events, or locales is entirely coincidental.

Grateful acknowledgment is made to the following for permission to reprint previously
published material:

Alfred Music Publishing Co. Inc.: Excerpt from "Do You Remember Walter?" words and
music by Raymond Douglas Davies, copyright © 1969, copyright renewed by Davray
Music Ltd. and ABKCO Music Inc., 85 Fifth Avenue, New York, NY 10003. All rights on
behalf of Davray Music Ltd. administered by Unichappell Music Inc. All rights reserved.
Reprinted by permission of Alfred Music Publishing Co. Inc.
Hal Leonard Corporation: Excerpt from "Killer Queen," words and music by Freddie
Mercury, copyright © 1974, copyright renewed 2002 by Queen Music Ltd. All rights for the
United States and Canada controlled and administered by Glenwood Music Corp.
All rights for the world excluding the United States and Canada controlled and
administered by EMI Music Publishing Ltd. All rights reserved. International
copyright secured. Reprinted by permission of Hal Leonard Corporation.

The math problems referred to in Chapter 6 have been culled from Gordon Raisbeck's
Information Theory and from David Harel's *Algorithmics: The Spirit of Computing*.

The Library of Congress has cataloged the Knopf edition as follows:
Guterson, David.
Ed King : a novel / David Guterson.
p. cm.
1. Orphans—Fiction. 2. Free will and determination—Fiction. 3. Fate and
fatalism—Fiction. 4. Millionaires—Fiction. 5. Psychological fiction. I. Title.
PS3557.U846E33 2011
813'.54—dc22   2011010255

Vintage ISBN: 978-0-307-45590-1

Book design by Virginia Tan

www.vintagebooks.com

Printed in the United States
10 9 8 7 6 5 4 3 2 1

Half sunk, a shattered visage lies, whose frown,
And wrinkled lip, and sneer of cold command,
Tell that its sculptor well those passions read
Which yet survive, stamped on these lifeless things,
The hand that mocked them, and the heart that fed.

—from Shelley's "Ozymandias"

Far off, far down, some fisherman is watching
As the rod dips and trembles over the water,
Some shepherd rests his weight upon his crook,
Some ploughman on the handles of the ploughshare,
And all look up, in absolute amazement,
At those air-borne above. They must be gods!

—from Ovid's *Metamorphoses*,
Book 8, "Daedalus and Icarus"

ED KING

Prologue

From KingWatch, twelve days post-crash:

7:47 A.M. EST BREAKING NEWS:

Ed King's flight data recorder recovered.
No evidence of mechanical failure.
Aircraft altitude at apex of flight: 54,500 feet.
Aircraft flight ceiling (manufacturer's recommended maximum
    elevation): 51,000 feet.

Comments? (20 words or less)

KingCrank: Might have guessed it: King flew too high. Rule out mechanical failure. This was pilot error.

grizpilot: I'm a pilot and can tell you—there's no defeating physics. Must have believed he was God.

pythiamist: What a coincidence. King goes down, queen disappears. Where do you get pilot error?

rudewakeup: Of course the conspiracy theorists tab queen as culprit. Oldest story in the world.

techtrappist: She's dead, too. They've both been offed. By us or the Chinese. Take your pick.

candydark: Queen survives. Even thrives. I say so in no uncertain terms. techtrappist—you're wrong. She goes on.

pythiamist: I agree w/ candydark. Queen told her pilot to cruise to Carlisle without her. Then disappeared. She had a plan.

techtrappist: And what was that? Walk away from billions? Give me a break, pythiamist. She's dead.

candydark: You must be a male, techtrappist. I smell dead-wrong male certainty every time you hit your Send key.

FiNancy: Speaking of walking away from billions, wish I'd run, not walked, from their stock 12 days back!!!

KingCrank: Pythia's toast.

FiNancy: I agree: history.

shanghairoller: Deal with it, folks. Just deal with the facts. Pythia's not coming back.

1

The Affair with the Au Pair

In 1962, Walter Cousins made the biggest mistake of his life: he slept with the au pair for a month. She was an English exchange student named Diane Burroughs, and he was an actuary at Piersall-Crane, Inc., whose wife had suffered a nervous breakdown that summer. Diane had been in his house for less than a week—mothering his kids, cleaning, making meals—when he noticed a new word intruding on his assessment of her. "Here I am," thought Walter, "an actuary, a guy who weighs risk for a living, and now, because I'm infatuated with the wrong person—because I'm smitten by an eighteen-year-old—I'm using the word 'fate.'"

Diane had been peddled to Walter, by an office temp familiar with her current host family, as "a nice girl from the U.K. who needs work to extend her visa." Walter, who at thirty-four had never left North America, thought "au pair" sounded pretentious—"You mean babysitter," he told the temp. Immediately regretting his provincialism, he added, "I could also go with 'nanny.'" The temp's comeback was sharp. She was younger than he was, wore formidable boots, and had an air of immunity to an office flirt like Walter. "No, definitely, it's 'au pair,'" she said. "She's here on a visa. She's from out of the country. If you take her on, you become her host father, and you give her an allowance for whatever she does for you—child care or housework or whatever."

"Au pair" it was, then. Walter took down the phone number, called Diane's host mother, then spoke to the girl herself. In no position to be picky—he needed help yesterday—he hired Diane on the telephone. "This is hard to explain," he explained, "but my wife's . . . hospitalized."

Back came the sort of English inflections he couldn't help but be charmed by. "In hospital," she said. "I do hope it isn't serious."

"No," he said, "but meanwhile there's the kids. Four and three. Barry and Tina. Out of diapers, but still, they're tricky to corral."

"Then allow me just a smidgen of shameful self-promotion. What you need is an English au pair, sir, adept with a rodeo rope."

"I think you mean lasso."

"A lass with a lasso, then, for when they're mucking about starkers."

"That's what I need. Something like that."

"Well," said Diane, "I'm your girl."

This flagrantly forward use of language—neat, cunning phrases and breezy repartee—from the mouth of a high-school girl jockeying for work was new in his American ear. Diane sounded quick-witted and cheerfully combative—qualities he'd always found winning and attractive—as in her screed on the U.S. State Department and its byzantine visa require-ments. "I'm still keen to go to college in America," she told him, "but at the moment I'm furious with your Seattle passport office. They're trying, actually, to throw me out."

The next Sunday, with his kids complaining in the back seat of his Lincoln Premiere, Walter went to escort this girl from her host family's large Victorian near Seward Park to his brick-veneered ranch house in Greenwood. He hoped Diane wouldn't be too disappointed to discover she was moving down in the world, and as he parked on the cobbles fronting the Victorian, he imagined himself apologizing for having noth-ing to offer in the way of gilding or ambience. Seward Park, after all, dripped old money and featured lake views; Greenwood, by contrast, was dowdy and decrepit, with summer-arid grass patches and sagging gut-ters. Walter, of course, would have liked a better neighborhood, but his was a notoriously mid-wage profession, a fact he hadn't reckoned with at Iowa State but was reckoning with now, too late. Not that it was bad at Piersall-Crane, where he held down a cubicle by a window. Walter took certain consolations there—in collegial hobnobbing, in crisply dressed women, and, not least, in the higher realms of actuarial science. That the predictive power of numbers on a large scale could be brought to bear on future events—for Walter, that was like an esoteric secret and, as he put it to himself, sort of mystical. Okay, it wasn't art or philosophy, but it was still deep, which almost no one understood.

When he first saw her, the au pair struck him as nowhere close to legal. She looked like a child, unfinished, a sprout—no hairdo or makeup, no jewelry, unadorned—she looked like the younger sister of a girl he'd dated long ago, in high school. Her abraded leather suitcases, strapped and buckled, and riddled with tarnished rivets that looked shot from a machine gun—a matched set, though one was a junior version of the other—waited for Walter on the porch. Propped on the clasp of the larger one was a transistor radio with an ivory plastic strap and ivory knobs. Feeling like a porter—but also like a honeymooner—he hauled her overstuffed luggage to the Lincoln's trunk while Diane, in dungarees, doled out last-minute hugs and delivered farewells in her disarming accent. "Lovely," he heard her say. "Perfect." Then he held the car door wide for her, and when she turned, brightly, to greet his kids in the back seat, he looked, surreptitiously, down the gap that opened between the rear waist of her dungarees and the nether regions of her back, at the shadow there, the practical white undies, and the reddish down along her tailbone.

It was so—you never knew; you couldn't predict. Not even an actuary knew what would happen —there were broad trends, of course, which he could express in tables, but individual destinies were always nebulous. In Walter's case, this meant his wife was out of the house while he, against the odds, on a fair summer morning, was collecting up this enticing piece of luck to install in the bedroom across the hall from his. How had this dangerous but fortuitous thing happened? What had he done to deserve this risk? With these questions and her underwear in mind, he chose, as his route, Lake Washington Boulevard; there might be an intangible benefit in such a sinuous and scenic drive. He also decided to take all three kids to the booming, newly opened Seattle World's Fair, because there he could function like a grandee, bestowing cotton candy and other largesse, before introducing Diane to Greenwood. With this plan in mind, he motored past pleasure craft and horse chestnut trees while, on the passenger side, hands twined in her lap, Diane answered questions, ingratiated herself skillfully and easily with his offspring, and brought to his mind the pert and perfect Hayley Mills, that upbeat, full-lipped, earnest starlet who, on the cover of *Life* in a sailor outfit, had puckered, naughtily, for a kiss. In fact, as Diane chatted up his children in lilting tones but with a teasing irony that, over their heads, might be aimed at him, she was a drop-dead ringer for the sixteen-year-old Disney darling who'd been in newspapers and magazines lately for turning down the lead role in *Lolita*. A morsel, a nymphet, in frilly socks and Keds, a junior-high date—the beach walk, for sodas—and at the kind of youthful sexual crest that even a four-year-old could sense. Sure enough, Barry, with a four-year-old's primal yearning, leaned over the front seat and settled his head on his hands, like a cherub posed for a Christmas portrait, the better to bask in Diane's nubile aura. Flicking two fingers against his bony shoulder, the object of his son's newly stirred affections chirped, as if on cue, "I love your name, Barry, really I do. And 'Tina,'" she added, "is so lovely." After that, she shot Walter a look, and winked as though he, her new employer, were instead her intimate chauffeur.

"You truly have great names," he tossed out.

"Tip-top, the best, brilliant."

"Barry and Tina: it's genius, it's beautiful."

Diane, and then Walter, laughed.

And she laughed an hour later—the same truncated notes, issued through her nose and throat—when, on the mammothly rising Space Wheel, they all rocked precariously in the apex tub, ninety feet above the mania of the fairgrounds. She laughed because, taking hold of the lap bar, he'd muscled them into rocking harder while Tina put up conflicted resistance ("Daddy!") and Barry applied a grit-filled assist. "Beastly!" hissed Diane, pulling Tina toward her. "Never mind such recklessness, love—he's only toying with your dear, precious life."

"But Tina absolutely adores danger. Don't you, 'luv'?"

To this his daughter had a one-word reply, delivered while clutching the au pair's stellar thighs: "Diane."

On the fairgrounds, Walter followed Diane like a dog, so he could admire how she wore those dungarees. There were a lot of bare-armed dresses on the midway, and peppermint tops, and circus stripes, but nothing that could beat Diane in dungarees. Nothing could beat Diane's tilting ponytail when she lifted her chin to pack in wads of cotton candy; nothing could beat her in the Fine Arts Pavilion with her lovely little hands at the small of her back, leaning toward a painting called *Oedipus and the Sphinx*. Barry stood beside her with his head on her hip, and Walter stood alongside with Tina in his arms. The odd and slightly uncomfortable thing was that Oedipus had been painted monumentally naked—two spears, points down, beside one foot—while the Sphinx, half in darkness, winged and severe, pointed her bare breasts, from startling close range, at his face. "Ace," said Diane, examining it. "I must say I like that running fellow in the corner. He's quite active—he fixes Oedipus to the canvas. It's arresting, so to speak, wouldn't you say?"

Walter nodded as if he knew what she was talking about, then set Tina down and crossed his arms, the better to brood on art.

"Look how he's brushed in the shadows of the cave," Diane said. "Look how the sun plays in those rocks, lower left."

Did he read her correctly? Was he getting her signals? Because it seemed to Walter she was skirting the obvious— the nudity two feet in front of their faces—so as to give them both a chance to linger. She seemed, at the moment—if he wasn't mistaken—a prick tease of the precocious-teen brand. He was confident that the point she meant for him to take was, As long as neither of us mentions nudity, we can go on standing here, looking at pornography together.

"Personally, for me, it's the blue sky," he said. "That amazing blue sky in the background."

Again her truncated laugh, as at an inside joke, which he was now laboring to solicit at every turn.

They went to examine the World of Tomorrow. The line for this exhibit was long and hot, but eventually they found themselves inside the Bubbleator with 150 other agitated fairgoers, ascending, as if inside a soap bubble, toward "The Threshold and the Threat." "The Threshold and the Threat" had been highlighted in press reports as a thought-provoking and instructional tour-de-force—Walter thought that sounded good for the kids—and was billed in the fair's extensive guide as "a 21-minute tour of the future." Yet, after a half-minute of ominously slow rising to a soundtrack called—Walter knew this from the guide—"Man in Space with Sounds," the Bubbleator arrived not in the future but underneath a strangely lit semblance of the night sky. Stars and planets were projected onto distorted cubes, or onto something like magnified cells in a beehive. What was this, anyway? Why had they been lifted to this surreal destination? Tina clung anxiously to his pant leg, and Barry looked frightened and aghast. In contrast, the new au pair only stretched her back, pointing her girlish breasts at the faux heavens. Then she dropped them, and joined him and the kids as they huddled together like an abducted family in the bowels of a B-movie spaceship. Everyone had to endure more "Man in Space with Sounds"—alarms, theremin wails, inharmonious strings and brass, much of it familiar to Walter as the sort of thing that backed Vincent Price—until, cast in celluloid on the weirdly curving cubes, a frightened family crouched in a fallout shelter. This was too much for Tina, who covered her eyes. Walter wondered who at the World's Fair had given the green light to "The Threshold and the Threat," because, whatever else it was—besides some pointy-headed goofball's dark view of the future—it was also, in his view, wrong. Subliminal, demonic, scarring, you name it, but best summed up as *wrong*. "We should have been told before we got in line," he thought angrily. "Somebody should have warned us."

And now, on the cubes, came one image atop another, kaleidoscopic, fleeting, discombobulating, dissociative—jetports, monorails, the Acropolis, a mushroom cloud—before, again, that pathetic cellared family, this time with JFK exhorting them, and all other Americans, in his Boston-brahmin brogue, to build a brighter world through technology.

The hallucinatory journey through apocalypse ended, and Diane said only, "That was fab."

"That was a nightmare," countered Walter. "Let's get out of here."

Outside, he felt reassured by the real world, and so, clearly, did his kids. They all breathed happily the June carnival air, pregnant as it was with cooking grease and promise. In the Food Pavilion, it was Orange Juliuses all around—the kids and Diane sucking away at jointed double straws while he, having bolted his Extra Large, ate a corn dog. Just let it happen, he told himself when Tina implored him for a Belgian waffle— be carefree and magnanimous, stay with the pointed humor ("How about the Girls of the Galaxy exhibit?"), and tease them all often, with easy tenderness. There were solid points to be earned, he felt sure, by riding the fine line between paternalism and friendship, between daddy and a nice guy with cash.

"Girls of the Galaxy?" Diane asked.

"According to the fair guide, they pose naked for Polaroids."

"Including Earth girls?"

"Especially Earth girls."

"That wouldn't do in England. Not at all."

Walter shrugged as if Girls of the Galaxy was just old hat in his world. "My, what do you call it, bonny lass," he said, "you're not in England anymore."

Diane separated her lips from her straws. "*Bonny*'s Scottish," she said, looking into her drink. "In England, you might try *stunning*."

"Stunning, then."

"Or *comely* would do—I would accept that."

They moved along until the kids got tired. It was time to go home, but, because he wanted to—it was the only thing he was really interested in at the fair—they visited the World of Science building and its Probability Exhibit. Here, in a glass box, thousands of pennies dropped mechanically down a chute and were shunted thereafter past equidistant dividers so as to demonstrate the inexorability of a bell curve. As the coins fell in essential randomness, they inevitably built up a standard normal distribution ("A Gaussian distribution," he told the kids and Diane), which never varied and was a fixed law of nature; the pennies made a perfectly symmetrical hill, the formation of which could be relied on. He admired this so much he got effusive about it and explained, to Diane, what a bell curve was, and in language he hoped didn't sound too actuarial delineated the "central limit theorem" associated with what they were witnessing. "Put it this way," he said, moving closer to her. "The sum of variables at work among those pennies follows a unique attractor distribution."

"How interesting," she shot back, mirthful at his expense, and mimicking his enthusiasm while flipping her ponytail absentmindedly. "An attractor distribution."

They were now six hours into their relationship, and already it was more than he could take.

Walter had needed no more than a year of marriage to get to where he'd felt the odds were decent that he could predict what his wife, Lydia, would say. When the McGuire Sisters were on *Ed Sullivan:* "Phyllis has gained weight"; when he asked what she needed from the A&P: "Nothing"; when he kissed her in the bathroom: "I have to get dressed now"; when he said "Good night": "I hope so." Walter was pretty certain he could see inside her brain, so he was caught off guard one Monday morning when he was unable to rouse Lydia. It unfolded that she needed hospitalization following an overdose of prescription sleeping pills he hadn't even known she'd been taking. A psychiatrist said she must now have complete rest from household responsibilities and duties.

It shocked Walter to see Lydia in a hospital gown, haggard, without makeup, without stockings, bereft of dignity, but there was nothing to be done about it, or at least nothing *he* could do. She was in the hands of head doctors at this stage, who put her, he thought, through strange paces. She scribbled pictures, modeled with clay, attended daily "group sessions," and played shuffleboard. On his visits to the ward, Walter felt out of her loop, estranged not just by virtue of her mental illness but by virtue of her therapy. He went daily, and always found her the same— drugged and incapable of speaking intimately or of explaining her problems to him. She wasn't a zombie, but she wasn't *there,* either, and he couldn't figure out how to act around her or what her illness portended. Nor could he trace her demise backward in time to how, and why, it had happened. Out of nowhere she'd simply gone off the deep end—Lydia, who'd long been steady and forthright; Lydia, who'd taken him into her arms in the middle of the three and a half Chicago years he'd enjoyed after Iowa State. He'd thought of her, in that era, as a poor man's Sabrina—Sabrina if half Norwegian, Midwestern, and plain-speaking— because she looked so much like the sensationally built British pinup who'd consorted with Fidel Castro. He'd married her eagerly. Then she got pregnant, and her cheesecake magnetism evaporated, never to return. Since Barry's birth, she'd struggled with weight gain in a way that drove both of them to the brink. Lydia was always riding the diet roller-coaster, up and down, up and down, which would have been all right with Walter if she didn't have to talk about it so much. He felt bad about his irritation when she brought up calories, but she'd become obsessed to the point of having no subject other than food. So what if she was too broad in the beam to make it as a calendar girl—was that any reason to starve yourself? After all, he'd gained weight, too, but was *he* going crazy about it? Didn't she know that he loved her despite her weight problem?

On she went, looking sadly in the mirror, counting calories, and buying new clothes. Lydia was so concerned about the heft of her behind, its geometry and sag, its silhouette in skirts and pants, that sometimes, in the wee hours, she jarred him from dreams because she was performing "clenches" in bed and the box spring was quaking under him from the stress of her exertions. The first time this happened he'd teased her about it, but before too long, it was troubling.

Now she was in a mental hospital, which he should have seen on the horizon. She'd been worn down by domesticity, by multiple sinks, kids, shopping lists, and dirty underwear in the hamper. That was Walter's theory, anyway. He thought that Lydia was resisting domesticity after four years of French with a minor in history, and two more as a good-looking single woman in Chicago with friends, dates, a downtown job, and a series—probably—of boyfriends. That made sense. After all, there were girls he missed and longed for. There were days when he didn't want to be who he was or do what he was doing, at home or at the office. So who could blame Lydia for going off the deep end? He himself could go off the deep end. For now, though, the main thing was, Lydia's illness was an all-out crisis. Lydia had left him juggling all the pins. It wasn't her fault, but the pins were in the air, and Walter only had two hands.

And that made the au pair, Diane Burroughs, a godsend. At just the right moment this dazzling girl, brimming with pluck and perpetual good humor, domestically energetic, chipper, and playful, had landed on Walter's doorstep. What a miracle! Here was this pretty young Brit in an apron, fixing wholesome meals, making up beds, and ironing, with charm, while listening to banal pop music. Walter didn't really know anything about her, but he wanted to know everything, right away. It was like his crushes in junior high—he felt a stomach-churning need to make on-the-prowl headway despite overwhelming trepidation. And so, when it seemed safe, he snooped among her things, starting in the bathroom she shared with the kids, where he pondered, alongside Lustre-Creme Shampoo and Junior Pursette tampons, a jar of coconut oil. He wondered about this oil, and how and why she used it. He wondered if Diane liked to—how did the English put it?—diddle. Was that their term?

One thing he did know was that Diane liked television. Nightly, when the kids were under their laundered sheets, tucked in with teddy bears, read to, and asleep, Diane made her way to the living room to watch, for example, *The Many Loves of Dobie Gillis*. When he called home at four-thirty, she would cheerfully tell him that she and the kids were watching *American Bandstand*. On Saturday mornings, wearing cotton PJs, she cuddled with Barry and Tina in front of *The Alvin Show* and *Top Cat*. Could you blame her for any of this? Did it make her less attractive? No, you couldn't blame Diane—she didn't lend herself to blame. Blame wouldn't attach to her peerless young body. Walter tried to roll his eyes at her and feel superior, but that was no use, because he didn't feel superior—he felt older, yes, but not superior. At the end of week one, after giving it careful thought, he paid Diane her right and proper tribute: a sizable cash bonus with a note confessing, "I feel lucky, Diane. You're worth it."

Sometimes, in the late evening, he listened hopefully—and pathetically—for the pad of her slim, slippered feet in the hallway, louder as she emerged from the children's bathroom and headed in his direction. Always, at the last, she turned left instead of right, shut the door behind her with a thoughtfully quiet click, and made the muffled, unextraordinary noises that went with arranging herself for sleep. At that point he liked both to listen and to imagine, conjuring scenarios involving coconut oil and Diane Burroughs in . . . a pink chiffon baby-doll with spaghetti straps? No. Her innocent white cotton underwear? Yes. If her box spring made the slightest noise, he ran with that and felt his heart jump a little—maybe she'd finally surrendered to desire. . . maybe, in a moment . . . But he knew this was ridiculous. Besides, he couldn't sleep with all this yearning, with the guilt and fantasizing and the laughing at himself. "I'm a fool," he thought, "thirty-four and a fool. The truth is, I'm lying here in a T-shirt and boxers, pining for a girl who watches cartoons and sings along to the Billboard Top 40."

When Diane took the kids to a park one Sunday, he looked around, delicately, in her bedroom. On the desk was a letter she'd written on ruled school paper: "Dear Club," it began, followed by "Hey cheeky Jimmie take a puff for the au pair. On the up side I've had a trip to the World's Fair." Walter skimmed ahead to ferret out "Club," which he took to be one of those silly English nicknames, in this case probably for a buck-toothed beau whose real name was Rupert or Lionel or Percy. Farther along, though, after evaluating evidence like "In answer to your question, I haven't kept in touch with John or Mum, or with anyone in Essex, for that matter," he surmised that Club was Diane's brother. And that was good, because a brother was no impediment to his chances.

Even though no one was in the house, Walter found himself being very quiet as he opened Diane's drawers. There were high-waisted panties and white camisoles, but what he liked best, and lingered over, was the mocha bathing suit with the long back zipper, a bust of tulip petals, a modesty panel draping its crotch, and leg openings in the style of a boy's briefs. Walter sniffed it—chlorine—and fondled its hook-and-eye closures. He pressed on the plastic bone between the cups, ran his fingers along the perforated lining, and caressed the metal slides of the shoulder straps before, in a pique of shame, arranging the bathing suit to approximate how he'd found it. After pausing to steal a look in the closet, he admonished himself and fled.

On the last Friday in June, Walter took the kids and Diane (with the blessing of Lydia's therapist, who assured Walter that there was no reason not to do it) for a three-day weekend on San Juan Island, where he owned a cabin with a sagging roof that was admittedly a money pit and a burden. Between the southern exposure and the steady sea wind, there was no way to keep up with the leaks, stave the drafts, or preserve the rotting windows that, in the best scenario, would be painted with a heavy preservative annually. This was not to mention the weeds between the pavers, the sluggish septic system, the well needing deeper excavation, the failing foundation, and the potholed drive. From the moment they bought the place, Lydia had encouraged Walter to think of its rusticity as charming and to let go of his urge to make it perfect, but he viewed a day not spent on chores as a day hastening the demise of their investment. There was no way he could let the place disintegrate, and as a result, only some of his island time was spent in a deck chair with a beer; otherwise, it was trips to the hardware store and unending, halfhearted puttering. This weekend, though, there was the stimulating consolation of Diane in her mocha bathing suit, cavorting with his kids on the beach.

On Saturday afternoon, Diane helped him paint the picket fence and pulled weeds out of Lydia's perennial beds. Lydia wasn't much of a gardener; every spring she planted a box of bulbs that by June lay under a morass. Diane took care of that cheerfully, wearing jeans she'd scissored into shorts, a baby-blue T-shirt printed DEWEY WEBER SURFBOARDS, and Keds without socks. At five, she disappeared into the bathroom, to emerge eventually with her hair combed wet, in a plaid sundress, barefoot. Walter, in the striped polo he reserved for painting, unshaved, sunburned, and smoking a cheap cigar—a look he could only hope had a manly summer charm—watched her from his post at the barbecue while she leaned on the porch railing and gazed at the water. "I ought to shave and change," he thought.

He did. At nine-thirty, Diane put the kids to sleep in the cabin's single bedroom. The plan was for her to bunk with Tina in the musty, soft queen-size bed that was Lydia's before he married her; Barry would sleep beside them on a narrow camp cot. Walter was to repair to the sleeping loft, with its spiderwebs, heat, and nocturnally active houseflies, but since this prospect had no appeal, he settled on the couch instead, his feet up and a beer beside him, to read *The Sand Pebbles*.

Then, around ten, Diane slipped out of the bedroom. Her hair, he noticed, was a little awry, probably from pressing against a pillow. She still wore the plaid dress, now wrinkled across the thighs. Without asking his permission, she went to the front door and propped it open with one of Barry's rubber beach boots. "Warm in here," she explained.

"Fortunately, we don't have mosquitoes," he replied.

"I'll shut it again if you want me to—do you? Whatever you want. It's your cottage."

He put down his book and said, "Diane, come on, now, it's not what *I* want, it's what *you* want. If it's the night air you want, then, by all means, let's have the door open wide."

Diane smiled and raised her eyebrows suggestively. "What *I* want? Is it, really? In that case, let's play a game."

Walter swung his feet to the floor and, taking up his beer, feigned confidence. "Which game is that?" he asked.

"Life," said Diane, pointing toward the cabin's shelf of tattered board games. "That's one I know how to play."

Together, they set up Life on the kitchen table. She accepted his offer of a bottle of Dr Pepper and, when he told her to pick first, selected the red car; he took the green. Off they went, following the track past mountains, trees, and buildings until, at the first junction, Diane chose the College route. In the name of competition, he teased her by saying, "College isn't automatically or always the right path. It might seem like it is, but let me tell you, it isn't."

"How would you know?"

"I'm older than you."

"How old exactly?"

"Old enough to know you shouldn't go to college without giving it some thought."

"Well," said Diane, and spun the wheel, "I've done that already. The thinking."

"That's fine," replied Walter, "but look where you've landed. I'm afraid I'm going to have to go with my Collect card and take half your windfall. Pay up."

Diane wagged a finger at him. "Keep your hair on," she said. "I've got an Exemption card I haven't played yet."

He bought insurance, she bought none, and eventually, his long-term approach proved superior. But just when he thought he had her on the ropes, Diane landed on the Lucky Day square. With twenty thousand dollars newly in hand, she opted for the game's penultimate gamble: lose all of it or, in one spin of the wheel, turn it into the lead-seizing sum of three hundred thousand. "Don't do it," he warned. "The odds are four to one against you."

"Just get the number strip," she answered.

When she'd lost the twenty thousand, she took a pull from her Dr Pepper and said, "Your turn, Walter. At least I tried."

Had she called him Walter before? "Walter" was a good sign. "Walter" meant he was getting somewhere. Yes, there was a definite warming trend. "You did try," he said, "And now you're broke."

Eventually, he retired as a Millionaire, and Diane, behind, risked it all on one spin, hoping to vault past him and become a Tycoon. Instead, she finished Bankrupt, then plucked up her car in a feisty capitulation. "Congratulations," he said. "Another round?"

"No," she answered. "You only get one go at Life. I went to college, got married, got a job, had kids, bought a house, bought a car, bought two cars—what more could I want?"

Was this code for ridicule? A condemnation of his choices? "Great," said Walter. "Now, not at all meaning to lead you astray—but could I offer you more than just a soft drink?"

"I'll have what you're having. A pint."

"You mean a beer."

"If you want to call that a beer, yes, thank you—I'll have an American beer, please, served from an American can."

He got her a beer. They went outside and sat on the stoop, where they listened to waves degrade the beach and gazed at the Big Dipper. Walter admired how Diane brought her knees together to prevent stray glimpses of her panties. What great legs she had, he observed, with just the right girlish taper. "You knock a beer back fast," he said. "I bet you had a good senior year."

"Absolutely. Tip-top, Walter."

"You went on dates, went to parties, ran around."

"I partook, yes. Indulged, shall we say. I enjoyed my year as an exchange student."

Walter—feeling like a teen-age boy again, one with the utterly transparent intention of getting his cute date drunk—went in for what remained of the half-case he'd bought that afternoon in Friday Harbor. "Partook," he thought. "Indulged. Enjoyed. This girl's talking about sex."

When he came back, Diane said, "Stars like this remind me of home. I used to look up at the stars quite a lot, for lack of better things to do."

"You're a romantic, Diane, so try this out: look at that moonlight, glinting on the sea."

She did that. Then she leaned on her turned-back palms with a tilted head so as to look at the sky more comfortably. Walter almost said, "Can I kiss you, Diane?" but opted instead for, "You're clever for your age. Incredibly mature. For someone just done with high school."

"Here," she said. "But at home I'm below average."

"I'm sure that's not so."

"Flattery gets you nowhere."

Walter shrugged like somebody defeated. "Changing the subject, then," he said. "I've been meaning to ask. Have you overwhelmed our State Department yet with your vast English charm? Because, if not, maybe I could help you with it."

She hadn't overwhelmed the State Department yet. "Though I'm still working on it," she assured him. "But, please, don't let's talk about it."

"You're on a little vacation up here. You don't want to think about the real world, do you. Well, then, long live the Queen, or whatever you people say. Drink up."

And she did drink up, with her fair throat bobbing. He offered her another right away.

"Declined," said Diane. "Not tonight—no." She grinned, rose, crossed her legs, and pressed her thighs. "Walter," she said. "Walt. Wally. I need to run a bit quickly to the toilet. Excuse me, then. I'm off."

Walter considered the meaning of "Wally" while listening to his au pair pee forcefully. Then she emerged, took their beer cans to the sink, and, under the kitchen lights, bent at the waist to pick up a dish towel that had gotten shoved under the toe kick. The thick, falling hair, the tanned legs, the nimble hands, the shadow of her junior bra beneath her plaid dress: a familiar panic from his pre-married years began churning in Walter's brain and chest. "Maybe," he thought, "the ball's in my court and she's waiting for me to take a shot at her—or maybe, if I do that, she'll scream." However he looked at it, one thing was plain—this little chick had him gripped by the balls. "Fun game," said Diane. "Good night."

Later, irritated by flies trapped against the ceiling in the loft, he jerked off while generating a mental slide show of Diane, in her underwear, meeting his needs.

The flirtation and seduction that played out in the coming days, both on San Juan Island and back home, in Greenwood, were built from the usual and inevitable ingredients: double entendres, verbal sparring, electrifying unease, fearful agitation, bated breath, and, finally, desperation before the inevitable plunge over the waterfall.

The kind of trouble that there was no going back from started before midnight on the Fourth of July, when Walter awoke to find Diane on his bed in light cotton pajamas printed with fire engines. "What is it?" he said, sitting up on one elbow. "What's the problem, Diane?"

"Oh, Walter," she answered, pleadingly.

He hesitated. "Bad timing," he thought, because he'd eaten two burgers and a lot of macaroni salad around eight, then worked his way through nearly a half-case of Pabst while Diane, in her scissored-off jeans, lit sparklers and Snakes for the kids in the back yard. In other words, he felt sluggish, not in optimal form, and too bloated for what might be about to happen. In the bed he shared with Lydia. Beneath portraits of Tina and Barry on the wall. Where either of them might come padding in, wakened by fireworks, scared, seeking solace. And, finally, with a girl who claimed to be eighteen but who might be, by the look of it, considerably younger. "What's the deal?" he said.

"Can I get in?" Diane asked.

She lifted his sheet, rolled onto the mattress, and tucked herself, urgently, against his side, as though she were his daughter and he was about to read a story. Walter, who wore only his boxer shorts, said, "Whoa-ho-ho, wait a second."

"Please," Diane answered. "I'm lonely."

She snuggled in farther. There was a big portable fan on in the room, and the window was open, but it was still hot. Already, between them, a film of sweat was forming. But that wasn't the main thing. The main thing was that Diane was making a strange noise now, a cross between a whimper and a shriek. Was that crying? Yes, it was crying. Not knowing what to do or say, Walter said, "Hey, come on, now, Diane," and patted her shoulder.

Diane blubbered, sniffled, and honked while twisting a lock of hair around her index finger and giving him—maybe not unwittingly—a boner. Yet, despite his dick's insistence on a selfish response, there was no way for Walter not to feel sorry for Diane, even tender, like a father. Until now she'd seemed so resilient and unsinkable. What was she crying about? He wasn't ready for crying. "Diane," he said, and stroked her hair once. "It's okay."

"No, it's not," she answered.

Then she let forth with personal information she seemed desperate to divulge. She was fifteen, she was "the daughter of the town whore," she was "never, ever going back to England," she'd lied to the State Department, her school year had been a social disaster, and nothing had gone right with her Seward Park host family, particularly with her host father, who'd ignored her. "How could that be?" asked Walter.

"He didn't like me, I know he didn't."

"That's impossible. He must be nuts."

Then she said that her own father was French or an American sailor—she didn't know which. She had a half-brother, Caleb, older by sixteen months ("So I was right," thought Walter, "about the letter on her desk—her half-brother Caleb is this 'Club' she writes home to"), who'd run off when he was fourteen to London, and another half-brother, John, older still, who was a constable. She had a grandmother in the countryside who, Diane said, was "a terrible witch," and a grandfather who'd called her "a bastard miscreant from a litter of bastard miscreants."

She described for Walter a scene from her childhood. She was twelve, it was summer, she was in the countryside, slopping pigs, and her grandmother said, when Diane asked who her father was, "Only the Lord and your mum know." Her grandfather added, "Before you was hatched she was consorting with a sailor." Vivid recall made Diane sob all the harder. She even remembered that, later, in the house, her tormentors had gone on pitching it about: "Dallying with a Frenchman at the time, wasn't she?" and "That sailor was a merchant-marine man and a sot." "That sort of talk," Diane told Walter, to which he replied, "That wasn't nice. That was just plain inconsiderate."

Next complaints about her "mum" tumbled out—her mum who'd once made a shameful few quid servicing the needs of any and all comers, and a few more dusting and scrubbing genteel homes. But her mum couldn't keep clients in either category, and went on the dole, and shut herself in, the better to monitor the phone and the neighbors. Thereafter, when forced to go out, she painted herself with a horrifying rough, and though she limped from sciatica, straightened up in the presence of men as though they still represented opportunity. They didn't any longer, and it was Diane's job to listen to her mum rant about it, and to agree with her about everything but especially about her remaining attractions, and to clean out her ashtrays and kitchen pots and toilet, and sleep on the sofa when the rooms were let to boarders, until, feeling taken for granted, she left.

"Diane, you're not taken for granted *here*," said Walter. "I would *never* take you for granted."

With this, she kissed his cheek, he thought in gratitude. Walter felt that the next move was his, but he was worried about his breath because of the macaroni salad. For this reason he hesitated, wondering how bad it was, and in that moment, with force and suddenness, Diane climbed on top of him. "Jesus," he said.

"Oh, Walter."

It was a little bit hard to get past the fire engines on her PJs—past the idea that he was in bed with a fifteen-year-old—but Walter got past them soon enough. The PJs came off—he made sure of that—the top first, and then the bottoms. His au pair, naked, was so sleek and untarnished, so gleamingly pubescent, and so unlike Lydia after two babies, that even as he flipped her onto her back, even while he asked her, twice, if she was sure, he knew, glumly, that he was doing the wrong thing. There was a name for this, statutory rape, which, he had to admit, excited him. He had moral qualms, but he ignored them.

Did she have moral qualms? She cried a lot while he went at her, but didn't resist or make him stop. Walter pressed on, determined to incite participation, to goad from Diane some clenching and clutching, some shortness of breath, any signal of his prowess or good technique, but somehow, at the end, she still seemed miserable, and the worst of it was her almost imperceptible orgasm, during which she squeezed her eyes shut. She fluttered under him, with effort, like a wounded bird, and immediately afterward, or before she was done, sobbed again in childlike catches, smelling of her tears and his spunk. "Diane," he said, "are you okay?"

"Oh, Walter."

To his surprise, she didn't say another word, and before long began to snore intermittently in an ascending nasal hum. He listened to that for fifteen minutes, running a hand along her back and flanks and admiring their youthful smoothness. Then, fearing that one of his kids might stumble in, he woke Diane and asked her to go back across the hall to her bedroom.

"Ask nicely, Walter."

"Okay," he said. "I don't want you to go, Diane. But for the sake of the kids, please, I think it's time."

She got on her PJs and exited. A bit later, he heard the morning paper land on his porch, and got up to read it. The French were tossing in the towel in Algeria, JFK was pussyfooting with the Russians. He found he couldn't concentrate on any of this, because he kept wondering if what had happened was a train wreck. "Of course," he thought, "it's a major train wreck. I better nip this in the bud and get a hold of myself."

But he didn't get a hold of himself, for a whole thrilling month, until the day his wife was discharged from the hospital.

Walter collected Lydia on the first Saturday in August. She kissed him in the doorway of her room on the ward—with a guilt-expanding, marital ardor—and he took in the view of the fine down on her forearms. Her hair was done up loftily—stacked high by an in-hospital dresser—and she'd put on, for her return home, a newly ironed floral shift and scarlet pumps. Lydia paused at the threshold of the hospital to say, "I never want to come back to this hellhole," took Walter's hand, and again kissed him. She kissed him a third time beside the Lincoln, and told him how wonderful it felt to be rested and to have lost ten long-resistant pounds. She wanted her life back, she said. She sounded hopeful. Walter said he wanted that for her, too, then asked her to explain what her illness had been about. What did the shrinks say? What was behind it? Lydia told him that it was very complex and without an easy, all-purpose explanation. It went back to her childhood, he gathered she was saying. Her mother had been beautiful and slim. Her father, a small-town accountant, had been distant. The main thing was, she felt better now.

Walter brought Lydia's suitcase into the house, while Lydia brought a regal calm. The kids greeted her with no less affection than if there'd never been a Diane Burroughs. Lydia got down on the floor with them right away, the better to deploy her newfound serenity, and so did Walter, miserably. Diane turned out to be a consummate actress, and introduced herself to Lydia wearing culottes, an apron, and pigtails she flipped to entertain the kids while extolling the "tasteful, modern decorating scheme" in the Cousins home and the "marvelously quiet" electric dishwasher. That was the full extent of her welcome. She kept aloof from the rest of the family reunion, as if to exercise English serving-class discretion. Then it was time to eat what she'd prepared—a summertime salad of cold poached chicken breasts laid on spinach leaves, with mandarin oranges and almond slivers. The kids had mostly Tater Tots, and, for dessert, a Duncan Hines chocolate cake that Lydia declined, claiming fresh resolve. Diane told Lydia she looked beautiful.

After dinner, Walter and Lydia sat in the back yard while Diane did the dishes and watched the kids. There was some talk about flowerbeds, about changing things, about a birdbath and pavers and less weeding. Walter felt half present for this dialogue, preoccupied, as he was, with marital angst. What to do? What came next? What was his future with Diane? He tried focusing on Lydia, who looked good on the patio—in fact, with her post-institutionalized, preternatural calm, and minus ten pounds, she looked better, in his eyes, than she had for a long time, and not at all furrowed, desultory, or anxious. Walter knew she hadn't "done it" for a month, which meant doing it with her tonight should be better than it normally was. Unfortunately, he was beset by morose feelings that he knew would detract.

When he thought he could do so without giving Lydia the impression that he was abandoning her on the night of her return to the family circle, he said, "I'll go check on the kids."

"Good," answered Lydia. "I'll take a shower."

Walter retreated. Being out of Lydia's presence was a reprieve—he didn't have to hold his face to a false expression, and he could anguish without worrying how it looked. At Diane's bedroom door, he gave a warning knock, then opened it and said, "Kids! It's time to calm down now and brush your teeth."

It took a while, but Barry and Tina finally went—right after he'd told them to, with severity at last, for the fourth time. Walter shut Diane's bedroom door behind them, stood against it, and said—to a teen-ager in culottes—"What now?"

"We'll find out, won't we."

"What do you want?"

"Plenty of things."

"What does that mean?" asked Walter.

He pinched her chin between his fingers, the better to admire her face before moving in to kiss her, but Diane pushed his hand off and stepped back. "Don't do that," she said. "Not now."

"Okay," said Walter. "I understand."

It didn't at all surprise him, forty minutes later, to find that he had trouble in the sexual department with the freshly washed, scented, and slightly damp Lydia. Under him she felt urgent for renewed affections of a sort that at the moment he was incapable of providing. After much effort, he softly snaked into her, where he found himself wallowing not in pleasure but in guilt. Lydia's familiarity and recent mental illness guided him into a sea of self-loathing, where he shrank to almost nothing, apologized profusely, felt grateful for his wife's reassurances, and finally did what he always did when, failing to get started or show self-control, he still felt a need to be a source of satisfaction. Walter became earnest with his hands.

The question developed, by Lydia's third day back, as to the future status of the au pair. Did they need her anymore? What was her role? Was Lydia now ready to resume her tasks as housekeeper, laundress, cook, mom? Was it prudent for her to plunge in right away—into everything that had driven her, recently, to exhaustion? Was it fair to the au pair to dismiss her without warning, or was it better to make a gradual transition, in which case Diane should stay on in the guest room as an ancillary figure, a mother's helper? Could they justify the continued expense?

About Diane's status—should she stay or go?—Walter thought it best to defer. "Don't argue it either way," he decided. "Leave it to Lydia." But Lydia insisted on his active participation, and coaxed him to express himself, until he felt forced to say what he knew he had to say, but didn't want to say, since there was no right answer—that it was time for Diane Burroughs to exit.

Together, they broke the news to Diane, explaining the simple, unsurprising truth that, with Lydia's return, they didn't need an au pair. Diane took this in stride, which hurt Walter's feelings, assuring the Cousinses cheerfully that of course it made sense—"Mum's home, so absolutely. My job's done." Lydia hugged Diane, told her how grateful she was for her "extraordinary and wonderful way with the children," praised her for everything she'd done for her family, and assured Diane that Diane needn't leave until she'd made arrangements for, as Lydia put it, "the next exciting phase of your young life." Through all of this, they were in each other's arms, patting, rubbing, and massaging each other's backs, with Diane grinning at Walter over Lydia's shoulder in a way surely meant to mock his wife, then forming her lips into the shape of a kiss before showing Walter the slick tip of her tongue, all of which childish display he endured with a bitter censure and regret. Then Diane said to Lydia, embracing her harder and staring Walter down, "For me, being the au pair in your home has been *deliriously* exciting. But you're right, Mrs. Cousins. I'm looking forward to whatever happens next."

What happened next came later that summer, after Walter had consigned Diane to the consolatory vault of sexual imagery he employed while doing it with Lydia. She called one morning at his office to say, "Are you ready for this? I'm pregnant."

Walter sat up straight in his cubicle. He was in the throes of a loss-cost calculation for a savings-and-loan under time-sensitive duress, and felt driven to get numbers out the door, but forget that now: Diane was *preg-*

nant. Pregnant and, he had to assume, fingering him as the father—but was he? Couldn't it be some other fool? Walter looked over his dividing walls to see who might be in hearing distance. Next door, to his left, was Duane Keene, chewing on a stem of his glasses; to his right was Rick Lubovich, with his hangdog shoulders, as usual doing little more than rubbing his head while pondering his IBM Selectric. Since they could both overhear him, Walter said, in a normal voice, "Okay, I'm listening to you."

"Well, what are we going to do, Walter?"

"That's going to take some discussion," he said. "Do you think we can set up an appointment?"

"This is so horrid," Diane replied. "I never wanted to be like Mum. Now look at what's become of me." He heard sniffles.

Walter said, "I absolutely understand. My calendar's open in front of me right now. I could meet you, really, any time."

"Why is this happening?" Diane asked.

"I'd like to help you to address that if I can. So let's get together and talk," said Walter. "I hear what you're saying—it's urgent for you, and I want you to know that I'm available with regard to it—in fact, I'm at your disposal."

"Oh, Walter," said Diane. "What will happen to me?"

That evening, he picked her up at the house in Laurelhurst where Diane was now installed as au pair. It was a night in mid-August when fall was discernible as a faint, crisp chill just after sundown. Diane was out front, arms crossed impatiently, wearing dungarees and a man's white dress shirt with its sleeves rolled. She didn't look well groomed. She hadn't primped to see him. She looked like she'd come from the kitchen sink, and probably had. She got in quickly and said, "Go," as if the Lincoln was an escape car, then watched the side mirror as Walter sped off. They left Laurelhurst behind. Walter chauffeured her along residential streets, going nowhere and—between long silences—speaking to the matter at hand. "I'm sure," he said, "that I could arrange for an abortion. If you want to consider that, I would love to discuss it with you. And the first thing you should know is that I would take care of everything, and pay for everything, and go with you, and take you home afterward. I'd be there with you throughout the whole business. You don't have to worry about that."

Diane rode with her head against the window. She looked—how did she look? Like he'd been stupid about rubbers? Like he was a total idiot? Like he disgusted her? It was impossible to know what Diane was thinking—he'd felt this way about her from the moment they'd met—because she was fifteen and foreign. "That all sounds great," she said, "but I could never, ever do it. I'm not going to have an abortion."

"I don't know," Walter replied quickly. "We shouldn't take options off the table."

Their silences grew longer as they rode past evening lawn sprinklers, dog walkers, and a few kids on bikes, asking, in different ways, again and again, "Now what?" Finally, though, Walter got Diane to agree to a plan—a far-from-foolproof plan, unwieldy and laborious, but the best he could come up with under the circumstances—which they put into motion in the middle of November, when Diane told her au-pair family that she was going home to England. A week before Christmas, her host mother and father dropped her at Sea-Tac Airport. She lugged her suitcases into the terminal, rode down the escalator to the baggage-claim level, then went back outside to meet Walter, who was waiting in his car. Yes, he felt oppressed by Diane's pregnancy, and fearful of how things might turn out, but he also felt steeled and ready at this point. He'd told Lydia—who was back to normal, well organized, and on the ball—that he was "going to Houston for a conference." She'd answered, good-naturedly, "That's what they all say," and he'd chuckled as if to acknowledge the truth of this. Then, feeling tender, and despising himself, he'd hugged her and insisted that he didn't want to go to Houston, which, if you construed it the right way, was a fact.

Now he and his knocked-up fifteen-year-old former au pair drove eighty miles north to Anacortes. Walter brooded at the ferry slip where they were going to embark for San Juan Island while Diane slumped, gray-faced, against the window. In a battering sea wind they drove onto the boat and ended up between a trailered backhoe and a wrecking van. Diane wanted to stay in the Lincoln, as opposed to sitting in the warm cabin up top, so Walter put a blanket over her legs and, self-consciously solicitous, another around her shoulders. The ferry churned into disagreeable seas, which became forbidding in Rosario Pass, eliciting, in Walter, fear of a roll. He said, "I'm sorry the crossing's so rough," and Diane answered, "Come off it, Walter. You sound pathetic." Then they disgorged onto broken tarmac and drove deserted roads to the cabin at Cattle Point, where Walter installed his soured teen lover, put a wad of cash in her hand, and started dinner—macaroni and cheese in a box.

Diane wouldn't eat. She wouldn't talk, either. The rain was louder on the roof because of her silence. She went in the bedroom, shut the door, and ignored him. Walter passed the night on the couch, awake with his clothes on, while she snored on the other side of the wall in a way that, despite everything, was moving and endearing. Somebody that young and beautiful could snore and it was charming instead of obnoxious.

In the morning, before she woke, he sped into Friday Harbor. After scouring want ads in his idling Lincoln, he made a call from a booth and, following a cursory test drive, bought a seventy-five-dollar beater. It had buckled seat springs and smelled of mildew, but, leaving his own car behind, Walter drove it back to Cattle Point and, with false enthusiasm, urged Diane to learn to drive. "Come on," he said. "This will be fun." As if they could be jolly about an automobile, as if they were father and daughter. Diane got behind the wheel and immediately demonstrated her driving know-how. "None of your business," she answered Walter when he asked her where and when she'd learned.

They went back for the Lincoln, then caravanned to a gas station, where Walter filled both tanks. He bought a quart of ice cream, a deck of cards, a book of crossword puzzles, and four bags of groceries. All of this went into Diane's topped-off beater. No, she said, she didn't need him to lead her back, because she knew "the way to jail." What she did need was twice the cash he'd doled out earlier. Walter forked it over. He stressed that she should enjoy herself, use the car when she needed to, and wait things out. "Brilliant," said Diane. "That's just brilliant."

One more time, Walter apologized, as if repeating himself would make things better instead of worse. "Look," he said, "I take full responsibility for my part in this. I have a duty here, I know that, and I plan to see that duty through, no matter what."

"Go home," she answered. "And lay off the subject of what a good citizen you are, all right?"

On the ferry, his tail between his legs, Walter rubbed his receding hairline and stewed behind his steering wheel. On the mainland, he battled homeward in rain so harsh he worried that an accident, if it happened, would be his undoing. How was it, Lydia would want to know, that he'd had an accident *north* of home when the airport was *south* of it—the airport he'd supposedly made use of for his supposed trip to Houston? "Right," thought Walter, "I've been in Houston," and he stopped at Northgate Shopping Center to look for gifts that would seem like Texan gifts.

That night, sleepless, with Lydia beside him in a cotton nightgown and high-waisted panties, he lay in bed worrying about ways his plan could fall apart. What scared him the most was Diane's clear ire and her potential for irrational behavior. She might go to a pay phone in Friday Harbor and call him at home, for instance, even though he'd asked her not to. This worried him so much that, in the morning, when the phone rang, he answered in a panic, sure it was Diane, but it wasn't Diane, and all weekend it wasn't Diane, and even though he still worried about a phone call incessantly, by Monday he'd succeeded in incorporating this worry into the larger, more generalized, apocalyptic worry he felt about the whole affair. How much more could he take?

On Monday, Walter contacted an obstetrician in Anacortes and an adoption agency in Bellingham about "a delicate situation involving our au pair." On Wednesday, he took a day off from work and ran up to San Juan Island with flowers, doughnuts, magazines, and a used television set. As it turned out, there was reasonably good reception at Cattle Point. To be polite, and to make it look as if he wasn't in a hurry to catch a ferry home—to add a layer of reassurance for Diane that he was a good guy—Walter served Jiffy Pop and watched *As the World Turns* with her. "I'm in prison here," Diane said. "There's nothing to do. I don't do a thing."

"Take walks," said Walter. "Get exercise."

The next time Walter came to the island, it was to collect Diane for her appointment with the obstetrician. An hour on the water to pick her up at the cabin, an hour back to the mainland with a seething girl for company, thirty minutes with the doctor in Anacortes, a hot dog and ice cream devoured in a parking lot, and then yet again to the interminable ferry, again to Cattle Point, again getting Diane to her cloister, and then, for Walter, once more to the mainland, once more the long drive home. The next week, he had to do it all over again for a trip to the adoption agency, so Diane could sign relinquishment papers and claim she didn't know who the father was, even though the father—actually, Walter still wondered—was sitting right there, pretending to be helping. Walter felt grateful that the woman in charge of things pretended not to have seen this before—namely, the pregnant girl accompanied by an older man who purported himself as strictly a good Samaritan. But he didn't feel grateful when she said that Diane would have to return the following week for an assessment of her features. This was so that the baby, when it came, could be placed in a family that had the right look, the better to allow for a successful sham, and to keep everyone not party to the deed—especially the baby, as it grew into a man or woman—from wondering what it meant that no one else in the family was, say, left-handed and cross-eyed. The next week came—another twice-circuitous journey. The assessment of Diane's features was demeaning, and though she mechanically went along with the process, afterward she was livid about such a soulless inventory of her features. Walter worried that her goodwill was eroding further because she seemed brimming over now with shame and wrath. "Like *meat*," she said. "It's humiliating."

She swelled prettily, though, as things progressed. They both went on lying to everybody involved in order to sustain the charade indefinitely, and in order to move forward without a hitch. Lydia, with her inner battery now fully recharged, took a wifely interest in what she called Walter's "distance." He told her that stress at work—preoccupation with "an upheaval" at Piersall-Crane ("Someone got canned, and somebody somewhere decided to dump his accounts on *guess who*?")—was the cause of his absence from their family life. Then he played with the kids, to lend depth to his remorse. Meanwhile, Diane metamorphosed. Her teen-age pregnancy was charming, yes, but she looked blotchy and had a burgeoning double chin.

What to do? How to get to where this thing was done and he could move on with life unencumbered? And in the meantime, how to keep an angry fifteen-year-old on his side? Out of ideas, he bought her, once again, a double ice-cream cone in Anacortes, but it just made him all the sadder to watch Diane, so buffeted by circumstance, lick away earnestly at her Rocky Road. He said, "I know all of this is tough, but, believe me, I'm sticking with you, and we'll get through it. These things happen."

Diane sighed. "A baby," she said. "And look what I'm doing."

"I'm looking at it," answered Walter, "and what I see is two people doing the best they can to do the right thing, Diane. We're going to make sure our baby has a good home. We made a mistake—I made a mistake—

but we're owning up to it together, and so far, I've been proud to stand beside you while you stay the course with so much . . . is the right word 'courage'? Look, I'm sure it isn't easy to be alone on the island day in and day out, especially at your age, but we have to bear up, and we're getting there."

"It's not just that it's a baby," Diane said, "it's that it's *my* baby, growing inside of me." Then she cried while her Rocky Road ran down the cone onto her hand.

Walter convinced Diane to opt for an induced birth. She was to say that she lived on San Juan Island and was afraid of having her baby on the ferry, but the real reason, of course, was that an induced birth meant Walter could schedule.

One week before the day he'd marked on his calendar as TRAVEL TO BALTIMORE, they had to listen to a lecture from the adoption agency's director. By law, Diane would have forty-eight hours following the birth of the baby to change her mind. After that, there would be a third day for the baby in the maternity ward, to make sure it was healthy. If there was anything wrong, if the baby didn't meet certain standards, the new family wouldn't come for it, as stipulated in their adoption papers. If nothing was wrong, as everyone expected, then, on the fourth day, the new family would take the baby without seeing Diane, or Diane's seeing them. Thereafter—out of this the director made a full-blown disquisition— Diane should think of herself as having done the right thing, as having provided love and a good life for her child by relinquishing it to adoptive parents, who subsequently would in fact be the *sole* parents in all legal regards. Was that understood? Did Diane know what she was doing? Did she get the nuances, the legal principles, the injunctions? Odds were that she did, thought Walter, because it had all been plodded through with Biblical depth and thoroughness. There it all was, a lot of spelled-out mumbo-jumbo, no doubt arrived at by lawyers and politicians and, he hoped, irrelevant in his case. Let the counted-on scenario begin, he thought, with no "if"s intruding.

The appointed day arrived. For the trip to the mainland hospital, they took two cars, Diane in her beater without a license or insurance, and Walter in his workhorse Lincoln-cum-taxi, so that afterward they could go separate ways. But not really separate ways, because Walter would remain tethered to Diane to the tune of—she'd made clear what she wanted—one hundred fifty a month. How would he swing that? It was a question for later. A big one—but later. For now, on the ferry, they sat in his car together, Diane with her hands supporting her belly, Walter in the driver's seat with his fingers twined behind his head, feeling, for the first time, that this episode might indeed draw to a close without ripping him apart. Maybe he would get away scot-free. Maybe, soon, the danger would pass. "Hey," he said, "how are you doing over there on the passenger side, Diane?"

"Scared."

Walter nodded as if he understood. "That's got to be normal. On the other hand, the odds of complications during childbirth that doctors can't handle are extremely low these days. What else?"

"Odds," sneered Diane. "Don't be so stupid. I'm not worried about the odds on what's happening today. I'm worried about the odds for tomorrow."

"I know," answered Walter. "I know, I know. But I think it's good for us to take this one day at a time. Right now's not the moment to plan your whole life. Let's think about what's on our plate today, and we'll think about tomorrow tomorrow."

Diane said, "Easy for you to say. Tomorrow you go back to your cute children, your wonderful wife, your summer cottage, your car, your house, your wage packet—all of that, Walter. It's no wonder you're not thinking about tomorrow. You know pre*cise*ly what tomorrow looks like."

"That's true," he countered. "Whereas you, young lady, when this unpleasantness is done, will be young and beautiful and have your whole life in front of you, an open book, a wonderful adventure, while I'm watching *Ozzie and Harriet.*"

At the hospital, the obstetrician delivered a last-minute bad surprise: induction could take "several days." This made Walter's anxiety skyrocket, because his lies were good for a limited duration. He'd counted on the baby appearing on day one, then disappearing—on schedule—ninety-six hours later, but now, if he had to factor in several days *prior* to the birth for labor induction—well, he *couldn't* factor that in. His whole ruse, at the last minute, would topple, or unravel. "What about a C-section?" he asked.

It turned out that this was not his decision. He was banished to the waiting room to hope for the best, and to sit with another prospective father—twenty-five and balding—to whom Walter explained, when asked, what an actuary does, before both of them descended into nervous brooding. After four hours, to his relief, an intern came to tell him that labor was under way. Five hours after that, around 7 p.m., Diane gave birth to an eight-plus-pound boy, who, the obstetrician came to tell Walter, squalled loudly, with healthy lungs. When Walter first saw him, through glass, held closely to the pane by a maternity nurse, he noticed that his son wore a beaded bracelet identifying him as "Baby Doe." Baby Doe, decided Walter, looked like his grandfather—like Walter's father—who lived in Cincinnati with his third wife. He looked sturdy, healthy, strong-boned, and handsome, like most of the Cousins men, and there was absolutely nothing wrong with him. "Wow," thought Walter, "that's my son," and for a moment he regretted that, as of three days hence, he'd never see him again. That was upsetting. That hurt a little. Another atrocious outcome of this swamp-march.

From a hospital pay phone—from "Baltimore," this time—he called Lydia. "Up late," he said. "Long day here. I've been burning the candle at both ends."

"At a conference?"

"I hate conferences."

"What's keeping you up so late at a conference?"

"I have to hunker down and prep for meetings. Otherwise, I'm not prepared, darling."

Then it was time for a visit with Diane, who was sitting up in bed in a blue hospital gown, a little peaked, with gray lips, greasy hair, and the amorphous torso of a completed pregnancy. "Diane," he said cheerfully, "you're looking good."

"How's he doing?"

"I was just there, checking. He's a handsome kid. I got kind of caught up in looking at him and had to make myself stop staring at the little guy. It was emotional, Diane. Pretty painful."

"I'm not asking about you, Walter. I'm asking about him."

"Not a peep," answered Walter. "Right now he looks happy. And how are you? Are you doing all right? Is everything looking like it should?"

"Just terrific," she answered.

The sarcasm worried him, and his worry deepened when she crossed her thin arms—one with its hospital ID band askew—and shook her head as though her disgust with everything, but mainly him, was total.

"I'm sorry," he told her, once again. "It's sad for me, too. It's really, really sad, actually."

Diane's sigh, on hearing this, was of the never-ending variety, and left him feeling, on top of worried, blue. Blue because this had to be the darkest day of her young life, and that he had a role in it—the main role, in fact—made him feel so sick about himself his eyes filmed. "Stop blubbering," Diane said. "There's still, you know, the forty-eight hours. The two days I have to change my mind."

Walter's stomach clenched. "I don't know," he said, in a panic. "I don't think you can change your mind at this point. I'm not too sure about that."

Diane pulled up her knees and hung on to them. "Of course I can," she said. "Forty-eight hours. There is a *law* that says I have forty-eight hours."

"True," said Walter, "but that's just because people get emotional. They see the baby and they get emotional and then they lose *objectivity*, Diane, they get all *embroiled* and they can't see straight, and for women—this is true—their hormones get stirred up. It's just not a good time for *anyone* to be making a decision about *anything*, it's really not."

"It's actually vice versa, Walter. You don't know what you really want until your emotions come into play."

This didn't sound too teen-agerish to him—its maturity was curious, even startling—but was that important right now? The whole thing just couldn't disintegrate like this, not when he was so close to slipping out of it. "Diane," he said, "come on, please. There's a family out there expecting a baby. There's more than just yourself to think about."

"That's ironic," Diane pointed out. "You telling me there's more than just myself to think about."

"Listen," said Walter, "I'm not a bad guy. I understand what you're saying about emotions. Your point of view is completely valid, but this just isn't *the time*."

"It is pre*cise*ly the time," Diane countered. "It's the forty-eight hours I've been allotted to reconsider. Walter, if you were named as the father— yes?—then you might call this a discussion between two people who both have a hand in a decision. But—Walter—you are *not* named. You might be the father, but you are not named. *If* you were named, then the two of us might be deciding this together, but you're not, so just stay out of it. I mean it."

"I'm not Norwegian, but Lydia is," said Walter, "and this is a really good time to say *uff da.*" With that he fell, hard, into a chair.

"Lydia who?" asked Diane.

Now what? A counselor? Someone from the adoption agency? More money? All of those were bad ideas.

Walter repaired to the hospital cafeteria, intending to see if a late burger and fries would help him think about what came next. But when his burger was gone, there was still no solution, so he returned to the buffet line for butterscotch pudding, and, while eating it, made a list of options under the headings "pro" and "con." Should he go back and argue? Try to reason with Diane? Remind her of her dream to go to college someday, which probably wouldn't happen if she kept the baby? Should he offer something? Ask what she wanted? Ask her, flat out, what it would take, in cash, to get her to keep to their plan? How about pushing the morality angle? He could already hear himself, he practiced a little: *You're giving the child a better life.* Nope. *When you promise someone something, make an agreement with people, you have a moral obligation to keep to your word*—but no, that wouldn't wash, either.

This Diane Burroughs was a tough little bird, but he'd known that from the first—ever since they'd played Life together. Clever and immune to manipulation. Always watching, thinking, weighing. What would she respond to when push came to shove, this girl who hailed from a gritty slice of England? He didn't have a clue. He couldn't tell.

Feeling hopeless, but armed with peanut-butter cookies, he returned to Maternity to plead his case. What Diane really liked were snickerdoodles, soft in the middle and doused heavily with cinnamon, but there were none of those, not even approximations, so peanut-butter cookies would have to do, delivered by a supplicant named Walter. "Eat one," he said. "They're not snickerdoodles, but they're good." Diane, in answer, glared, shook her head, and then, with clear disgust, said, "*Please,* Walter."

He retreated to a chair underneath her room's mounted television. Diane had been watching a serial drama he wasn't familiar with—about rich people and their alluring money—with curious avidity, he thought, given the pressing real-life matters at hand. How could she do that? He could never do that. "There's something," he said, getting up to take a cookie, "that I want you to have a little think about."

"And what might that be?" asked Diane.

"Just this," said Walter. "Try doing this. Try seeing yourself, I don't know, a year from now, then three, five, ten years out. Try asking yourself what things might look like."

"What for?"

"It's a good exercise. I do it all the time. Humor me, Diane. Bear with me."

Diane shrugged her wonderful, girlish shoulders. "Ten years," said Walter, "*snap*, like that. And now you're twenty-six—okay?—with a ten-year-old kid in your life."

"Is your point that you know how to add up, Walter?"

Walter threw up his hands, one of which had a cookie in it. "Is that what you want when you're twenty-six? I'm thirty-four, and I can tell you, you don't. What you want to do—what you tell me you want to do—is attend a good American college and really *make* something of your life."

"That would be good, but—"

"Listen," said Walter. "Do yourself a favor. Don't decide anything at the moment, okay? Just do that, please. For your own good, Diane. Rest, watch TV, get a good night's sleep, then let's get together and have a talk about your future. A really good talk, you and me."

She didn't reply. She didn't even look at him. "Diane," he said, "you have to believe me when I say to you that, whatever you decide, you can count on my support. If it's college, I'll help. If it's not, I'll help, too. I'm not going to shirk my duties, believe that. I only want beautiful things for you."

And how did she react to this? To this fresh reinforcement of his gen-uine sincerity? To his grasping, once again, at the straw of his own decency? She reacted by saying, "Not again, Walter. *Please,* not again. *Please* don't feed me that stale line."

The next day, to his overwhelming relief, Diane decided to stay the course. Who knew why? It didn't matter why. Baby Doe, without a doubt, was going to be adopted, and he, Walter, was going to go home, like a sailor who'd been on a long sea voyage that included sharks, scurvy, pirates, a typhoon, and a broken mast en route.

"Diane," he said, "I think you're doing the right thing in a situation where, really, there's no right thing, only lesser evils and greater evils, and that's the problem with life, for me—it doesn't always go the way I think it should, it's not always under my control."

He thought he was speaking to her from the same corner of the ring, or from a page they shared, but Diane held her gut as if sickened by his observations and said, "I don't need a lecture, Walter."

"Okay."

"Your problem with life—it'll have to wait."

"I see that."

"I'm incapable of talking about your problems right now."

"Let's not talk about them."

"The deal is, Walter, you're the definition of a wanker. You need to understand this: *you are a wanker*. Wanker, okay? What's the American? Just look it up. Wanker."

"I'll look it up," he said gruffly, and left.

Exhausted, he called Lydia from "Baltimore." "I'm worn out," he said, "and looking forward to getting home. I'm really, really looking forward to getting home."

But he couldn't go home. Not quite yet. There was one more night of this mire to be endured, and of watching motel television with a headache. He felt buoyed, though, because the whole thing was nearly over—all of it except for the blackmail part, the paying-through-the-teeth part, the arm-and-the-leg part that there was nothing to be done about. But the dangerous part, the heart-soul-and-life-rending part, Walter believed that was done.

That night, Walter dreamed. He dreamed he was standing in the Newborn Viewing Area watching Baby Doe through glass. Then a nurse appeared, plucked up Baby Doe, brought him to the window, and displayed him for Walter's benefit. "The logical thing would be to kill him now," she said through the pane.

In the morning, Walter mulled this while he shaved. "Interesting," he thought, "but dreams aren't valid. They have no legitimacy. They're just strangeness while you sleep. A dream is just your brain with its signals crossed. Oh well, so there you have it. Another weird dream. It's meaningless."

Walter checked out and returned to Maternity, where Diane and Baby Doe, he found, were gone. They'd left the hospital—but that couldn't be. What was she *thinking*? What was going on? "Oh no, no, *no*," thought Walter, and called the adoption agency. He was put on hold twice, passed along twice, until the director informed him that she knew already. She'd gotten in touch with the prospective adoptive family, and the prospective adoptive family was opting out for reasons it wasn't obligated to divulge, but also didn't mind, in these circumstances, divulging—namely, that the birth mother had had a change of heart, and they didn't want a birth mother who couldn't let go, and also, what about the birth mother's state of mind right now, how was she treating the baby? There were too many danger signals.

The beater car was gone from the hospital parking lot. It was the middle of April—a chilly wind, stirred pollens. Walter scratched his head and weighed his choices. He could just go home and take what fate dealt him, or not go home, never go home, or— "Wait," he thought. "What am I doing? How many times am I going to do this? What have I gotten from evaluating options? Look where it's gotten me—to this, right now. God, what a misery it's been, and what a breath of fresh air it would be if somehow, some way, I could just *live* again, free of all these problems."

He sat in his car feeling cheated by Diane, and banging his hand against the steering wheel. "I navigated so carefully through everything," he thought. "I did everything right. I did everything I could. And look at me now, I'm sitting here like an idiot. And now I'm thinking about sitting here like an idiot. And I don't have a reason to start my car. What would I do? Where would I go?"

Diane, he remembered then, had only a little money—whatever she'd saved from the cash he'd bled. It couldn't be much. Maybe enough for a few motel nights, but then what? She didn't have an income. She had a new baby, and—she had Walter over a barrel. "That's the key," he thought. "That's the main thing. She has me on the hook for three hundred a month. Why would she run away from that? She wouldn't run away from that. No way is she running away from that. Why didn't I think of this? If I just sit back, I'll hear from the little minx—she'll call me at the office and soak me good." In fact, he saw, she would soak him good indefinitely, milk him for whatever she thought he was worth. He was going to be paying through his teeth for a long time, that was just the way it turned out.

Walter drove to the final station in his journey: the Northgate Shopping Center, for gifts. For Lydia, Chanel No. 5; for Barry, the Lego Town Plan Set; and for Tina, the Happy Hippo, with a movable mouth and springy tail. Wonder of wonders, he felt buoyant walking the mall, amazed by Planet Earth and its intricacies, and by the singularity in all that had happened, and that night, at home, in bed with Lydia, he performed adequately, maybe even better. Afterward he even felt ready to turn over a new leaf, and prepared to live with himself.

As he'd predicted, Diane called him Monday morning at Piersall-Crane. In a disembodied voice, as though reading from a script, she gave him instructions the way a kidnapper would give instructions: how much money she wanted—250 now, monthly, because of the kid—the date each month she wanted it, the post-office box in Portland where he had to send it, what would happen if he tried to play games or manipulate things or send money late or not send enough money or claim that this or that, an emergency or something, had gotten in the way of sending it *even once.* "You're being blackmailed," Diane advised him sternly. "If you don't follow through or hold up your end, all right, then, I'll pick up the phone and—what's her name again?—that's right, Lydia. I'll call Lydia. Lydia, you wanker. And no more apologizing," said Diane, "because I've had enough of your apologizing."

"I've got it," said Walter. "But just one thing. Two hundred fifty a month? That sounds like a heck of a lot of money, maybe more than—"

"Listen," she hissed. "I didn't call to negotiate—that's not what's going on here. Do you think I'm one of your stupid clients? This is the girl you got up the duff, Walter, this is me, Diane Burroughs, calling on behalf of your illegitimate son. This is about your *son,* you bloody arse, and what I want is *more* than reasonable when you think of it in terms of child support."

He couldn't argue and didn't argue. It wasn't his show: he could see that. So instead he said—after peeking into empty adjoining cubicles— that he only wanted the best for her, that he had never wanted anything but the best for her, and that, no matter what, he would always do his part. In short, he fed Diane the same lines he'd fed her for months, which, it turned out, had gotten him exactly nowhere. "Shut up," said Diane, "and send the money."

After putting down the receiver, Walter shook his head for a long time. "I'm an idiot," he thought. "What just happened? And the whole time I thought I was smarter than her! Come on, Walter, clean up your act. Get a grip, buddy. Grow up—it's time. You're lucky this mistake didn't blow up in your face. Lucky to get out of it alive."

2

Candy Dark

Certain nurses in Diane's maternity ward doubled as self-appointed counselors. If a nurse was prone to even ordinary sympathies, much might incite her in those halls of extremes—stillbirth, say, or a pregnancy that ended in sterility, or a newborn with a handicap or harelip. Often it was just the birth of a baby whose mother hadn't meant to get pregnant; on other occasions the mother held in her arms the product of her rape. Then there were the girls like Diane Burroughs, children who'd been kept under wraps until the end of their interludes as embodiments of shame. The maternity nurses all knew that poor, waifish Diane had to give up her son and not see him again—ever. That she'd have to wonder, for the rest of her life, where he was and how he was faring. That she'd yearn for him. That she'd entertain fantasies about boys she saw who called him to mind. The toddler glimpsed in tow at Sears, the teen-ager mowing a lawn on the next block, the excellent young actor in the community-theater production of *Our Town*—all of them might be, in her head, her son. It was hard for most of the nurses in the ward not to sympathize with Diane, or, for that matter, with many new mothers. They couldn't keep themselves from holding hands, doling out tissues, listening with the private conviction that there was more to their work than medicine, and talking to new mothers with the sense that, like Florence Nightingale, they were ladies with lamps.

In Diane's case, the lady with the lamp was named Nurse Carol, so it was Nurse Carol who succumbed to Diane's appeal, four hours before Baby Doe's adoptive family was to arrive, for an hour with her son. One hour and then Diane would be done and could start putting her loss behind her. One hour just to hold her baby so she could remember his face, his smell, his skin; one hour because an hour like that would help her come to terms with what was happening. What could Carol say to such a plea? There was no harm in what Diane was asking. She went to the ward, plucked up Baby Doe, brought him to Diane, and, after expressing her sorrow and hope, left and shut the door.

Diane had it all minutely orchestrated. She'd made Walter, the day before, haul her junior suitcase to her beater car and leave it in the trunk beside its larger partner. She'd gotten her things down to where they fit in half a grocery bag. Now all she had to do was wait until things quieted in the hallway. Meanwhile, Diane cooed at Baby Doe. She put her nose to his and said, "Hi there," softly. She drank him in up close and rocked him. Her son looked rather like her half-brother John—he had John's constabulary brow, nose, and chin—but his green eyes were more like her half-brother Club's. Did he look like Club or did he look like John? She hoped he'd be more like Club than John, because John was dense, and Club was charismatic. Who else did he look like? Did he look like her? Diane held him out, carefully, at arm's length, the better to observe his features while he hung there. She decided that one day he'd have powerful shoulders. Plus, his birth height was in the seventy-fifth percentile, so he was going to be tall, and, she could see—after all, she was his mother—very, *very* handsome. All of this without forgetting the important point: that she hadn't planned on being a sixteen-year-old unwedded mum, especially not of a child whose father was Walter Cousins. Nevertheless, she opened her blouse for her son, and let him take her nipple for whatever he could get—she gave him both breasts, and held him with affection. Then, after buttoning up and getting on her coat, she put a folded sweater in her half-full grocery bag, gently set her baby on top of it, and, carrying the bag against her chest, went out to the parking lot.

Down the road three miles, Diane pulled over in the parking lot of a Chinese restaurant. The coast was clear, so she went to the trunk for a suitcase, emptied it, lined it with her coat, propped it open on the passenger seat, and settled her baby inside. In his intermittently loud company, she drove south, because north lay Canada and, maybe, a border request for her nonexistent driver's license, and east and west lay, respectively, mountains and water. South it was, then, at a steady, modest clip. Leaving the freeway once for gas, once for nappies, pins, a terry-cloth washcloth, and baby powder, and once for a baby bottle and a quart of milk—which she had no way to warm other than to leave it by the car heater—Diane obeyed every American driving law. When her baby cried, she felt anxious and ill-equipped. Twice she pulled over to put the bottle's rubber nipple in his mouth, twice to change his nappy and toss his old one in the weeds, and twice to burp him with soft jolts to the back, which she thought was proper technique. Too bad, she thought, that her au-pair year hadn't included infants. She'd have to do what she thought was right and hope for the best. She turned on the radio, talked to her baby, stroked his head with one hand, and worked the steering wheel with the other, all the while fretting about being pulled over, because, it occurred to her, not only was she driving without a license, she also couldn't produce a birth certificate if asked, just a passport with an expired visa. What she did have, though, was $250, and a plan.

That afternoon, in Portland, Oregon—in the wrong part of town— Diane paid cash for a motel room rife with spiders and saturated with tobacco. She got herself installed in this squalid fleabag, removed both hospital ID bands—her own and the baby's—changed another nappy, worked the bottle, watched television, took a shower, and then, for the umpteenth time already, burped her son—who spat up on her, wailing— and slept when he did. In the morning, bleary, she bought a twin packet of cupcakes and ate them with chocolate milk in the car. Well into afternoon, she drove broad circuits, surveying Portland, while the baby, swaddled in his suitcase-nest, rode shotgun with, unfortunately, distress, odors, and complaints. Portland seemed smaller than Seattle, but leafier and just as prosperous. There were plenty of grand Victorian homes in neighborhoods where the streets were shaded by large trees, but also plenty of dutifully kept ranch houses like the Cousins home in Seattle. Diane cruised neighborhoods with an eye toward their amenities before renting a post-office box in Sullivan's Gulch, not far from Lloyd Center, a new shopping center. She wanted to go inside Lloyd Center and have a look around, but instead, with her baby on her arm, she went into a battered-looking secondhand store and bought him a wicker basket, a blue baby blanket, a grow suit, and corduroy booties. Lloyd Center would have to wait.

That night, Diane parked her beater beneath a streetside elm in the Eastmoreland neighborhood, where she could see downhill a long way. For an hour and a half she watched the scene in front of her and in her rearview mirror. People came and went, cars pulled in and out, lights went on, lights went off, people walked with dogs on leashes, a cat prowled cryptically. Around nine-thirty, Diane selected the third house from the end on the east side of the block, a large, red-bricked Tudor with tall hedges. Now came the hard part—the disturbing crux of the deed. She got out, looked around, collected herself with one deep breath, then opened the passenger door and gathered up the wicker basket containing her sleeping son, who was tucked into his blue blanket and warmly dressed in his baby grow and booties. As calmly as she could, but steadily, she walked down the sidewalk through intervals of yard lamplight that illuminated her son's perfect face. And it *was* perfect. Why was her son so perfect? She looked, alternately, at him and at the Tudor. From its front window, a purple light emanated; the people inside, she understood, were watching TV. TV watchers in a red brick Tudor were going to have to do the right thing. "Okay," Diane thought, "this is it," and then, suddenly welling up, she climbed the stairs and left her son on the stoop.

It was bitter-hard. But, driving off, she bucked up within minutes. The TV watchers, upstanding people who lived in a good home in a good neighborhood, would squire Baby Doe to the next step along his way. All he had to do was cry how he did and they would give him what he needed and take him where he needed to go. And that left her free now—free, foremost, to call that toff Walter on Monday morning and bleed him for everything he was bloody worth. For now though, she returned to her dingy quarters, where she passed a night equal in sleeplessness to the one before it, if for different reasons. Her baby kept her awake not with intermittent squalls but with his absence.

The following afternoon, with Walter on the hook, a bag of chocolates beside her, the television for company, and a pillow behind her head,

Diane sat on her motel bed circling rooms for rent in the *Journal*. She looked at the comics, did the crossword puzzle, and read "Hints from Heloise" and "Dear Abby." Below the fold in the local section she came across the headline POLICE SEEK PARENTS OF ABANDONED BABY. No witnesses or clues were mentioned in the story. The infant was in the care of the Boys and Girls Aid Society of Oregon. Diane felt relieved to know that Baby Doe was settled. Her plan was a success.

Two days later, on a sunny morning, standing in the post-office foyer, she tore open Walter's first installment with giddy pleasure, counted and then folded his fresh bills into a fat wad, noted with interest but not disappointment the absence of a note or letter, then walked down the street and leased a safety-deposit box at a branch of Portland Trust and Savings. The next day, she took a furnished room in Sullivan's Gulch, dank and dreadful but dirt-cheap, and certainly no worse than what she'd known growing up. Determined to save what she could on rent, she shared a bathroom with other tenants and cooked soup and oatmeal on a hotplate. The landlord didn't ask for references or a damage deposit, and the building was in walking distance of her post-office box. Lloyd Center was a bit of a trek, but the weather was fair, the days were long, and she had time, suddenly, to do as she pleased, which meant reading in bed all morning if she felt like it, sitting in a cinema in the middle of the afternoon, eating in restaurants, and shopping. Diane, settled in, sent Club her mailing address, saying, "Write to me here—I've gone a bit south." A month later, he replied with a postcard from Liverpool depicting, in sepia, its long-ago canning dock. "Scraggy-neck," it read. "Right enough for the moment. Studying electrical from mail order manuals. Wouldn't mind putting to sea as a joiner, something in an engine room, thank you please, what I would like is electrical greaser, out of the wind, where it's snug." In a second paragraph he asked, "What's all this with them thrashing up their Negroes? Cattle prods and hoses? God save the Queen, Luv!—Club."

Lloyd Center was American and fantastic. At a kiosk, she counted one hundred shops and read a sign claiming that no shopping center in America was larger. There was an ice rink with a viewing balcony. Lipman's sold fine apparel for women, as did Meier & Frank. Diane spent a lot of time combing the racks, contemplating the displays of fashionable clothing, and trying things on in tiny dressing rooms. Everything was a no-go—even though she was snapping back from pregnancy—but she still liked rhythmically sliding the dresses, skirts, and blouses on their hangers, pulling out a possibility, eyeing it critically, checking the price tag, assessing the fabric, reading the label, and slipping it back in place before rifling, once more, through the rack. If she lingered long enough, a floor clerk might come round to suggest the girls' department for a proper fit. There were a lot of tucked bodices, and gloves for evening wear, and seersucker suits, and dozens of variations on Jacqueline Kennedy's pillbox hat, but none of that seemed right to Diane. What seemed right was a look she came across while passing the toy department at J. C. Penney: Blonde Ponytail Barbie, in a maroon velvet sleeveless top and a white satin skirt, complete with glossy lips, painted fingernails, and maroon wedges.

Three weeks later, costumed as Blonde Ponytail Barbie, Diane sat in the tea shop on the tenth floor of the downtown Lipman's, eating tuna casserole and, with a pencil, designing a business card on a napkin. A week later, after picking up a hundred freshly printed cards at a stationer's, she bought a handbag, earrings, necklace, bracelet, and watch. These were of good quality, as was her hairdo—glossy, with bangs—which she'd paid an expensive dresser to put together. On a side street, in her mildewed beater, Diane adorned herself with the jewelry, tucked a dozen of the fresh cards into her handbag, and made a last assessment in her rearview mirror. Then, wearing a straight face, she got out on the passenger side, looking, she hoped, supremely confident.

Diane walked down Eleventh drawing glances. At the Seward Hotel, with no hesitation, she glided through the door held open for her and sat in the lobby with her legs crossed, as if she belonged there, under the rustic chandeliers, the gilded archways, and the murals depicting the Lewis and Clark Expedition. For a half-hour, she monitored the front desk and the concierge stand, the comings and goings of the bellboys with their carts of luggage, and the Seward's guests, with their gaiety, fine clothes, and need for taxis. The concierge, in a tight serge suit, with a scarlet face and a walrus mustache, stood at a kind of podium. Diane, after smoothing down her velvet top and brushing at her satin skirt, approached him, half curtsied as part of her act, and said, "Pardon me. I wonder if I might inquire."

"British," said the concierge. "Am I right?"

Diane snapped open her bag and produced her business card, which he studied suspiciously, with pursed lips. It read:

First Class Service
CANDACE DARK ESCORT SERVICE
Portland's #1 rated agency
Sophisticated, refined, and high-class escorts,
strictly for gentlemen
We Are Happy to Serve You
Call CA7-4223

"We run a very professional and aboveboard operation," said Diane. "On top of that, we offer a ten-percent commission for client referrals."

The concierge licked his lips as if consternated. "How old are you?" he asked.

"The escorts we employ are all between the ages of twenty-one and thirty-five," Diane answered. "No minors, we don't employ minors, that goes without saying."

"I'm guessing you're sixteen, tops."

"Please do give my proposal some thought, sir. Our ten-percent commission is competitive in the industry. Our agents have been known to make as much as twenty dollars per referral, even more. I'm sure you must have guests who inquire regarding escort services, and when they do, why, perhaps you'll think of me." She smiled, and once again curtsied.

The concierge's eyes made a sweep of the lobby before he said, "We'll see what happens," and put her card in his jacket pocket.

It was the same at the Benson, with its marble floors and fireplaces, and at the Imperial on Broadway, and at the Heathman. At all of these fine hotels, a concierge took Diane's card, each with his own we-both-know-what-this-is-about-but-we're-not-going-to-acknowledge-it mien. It was fine with her for them to handle it that way. She concurred, silently, with their need for discretion, and let them know, without saying it directly, that she intended to be so impeccably discreet, at every turn, that nothing about her would ever threaten their good reputation, advantageous position, or employment.

She was in business after that, with some success. It was what she'd seen her mum do, after all, on a different scale, at home. Instead of entertaining men in a parlor, Diane went with them to dinner, the theater, the symphony, and piano bars where richly colored drinks were served. Never did she announce herself as a purveyor of sexual services. The safer thing to do was to accept the offer of a hotel-bar nightcap, and then the invitation to the room. Then, behind the locked door with the security chain latched, and with no mention of money changing hands, to take control of the transaction. Diane did this by giving her client what he needed, even if he was blind, beforehand, about what he needed, and was only seeing it right now through the ministrations of "Candy Dark." Sometimes, as soon as a client was sufficiently serviced, he'd ask her to leave with a gift for her trouble—the late-night cab, the prearranged "escort fee," and "a gratuity," as Diane taught them to call it—and sometimes she had to stay on until morning before, needing to get on with whatever it was that had brought him to Portland, her client, maybe half dressed, or in his underwear, or shoeless, or with a loose tie, would pull out his wallet. If he was cheap, she would prod him. Usually it was productive to prod a man who came up short in the cash department—to make him feel bad about that, but good in bed, was the right combination. There were skinflints, to be sure, and the expense of commissions—Diane paid her concierges with a punctilious discretion, if not always with a completely honest 10 percent—but in the end, she was rewarded handsomely for what she did. Before long, she was able to get a nice apartment and—with the help of a client who sold upscale trade-ins—a more respectable car.

One night, she escorted an attorney who specialized in immigration law, and made sure it came to pass that he requested her services for the following evening. This man, whom she found attractive, which was rare, insisted that it was important to him, erotically speaking, to know who he was sleeping with, it couldn't really be "Candy Dark." She told him her name, because she liked him and wanted to, but more because she thought he might take on her visa problems free of charge. He did take them on, this well-toned repeat client with broad shoulders and a slim waist, who was given to gasping, "Diane . . . Fucking . . . Priceless . . . Burroughs!" when his big moment arrived. Soon, with the right papers in hand, Diane got a driver's license and a long-term visa.

There were problems, of course, with this manner of living, like worrying about arrest for solicitation, and concern about getting pregnant again. Then there were the clients who seemed like potential murderers or, less frightening but more common, clients with sexual difficulties. There were men with ghastly halitosis, men whose proclivities were pathetic or onerous, and, worst of all, men who went too far despite her firmly articulated prohibitions, inflicting pains that weren't artfully constrained or merely of the moment—injuries, sometimes, of the kind you limped home with and then recovered from with bed rest and ointment. Which wasn't so bad, the days off and the unanswered telephone, the books, naps, TV shows, and American-cheddar tuna melts, the luxurious baths, the towel wrapped around the head, the robe and slippers, the indulgent home manicures—in sum, the life of a B-movie starlet. During these interludes, though, Diane felt lonely. Wallowing in the wounds of high-end prostitution, she remembered her son, wondered about his welfare, and regretted her decision to abandon him.

Diane moved into a new apartment, significantly more posh and with a view of the Willamette, and traded in her car for one more daring. She also made some updates to her wardrobe, not because she needed to, but because shopping was fun—shopping, crossword puzzles, dime-store novels, television, and desserts filled her days, just as needy men filled her nights. She bought Junior Miss light pajama sets in both black and pink, carried them in her bag, and sometimes emerged from a hotel bathroom with one or the other on, and, with her ponytail tightly banded and her face freshly scrubbed, purred, "I was naughty and got my other PJs dirty." It was fair to say that playing Candy Dark was satisfying, since it included turning men around and exploiting them whenever possible.

Diane took a vindictive delight, too, in Walter Cousins's payoff packets, which now always arrived with an accompanying note wishing her and "the baby" well, or with an inquiry about visiting her when next he was in Portland. She never answered these. She tossed them in the trash. Sometimes, in the grip of melancholy, she drove past the Tudor in Eastmoreland where she'd left her son, slowing so as to hurt herself, once again, by drumming up the disconsolate feeling of leaving him on the stoop. Sometimes she parked outside the Boys and Girls Aid Society of Oregon Home—actually three cottages, quite charming, on Southeast Powell Boulevard—for no reason other than to share her baby's world: the grounds he knew, just visible through a gate, the trees, gardens, squirrels, and calling birds he was becoming aware of as he grew. Or maybe not, since by now he could have been adopted. She hoped that, if so, he was somewhere wonderful. She hoped he'd landed in the proper sort of family, with a mother who served good suppers every night and a father who tucked him in and read him stories. These homey images comforted Diane. She was entirely for them, for every middle-class convention, for all the stock concepts of sound child-rearing. It pleased her to think that at least one Burroughs might escape the impoverished fate of her clan. Hurrah for Baby Doe, slung from that impossible English mess as if from a catapult. He would soar, she constantly hoped and prayed, while following an American arc.

In the summer of 1970, a client took Candy Dark to a soirée at the Riverside Golf and Country Club. Along the way, in a hired car, he explained who would be there—rich people, in a nutshell. He said he needed her "to hold up her end." He added that introducing her as Candy Dark was "not going to wash," and that he wanted her to choose a different phony name that was "a lot more plain." "What about 'Diane'?" Diane suggested. "Would 'Diane' be acceptably unremarkable?" And so, at this soirée, she was introduced as "Diane Davis" to men in cummerbunds and women in summer gala dresses. Her client, it emerged, was loud and overbearing, and went about asking people, regarding Diane, "Ain't she cute?" The more he drank, the more unacceptable he became, and the more uninhibited. He put his arm around her waist and his lips around her earlobe. His ranging mitt stopped, now and then, to squeeze her neck below her ponytail. Eventually, and drunkenly, he lost track of her whereabouts, and this left Diane free to sit with a decorated drink, waiting for the night's dénouement.

She was people-watching at the verge of a great pulse of revelers when a tall, not bad-looking young nob approached, introduced himself as Jim Long, and asked if he could sit with her "while these people make fools of themselves." Diane pointed out a nearby chair.

Jim Long had dark, curly hair, aquiline features, and a prominent Adam's apple. He was twenty-seven. He was the fourth of five brothers and had two sisters—one older, one younger. The month before, he had been appointed vice-president of marketing at Long Alpine Industries, Inc., the company his father had started after World War II, which specialized in alpine skis, though they also made Nordic, touring, and tele-marking skis. They had a factory in the area, and were just beginning production of a new line of fiberglass skis after having used laminated wood for twenty-two years. Long was in a period of change, risk, and new investment that made the future feel, Jim told Diane, "like a game we're in without a playbook."

Diane acknowledged that skiing was not particularly popular among the English but claimed that it had always excited *her*, especially after see-ing what the Goitschel sisters had accomplished at the Innsbruck Olympics. She mentioned the handsome Frenchman Jean-Claude Killy—whom she'd read about in magazines—but pronounced his name with-out refinement, not wanting Jim to think she was a snob. Jim replied that he'd met Kill-*ee* at the '67 World Cup race in Berchtesgaden, and that there'd been a follow-up discussion with "that self-infatuated playboy" about endorsing Long's new fiberglass product. Which went nowhere, because a rival nabbed "the Frog" by agreeing to name a ski for him—in fact, a whole line of skis. What were Diane's special interests?

European travel. American baseball. Outdoor recreation. Water ski-ing. As a girl, she'd roamed often in the Lake District.

Jim drank Miller High Life from a bottle. His fingers ended in broad nails, his expression suggested an amused judgment of the world, and he wore a checked shirt and blue blazer. He reiterated his distaste—demon-strated by this casual attire—for country-club parties of the sort now unfolding. He said that he liked to ski, play golf, and fish for salmon, that he liked to do all of these things with friends but that large gatherings didn't appeal to him because at large gatherings the conversation was superficial. Diane had heard this come-on before, but she agreed anyway, pretending it was novel.

What did she do? She'd done many things, mostly for firms in Lon-don, New York, and now in Portland, where she'd relocated because of an attractive offer at a pharmaceutical firm and for its proximity to the out-of-doors. Jim would chalk up this circumspect story, she knew, to femi-nine evasiveness, but a woman, after all, had a right to mystery. Later, she could admit to exaggerations, if she had to—it would be easy to do and he would love it.

They repaired to a veranda with a view of the golf course, where night bugs agitated the lamplight near the top of a pole, and where a fairway appeared endless and moonlit. Jim put one hand on the railing and made a comment about Canada geese fouling a green that was too close to a water hazard. Then he confided that, for the past few months, he'd been struggling against fogies both at the club and at the company. He was on the Greens Committee, and there was considerable expense involved in addressing the Canada-goose issue permanently. The problem was that most of the executive positions were held by old duffers who opposed improvements that might increase dues. Now Jim slid one hand into the pocket of his slacks and, with the other, aimed his beer bottle at the golf course. "These guys are old-school," he said. "I'm not old-school. It's a little bit never-the-twain-shall-meet. A little bit rock-and-a-hard-place."

Jim talked next about Autzen Stadium, where the University of Oregon Ducks football team played; the Long family had been a major contributor to its construction. And about Timberline Lodge at Mount Hood, where the rooms were Spartan but the setting spectacular. It had sunk, years before, into disrepair, and closed, but the Longs had put money there as secondary investors, and for ten years now, Timberline had turned advancing profits. At the moment, the ski industry—the entire recreation industry, in fact—was "booming along nicely," even as Nixon led the country into recession and inflation, and deeper into a war that was "going south." Americans, Jim argued, felt a need for escape.

Broaching Vietnam made him grave. A friend had died there; two more had been wounded. This left him "pissed off enough to want to do something about it," he didn't know exactly what, but he was thinking of voting for Bob Straub for governor, and he was lobbying his family to increase its support for Mark Hatfield now that Hatfield had teamed with George McGovern on troop-withdrawal legislation. "Enough," he said. "Should we walk on the golf course?"

Diane said she would like that enormously, but she was here with someone else, and even though this someone else was absolutely paralytic, she—

"Absolutely paralytic," Jim said. "I like that. In fact, I love it. Who are you here with?"

"Nobody who matters."

He smiled and ran a hand through his curly hair. "I hate these parties," he said as though he wasn't repeating himself. "Duffers and drunks. They ought to be moving on improving this place and doing something about the damn war."

Diane looked at her watch. "Midnight," she said. "As in 'Cinderella,' Prince James. I'd better make an appearance inside; His Lordship might fret—assuming he's still conscious."

She opened her little handbag, produced her silver pen, and wrote her name—Diane Burroughs—and phone number on the back of a Lipman's receipt. "As opposed to a glass slipper," she said, before stuffing it into the breast pocket of Jim's blazer. "But then, this is reality."

Jim, she soon found, had a beautiful family. His parents, Nelson and Isobel, warmed immediately to their son's new British girlfriend—Nelson in particular, who looked like a butler, with his thin upper lip and gleaming pate. Nelson had been stationed, during the war, at Debden, where he "grew fond of the English," but, more to the point, he told Diane, where he met plenty of English girls who looked and sounded like her. "Ergo," he added, winking, "I can't help but associate you with that period in my life, which was so stimulating and formative." Isobel said that Nelson had a photo album in the attic with pictures in it of the pretty English bachelorettes he'd dated while she herself was finding dates few and far between, because all the young men were overseas. But how wonderful it had been when they came home in '45, and she'd had the pleasure of dating "a host" before meeting Nelson at Sun Valley Lodge on New Year's Eve of '46. It had just reopened after having served, for the duration, as a war hospital. They'd skied together for three blissful days.

The Longs, in concert, embraced Diane as right for Jim. Within a month she was an integral part of this prominent ski clan's relentless social calendar. Jim's brothers—Rob, Tom, Will, and Trip—all resembled each other, though Jim was the most fit, and Tom, the youngest, and a bachelor like Jim, had by far the most hair. The married men were varyingly flirtatious with Diane but uniformly cautious and unthreatening; Tom, the baby of the family and its self-appointed rebel, was too self-involved to see anything in Diane except, she sensed, what he wanted to see—namely, English decoration. Jim's older sister, Sue, was married to the president of sales at a company that built long-haul trucks, and his younger sister, Lynn, was a Tri Delt at U of O who took easily to her role as Diane's default roommate when the Longs descended on Timberline Lodge, or stayed overnight at the Hilton in Eugene after a Ducks game and its consequent revels. Lynn wore a billowing auburn ponytail, and in hotel rooms liked to sit on her bed drinking rum-and-Cokes, talking about sex, and goading Diane to be revealing about her love life: what she'd done or hadn't done, what she was thinking about doing next, if it was true that foreign guys were better in bed—especially French guys—if she liked lingerie and, if so, what kind, and, eventually, if she could keep secrets. And then there were the secrets themselves—for example, that Lynn had been on the pill until the weight gain and headaches got to be too much (now she had an IUD that was only borderline comfortable and might have to be refitted), and that she'd lost her virginity during high school but had since then slept with just one guy besides the guy she was sleeping with now, who was better at it than either of the other guys.

Jim was only mildly aggressive when it came to his need for sex. Diane let him inside her bra early on but drew the line at her panties until, after three months of dating, he gave her a garnet ring one evening in a seafood restaurant—an "I'm in love with you" ring, as he called it. That night she didn't stop his southward-moving fingers, which, on reaching their destination, flailed away at high speed. Unable to respond to Jim's overzealous efforts, Diane emitted a few fake ecstatic squeals while clenching her buttocks, after which he whispered, "My turn." His turn took no more than thirty seconds, and ended with him gasping, "Holy Jesus." Henceforth a swift approach kept Jim maintained—après-ski, post-golf or post-swimming, or at the end of long hours at Long Alpine headquarters, he did what he did for Diane, and then she did what she did for him. She did it without complaint, but also as if it were not her favorite thing in life, not exactly a necessary evil but also not exactly something she looked forward to.

It wasn't hard to steer Jim toward a marriage proposal. If he wanted to think of himself as a hero who was improving things on the golf course and in Vietnam, fine, because Diane could play his lady in distress without thinking about it, be the princess in the long satin dress who was always pulling its embroidered hem higher to go up and down stairs, the lovely girl in one of those tall, conical, pointy hats with the sheer veil attached to it who was also excellent on horseback. She could be what she knew he wanted her to be: chipper, bright, British in affect, sparkling, effusive, charming, sexy (but sexy without going overboard into slutty, and without suggesting dark and dangerous). She gave him the whole act, everything he needed, and after a year—he had it marked to the day—he got down on one knee, brought out a diamond ring, said what he had to say—to which she at once said yes—and finally, since Diane had led him to believe that she was parentless because of a car accident when she was seven, asked whom he should contact for permission. Diane just giggled, kissed his cheek, slid a hand down his pants, and said, "I'm all the permission you'll ever need, Jim."

The next morning, with Jim in the bag, she fended off phone calls from a succession of Long women who wanted to talk about wedding plans. The outlines emerged of a Congregational church ceremony to be followed by festivities at the Riverside Club, the details of which, in the ensuing months, she felt no need to put her stamp on. When the big day arrived, Diane found herself covered to the throat in virginal white and hauling about a train of female Longs: Jim's two sisters, three sisters-in-law, and a niece strewing flower petals as the extensive Republican gathering in the pews smiled about how cute she looked. In front of them all, trying hard to appear poised, Diane put a gold band on Jim's thick ring finger. His kiss-the-bride kiss was tender, not acquisitive; friendly, not lusty. On their way down the aisle as man and wife, he nodded, waved, and shook hands with happy force. Then they were alone, momentarily, in an anteroom, where he exclaimed, "Jesus, we did it!"

It was May of 1972. In a brand-new Olds 442 convertible, Mr. and Mrs. Long motored to a lodge on Cannon Beach for a simple honeymoon (to be followed by a three-week tour of Italy that Jim couldn't work into his schedule until June). That night, with an uncorked bottle of champagne and two new glasses, and Diane decked out in the red lingerie Jim gave her, they moved beyond digital manipulations. Jim wasn't bad—a little bland, a little hurried—but his rubber had the wrong ring size, and after it came off inside her, she couldn't get it out. In the morning she sent him for a package of cotton swabs because she still couldn't retrieve it. With Jim away on this husbandly mission, she got up, peed, and went out on the veranda so she could look at and smell the ocean. A seagull prodded something below her in the sand, and after a while she realized it was a plastic bag. That seemed sad and unromantic, a reminder of the bleakness of life on earth, which was how she often saw things when alone, and which led her, inevitably, to think of her son. Gravity, or maybe peeing, made some kind of difference, because suddenly she felt able to extract Jim's rubber, and went in and did so, much to her relief, since if it stayed any longer it might incite a yeast infection. Again on the veranda, she saw there were more gulls, and on a whim dropped the rubber in their squabbling midst before looking up and down the wide beach. To the south, a family was on a morning constitutional, Mum and Dad holding hands, their boy and girl trotting in arcs along the wet part of the strand. Every once in a while, the boy dashed into the surf. Finally, he fell and tottered up, wet. This made Diane think again of her son, who would be nine now, nine and a month. For all she knew, that was him below, wringing out his shirt and looking stunned.

3

The Adventures of Baby Doe

The people in the Eastmoreland neighborhood who found Diane's baby on their stoop were the Crofters, Arnie and Stacy. There was a troubling noise just outside their front door—Stacy thought it might be clashing cats—which caused Arnie, since he could no longer ignore her or it, to turn down the volume on *The Nurses*. Standing by the TV with his hands on his hips, he said, "Shhhh," a little angrily, because Stacy was blowing her nose into a handkerchief. "Sorry," she whispered. "Quiet!" Arnie answered. They regarded each other with bitter familiarity. "Something isn't right," Arnie observed.

All Arnie had to do was go outside and look, but he hesitated, hoping the noise would resolve itself so they could get back to *The Nurses,* and Stacy beat him to it. She threw open the door and, after gasping, said, "Arn!" By the time he got there, she had a crying baby in her arms and was whispering to it, warming it against her chest, rocking it, and patting its back. "Poor baby," she said. "It's a *baby*."

Arnie answered, "Wait a second."

He stood on the stoop and scrutinized the block. Then, spurred by what he recognized as a closing window of opportunity to find out who had abandoned a baby, he hurried to the sidewalk and looked more thoroughly. There was no one walking, running, or driving away, just the same old quiet street, still, as always, after dark.

Arnie went in, dialed the police, and said, "Uh, the strangest thing just happened right now—someone left a baby on our porch." Then he and Stacy sat on the couch, taking turns holding it. There was the ammonia smell, emanating from a diaper, that Arnie, at fifty-eight, remembered from his own kids, and that made him hand the baby back to Stacy. He went to wash his hands, and when he came back, Stacy was talking soothingly to it, calling it, over and over, "you poor, poor thing," and "you poor little baby," asking it, "Are you better now?" and apologizing by saying, "I'd change your diaper if I had one around, but I don't anymore, you little sweetheart."

Arnie said, "This is unbelievable."

"Look at his little blue blanket," answered Stacy. "It's a boy."

They leaned in to enjoy the little foundling together. Their own kids were both married, but there were no grandchildren yet. Stacy said, "This guy is really, really *darling.*"

"He's cute," agreed Arnie, "but what baby isn't? When did you see a baby you didn't say was cute, you pushover?"

"Just *darling,*" Stacy answered. "Who would *do* a thing like this?" She stroked the baby's chin. She smelled his hair.

Arnie stroked the baby's chin, too—their hands alternated. "Unbelievable," he answered. "Someone not right in the head, I guess. Their own *baby.*"

Stacy slid her index finger into the baby's fist. "Wow," she said. "My, my, sweetheart. Strong boy."

"He does look strong. Look how thick his neck is."

"This is really sad," said Stacy.

They sat there, asking questions and admiring the boy, until two policemen arrived. After a series of radio and phone calls, one of them finally took the baby from Stacy's arms and returned it to its basket, where it wailed. Stacy wanted to explain to these young men what the baby needed, but the whole thing was so sad now that she was rendered mute by it, and could only watch from the stoop while one of the policemen carried the basket out, put it on the back seat of his patrol car, and shut the door, not gently. Stacy's eyes welled. She nodded silently at the officers while they said their farewells. "That's what happens," she told Arnie later. "That's the world. Someone leaves a baby out in the cold, next a cop slams a door,in his face."

"Okay," said Arnie.

"That poor kid ought to be nursing right now instead of riding downtown in a cop car. I mean, Arn, come on, tell me, where is God at a time like this? All these people blabbing how God has a plan, it's all for the best, we shouldn't try to understand—well, no, I *don't* understand. A God who lets stuff like *this* happen—what kind of God is *that*?"

Arnie said, while reaching for his pipe, "I don't know. You do the best you can, I guess, and the rest is out of your hands."

"What kind of God?" repeated Stacy.

The Boys and Girls Aid Society of Oregon Home on Powell Boulevard Southeast was staffed by women who believed, based partly on intuition and partly on research, that an orphanage should feel like a home. This was fortunate for the abandoned boy handed over to them by the Portland Police Department, who in the Infant Cottage was lavished with attention. Loving women nurtured waifs like him around the clock until they could be placed in foster homes or adopted. In other words, in the first weeks of his life, the son of Diane Burroughs and Walter Cousins had the copious and intimate contact with women recommended for infants by psychologists. He didn't have this sort of contact with just one woman, or achieve the kind of bonding with one woman that was considered, also by psychologists, essential to well-being; instead, there were five women, attentive, trained, and committed to their work, who held him, spoke to him, fed him from a bottle, looked him in the eyes, swaddled his bottom, and, when he cried, soothed him with the right intonations. Administered to thusly, he thrived, reaping the benefits of advanced child-care theory. He was prized, cuddled, rocked, and sung to. As the youngest ward of the state on the premises, he led a princeling's life, attended by adoration. The story of his abandonment provoked maternalism in his caretakers and played on their sympathies. None of them wanted the poor, unwanted child who had no name to fall through the cracks or endure the tiniest deprivation. He was, they felt, so young that it was not too late for their compassionate ministrations. Bad influences hadn't impaired him, as they'd impaired so many of the older kids in the home. He could be set on the right path by the power of their loving-kindness. And, since a nameless child was too abstract to function as the right vessel for their feelings, they dubbed him, at first, "our little lost lamb," and then, for short, "Little."

A singular and fantastic season for Little. Eleven and a half weeks of the royal treatment, including a lot more warm milk than he needed and a lot of talcum powder between the waist and knees. Little quickly developed chin blubber and passed his waking hours in a satisfied dolor that smelled of Breck, Crest, Yardley of London, egg-salad sandwiches, and Diet Rite. Then, one day, out of nowhere, he was dressed too warmly and carried outside by his new adoptive mother, Alice King, who afterward would always associate the smell of roses with his first hour in her arms. This was because not far from her car door were wildly proliferating coral-colored blooms, long-thorned and red-tipped, with a thick, tangy scent. They were so beautiful and perfect she wanted to have one to dry and press in a keepsake book, and so, with her free hand, she reached for a likely flower, one with time left on it, thinking she might twist it free or bend it over a fingernail. Instead, she was painfully pricked in her thumb, which she withdrew and sucked. A single dark drop of her blood, she saw, had fallen on, and stained, her new baby's blanket. This seemed to her an unhappy omen, and she said as much to her husband, Dan. "You don't believe in omens," he reminded her.

Until now, the Kings had been childless. Dan had been in medical school, in residency, taking boards, volunteering for the UN Medical Services in Madagascar, and establishing his family practice in a Seattle suburb, while Alice took a master's in political science and worked for the mayor's office. In their early thirties, they tried to have children, and then—worried—got serious about the effort. They did what a specialist told them to do, which didn't help, because, as it turned out, Dan was shooting such a high percentage of blanks that the odds of success were almost nil. He was devastated by news of his insufficiency, and told Alice and the fertility specialist who'd delivered the guilty verdict that no one, obviously, felt good on hearing that he was an evolutionary failure. After that, his inability to impregnate Alice affected his sexual performance. When Dan tried to do it, he would find himself thinking about his sperm's bad motility, about all those sluggish, unmotivated losers wandering into blind alleys or just losing steam, dissolving in place, uninterested in destiny. In a depressing and insidious way, he identified with their incompetence. "That's me," he thought. "It's a metaphor for me." In that frame of mind, he couldn't consummate.

Then a light went on. Dan and Alice, though only nominally Jewish and avoiders of synagogues, went to visit a young rabbi recommended by friends. He was dressed in shirtsleeves to see them in his office, a beardless guy named Nathan Weisfeld. A popular recent addition to Temple Beth David, Weisfeld was a supporter of John Kennedy even if Joe Kennedy was an anti-Semite and Nixon was maybe better for Israel. John Kennedy had a nice wife and children, John Kennedy had been wounded in World War II, John Kennedy came from immigrants, John Kennedy was a liberal. As for adoption, "He who raises someone else's child is regarded as if he had actually brought him into the world." It was an act of *chesed,* it made a contribution, it served so beautifully the endeavor of world repair, "which we call *tikkun.*" Weisfeld shrugged. "Of course you should adopt," he said. "Nothing in Jewish law says no, nowhere is there an admonition." He shrugged again. "I can only say *mazel tov.* Wonderful news. Now go and build a Jewish home together."

Conveniently, it was time for the annual Passover trip to Dan's parents. They lived in Pasadena with air conditioning, but were originally from Pinsk. "In Pinsk," Dan's father, Al, asked, when Dan told them what he and Alice were considering, "was there a Jew who adopted, Beryl?" Dan's mother said no, it was unheard of in Pinsk, this was not something Jewish people did. "She's right," said his father. "Your mother is right, Daniel." "Adoption!" said his mother. "Did your brothers or your sisters adopt? They didn't adopt. No, every one of them with their own children, our grandchildren, seven grandchildren, *and not one is adopted.*"

"This is what I live with," Dan said to Alice, as soon as they were out the door. "Textbook Yids."

They set out for San Jose to see Alice's father. Dan stopped at pay phones to check on his patients. Alice read *So You're Thinking of Adopting!* At a roadside picnic table they ate sandwiches and potato chips, and talked about the new pieces of contemporary furniture they were considering for their living room. Alice wanted to donate the old pieces to the Jewish Family & Child Service. They talked about their exasperating parents; Alice's sister, Bernice, and her marital problems; the cost of joining a private swim club where Alice's best friend and her husband were members; and, more than the rest of it put together, adoption.

In San Jose, Alice's father, Dave Levine—sitting on his deck in tennis shorts, thighs splooching where they pressed against his lawn chair— said that someone named Marty Ashkanazi had been adopted after his family got "wiped out" in the Holocaust. This Marty was "today a perfectly good guy," which Pop felt was proof of something. If Marty could be adopted and turn out so well, who was to say about adoption? "Only an idiot could say yes or no," said Pop, "adoption yes or adoption no, so let me be an idiot and say to you something—when you adopt, it's true, you take your chances."

"That's obvious," answered Dan. "But isn't it also taking a chance to have biological kids? Either way, you do the best you can, but you don't really control what happens."

"Take Alice, for example," Alice's father agreed. "Look what happened to my baby girl Alice. She marries a guy who is admittedly a nice guy, only problem is he carts her somewhere else, then she forgets back home in San Jose, now I only see her maybe twice a year, three times if she has *tsuris*."

"We come more than that, Pop, so stop with the guilt."

"Four times."

They hauled him all the way up to the city so he could visit his ill sister in the Mission District, where she lived behind barred windows and a double lock. "Only one more thing," Pop insisted, when Dan told him for the third time that he and Alice had to get on the road, and so, before taking him all the way back to San Jose, they stopped at Home of Peace in Colma. "Please God, this is where I end up," Pop said, "in the ground beside your mother. When it's my time. Which might not be for a long time, or which might be driving home in a few minutes with this *meshugenah* here." He pointed at Dan, then threw up his hands. "Okay, here, my final word," he said. "My commentary, take it or leave it. And what I'm thinking is, an adopted is like the Jews, okay? Without a country, because he has two countries, his home country and the Promised Land. 'Next year in Jerusalem'—maybe an adopted is saying this in his head, he thinks something is missing, always something is not right or perfect, he has longings. Maybe his parents are Dr. Daniel and Alice, perfectly nice people, loving people, concerned people for the good of the whole world, liberal people who care about other human beings, which is a wonderful way to be, I'm not discounting it; still, here is this adopted, wondering always who he is, not at peace in his heart, restless about everything, a striver, a historian, a what-do-you-call-it, a genealogist type of guy, never satisfied, always asking questions, maybe even rebellious against his perfectly loving parents. Why? Because they aren't his parents and he knows it—and also he's mad at his real parents."

"We wouldn't tell him," said Dan. "He wouldn't know he was adopted."

"Nobody would tell him," Alice added. "Everyone would have to keep the secret."

"*Oy*," said Pop.

But in the end he hugged his daughter and stroked her hair, which was honey-colored, thick, and worn loose, to her shoulders. "Alice," he said, "if you and Dr. Daniel must do this, adopt, please do it with both eyes open, can you promise? Both eyes open, please, knowing ahead maybe you can't see what there is to see, maybe it's a wrecked train, maybe not, who knows?"

"We know," said Dan. "Things can go wrong. It isn't news to us, the risks of adoption."

Pop shook his finger at him over Alice's shoulder. "This is what I mean," he said. "This is what I'm nervous of, *exactly*. Listen to Dr. Daniel when he speaks. He thinks this will happen to *other* people. He doesn't think it will happen to *him*. How could it happen to the wonderful Dr. Daniel, who has such a wonderful life?"

"You're right, Daniel's like that," said Alice.

They situated Pop in his quarters again, and finally, relieved—their forebearers in their wake—got on the freeway. For fifty fast and therapeutic miles they shared their generational amusement and gave their familial irritation full rein, laughing because their parents were archaic, and angry because they were know-it-alls. When that was exhausted, and for the next two hundred miles, they talked as if against a deadline about adoption, and, partly because their parents were so difficult—because their parents' concerns about adoption were so ridiculous—they decided to go ahead with it. That night there was motel sex as confirmation. There were earnest convictions, virtuous feeling, outrage, and the will to make a statement. Let their parents think what they want to think, let them be oppressed by tradition and reservation, by Darwinian smallness, and by fear of the unknown—they, Dan and Alice, were adopting.

Without delay, then, they started the process. They had to jump through hoops, waste reams of paper, and, Dan felt, put up with nonsense. They had to answer every question, fill in every blank, and be patient while invisible wheels turned; they had to expect things to proceed in tiny increments that inevitably triggered another invoice. During all of this, Alice got up to speed on adoption. She read studies and how-to books. When Dan complained about exasperating forms, Alice said that people who gave up because adoption was tediously bureaucratic, not to mention expensive, couldn't be counted on as parents anyway, and if they were going to complain, as Dan was complaining, about the "home study," if letting someone in the door to poke around a little was going to be treated like a deal breaker, well, said Alice, there were plenty of other people who wanted kids. Dan, demurring, left the details to Alice, except for the writing of checks, which he complained about, too. The whole thing was one big ongoing eye opener, but he felt vindicated when, in the same hour Alice pricked her finger on a rosebush in front of the Aid Society Home, he, like his wife, fell in love with their adopted son.

Driving home from Portland with their miracle child, Dan and Alice had fun with names, then chose Edward Aaron King, after her mother, Eidel, and his grandfather, Avrom, but also, just between the two of them, because the middle name was Elvis's middle name, and Dan, especially, was an Elvis fan.

The next day, at the hospital to which he was attached in Seattle, Dan took the elevator up to Maternity and dug out a blank Certificate of Live Birth. He filled it in to convey that Edward Aaron King was the son by birth of Alice and Daniel King, and forged the unreadable signature—approximated from one that was prevalent in the files—of an attending obstetrician. After putting this in the mail to the Seattle–King County Department of Public Health, Vital Statistics Section, he called Alice, who told him that she was "busy, busy, busy." First thing that morning, she'd done what a friend advised, which was to dribble warm formula from a baby bottle onto her breast and let it roll toward her nipple for Eddie. Eddie had taken from a bottle with greed, but during lulls she'd doused her areolas with formula and encouraged him to latch on by poking him with her nipple. The sequence—she didn't tell Dan this—gave her gooseflesh. It was like trying to catch a nibbling fish. She said, "Come on, come on, that's right, good boy," and "Mama's so sorry she doesn't have her own milk for you," and "Look at you, such a handsome, handsome boy," and "Do you know Mama loves you and will always love you, my baby Eddie, no matter what?"

It surprised Alice to discover that she enjoyed changing Eddie's diapers. What a pleasure it was, after wiping him clean and dusting him with Johnson's, to coo at Eddie while he aired out on the changing table, and to tell him how beautiful he looked. Tidying him up, taking care with the pins, nosing his belly, and smelling his skin—it was thrilling and a little bit addictive. At the first sign of rash, Alice was there with ointment; at the first cough or cry in the night, she popped up. How quickly the meaning of her life changed from staffing issues at the mayor's office to every new wrinkle, each fresh manifestation, of Eddie's needs. And what a revelation it was to find that she enjoyed this more than anything else, the faux suckling, the wiping, the rocking, the holding, the scent of him, the miracle of Eddie, especially when he gazed into her eyes, curiously at first, as if studying her essential mystery, but then to behold her with what she knew was a deep, maybe even a spiritual, sense of who she was, at a level so basic it was beyond what words could express. There was no point in trying to explain it, except to say how much she loved their adopted boy, what a miracle he was, how devoted she felt, and how unexpected this all was, this change in her from one person to another, one woman to another; still, none of these avowals got to the heart of it, which was the feeling she had when Eddie looked her in the eye as if to close an unclosable gap.

Her days now passed in a succession of achievements— not her own, but Eddie's. Eddie discovered his thumbs, which was astounding. Then he squeezed Alice's finger, smiled—or maybe smiled—lifted his head, and got the hang of a pacifier. Then his eyes followed the little monkeys, elephants, giraffes, and zebras when she set his mobile in motion. Then he held a rattle and threw it. He flopped over and squirmed, and at the pediatrician's he was off-the-charts tall. Whatever happened, Alice basked in it. His hair was the same color as hers—honey-hued—which meant they were meant for each other. When she cleaned his navel with a cotton swab, Eddie giggled. Giving him a sponge bath in her lap was fun, and so was cutting his nails while he dozed. He was adorable in pajamas, and the soft spot in his head, his fontanel, pulsed with the beating of his heart.

Nine a.m. and she's bathing Eddie. Ten a.m. and she's using a toothpick to clear a baby-bottle nipple while on the stovetop sterilized formula cools. Eleven a.m. and she's searching in Dr. Spock for the meaning, if any, of Eddie's erections. Noon—scraping Eddie's bowel movement from his diaper into the toilet. Twelve-thirty, folding Eddie's diapers, fresh from the dryer. One-thirty, fresh air for Eddie in his accordion-roofed stroller; two-thirty, with Eddie at the A&P; three-thirty, reading *One Day in the Life of Ivan Denisovich* while Eddie takes his nap. Five-thirty, cooking liver and onions with peas and rice while holding Eddie; six o'clock, tossing a salad while Dan holds Eddie. Eight o'clock, watching TV beside Dan—with Eddie in her arms; nine, taking a shower but not shampooing, because Dan liked her to come to bed showered but not with wet hair. That was her day, and as for her nights, the doctor was now back in business in a big way, and told her that the smell of formula on her breasts was fantastically arousing—in fact, he loved it, in the wee hours, when she brought Eddie to their bed so he could watch her dribble formula down her breasts.

Her husband, she discovered, was an excellent father. When he came home from his constant, consuming family practice, he went immediately to Eddie. He held Eddie in his lap, talked to Eddie, and fed Eddie from a bottle. On weekend afternoons, he napped with Eddie. They'd found bliss, Alice and Dan, even if it was with someone else's child—but was Eddie *really* someone else's child? In the ways that mattered? In the deep and soulful ways? As Rabbi Weisfeld had said, "He who raises someone else's child is regarded as if he had actually brought him into the world." "Now we get that," Dan said to Alice. "It feels like it was always meant to be."

Maybe there was something in all of this that quickened Dan's sluggish swimmers. Or maybe it was that, one December night, Dan and Alice ended up on the floor, coming in unison, while Alice had two pillows stuffed under her hips. Maybe it was that, afterward, because it was warm by the heat register, and because Dan was in the kitchen eating a bowl of cereal—which meant she was alone and could completely relax—Alice stayed on her back with her legs up for a half-hour. Whatever the reasons, a miracle ensued: fourteen months after adopting a son, Alice gave birth, by C-section, to another, whom she and Dan named Simon Leslie King, after Alice's uncle Shimmel and Dan's grandfather Eleazar.

Again the Kings went dutifully to California—this time, since there were two babies, on Western Airlines. In Pasadena, Dan's mother insisted that "Shimmel" looked like Dan, but even more like her brother Morton in Atlantic City. Dan's father said, "You're nuts, Beryl, he don't look like that shlep brother of yours. Just notice his fingers—with fingers like that, he's Isaac Stern playing Carnegie Hall, he's Sandy Koufax with the fastball or somebody else good, but Morton, please, don't say Morton, this way you bring bad luck around his head."

In San Jose, Pop held Simon in his lap and examined him critically. "This one," he said, "this one looks like your mother, Alice. The same eyes, your mother, and, see, the earlobes? Your mother's earlobes. I don't believe it. So much your mother I can't take my eyes off. I don't *wanna* take my eyes off. Look at this, will you look already? Edeleh, what do you think of your baby brother? What do you think, of all the good luck, now you have someone to throw a ball."

There was no need to buy formula this time around, because for Simon there was milk so constant and profuse it dripped into Alice's sturdy bra. When she did it with Dan she was two leaky faucets; either that or, if she was on top, he squeezed milk out of her nipples as if they were squirt guns. It was good he still wanted to have sex with her, Alice felt, because since her pregnancy she was *zaftig* in her hips, rear end, and thighs. She had love handles. She had cottage-cheese skin on the backs of her legs. There was a saving grace to her general expansion, though—her breasts were swollen and, to Dan, sexy. When she wore something low, her cleavage shone as if there were a lamp down there, and in her bathing suit at the View Ridge Swim Club her big boobs tried to spill out of her top. Alice felt like Marilyn Monroe, and even went to a stylist for some chin-length curls reminiscent of Marilyn's.

Two babies—that was twice as complicated. Still, Dan and Alice shared an ecstasy that, punctuated by upsets, astonished them with its potent, strange embrace. When Eddie started walking, Dan said, mimicking Jimmy Durante, "That's my boy!," and took Polaroids while Alice recorded the event in a baby journal. In fact, everything Eddie and Simey did, all their firsts and triumphs, were noted with like exultations and recordings, and with clamorous approval and long-distance phone calls. California was notified when a boy placed a square peg in a square hole, beat a relatively rhythmical tattoo on a drum, peed in a toilet for the first time, took off his shirt and flexed his biceps, or did a somersault. When Eddie posed for a high-chair photograph slathered in spaghetti sauce, that amusing snap got sent to California, along with snaps of Eddie and Simey at the park, at the pool, in the back yard enjoying a sprinkler's spray, in the front yard clutching red plastic baseball bats, in Dan's arms, in Alice's arms, in snowsuits, on the ferry to Victoria, at the Space Needle. Dan would call home from his clinic and say, "How's Simey and Eddie?" or "How are my kings?," and if there was something to report, Alice would: "Eddie actually *ran* today." "Simey's teeth look beautiful." "Eddie is clearly ambidextrous." "Simey ate two bananas this morning." "Not a peep when Eddie got his diphtheria shot—not a sound."

Dan liked to stuff his sons on weekends: oatmeal with brown sugar, melba toast, scrambled eggs from his own plate, graham crackers spread with jelly, macaroni or Rice-A-Roni, chocolate pudding after dinner. He liked to jostle Eddie and Simey in his lap while watching *Saturday Night at the Movies.* He liked to drag them around the pool while making speedboat noises. He liked to tickle their plump, dappled thighs above the knees. But then he noticed something that, as a doctor, he was concerned about—Eddie, it seemed to Dan, had excessively turned-in feet, which was affecting his gait as he toddled and scrummed and might one day affect his hips, knees, and ankles if nothing was done about it.

Alice took Eddie to a pediatric orthopedist. Yes, the boy was pigeon-toed, but that was normal, the orthopedist said, because of how the fetus sits in the uterus, and in most cases it corrected spontaneously within a year of independent walking. Three weeks passed, though, and Eddie seemed, to Dan, more pigeon-toed. To him, the boy had the excessively turned-in gait of a child with an actual orthopedic problem. Again to the specialist, who this time, under pressure from Dan, took measurements and found severe in-toeing. Eddie had lower-body X-rays showing neither a rotated hip nor a rotated calf bone, but revealing an emphatic *metatarsus adductus,* otherwise called curved feet.

Curved feet! That sounded to Dan like a congenital anomaly, and the idea that Eddie's birth parents had passed to Eddie a congenital anomaly like *metatarsus adductus* left him upset—unfairly, he knew—with those invisible people. Chagrined, he had his adopted son fitted for night splints, which meant his feet were joined, while he slept, by a bar fastened at each end to special shoes. So stoic was Eddie, asleep on his back, that he seemed at first not to notice this circumstance, but then his right shoe began to chafe at the ankle, and since his room was too hot, as a matter of course, his ankle got damp and stayed that way, and the tender, pink spot there became infected. Dan tried gauze, iodine, moleskin, and an antibiotic, but it was too late, Eddie had staph, his foot ballooned, and he had to go to Children's Orthopedic, where the treatment included the draining of pus from his ankle, warm dressings, intravenous feedings, stronger antibiotics, and infant doses of codeine. After twenty-two days of this, Eddie went home, but his right foot now looked a little disfigured, and when the treatment with splints was tried again, it was implemented with footplates instead of shoes.

A silver lining: the fastest runners in the world were pigeon-toed, like Eddie. So, when the Kings got together with other young families and someone made a comment about Eddie's gait, Dan would respond with world-record holder Bob Hayes, the hundred-meter winner at the '64 Olympics. If that didn't ring a bell with people, he would suggest next the image of Jackie Robinson stretching a single into a double. Alice, at the swim club, holding Eddie in the water, or watching him splash in the kiddie pool, referred to his disfigured foot, when someone asked about it, as "his little Achilles' heel." Often, at bedtime, she rubbed his foot with baby oil, and his persistently swollen ankle made her sad.

But really there was little to be sad about. Both Simey and Eddie started reading at an early age, each sounding out the words in a Dick and Jane primer while sitting on Alice's lap. Both were mathematically precocious, good with puzzles, gentle with the cat, and problem solvers on a playground. Eddie was well coordinated and could throw a tennis ball over the net from the midline, whereas Simey was prone to earaches on the plane to California, and to car sickness when they drove. At four, Eddie dove off the low board into deep water. His baby fat was gone, and, flying through the air with eager courage, suntanned, arms spread, muscles wet and gleaming, he left Dan and Alice giddy with pride. This fearless, charming, intelligent, and enormously nice-to-look-at child was a spring of good feeling that never stopped flowing, an answered prayer, a gift from God—just like Simey, their birth child.

Eddie and Simey, Simey and Eddie—they had their portrait taken by a professional photographer, Eddie in a bow tie and sweater vest with Simey in his lap, then Eddie and Simey under the cherry tree in the back yard, then Eddie and Simey with Lincoln Logs and Tinkertoys. The best one was Eddie and Simey on the living-room floor, cheek to cheek, giggling. "Such a nice big brother," Alice said as the photographer snapped away with a camera on a tripod. "That's my big, good boy, my darling Eddie."

"Ick," Eddie answered. "Simey smells bad."

They sent the photograph to San Jose and Pasadena, framed and ready for hanging. Pop called long-distance on a Sunday night, because Sunday night was cheaper than other nights; already the picture was on his wall, he announced, adding that he'd gone to the hardware store for hooks, which came "in a package of total five hooks, the other four are now in the drawer where I keep the screwdriver and pliers, but that's not the main thing, the main thing is, a very nice picture, but different, those two."

"Kids don't have to look alike," said Alice.

"What's the big deal?" added Dan.

"Maybe one day they ask," said Pop. " 'How come he's tall, I'm not so tall, he's got his nose, I got my nose, his hair, the other hair'—what you gonna say to your boychiks then? Huh, Dr. Dan? I'm waiting for you! This one, he's hitting home runs from the left side of the plate; the other, he's making like Einstein in science class; one allergic maybe to nothing, one don't leave home without having asthma; one is this, one that, one up, one down, one yes, one no—so what do you say, Mr. Know-It-All?"

"We stick with the mystery of genetics," answered Dan. "It couldn't be simpler, Pop."

"Simple?" Pop said. "How is it simple? One day, Edeleh finds out."

"We stick with the mystery of genetics," Dan repeated. "If no one slips up or spills the beans, he isn't adopted. Let's all remember that."

Pop sneezed into the phone. "Excuse me," he said. "It's lying, this business. The tooth fairy's lying, the *golem* is lying, Santa Claus is lying, all of it lying, but this, Mr. Eddie, not adopted, that's *lying* lying, that's Number Nine of the Ten Commandments lying. Listen, Daniel, I'm telling you from my heart, you want more *tsuris* than you already got? Go ahead—tell this lie!"

Dan looked at Alice, pointed at the phone, then made the loony-bird sign at his ear—a rotating index finger.

"Pop," said Alice, seizing the receiver, which until now Dan had held at an angle while both of them tipped an ear toward it, "you're having a heart attack over nothing. All of the specialists say the same thing, better that the child doesn't know about adoption. This is like a white lie or a lie of omission, this is for the good of our Eddie."

"Okay, forget it, I don't know nothing," Pop answered. "Since when is it up to me yes or no, Alice and Dr. Dan should lie or not lie? Go ahead, it isn't my business, not the *alter kocker*'s business. Only, *a glick ahf dir*, see what comes of it!"

Alice and Dan did what many American Jews did when, after fleeing their parents, they themselves became parents: join a Reform synagogue and celebrate a few holidays. At Temple Beth David, where Nate Weisfeld was now rabbi-in-chief, Sukkoth came with fruit pies and ice cream eaten in a sukkah constructed by sixth-graders, Purim brought a carnival for kids and a costumed musical extravaganza, and Hanukkah was funded to compete with Christmas. Dan and Alice approved of the ambience. They paid for access to it. Neither believed in the God of the burning bush, or even in his modern, more nebulous iteration, but both believed there was vaguely more than met the eye, generally speaking, in the universe. Belief, however, was beside the point—what mattered was that Eddie and Simey should have an identity and not just wander through their lives like lost sheep; Eddie and Simey should know whence they came (even though Eddie came from who knows where, technically); Eddie and Simey should have a cultural experience and be nurtured in the embrace of a community. When push came to shove—when it came to their kids—the community the Kings wanted was a community of Jews, not bearded Jews who made no sense but rational Jews who didn't believe in the God of the Torah or, for that matter, in the Torah itself. The earth was made 5,728 years ago? Come off it, no one in their right mind could believe such crap. Adam and Eve? A curse on the sons of Ham? Lot's wife turned into a pillar of salt? Please. Spare us. Ancient tribal myths. Fortunately, Rabbi Weisfeld could spin Torah dross into contemporary gold, and do it at a level kids could understand, complete with life lessons, liberalism, and a seasoning of eternal mystery. Things at Beth David were at the right pitch, not too irrational, laughable, or boring, not too embarrassing, ancient, or foreign. Secular as it was, though, watered down to nearly nothing, Beth David remained strong on the Chosen People motif. God liked Jews a notch more than anyone else. God had made a special pact with the Jews, which explained their smarts, Israel, and pastrami. At Beth David, the King boys learned that Jews were special—the smartest, the most sensitive and moral, the greatest artists and writers, the greatest scientists and scholars, the best at making money and at giving it away. Einstein, Marx, and Freud were Jews, so were a lot of the the Bomb inventors, and so was nearly everyone in show biz. Yes, there'd been a Holocaust recently, during which Jews had been marched into gas chambers, but since then they'd risen from the ashes, won the Six-Day War, garnered Nobels, and beat polio. Still on top!

Alice and Dan liked the Chosen People concept so much that they put Eddie in Beth David's half-day kindergarten. On his first afternoon, he didn't want to go, and cried, and clung to the car-door handle. Alice bribed him by saying that after school he'd get a toy and ice cream, and he calmed down and went to Beth David.

As it turned out, kindergarten wasn't bad. Finger painting, building blocks, story time, and kickball were good; playing house, nap time, and singing weren't. Clay was so-so, the matching game was good because he knew the answers, and what happened on a kibbutz was okay because they saw a movie about it. Eddie felt impatient saying his *bracha* before he could guzzle grape juice and wolf down his challah, but he liked to give *tzedakah,* because the sound of a coin clanking against the wall of the can was satisfying. The money was going to plant trees in the Promised Land, as shown on a poster labeled "Miracle in the Desert" taped to the classroom door. Eddie liked the idea of those trees, but he didn't like it when Miss Cohen got out her guitar and, sitting on the floor, made them sing, in Hebrew, "Hatikvah," the national anthem of Israel. Even worse, they had to make hats out of construction paper and wear them, along with sheets, for little plays about Abraham and Moses. Worst of all was Israeli dancing with Rabbi Weisfeld, who turned pink doing the *hora.*

"Not enough academics," said Dan, after an open house in Miss Cohen's room. "Whatever happened to the ABCs? Since when does Ed need Joan Baez Junior if he's already reading like a fourth-grader? They're charging us tuition like he's going to Harvard and this is what we get?"

"I agree," said Alice. "She's too young."

They moved him, briefly, to a Montessori school, and when that turned out not to be a good fit, they found a school for the academically gifted whose motto was "Great oaks from little acorns grow." Acorn Academy's teachers were specially trained to help exceptional children become more exceptional. Eddie was finally where he was supposed to be—with twelve other kids like him.

Acorn Academy encouraged extracurricular activity, so Alice and Dan added Tuesday piano lessons, Wednesday modern Hebrew, and Sunday mornings—for both Simey and Eddie—at the Jewish Community Center, which offered tumbling and basketball. Within three months, Eddie was playing "The Pirate's Hornpipe" at a recital and mopping up the other boys—including Simey—when it came to layups on a six-foot hoop ("Havlicek Junior," his coach called him). Simey showed little interest in sports, but it was apparent early that he was extremely intelligent. Simey, in fact, was a veritable whiz kid, prodigious in his ability to multiply long numbers without pencil and paper. Given his unusual brilliance, Dan and Alice paid for testing to determine if he should start school early. A specialist at the University of Washington thought Simey had "exceptional blood flow in his cerebellum" as well as a trait often found in prodigies known as "the rage to master." In other words, the answer to the early schooling question was, as Dan put it, "an unqualified definitely"— Simey should join Ed at Acorn Academy, despite being seventeen months younger. So he did.

The next year, Ed and Simey went to Gladys Glen, with its special program for gifted children and its ten-acre wooded campus. Monday through Friday, Alice drove them to Bellevue at eight and picked them up at four-thirty. This meant no more Wednesday modern Hebrew, so Dan and Alice shelled out for Saturday school at Beth David. A tradition developed for after Saturday school: the Kings ate corned beef on rye with potato salad for lunch, followed by macaroons and halvah from Israel.

Simey and Eddie each got a weekly allowance of twenty-five cents, which Dan parceled out on Saturday mornings in the form of two dimes and a nickel. The nickels were meant for *tzedakah* at temple, but the dimes were theirs to spend as they wanted, and what Eddie wanted, each week, was a package of Sugar Babies and a comic book. Always on Saturday he was impatient for these purchases, and begged Dan, on the way home from Beth David, to stop at a mom-and-pop store where, before long, he and Simey were expected. Simey took forever choosing candy, but that was perfectly fine with Eddie, because it gave him time to read parts of comic books while standing in front of a display rack. Back in the car, the boys tore into their candy and stuffed it down greedily. Eddie usually had his comic book read, or partially read, before Dan pulled into the driveway. If he hadn't finished his intense examination of the latest *Adventure, Action,* or *Green Lantern,* he sat there deaf to Dan's entreaties—"I want you inside *right now,* little man"—and read and finished his candy. Simey went in to watch cartoons, and Dan and Alice prepared the Saturday delicatessen lunch, so that a sandwich and potato salad, on a paper plate, would be waiting for Eddie when he came inside to reread his comic book while eating.

Sometimes Eddie tossed out snippets about the Legion of Super-Heroes. From the back seat he would let Dan know that he didn't like Triplicate Girl, or that Colossal Boy was in love with Shrinking Violet. At school, Eddie wrote illustrated stories about Cosmic Boy, who creates magnetic fields, and Lightning Lad, who's killed but resurrected. In her end-of-the-year report, his teacher wrote, "Eddie has a terrific imagination and a real talent for drawing with crayons. I would venture to guess that for him the Legion of Super-Heroes is something like the panoply of Greek or Norse gods, and I have not discouraged his interest in this direction. His absorption in these figures has been a gateway for him to art, narrative, and much creativity. The resurrection of 'Lightning Lad' in particular, I thought, was truly wonderful, and indicative of a mind that is stretching itself. For Eddie to be playing so powerfully with myth and story at such a young age is, I think, an excellent sign. I've enjoyed listening to him as he explains the meanings behind his pictures."

That summer, the Kings spent three days in Pasadena and a fourth, much anticipated, at Disneyland. As soon as they entered, here came the Dapper Dans, strolling along Main Street in their candy-stripe vests singing "Down by the Old Mill Stream." Eddie, though, kept looking for Legion of Super-Heroes figures, even after Alice had explained, twice, that there were none of those at Disneyland. "A different company," Dan added, exasperated. "The Super-Heroes aren't Disney, they're DC Comics, which is owned by Warner Brothers, which is a Disney competitor. Now, look at those animatronic bears there, boys—they're wearing what look to be actual bear hides."

"Where can we see the Super-Heroes?" answered Eddie.

In the first grade, Eddie decided that, though comic books remained glorious, baseball cards reigned supreme. Baseball players, like superheroes, wore colorful uniforms, but they also wore five o'clock shadows. Eddie filed his cards in shoe boxes. Dan encouraged him to create a special category for Jewish ballplayers, but what Eddie really liked were MVP cards. There was a "Classic" series of MVP cards that a collector could compile with luck, cash, and determination, and Eddie, by Hanukkah, was dead-set on filling his few remaining gaps—'34's Mickey Cochrane, '43's Spud Chandler, '58's Jackie Jensen, and a frustrating three in a row, '63–'65, Elston Howard, Brooks Robinson, and Zoilo Versalles. On the first night of Hanukkah, after fidgeting through Dan's recitation of the three blessings in Hebrew and English and Alice's candle lighting, Eddie tore into the fifty packs of Topps his mother had wrapped in festive paper. Cochrane, Robinson, and Versalles, yes; Chandler, Jensen, and Howard, no. "Don't give up," advised Dan. "You hit five hundred on opening night of an eight-game home stand."

Next it was movies. Somehow, Eddie knew his movies. On Friday nights it was mandatory for Dan and Alice to take their sons to see, for example, *Escape from the Planet of the Apes*. All four Kings went to a matinee of *Fiddler on the Roof* and to the opening night of *Charlie and the Chocolate Factory*. By early February, Eddie was putting his Oscar predictions in writing, hitting on *Bedknobs and Broomsticks* for visual effects and *Fiddler* for cinematography, but striking out on all the big awards, which left him irate. "It wasn't me," he said, before going to bed. "The Academy made idiotic choices."

Then Eddie wanted to play football. After his first game, in the car, on the way home, he said to Dan, "I hate playing guard, I want to be quarterback, how come I can't be quarterback?"

"Are you good at quarterback?"

"*Way* better than Timmy."

"I don't know why, then," Dan said. "If you're better than Timmy, and I'm sure you are, how come your coach plays you at guard?"

"It's *unfair*," said Eddie. "I should be quarterback."

There were also problems, that spring, in baseball, because Eddie couldn't seem to get a hit. An optometrist said he needed glasses for nearsightedness. "No, you look very handsome," countered Alice, when Eddie tried some on for the first time and declared, "I look like a retard." The optometrist's assistant explained that, for sports, glasses could be secured with an adjustable band. "I don't want an adjustable band," said Eddie. "I don't want glasses. I'm not wearing glasses." Alice had him fitted for contact lenses.

Where Eddie truly excelled was in the swimming pool. His swollen foot was no longer swollen, just a little thicker than the other foot. Each summer he became more dominant in the water; each summer he smashed club records. He began to call himself Ed, not Eddie, and recoiled now when his parents called him *Edeleh*. Still, it was fun for Dan and Alice to sit on bleachers—while Simey ran around with other kids—and watch Ed, in his racing suit, outdistance the field in the butterfly and freestyle, and anchor the swim club's medley relay team to a Seattle private-club historical best. With his rangy shoulders and narrow waist, wringing out his hands and curling his toes around the edge of the starter's block before the firing of the pistol, Eddie gave Dan a new take on his birth parents, who were present—for Dan—at a moment like this, as the true font of Ed's success. Alice was less prone to give them the credit and believed that her efforts in getting Ed to 6 a.m. turnouts—not missing one—was essential to his glory. She glowed with each of Ed's swimming triumphs, enjoying them, sometimes, with tears in her eyes. Now when she called Pop he liked to say, "Put Mr. Mark Spitz on the telephone with his *zaydie,* I want to ask him how are his seven gold medals and if the girls already are crazy for him."

The girls were; Ed King was popular. There were two bathing beauties on his swim team, both older, who liked to sit with Ed on adjacent towels during meets, play Crazy Eights with him in the clubhouse, double up against him during splash fights, and alternately challenge him to games of tetherball (high-speed and giddy bouts, Alice saw, from her post in a chaise longue under an umbrella). There was a well-developed girl at Saturday school who turned crimson in Ed's presence and who showed up to watch him play basketball at the Jewish Community Center, where Ed commonly scored twenty or more points while leading his team to summer victories. There was a girl down the block, a year older than Ed, who was fanatical about music and had a record collection, a stereo, and posters of David Bowie and Patti Smith in her bedroom. And there was a girl from school who called to ask him if he wanted to join a group of friends for a trip to the Northgate Mall. Ed went, and they wandered—

Ed and two blondes. After lingering on a bench, where they ate bags of French fries, they saw *Jaws*. Ed sat between his tandem dates, holding in his lap a box of popcorn into which they dug their fingers, giving him a hard-on.

Ed and Simon now attended Gladys Glen's new middle school, where, in the back of a math classroom sat four bulky computers—a first in the area for students their age. There they discovered video games, and because they talked about video games so much, and pointed their parents in the right direction, Dan and Alice bought them a *Pong* console for Hanukkah. The boys wore out the paddles within three months, damaged the television, and made so much noise playing *Pong*—hooting, hollering, arguing, even screaming—that Dan and Alice had to institute a *Pong* curfew that began, on school nights, at ten. Ed and Simon started going to an arcade on weekend afternoons to play *Jet Fighter*, *Shark Jaws*, *Stunt Cycle*, and *Gun Fight*, competing to see their initials digitally emblazoned next to the term "Hi Score."

Suddenly Ed's Bar Mitzvah loomed. He had to meet with Rabbi Weisfeld to go over his Torah and Haftorah portions and to discuss their interpretations. Weisfeld, keeping a straight face, grilled Ed mercilessly. Knowing that the boy wasn't born a King, he was impressed all the more when Ed memorized with such rapidity that, as he put it while lauding this stellar student to his parents, "not even a *yeshiva bucher* could do better." "It's easy for me," Ed explained, when they passed on such rabbinic compliments.

Five hundred fifty people filled the sanctuary on the day of Ed's Bar Mitzvah. There he stood at the head of the congregation, in a new suit and gleaming shoes—the birth son of Walter Cousins and Diane Burroughs and the adopted son of agnostic Jews—reading, in Hebrew, about the ritual for cleansing lepers, which included pigeons, hyssop, shaved hair, and dead lambs. When that was done he read the speech Alice had slaved over for three nights: "My Torah portion from Leviticus 14 and 15 tells us that God, in his infinite wisdom, makes way for the return of the healed soul into the community of Israel. Why one *ephah* of flour mixed with water as a grain offering? Why does God allow for either two turtledoves *or* two young pigeons, according to what the sick man can afford?" He paused to let those questions sink in. Almost everybody was smiling at Ed, and his view from the pulpit was of widely approving faces. "Today, in our world, questions like these don't make any sense, not if we ask them literally," he read. "It is their meaning and symbolism that we are meant to explore. God always has a deeper purpose, and when He says that a priest should put the blood of a lamb on the tip of the right ear of a leper, and on the thumb of his right hand and on the big toe of his right foot, we need to ask ourselves what God is really saying."

He paused again. A few people were nodding. Ed turned the next page of Alice's script. "The Lord is mysterious," he read. "It's no fault of the leper that he's a leper. In olden times, lepers were banished. They had no chance. They were shunned and died alone. Find yourself a leper and your life was over. One day you woke up with a sore on your arm, and that was the end for you."

More nodding. Ed nodded, too, as if commiserating with the congregation about the dark, unjust past. "All right, the ritual sounds completely strange. The ritual is even ridiculous and stupid. Here's God telling Moses that if a Jew wants to make the house of a leper clean he needs to find a priest, and that priest needs to find two birds, cedar wood, scarlet, et cetera, bring it all to the house, kill one of the birds in an earthen vessel over running water, dip everything else in the blood of the dead bird, and sprinkle the house with the blood and water seven times." More smiles, more laughter, more inside-joke nodding. Ed smiled, too, then waved at his grandmother. "Here," he read, "we have to think of God like the Wizard of Oz, handing out medals and certificates of achievement. Abracadabra, two birds, seven sprinkles, a little scarlet, a touch of hyssop, and presto—the leper's one of us again, he doesn't have to go into the desert, God makes the way for his impossible *aliyah,* just as he led the Jews to the Promised Land and, in 1948, to *Ha'aretz Israel.* God has a plan and a method to his madness, even if it looks like just smoke and mirrors, even if to us it's dead birds and water. But if you think about it, is that different from a Bar Mitzvah? I stand up here, I say the magic words, and—presto!—today I am a man."

Another pause. Ed turned the last of Alice's pages. A few "hmmm"s, more chuckles. Pop, Ed saw, had his handkerchief out and was wiping his eyes while holding his glasses. A few other people were crying, too, but most of the congregation was beaming.

"Actually," Ed read, "I'm the same kid I was an hour ago, except there's now been this ritual, my Bar Mitzvah, my own personal dead birds and slaughtered lambs, with you, my friends and family, as witnesses. Thank you all so much for coming."

Clapping in the synagogue wasn't generally done, but a number of people couldn't help themselves. Someone even called out, "Brilliant, brilliant!" and from there Ed launched into his list of specific thank-yous.

Ten-year T-notes, savings bonds, checks for fifty or a hundred dollars, and cash tucked into gilded cards—Ed, in his reception line, standing between his parents, stuffed all of these into the side pocket of his coat while shaking hands and suffering hugs and kisses. The well-built girl who attended Ed's basketball games turned crimson again while congratulating him inaudibly. Later, after lunch, and after Dan had stood up at the head table to thank in particular the friends and family who'd traveled far to be there, Ed lured her into the empty choir room, put his hands inside her blouse, and squeezed. She told him no, he did it again, she insisted no, he squeezed even harder. Then she pulled his hair, kicked him in the shin, called him a jerk, and fled in tears.

That summer, Ed went girl-crazy. Swim team was impossible. The girls in their racing suits, with their wet thighs and tan lines, plowing through a hundred laps before hauling out at poolside—where they giggled, whispered, breathed hard, rolled, and made wiggling adjustments to the nylon across their butts—for Ed, they were live pornography. Almost every day after swim team, he jerked off in the Kings' basement bathroom. Sometimes he took a mythology book with a full-page print, *Hylas and the Water Nymphs,* that depicted naked naiads emerging from lily pads to lead a young hero to his doom. Sometimes he took a Dionne Warwick album. He also liked Herb Alpert's whipped-cream girl, and Peggy Lipton from *The Mod Squad.* Then there was Raquel Welch as a mute cave siren in *One Million Years B.C.* and, even better, Welch attacked by antibodies in *Fantastic Voyage.* All of this was mixed up with the fifteen- and sixteen-year-old mermaids with whom he cavorted six days a week in the pool, especially a girl named Tiffany Wicks, who had a lithe, blond swagger like Peggy Lipton's. And Samantha Caldwell—Sam—with swimmer's shoulders, a nose plug, a latex cap, and a ritual of elaborate crotch adjustments each time she hopped onto a starting block. And Terry Tomlinson, who was as skinny as Twiggy and had a face like Mia Farrow's. And Barb Marconi, whose sunburned nose, blue eyes, and round butt popped up in his imagery constantly.

Then there were the Jewish girls at B'nai Brith Camp, where Ed jerked off quietly in a cabin full of fellow campers also quietly jerking off. It was the summer of the American Bicentennial, and these thirteen-year-olds liked fireworks and masturbating.

From the boys' showers, through a hole in the concrete, Ed and his cabin-mates watched girls going at their soap and shampoo, and caught glimpses of their shining wet—the term was—muffs. Best, though, were the late-night dances, held in the dining hall with the tables pushed aside and a rotating strobe light overhead. As soon as the main lights in the hall went out, Ed would head for a girl named Susan Weinbaum, whose principal features were long arms, long hands, long hair, a long waist, and, everyone in his cabin agreed, great tits. Ed hung on to her with the objective of making it to the night's first slow dance, usually four or five numbers in, during which he felt he had every right to press Susan Weinbaum with his trapped, straining boner. She never said a word about this, not even when—it had to have been obvious—Ed splooged in his underwear. Finally, one night, on a tumbling mattress in a dark corner of the rec center, Ed got his fingers inside her panties. Believing the point was to simulate a penis, he poked at her until Susan Weinbaum said, "Ow, you're hurting me. Don't do that!" Then he went back to what he preferred anyway: squeezing her breasts, pinching her nipples, and grinding against her crotch.

That summer there was also the girl down the block with the stereo in her bedroom. She had a boy's flat body and a bad case of pimples, but she also liked to lock her door, strip off her T-shirt, and give Ed a handjob. He asked, then begged her, to take him in her mouth, but she refused him with "No way, that's gross." She did, however, with her hand over his, teach him not only how to locate a clitoris but some good things to do once he found it.

Great information. Ed would get with a girl and, guided by her breathing, squirming, and clenching, do what it took to make her happy. Sometimes his attentiveness led to reciprocity, sometimes not, but his percentage of handjobs definitely went up, so the effort was worth it. He kept count of the girls who gave him handjobs—seven by the time he turned fourteen, including a straight-A ninth-grader whose secret was a tube of K-Y Jelly. After school, Ed and this girl would "study" in his basement, with the television on and cans of pop. She was good at what she did, so good that he always checked in at lunch to make sure they were still on for after school. All fall, she and Ed studied hard in the basement, until, one afternoon, Simey popped up from behind a chair and said, "I'm telling Mom!"

Ed quickly stuffed himself back into his underwear. The straight-A student put her lubricant behind her back. Simey ran for the stairs, but Ed caught him by the shirt. Simey was pencil-necked, knock-kneed, and uncoordinated, so hanging on was easy. He was also a crybaby. "No!" Simey screamed now. "No!"

"Wimp," said Ed, still holding Simey by his shirt. "You Peeping Tom. I ought to thump you."

"I hate your *guts*," answered Simey. "Let go."

"Ouch, I'm so wounded," Ed sneered. "Whatever, ya crybaby, but if you wanna get thumped, go ahead, Simey—tell Mom."

"I *am* telling her."

"See what happens."

"I'm telling her *right now*."

"Go ahead, wimp."

Simey told.

Ed got an Apple II for his birthday and began to play, obsessively, *Dark Planet*. The object of the game was to storm a cavern protected, vigorously, by the vassals of the Shadow Lord—each of whom wielded a medieval weapon—and, once past them, to rescue a maiden. This mostly naked blonde was handcuffed in a lair replete with instruments of torture, and guarded by a salivating, red-eyed wolf-man—the evil Shadow Lord himself. Ed, battling away furiously, found himself admiring the Shadow Lord, and prolonged his duels with this trying foe in order not only to assess his bag of tricks but to watch the cuffed maiden writhe against her chains in orgasmic ecstasy.

As high school approached, Dan and Alice chose University Prep for their sons, because of its fine academic reputation and its record of sending grads to first-tier colleges. This was all fine as far as Simon was concerned, but Ed wanted to go to a public school, because, he said, he was tired of snobs and rich kids. Dan thought public school was a bad idea, but Alice thought Ed should make his own decisions, so Ed chose Nathan Hale High. He quit sports, took up smoking, and got interested in fast cars. One Thursday night, when Ed walked in the door at twelve-thirty, he found his parents waiting sternly on the couch. Dan referred angrily to Ed's friends as "greasers," but once again Alice rose to his defense, this time by lauding the fact that he "embraced people from different socio-economic backgrounds." Ed laughed at both of them and said, "Get bent," which angered Dan so much he grounded Ed until Monday. Ed spent the weekend with his stereo on. Its bass thump could be felt in the kitchen.

"What the hell happened?" Dan asked Alice. "It's like taking in a wolf cub—he grows up to be a wolf."

"It's just a phase," Alice answered. "He's a teen-ager."

The phase intensified through Ed's sophomore year, during which his parents were completely in the dark about weed, beer, LSD, and cocaine. Ed kept his stash of drugs and paraphernalia where they would never find it, and employed eyedrops, gum, sunglasses, and breath mints. He gravitated toward juniors and seniors, and became a regular at late-night house parties and at keggers in the deep lairs of public parks. Mostly, though, there was nothing to do at night except drive around at high speed, high or drunk or both, with guys who had licenses. One Saturday, in a downpour, Dan had to go to a police station at 2 a.m. to collect Ed, who could hardly stand up. "We'll talk about this later," Dan said, through clenched teeth, on the way home. "For now, the main thing is, don't vomit in the car." Ed did.

After a prolonged consultation, and then a rift, with Alice, Dan grounded Ed for four weekends. Incarcerated in his room, he combed his quiff and plucked at a guitar attached to a used amplifier. For Ed's six-teenth birthday, Alice made reservations for Sunday brunch at the Roosevelt Hotel, where she and Dan ate eggs Benedict and lox while Simon read *Children of Dune* at the table and Ed, appearing hungover, drank black coffee, yawned, and made trips to the bathroom. They gave him a card—*We're Proud of You, Son*—and a check for two hundred dollars.

With this money, his Bar Mitzvah haul, and some cash he made selling pot, Ed bought a '66 Pontiac GTO, fitted it out with a quadraphonic 8-track, painted it black, and added racing stripes. Behind the wheel, in his bucket seat, fondling his stick shift, Ed liked to irritate and anger other drivers. He also liked to go to empty parking lots to practice dangerous turns. Dan reluctantly paid for Ed's car insurance, and Alice gave him gas money when he asked for it. She also paid for his guitar lessons and for the karate class Ed decided to take after seeing Bruce Lee in *Enter the Dragon*. Ed, it turned out, was good at karate, with quick feet for someone who was six foot three and weighed two hundred pounds. His lessons should have had a silver lining for Simon, because Ed's sensei emphasized "winning without fighting." Instead, Ed took a fresh fraternal pleasure from inflicting pain on his younger brother in the guise of passing along self-defense tricks.

Near the end of his sophomore year, Ed met a girl named Tracy Stolnitz who'd just graduated from Nathan Hale and bussed tables in a Mexican restaurant. They did it in the back seat of Ed's GTO, and then, for the rest of the summer, they did it as often as they could. Tracy not only was on the pill, she delivered in ways Ed hadn't thought of. There were finer girls around, Ed knew, but Tracy was mouthy and droll as she talked around her cigarette. Her comportment was sallow, but her style in the sack was wild. She wore studded black leather and kept an elbow in a car window frame so that it was easy to flick ashes; either that or she dropped them in a beer bottle. She and Ed saw bands that summer in Vancouver, Portland, and Spokane.

They planned an end-of-summer road trip. There was a Battle of the Bands to hit in The Dalles, and this Stonehenge replica thing somewhere near The Dalles a guy had told Ed about, and there were some friends of Tracy's with a house in Pullman, so they could stay there for a couple of days and go to this other Battle of the Bands, and then, on the way back to Seattle, Tracy knew some guys who had three-wheelers, and they could ride them or whatever. Ed told Dan and Alice he was going camping in the Blue Mountains, which wasn't far from the truth.

With Tracy managing the 8-track, Ed drove east on the interstate at eighty-five, sometimes at over a hundred. That afternoon, he replaced his fuel filter on a butte while Tracy, with a beer bottle in her hand, hugged him from behind. The Battle of the Bands in The Dalles was a dud. For the Stonehenge thing, they split a tab of acid. Later, they slept near cottonwoods, under stars, Tracy wearing only her black leather jacket and a mastodon-tooth necklace that hung in Ed's face when she climbed on top of him. Ed felt that he was living in a dream and that this was the high point of his life.

In Pullman, they went with Tracy's friends to the second Battle of the

Bands in their plan, taking along some piquant Thai stick and a bottle of mescal with a worm at the bottom. The next day, at about eleven, after a last session in the sack that was dulled by a hangover, they started west-ward, with Ed speeding—of course—and with his 8-track blaring, through the low, rolling hills of the Palouse. The roads were lonely and ran between wheat fields. There were farmhouses, barns, stables, railroad tracks, and rows of implements, but despite all these signs, they saw few people. Sometimes they saw a huge farm machine at work, usually so far away it looked no bigger than a toy; once they passed a truck parked beside a grain elevator; once they had to slow behind a farmer on a trac-tor, but otherwise, there was no one. With opportunity knocking this way, Ed went joyriding on dirt tracks with no names or signage, leaving behind him a rooster tail like a tornado. These were roads with persistent washboards, good for forty tops, but Ed was taking them at ninety with his rear end drifting, scouting ahead for potholes that might demand maneuvering and for intersections where he could show off his sudden turns. "Watch this!" he'd say, Tracy would brace, and Ed would send his GTO perpendicular to the road in a geyser of dust and a spray of flying gravel, his inside tires nearly airborne. Yelling and hooting, he'd regain control during a series of decreasing fishtails, after which he'd be driving east or west instead of north or south, or vice versa, all the while working his Hurst shifter.

They came to a two-lane meander, with wires overhead, eroding between wheat fields. Ed drove it like it was the Indianapolis Motor Speedway, timing himself on a zero-to-sixty twice but dissatisfied with the results. Pigeons flared at their approach, doves hopped off power lines, the chaff at the roadside swirled, but still there were no other driv-ers in this region, so Ed took it up, in a straightaway, to a personal best of 135. Satisfied, he stopped to piss by an abandoned barn, leaving his car, with Tracy in it and the 8-track blaring, idling in the middle of the road.

He was pondering what might have been the remains of a grain mill and peeing on a pile of sun-dried beams when a BMW approached, its tinny little engine whining. The driver careened around Ed's car and, lay-ing on his horn, gave Ed the finger. "What's up with that?" Ed asked him-self, returning the gesture with both hands. Then he zipped up, climbed in, and said to Tracy, "You know what? This guy's toast."

For a few miles he drove up the Beemer's license plate, castigating its driver continuously and in concert with his nervously laughing girl-friend, but the guy refused to do more than sixty unless he came to a passing situation, in which case he sped up so that Ed couldn't get around him, afterward slowing back to sixty and giving Ed, again and again, the finger. "What's up with this asshole?" asked Tracy.

"He's toast," answered Ed. "I'm gonna toast him."

At last they came to a straightaway between wheat fields. "Okay," thought Ed. "This is it. *No one* gets away with giving *me* the finger." Then he punched his pedal to the floor and veered, with a roar, into the oncoming lane. Quickly he was hood to hood and face to face with his adversary, where he took a penetrating look: an old fucker of the type who was arrogant and overconfident. A bastard completely full of him-self. God, what a loser! Like he owned the road! Like Ed was nobody! Fuck that!

"Goddamn it," said Ed. "I'll kill this bastard. This goddamn bastard *deserves to die!*" And twenty seconds later, at a crossroads, he did kill him, by running him off the road into a wheat field, where the Beemer, after rolling four times—the first three sideways and the last end to end—came to rest on its flattened roof.

4

Poor Walter

Having gotten started with Diane as an adulterer, Walter Cousins found cleaning up his act harder than he'd imagined. The discipline to resist a new liaison faltered in proportion to passing time, and the further he got from his affair with the au pair, the harder it was to feel admonished by it. After a while, he forgot how he'd felt on the Monday morning when he was blackmailed by a teen-ager for $250 a month in perpetuity, and shortly after that he broke down altogether and began a dalliance with a married woman. This new fling proceeded amiably. When it dwindled, there followed three more like it, all casual, experimental, and pragmatic. Finally, though, in his sixteenth year of marriage, Walter was caught in an indiscretion with one of his wife's friends. Lydia and the other woman had been close for a decade, and Walter had been jocular and easy with her husband, so it took eleven months of pretty good acting before the affair was undone by carelessness. Of course, that was the end of the couple-to-couple friendship, and of Lydia's trust. He and Lydia went to couples counseling, but quit when it became apparent that the money they were spending on it would be needed to put the kids through college. Besides, after all those expensive fifty-minute sessions, they'd at best reached a stalemate. Or maybe the better word, thought Walter, was "détente," as in Nixon with the Russians. At any rate, détente was what was on Walter's mind lately, when he lay with Lydia in their connubial bower feeling anguished about their very meager sex life. Once a week, or maybe every ten days, he tried to get something going with Lydia, but three out of four times he was explicitly spurned, and the fourth time there was rarely much to it. Lydia, like him, was in sexual decline, but, though back to obsessive and anxious dieting, seemed clear of the more severe mental-health problems that had besieged her in 1962. These days, she Jazzercised and, after seeing Nathan Pritikin on *60 Minutes*, subscribed to his diet plan. As a result of proximity, Walter ate better, too, lifted dumbbells a little, and logged minutes on a treadmill in the bedroom. He also now found gardening relaxing, and sometimes dug weeds beside Lydia. Together, they went for fast walks on weekends, both dressed in sweats and swinging two-and-a-half-pound weights, cotton towels around their necks. On San Juan Island, they walked in the morning, worked on the cottage in the afternoon, and did very little in the evening. Walter had stopped caring that the place wasn't perfect. He and Lydia milled there, feeling lonely. The kids, grown, rarely joined them on the island, leaving Walter with time to stare at the water, usually with a beer in his fist. There was always something to irk or perturb him during these ocean-view meditative sessions. The bottom line was that he didn't want to die. As far as he was concerned, death was the problem. The basic human problem. Everyone's problem. He wasn't any different from anyone else, but there was no consolation in that.

Occasionally, Walter and Lydia were able to coax Tina to the island, mainly because she had a friend in Friday Harbor who had summer work waiting tables. Barry, though, for three years in a row, came up only for the Fourth of July weekend, when the taverns in town went crazy. In other words, even when the kids were there, they weren't there. Lydia said that having them around was like running a bed-and-breakfast—which, she added, she was happy to do because she loved them so much. Mostly, though, it was just Walter and Lydia, reading, eating, walking, arguing, and doing their onerous second-home chores before settling into long, fruitless evenings. During all of it, Lydia talked about the kids so much—strengths, weaknesses, challenges, temperaments, marriage prospects, jobs, careers, schools, and the odds of producing grandchildren while continuing to live within driving distance—that they might as well have been there in the flesh. Walter, tiring of the subject, did zero to egg her on, but still he found himself thinking about his kids whenever he stared at the water. It seemed to him that, in the early years, things had been okay with them, the problems he'd had with the kids had been normal— the occasional tantrum, some spoiled behavior, some crying, yelling, lying, and disrespect, but nothing serious or out of the ordinary, nothing demanding special attention. But then, when Barry was fourteen and Tina thirteen, Walter was exposed as a breaker of vows, and after that, things changed.

Was there a connection? Lydia was certain of it. Walter, professionally accustomed to manipulating factors, pronounced himself ambivalent on the question of his culpability, but at the same time, privately, agreed with Lydia. After all, could it be a mere coincidence that, on the heels of the father's fall from grace, the son had changed so dramatically? After a boyhood of excelling as a Little League pitcher and getting pretty good grades at school, Barry had suddenly withdrawn into his bedroom. He became a Dungeons and Dragons devotee, a collector of pewter fantasy figurines, and a dope smoker. In fact, it soon emerged that he was not just a dope smoker but a *daily* dope smoker, and, more distressing, the kind of kid who needed counseling for depression. All of that would have been okay if he had just shown a sign of bucking up after "graduating" (Barry's diploma was from a pass/fail alternative program). Instead, he became a repeat watcher of *Star Wars* on a Betamax, a committed fan of punk and New Wave, and a regular at a midnight *Rocky Horror Picture Show* fest at the Neptune Theatre on Saturdays. On the wall above Barry's desk was a poster of Devo—four guys in belted yellow radiation suits with "energy domes" on their heads and black whips—and another of the Sex Pistols. Even all of *that* could have passed for sort of normal, as far as Walter was concerned, if Barry hadn't gotten as skinny as his hero Sid Vicious, and if he hadn't started dressing in what Walter thought of as his *Night of the Living Dead* attire, which meant he looked like he'd just popped out of a grave.

Then there was Tina. Blonde, chubby, cherubic, and serious, she began keeping a journal after intimations of Walter's debacle filtered down to her. Gradually, she went from selling Girl Scout cookies to editing her high school's "literary arts" publication. This meant that a gaggle of arty kids showed up at the Cousinses' house once a week and, behind

Tina's bedroom door, murmured about poems. Sometimes Walter overheard them in the kitchen, tearing into the Oreos and drinking all the 7 Up while—for example—making fun of Lydia's milk glasses because cows were etched into them. Tina's own poems were well received by the teacher in charge of Student Achievement/Art Night Open House, who displayed them in the library alongside student photographs and paintings. Her subjects were mass suicide, the Khmer Rouge, corrupt military contractors, and love, the latter, Walter knew, due to her experience as a girl with a new soulmate every month. In many of her verses she was ecstatic about a new soulmate, in mourning about the last one, or both. Yet, whether rapturously mournful or mournfully rapturous, Tina always seemed to listen to the same albums, including *The Concert for Bangladesh,* over and over again, and to music that sounded to Walter like monks humming in a cistern. This last was because she dabbled in spirituality. Whereas before Walter's infidelity cataclysm she would innocently assert that "science explains everything," afterward she was more inclined to say that "science is just another religion."

In 1975, on his forty-seventh birthday, Tina gave Walter a used album called *The Kinks Are the Village Green Preservation Society.* With a felt pen she drew an arrow, on the jacket, to a track called "Do You Remember Walter?" and beside it she wrote, "YOU!" Walter took a sip from his birthday martini, scratched his head, and said, "Oookay, me." Then Tina put "Do You Remember Walter?" on the stereo and made Walter sit there while she smiled at him. They listened—at her urging—to the song's lyrics, which began:

> *Walter, remember when the world was young*
> *And all the girls knew Walter's name?*
> *Walter, isn't it a shame the way our little world has changed?*

And ended with:

> *Yes people often change, but memories of people can remain.*

After they listened, Tina said, "It's not *exactly* you, but it's got your name and it's about a guy who's out of it, like you, so I thought you'd like it."

"Um, what?"

"So that's my birthday present."

Walter wouldn't have minded that his daughter had turned out this way—a poetess in an alpaca shawl scrounged from a thrift shop, drinking kefir with pale bards at the Sunlight Cafe—if a few of her poems didn't so flagrantly indicate that she despised him. Tina wrote a series of verses about a guy in Bermuda shorts barbecuing human limbs while smoking a cigar. Her coup de grâce, though, was a long, even epic, narrative denunciation, called "Walter," with references to Richard Cory, Walter Mitty, Willy Loman, Casanova, and Nixon. After that, Tina dropped him as subject matter.

Too bad for her, he told himself. Because, actually, at the moment, he was ripe for poetic skewering. On the approach to the terrifying Big 5-0, he had significant regrets. He didn't want to be an actuary anymore, and didn't know why he was an actuary. What was the point of all those statistics? Nothing important, that was for sure. Charts, graphs, tables, analyses—what a colossal, and egregious, waste of time, this math with which he'd elided his own life. Poetry writing, by comparison, sounded sort of fun. If it gave you a way to let your emotions out, poetry might be really worth doing. But where did you start? Poems didn't just *come*. And meanwhile, while he hadn't been looking—not in the way he saw now he should have looked—he'd risen to senior vice-president of research at Piersall-Crane. "Senior vice-president of research," he said to Tina. "You ought to write a poem about that." In jest, of course, though he wouldn't have minded. Better than nothing, a poem about him. So he was glad when Tina answered, "All right, a poem about it. What exactly is it you do for a living?"

"I'm in the numbers game. You know that."

"I've never really understood the term 'numbers game.' Why don't you be more specific?"

Walter decided to explain loss reserves and Financial Analysis of Insurance Companies by walking her through all the high points methodically, but hardly was a sentence out of his mouth when she demanded a definition of "liability." "Put it this way," he said, cutting to the chase. "People in business want hard information about the past and present so they can make predictions about the future."

"Why?" asked Tina. "Why don't they just *live*?"

Walter resigned himself to the removal of this conversation from the intricacies of his daily labors to . . . what would he call it? Soft teen-age thinking? Sophomoric value judgments? "What," he said, "business people are dead? Business people don't have lives?"

Tina, he could see, was holding back a smile—that scoffing know-it-all vegetarian poet smile with which she beleaguered him sometimes. She looked, he thought, something like Lydia, but this was beyond what Lydia ever did, this insulting, condescending, internal laughing, this snide, superior, and silent ridiculing, this wholesale dismissal, this contempt. "You're pissed off at me," Tina said.

"Maybe you should write a poem about it."

She did write a poem, called "Lost Reserving"—the intellectual poetess thought "loss" was "lost"—which began by saying, "He does Lost Reserving / for the undeserving, / this drone who has made his Faustian bargain / with the Capital for Captains Company of Amerika," and ended with "There will be nemesis."

Walter told Lydia that Tina despised him, and Lydia replied, in her long-suffering tone, "What do you expect, Walter? Another chicken's coming home to roost."

When Barry turned nineteen, Walter and Lydia bought him a used car with under fifty thousand miles on it. Barry, after two years of food prep in restaurant kitchens, was thinking of trying a community college. He now wore exclusively black, including, for a while, black fingerless gloves and a bowler. He also liked wrist bands, safety pins, studded belts, spiked bracelets, dog tags, and combat boots. His pants were festooned with chains, rings, buckles, a small skull on a strap, and a pair of handcuffs. In the rear of his pants was a large button-up flap. Barry had gone through a number of hairstyles before settling on Statue of Liberty spikes—black—held in place with Aqua Net hairspray. He wanted to try North Seattle Community College, since it wasn't too far from some friends he could live with, but the only thing was, he didn't have the money.

They gave it to him. That fall, he took Music Appreciation, Sociology, and English, and that winter he took Music Appreciation II, Music Theory, and History of Modern Music. Every so often he called home and, after saying, "How's it going?," brought up a problem he was having with the car, elaborated his penury, or asked Lydia to sew something for him.

Most of the time, when Lydia invited Barry to dinner, he answered that he had other plans, but once in a while he said yes and showed up with baskets of laundry. Over dinner he made use of face time with his parents to reiterate his car problems, until Walter offered to look under the hood. Before leaving, Barry ritually went to the basement to search for things he wanted in the junk pile he'd left behind.

In 1977, Barry didn't make it home for Thanksgiving because of a car trip with friends for something music-related. For Christmas, though, he showed, and so did Tina, who now lived in a dorm at the University of Washington instead of with her parents, which would have been cheaper. "Ingrates," Walter muttered to Lydia in the kitchen, after the kids responded to their gifts with nonchalance. "At least they're here," she replied.

Tina gave Walter a used tennis racket and tennis balls, and Barry gave him a pine-scented car freshener, three twenty-four-ounce bottles of beer, coasters, and a harmonica he blew demonstration riffs on with expertise. Praise from Lydia led later in the day to the loud revelation that Barry was a good guitarist and an even better drummer. Barry now wanted to apply to Washington State, about three hundred miles away, in Pullman, to study political science. Also, he knew a couple of guys there who wanted him in their band, playing drums. "A band," said Lydia. "What's its name?"

"They started out as Vomit in high school but now they're called Kill All Parents," answered Barry. "Just in case you're clueless, that was sarcasm."

"Okay," said Walter.

"I actually want to go to WSU just to get stoned and rock out."

"Barry," said Lydia.

"And take acid and get arrested and hang out with devil worshippers."

"*Barry,*" repeated Lydia.

"And fuck some farm girls—preferably virgins."

"Hey," countered Walter.

They made a deposit to hold Barry's place at WSU. That summer, Barry quit his restaurant job and played gigs with—the real name—DeathTrap. DeathTrap, explained Barry, was "parody of heavy metal. Really bad metal. Doom metal. We're a parody band." They heard from him only once all June, when he called collect to say his car was over-heating and to ask Walter for suggestions about addressing this problem;

he wanted to know what cheap solutions he could try before taking it into a shop. Walter made a phone diagnosis of "either thermostat or water pump," then asked, at Lydia's urging—and scrutinized by her as if she was sure he'd say the wrong thing—if they would see Barry on the Fourth.

"Lemme get my car straightened out," he answered. "I can't think that far ahead right now."

"It's next week."

"Okay," said Barry. "Good to know. But right now my car is, like, steaming all the time. It—"

"Bring it to the island," Walter urged. "Keep it topped off between now and then, and when you come for the Fourth, we'll work on it."

Barry said, "Uh, I'm pretty sure we have, like, a huge gig then. Like a huge, patriotic, America thing. A Mom-Dad-and-apple-pie thing."

He called the next time in mid-July, saying, "Now something's *really* wrong with the car," before describing, at Walter's behest, all the noises it made while dying on a lonely highway in eastern Washington. Lydia, on the other line, said, "So how did you get to a phone?"

"Hitched."

"You should *never* hitchhike, Barry," said Lydia. "Never, ever, ever. Please."

"Okay, great, good advice, I got that. But the main thing is, my car's fucked."

Walter sighed loudly into the receiver. "How often," he asked, "did you check the oil?"

"How would I know?"

"Did you ever check the oil?"

"I don't know."

"You either checked it or you didn't check it. It's not that complicated. It sounds to me like you never checked it."

"Oh," said Barry.

"You can't just drive and not check the oil."

No answer came.

"That was a good car before you didn't check the oil."

"Right," said Barry. "I fucked up the car. I totally fucked it up."

"Help him," put in Lydia. "He needs help, Walter. This is a cry for help."

This was also, thought Walter, typical of her, typical of his marriage, and typical of what happened, every time, with the kids—this was typical of everything. "I *am* helping him," he said.

"You're not helping *any*thing," Lydia snapped. "Barry," she went on, "let me give you a credit-card number. That way you can have it towed."

"Go ahead," said Barry. "I'll write it on my hand. I'm in a phone booth in Walla Walla, and it's a hundred degrees—I'm fucking boiling."

"Drink water," said Lydia. "Are you ready?"

She gave him the number, and when she was done, Barry said, "I gotta go. It's way too fucking boiling."

"The *language*," answered Lydia. "Your language *really* hurts me. I know you use that language in your world, but I would appreciate it if you didn't put it in *my* ears, *please*. It's like I'm being stabbed in the heart when I hear you talk like that. You're my *son*."

"Okay," said Barry. "Gotta go."

He went. Lydia and Walter remained on the line, though, in different parts of the house. "I suppose this is my fault, too," said Walter, over a static-filled and freighted dial tone.

"He called for *help*."

"I'm right," said Walter. "Everything's my fault. Nothing that happens isn't my fault. Dear."

"Now you're being sarcastic again. Why are you being sarcastic again? I don't understand why you do that."

"I'm sorry if I'm being sarcastic again. I didn't mean to be sarcastic," said Walter. "My sarcasm is something I battle with."

On they went, in that vein, as they always did.

In late August, Walter got the chance to do something good, because Barry called from WSU, and the upshot was, there were things Barry needed, mainly an amp he'd stored in the basement, but also some clothes he'd left behind, and all of his Dungeons and Dragons stuff, which he was going to sell. If anyone, said Barry, happened to be coming this way in the near future, maybe they could "just throw it all in" and Barry could "meet them or something."

Lydia leapt at this opportunity and made a plan. She would bake peanut-butter cookies, because Barry liked them, and Walter would take to Pullman the cookies, amp, clothes, Dungeons and Dragons box, and a new men's winter coat Lydia had bought at Penney's. He would leave on Saturday morning, meet up with Barry—Barry had told Lydia, "Dad can come up to my room or whatever"—they would tour campus together, eat a restaurant meal, and, said Lydia, "most importantly, connect." Then Walter would turn around and drive back, even though a normal person—obviously—would stay overnight after a trip of nearly three hundred miles. But, having wandered out of his marriage, and having gotten caught at it, Walter was in no position to argue about the plan. He would have to drive ten hours in one day. Overnight was for trustworthy husbands.

On Saturday morning, Lydia was up at four. She told Walter, getting out of bed, that she needed time not only to bake the cookies but to let them cool before putting them in a tin. "She makes such a big deal about everything," he thought. "Barry doesn't care about cookies."

Lydia pecked Walter on the cheek before he left. "Be nice, now," she said. "Give Barry a kiss for me. Will you give him a kiss? *And make sure he gets his cookies.*"

Walter did what he always did while driving—fiddled with his radio, got irritated at other drivers, changed lanes a lot, and thought about his problems. There were a number of late-summer RVs on the road, driven by retired guys who, glimpsed in passing, made Walter's heart drop. "I'm not there yet," he said to himself, "but the fact is, I'm getting there, either that or die first—please, God, don't let me ever buy an RV, let me die before that happens; if I ever start thinking about buying an RV, kill me."

After ninety minutes, Walter's discipline broke down and he ate two peanut-butter cookies. He noted how they'd been arranged carefully in the tin, with wax paper between the layers. After taking a third, he did some rearranging to make it look like he hadn't pilfered. At Ellensburg, where the usual strong wind was blowing from behind a slaughterhouse, he stopped for gas and ate a fourth cookie. Thereafter, he had minor fun passing other drivers, but mostly it was just a long grunt over bad roads with no cars on them. Tired of driving, and knowing he shouldn't make any more incursions into Lydia's sacred tin, he stopped in Washtucna and bought a package of Chips Ahoy! Walter ate them on a park bench while watching, as if not watching, two young mothers pushing kids on swings. One had a well-shaped, elegant ass—too elegant, he thought, for a woman in a wheat town. He imagined she wanted to leave Washtucna for a bigger place with more interesting people. He imagined he might represent this opportunity to her. Eventually, he just felt ridiculous— a grown man sitting by himself on a park bench, eating Chips Ahoy! and leering at innocents.

Back on 26, after passing through what felt like limitless wheat fields, he arrived in Pullman. Pullman turned out to be a few blocks of brick buildings plus some sprawl and a good-sized campus. Walter tracked down Barry's dorm room, but Barry wasn't there, and none of the diffident denizens Walter encountered, on Floor Three or elsewhere, knew a thing about his whereabouts. Walter retreated to the passenger seat of his car, where he lay back with his windows open and watched girls from behind his sunglasses. "They wouldn't give me the time of day," he thought. "I'm too old." On the other hand, the sun felt pretty grand, and a golden late-summer light suffused the youthful scene. The kids were winsome. The air was clean. Nevertheless, still no Barry, so after a while Walter went back into the dorm and explained himself to the farm boy in the office, who just sat there looking at Walter's driver's license and tapping an empty Pepsi can. Walter, taking the bull by the horns, asked if there was a storage room on the premises. "No, not really, but I guess you could just like leave your stuff here in the office," the boy answered, and giggled nervously.

Wondering why this labor had fallen to him, Walter hauled Barry's crap inside, but left the tin of cookies on the car seat for—at some point—a direct hand-over. Then he sat in a dorm commons watching televised golf with two Cougars. He said, "You guys have a blowout last night?" and one answered "Mmmmm," and then he asked, "Big party?" and the other guy answered, "Massive." They henceforth ignored Walter so completely that he began to understand his presence as an offense. Between that, the waiting, the long drive, and the farm boy in the office, Walter now felt darkly angry. Where was Barry? What was going on? "I'm not a delivery service," he thought, "and I have a right, at the very least, to a timely greeting from my son, and maybe even to some gratitude for the fact that I drove all the way out here." Then he got up and stuffed coins in a pay phone. "This is what I mean," he told Lydia.

"Try to be patient."

"I am being patient."

"You don't *sound* patient, Walter."

"You're reading my tone again. It's my words, not my tone."

"You're never patient, though. It's not just now."

"Where's Barry?"

"Patience."

Walter drove around until he found a café, where he ate a patty melt and scanned the campus newspaper. Every page was poorly laid out, and most of the articles, instead of supplying news, hammered readers with sophomoric opinions rendered as the final word. Barely engaged, Walter flipped from "Campus Life" to "Letters and Comments" and finally to "Arts and Entertainment," where the lead story was a double movie review—Bill Murray in *Meatballs,* Roger Moore in *Moonraker.* Walter wished he had a different newspaper.

Then, lo and behold, in the bottom corner of page 8, an article promoted a "Battle of the Bands" to be held at Ensminger Pavilion that night, and one of the bands, it said, was "eclectic, cerebral, hard-core DeathTrap."

Once again, Walter called Lydia. "Overnight?" she said. "I guess you have to, if you want to see Barry, and I support that kind of thing completely, you know, you spending time with Barry."

"It sounds like you still have a big trust issue, though."

"I still have a *gigantic* trust issue, Walter."

"Lydia," he said, "I love you."

He hung up and got a room at the Cougar Land Motel, where he watched the second half of a Rock Hudson movie. When it was over, he called Barry's dorm and let the phone ring interminably. Finally, someone picked up and said, "He's not here. I don't know where he is," over the top of loud music, and promised unconvincingly to tell Barry that his father was in town, staying at the Cougar Land, in Room 15. Next, Walter watched bowling and toyed with the idea of finding a decent happy-hour bar. It was just a thought, though; instead, he took a nap and a shower and, after eating a hamburger from a bag, found his way to Ensminger Pavilion, which looked like what it was—a hayseed concert hall smelling of livestock, with five hundred college kids packed in like cows, yelling, reeling, drinking, and smoking pot, while something vaguely resembling music was emitted by a band with no talent.

At ten-thirty, DeathTrap came onstage, and there was Barry in black leather pants, shambling toward a battered drum set, shirtless, pale, stringy, even gaunt, but with a splooch of stomach hanging over his pant waist and a drumstick between his teeth. He'd changed his hairstyle to bald, and, if Walter was seeing right from the back of the hall, he'd painted his lips like Dracula's after a kill.

There was nothing for Barry to do at first except beat on a tom-tom and crash a cymbal while six college girls in white dresses were "sacrificed" onstage, one at a time, by a studly-looking guy—the band's lead singer—who bit each, from behind, on the neck, hard, which appeared to elicit, from each, a fantastic orgasm. All of this while a dwarfish sideman chanted things like "The dark one has come!" and "Lusty wench, let thy blood feed Lucifer!" "Lydia would hate this," thought Walter.

After each girl had come, and dropped to the floor, they suddenly all rose from the dead as one and, standing at six mikes, sang, to Barry's beat, "Kill! Kill! Kill! Kill! KILL! KILL! KILL! KILL!" With that, the lead singer took center stage.

The other bands had been loud, but DeathTrap was louder. The resurrected girls got down on all fours, and the lead singer, sporting a codpiece, cavorted among them with theater and irony, stopping now and then to straddle one and hump her, much to the delight of the crowd. Barry pretended not to notice, and wailed away primitively, and threw and broke sticks. To Walter he seemed desperately self-aware, as though, instead of playing the drums for an eclectic, cerebral, hard-core band, he was making fun of someone who played drums for a group like that. Walter felt hollow—ill in his soul. It was so inexplicable, wounding, and tragic that his son had chosen such dark perversity from among all the choices life offered.

After its forty-five-minute assault on good taste and social norms, DeathTrap gleefully left the stage, Barry *sieg-Heil*-ing and goose-stepping away with a drumstick protruding from the fly of his pants like a long and very thin erection. Walter hurried outside, to a set of double doors at the back of the pavilion, where he was stopped by a bouncer with a badge reading MANAGER—actually, a kid who'd spent a lot of time in a weight room. "I don't care if you're God, sir," he said, "you have to have a pass to go in here."

"Come on," said Walter. "Be logical about it."

"I am being logical. And the logic is, you can't go in without a pass."

"But that's not logical," Walter insisted. "Obviously, you don't care about being logical, because if—"

"Hey," said the bouncer, blocking Walter's way when he tried to bluster past, "get the fuck out of here."

Walter sat in his car for over an hour, watching the back entrance for a sign of his son, who finally came out with a cigarette between his lips and his arm around the waist of a girl Walter recognized as a sacrificed virgin. "About time," thought Walter, then struggled out from behind his steering wheel and, feeling heartless now, headed for a showdown. The tang of pot hung on the air, and the stars and moon looked more vivid than at home. Many of the Battle of the Bands fans were leaving. Walter, despite his foul mood, saw beauty in the moment: the concert dénouement, the August warmth, the young people showing off attractive skin, and—the main thing pervading all of it—the probability that a lot of them were going to have sex in the next hour. It was great, except that he was so pissed at his son that everything else was in the background.

"Barry!" he called. "Jesus!"

Barry turned toward his father's voice, took the cigarette out of his mouth, tossed it, and disengaged from his virgin. "Barry!" repeated Walter. "What the hell is going on with you?"

When he got close—close enough to smell pot on his son's breath— Barry was staring at the ground. The virgin, who wasn't really all that cute, looked Walter over and then looked away as if at something across the parking lot. He could see, in her face, that she'd decided to keep mum, and to stay invisible, through whatever was about to happen between this middle-aged guy and Barry. "Hey," said Barry, "how's it going?"

Walter sighed. "How's it going? How's it *going*? Jesus, Barry, what *happened* to you?"

"What?"

"I was there at two."

"Whoops! Sorry, man."

"Jesus, Barry."

"I fucked up, I guess."

"Barry. *Jesus.*"

"I'm a fuck-up."

Walter thought the virgin might be laughing now, in a private way that barely showed. She was young, in her prime, with nice breasts and a horse face, and still wore the white dress she'd been sacrificed in that night. Despite his wrath, Walter thought first and foremost that he'd like to fuck her. "Sorry," he said, "whoever you are. You shouldn't have to listen to all of this."

It was as though he hadn't spoken. She didn't even say "Whatever," or shrug. Not a flicker of an eyelash, nothing to acknowledge him. And this nothing was the worst, the most disappointing response of all, which he was sure she understood. She was wielding the weapon, so female, of disdain, and that made Walter even more furious at Barry. "What's your name?" he asked.

"DeeDee."

"Well, DeeDee, Barry is my son, and Barry was supposed to meet me in his dorm room, but Barry never showed up."

More nothing—and so intensely was it nothing that it was also, from Walter's point of view, everything. "I suppose you guys are headed off to fuck," he heard himself say—and he was saying it to DeeDee. "Well, go ahead."

"Dad," said Barry.

"I hope you enjoy yourselves," said Walter.

Now DeeDee—at last—put her head down, where it belonged, and he and Barry were face to face. "Hey," said Walter, "you're shaking."

"Dad."

"I pay for everything, remember?" said Walter. "If I stop now, you're in trouble, Barry, because then you'd have to get a job."

No answer. It was satisfying, for Walter, to humiliate his son in front of DeeDee. To see him on his heels, shaking in his leather pants, devoid, for once, of a comeback. At the same time, Walter felt terrible, because letting loose on Barry wasn't good parenting. It was something he was doing because he'd lost control of himself. He'd always held back, sensibly—until now.

Barry, scowling, spat on the concrete and said, "Why are you so fucking *blind*?"

"What?"

"I don't want your money. Keep your money, Dad. Wake *up*, okay? Take a look at yourself."

Walter answered, "Nice meeting you, DeeDee," and walked away.

It was a rough night in Room 15 at the Cougar Land. From Room 14 came another Battle of the Bands, and when that finally drew to a merciful close, the relative quiet revealed that in Room 16 someone was snoring with the television on. Walter, a pillow over his head and wads of crumpled paper in his ears, lay awake replaying the parking-lot confrontation, particularly his part in it, which he felt acutely. By the time he fell into an unsatisfying half-sleep, there were cleaning carts rolling along outside, car doors opening and closing in the parking lot, and the voices of people walking past. Walter woke after ten with a headache, showered, and lay on the bed again.

At eleven-thirty, he paid his bill, then bought doughnuts in a bag for the road, and got out of Pullman. Passing between wheat fields, he festered over Barry, and over himself, and over Lydia and Tina, and the more he festered, the more disconsolate he felt. What a mess it all was, and what a waste of time, coming all the way out here like a good Samaritan, or like an envoy—of Lydia's—on a peace mission. Time, money, goodwill, all wasted, and now, blue and at a loss, he was going home to Lydia with her tin of peanut-butter cookies admonishing him from the passenger seat. What would he say about the fact that her cookies remained undelivered, despite her repeated exhortations? And why did there have to be repeated exhortations? For that matter, why Lydia's vapidity, condescension, sentimentality, and moral superiority? Why her constant leveraging? Why the guilt and punitive slavery? Why was she doing all of this constantly? Why did she treat him like he was serving a life sentence? What was in his oppression for Lydia? Walter, of course, knew the answer to these questions. It was that—as Barry might have put it—he was a fuck-up.

"What have I ever done right?" thought Walter. "My son despises me, my daughter hates me, my wife doesn't trust me, and everyone at work probably thinks I'm a jerk. On top of that, I'm a serial adulterer. I'm a shitheel who slept with his wife's best friend. I'm a chronic, fucking liar. I got blackmailed to the tune of two fifty a month by a goddamn teeny-bopper. It's been payola through the teeth for . . . for more than sixteen years. That's, what, almost fifty grand? Jesus, what else? How low can I go? I know how low—I'm a fucking statutory rapist. I've got a kid out of wedlock who I don't know a thing about. That's the real story of my life."

A fat rodent ran across the road in front of Walter and, while he hovered between speeding up to hit it and slowing down not to, made it to the safety of the wheat. Now and then he saw doves on the phone lines, as still as glass insulators, inert in the heat. Nothing else seemed to live here, especially not people, and the farther Walter drove into this stark, friendless landscape, the more deserted it felt, and the more deeply he experienced it as a last hiatus of relative peace before, as he thought of it, Lydia's hammer fell.

"I should just lie back and enjoy the ride," he thought. "I should be grateful for the beauty of this drive in the countryside, savor my freedom, and forget all the rest, since it isn't here right now."

At a dilapidated barn, he slowed to thirty, because in front of him a car was in the middle of the road, straddling the centerline. Maybe it was someone having engine trouble, he thought, or a photographer interested in the rural picturesque who'd stopped to weigh the barn's merits as a subject. Walter saw the silhouette of someone by a tree, and was prepared to give whoever it was a pass, cut him some slack, until it turned out to be a young punk taking a piss. Who did the little fucker think he was, hogging the road like that while someone—Walter—needed to get past, and had every *right* to get past? How could anyone be this *dumb*? Didn't this kid have any sense?

"Asshole!" thought Walter, and, pressing the accelerator, laid on his horn with the same irritation he'd felt when he'd let Barry's dorm phone ring a million times. He gave the kid the finger furiously. Until now, irritation had been as far as it went for him when it came to other drivers, but this time he was seized by rage. He felt murderous, capable of anything. Unbridled, cut loose, he screamed "Fuck you!" and punched it. Passing, he noted that the car had racing stripes, and that a girl in a leather jacket was watching him from the passenger side. There was freedom, he knew, in reckless speed, and the whole operation, his defiant pass, left him with a keen sense of victory.

But he wasn't victorious. The kid gave him the finger back—two fingers—ran, and jumped into his car. "Oh, no," thought Walter. "Stupid of me *again*." Fearfully, he watched the kid gain in his rearview mirror, and then, even more fearfully, watched him ride his bumper. Walter rolled down his window in a panic and waved him off, gestured for surrender, but the kid just rode his bumper all the harder. There was no way to shake him, because his car was souped up. In a straightaway, the kid pulled neatly alongside so his girlfriend could flip Walter off with both hands. Walter had a fleeting view of his adversary's face—the face of a raging, powerful young warrior—and the remaining manliness and heat went out of him. He felt scared into a thorough and quaking submission. Trembling, he hit the brakes to indicate docility, but as he did the kid forced him off the road into a wheat field. Poor Walter. He was turned upside down. He hung from his seatbelt with his head against the roof. He survived, in terror, the first of four rolls, but as the roof overhead hit the ground a second time, it caved in and broke his neck.

5

Mrs. Long

Jim Long was disciplined and didn't drink insensibly, especially compared with his brothers. He'd come home in the evening from Long Alpine headquarters, ask Diane about her day, listen to her answer, ask follow-up questions, make her a cocktail if she wanted one, and, if she was at the sink in the kitchen or bathroom, pin her from behind and plant a kiss beside her ear. She liked Jim, at first, despite his conventionality, because he treated her like a princess. Jim was her hero, defending her against the pettiness and testiness in his clan of snobbish ski barons, and enjoying, literally, kissing her feet, due to what emerged as a foot fetish. He squired her to concerts and plays, and took her out for prime rib, king crab, or oysters on the halfshell. When they dined at the Benson, Heathman, or Seward, Diane felt self-conscious and feared she'd be revealed as the onetime consort of well-to-do hotel patrons. On the other hand, she'd left behind Blonde Ponytail Barbie and, on her way toward thirty, embraced Impeccably Arranged. Impeccably Arranged meant that, with enough money on hand and time to spend preening, no one would notice that she wasn't perfect anymore. Why this was so important to her at such an early age was a question Diane pondered in a self-punishing way; she wondered if she was neurotic or normal, an obsessive narcissist or an average woman with an average concern about the degradations of time. Sometimes she felt like the victim of chauvinism, someone who had thoroughly objectified herself because of forces beyond her control. Other times she felt that she was pulsing with power—that, because she still looked relatively spectacular, men were putty in her hands. Looking spectacular was a fascinating game—without it, Diane felt, life might be boring. The only problem was that looking spectacular got harder as she got older. Gradually, adjustments to makeup, hairstyle, and wardrobe became less like fun and more like work, demanded rigor as the window for good results began to close, and took not only too much time but too much emotion. On any given day, Diane could be made to feel good or bad by the results of her labors at her mirror. That made her feel like a shallow twit, someone who spent time wondering if her current bad-hair day was a harbinger of unending bad-hair days to come instead of spending it wondering what she was going to do with her life. Diane thought about her looks with a terrible constancy. It was the monologue in her head for lonely hours at a time, the one that animated her current persona as the Impeccably Arranged Mrs. Long.

Mrs. Long's life was a veritable vacation punctuated by actual vacations. Her in-laws liked holidays at upscale destinations, and also liked to argue about upscale destinations, so usually airline tickets couldn't be reserved until a spate of factional politicking had subsided. One brother would argue for Lake Tahoe, another would speak for Jackson Hole, a third would stump for Vail. Diane pretended to have opinions about the resorts, hotels, ski slopes, beaches, and golf courses in play, but really it was all the same to her as long as no roughing it was involved. While her in-laws skied, golfed, or snorkeled, Diane idled in shops or read in a chaise longue. Eventually, they'd limp in from their exertions, and then it would be time for cocktails with pupus, chips and dip, or fondue. Listening to the Longs relive their day—the transparent boasts, the fraternal animation—left Diane more antagonized than the day had.

The Longs were energetic social drinkers, and when they got on a roll, they loosened up. The vacationing clan would gather at poolside, and the brothers would compete as cannonball artists or shove their wives into the water. The characteristic family laugh was a cackle that, at these times, moved up the registers of frequency and decibel and spread like a contagion. It ricocheted from one side of the pool to the other when the Long wives perched on their husbands' shoulders, grappling, grunting, giggling, and cursing while their lesser halves made uproarious comments. The commentary became more subdued and solemn when the men engaged in underwater contests of aerobic capacity, only to devolve again toward the bawdy and inane when the women tried synchronized swimming. Finally, the Longs would haul out at poolside to chat, snack, and bask in the late sun. After showering, they'd eat on a terrace. Then they'd descend on a bar or a club, where one or more of Jim's brothers might parody disco and, as the night deepened, strip-tease. The day after raucous benders like these, the Longs emerged from their rooms around noon, drank plain coffee, and described their hangovers. Soon, though, they were arranging to make their headaches go away via tennis, golf, or a run.

At home base—Portland's Riverside Club—Impeccably Arranged kept most men at bay, but it didn't slow down the "alpha males," a term Jim used to describe the more aggressive players on the club's tennis ladder. They flirted with Diane at dinner dances and cocktail parties, on the golf-course veranda, and on the terrace by the pool. Unimpressed by well-to-do pretty boys who, in the end, could do her no good, Diane focused on her complicated cosmetics, artificial nails, elaborate salon work, and faultless, stiff wardrobe. At least once a week, she made an appointment—for electrolysis, say, or to see a dermatologist, or for a pedicure or exfoliation. She knew that all of this was extravagantly bankrupt, because eventually you had to get old and maybe hideous. And how could you face being old and hideous if you didn't practice for it when you had the chance? Mostly, though, Diane dismissed this line of thought, and told herself such questions didn't need to be answered, that they mercifully came later and could stay in the background, that they could be met head-on when old age arrived. For the moment, though, the battle should be waged, because the battle—if not the war—could be won, hands down. In the name of this sort of limited victory, Diane had a lit mirror installed in her bathroom on an accordion-style hinge, the better for self-scrutiny. She tortured herself with tweezers to prevent pubic hair from showing near her bathing suit. She plucked down from her chin. She was meticulous with mascara. At the end of a long session of intensive primping, Diane looked so good, in her own eyes, it was thrilling. "Yes," she sometimes said to herself, "all is vanity, it's true, but I'm the May Queen."

Jim was openly glad that she looked spectacular. She also knew he had no idea how much effort was involved, and how much anguish and ambivalence. One day, as soon as he left the house, she stripped and stood before a full-length mirror without holding back her shoulders, sucking in her gut, or adjusting the lights beneficially. What she saw was shocking. Her side view in particular was horrifying, because it showed how clearly everything was sagging, how her body was getting wrinkled and dimpled. Face-to-face with herself in the mirror, Diane hated herself for hating herself, because it was one thing to be ugly, another to be fixated on it. Who was it who said that, whatever the inroads and humiliations of age, the inwardly graceful remained beautiful by definition? Mahatma Gandhi? Mother Teresa? Whoever it was, Diane didn't believe it, because the evidence for error in this theory of beauty was everywhere to behold. What made more sense was whoever had said that there's melancholy in seeing yourself rot.

Jim, on the other hand, by the time he was thirty-four, seemed perfectly able to go about in a bathing suit looking like a five on a scale of ten, as if flab, sag, back hair, narrow shoulders, spindly legs, and a droopy chest were not embarrassing. Diane could see that Jim wouldn't avoid the destiny of the Long males, which was to be thin at the lip, high at the forehead, and swollen in a way that looked painful at the belly; these signature flaws would pronounce themselves as Jim aged, in fact already pronounced themselves. No matter what he did at the health club or on his fields of play, Jim had the depleted look of his Anglo-Saxon forebearers. Before long, like his father, he'd lack a posterior presence—it would look as though, inside his pants, his rump had dehydrated and shriveled. The older brothers were increasingly like this, junior versions of their faltering dad, whose knees were obviously killing him as he battled down slopes and returned tennis balls. Yet Jim grew older the way Diane knew you were supposed to grow older—he let go, somehow, of the need to be perfect, and he didn't let it bother him, on the beach or by the swimming pool, when other men, younger and older both, looked better than he did. "I can either let it bother me or accept it," he told Diane. "I golf, try to eat well, go to the weight room, and play tennis," he droned on. "I work at keeping my perspective on life humble, and if I'm lucky enough to one day have children, I'll feel completely at peace and really blessed."

Diane was on the pill but didn't tell her husband. It seemed to her the least damaging way, for both of them, to deal with something she didn't want him to know about: that she didn't want to have kids. The pill, thought Diane, meant at least five extra pounds. She was past thirty and her thighs were getting bigger. Also, her butt was expanding. It was time to put up a more serious fight, so Diane began to use Jim's Ab Blaster and to walk on the treadmill in the basement. It cut against her grain to do these things, but the facts were plain now in the mirror.

Exercise, besides hurting, had another downside—after ten minutes of ab work and twenty minutes of treadmilling, Diane wanted to go out and order nachos. She began shopping at a health-food store, so that when the fatal urge hit her, there was something around that didn't go immediately to her backside. For about six months, she held the line—sort of—but not without having to increase her efforts and face up to her propensity to avoid exercise. Then it became necessary to join Jim's health club and to suffer on Mondays, Wednesdays, and Fridays through an hourlong, deafening aerobics class.

Difficulty in conceiving began to needle Jim, who said he'd always thought that by the time he was his age he would have had at least two or three kids. When his patience with God and destiny wore out, he broached the idea of a fertility specialist. Diane treated this as a rhetorical suggestion for as long as she could, then told him she would "do a bit of research," while hoping—in private—that time would do the trick. But Jim's campaign was just beginning. There began to be enthusiasm for the prospect of his progeny in other quarters of the family, most assertively from Jim's sister Sue, the one who'd married into long-haul trucks and, for reasons Diane never understood, was deemed a wise voice by her clan. Sue was the Long who spearheaded vacations, spoke to travel agents, and reserved blocks of rooms. She was also the one who arranged loge seats for *The Nutcracker* every year. Whenever a Long daughter reached thirteen, Sue made sure that the females in the family were invited to an elaborate afternoon tea in a reserved room at the Heathman. Sue had two daughters of her own, and three sons, and her husband was such a talented golfer that he gave eight strokes to Jim when they played. Sue golfed, too.

Sue called Diane to suggest they go to lunch. Over bay-shrimp-and-avocado salads, she beat around the bush before coming forth with sympathy, encouragement, and the names and phone numbers of fertility specialists. Sue passed this information to Diane on a memo sheet with "From the desk of . . . Sue Strom" printed on top. She'd written the names and numbers in her large, looping, unslanted hand. Below she'd added the words "God Bless!" next to a smiley face.

Still Diane didn't act. Jim, now desperately on the offensive, went to a specialist of his own, and "checked out," as he put it, "all systems go." Diane had the feeling he read his test results as a kind of report card on his value as a man—semen volume, sperm count, motility—and also that, by extension, he saw her as a failure. In response, she claimed to have seen a specialist, too, and to have heard that, for reasons unknown, she was "subfertile." This, she added, meant that they should try harder, which, for the moment, was good enough for Jim. On Super Bowl Sunday, at his brother Will's suburban castle, he jocularly described, to his smirking clan, his assignment "to work overtime with Diane."

Extra exertions of course got Jim nowhere. Fecund as he was, and willing, and hard-charging, he couldn't get the better of Diane's "subfertility." She kept hope alive, though, by pretending to be taking a hormone stimulator. She bought *The Joy of Sex,* which at first embarrassed Jim. Undaunted, she picked up a pornographic manual on positions that might improve their odds, and encouraged Jim to try them all. This he did with no lack of enthusiasm. He bought in wholeheartedly. He aimed for deep penetration. One night, he brought home a Xeroxed research paper establishing the relationship between the quality of a woman's orgasm and her odds of pregnancy, built around the theory that—he read this to her—"strong female contractions are like powerful waves on which sperm ride toward the cervix." Intrigued by the idea of focusing on his partner's pleasure, Jim next brought home a vibrator and a dildo. Diane, who'd borne up under plenty of partners interested in accosting her with these and other tools, not only let him go at her with them but dutifully pretended to contract in more powerful waves.

Jim, ever clueless despite his wealth and privilege, had no idea what he was up against, and, despite his unplanted seed, enjoyed his expanded sex life. At the height of his powers, he was on a roll, and so was Long Alpine, which had become so successful that it was written up not only in the fawning *The Oregonian* but in *Fortune* and *The Wall Street Journal*. Soon, the Long plant was enlarged and streamlined, and the marketing department got imaginative and savvy under Jim's energetic management. Long hosted contests at major ski resorts, gave away skis, vacations, and season lift tickets, bought out a rival, expanded research and development, and, at Jim's insistence, started a line of "cutting-edge" winter wear. Soon a new company catalogue had been developed featuring bold and athletic models, expensive photographs, and clever product descriptions. Long sold not only clothes, skis, and poles, but goggles, helmets, travel bags, boots, sunglasses, and other top-of-the-line fashionable accessories. All of it carried Long's updated logo, featuring the word LONG as if engraved inside an oval belt buckle. Jim closely monitored Long Alpine's ad development and spent a lot of time thinking about storyboards. He told Diane that his interests had turned creative and that he felt himself expanding as a human being.

Despite the rising fortunes of her marital community, Diane remained privately averse to the Longs and to their upbeat mercenary endeavors. She sat in judgment of them with growing severity. When she wrote to her half-brother Club to complain about her in-laws, she made what she knew were unfair exaggerations, subsuming them under the heading "Rich Americans" to make things clear. He wrote back to say that he'd never been to the States but that these monied in-laws sounded familiar from television. He wrote that he was "hod-carrying for shit money" and that this line of work was doing his back in. He had "a mate who does up gypsy caravans" and was thinking of making his way down to Dorset to help him with the painting. Maybe he was going to travel, he claimed; maybe he would visit her one day. All of that was refreshing to Diane, who otherwise had to put up with the band of philistines she'd married into. Her critique of her in-laws eventually extended to the way Isobel's breath smelled ("tonsillar concretions" was the name of her malady) and to the make and model of Nelson's tennis racket. The phrase "ruthless buggers" sat high in her head when the arrogant Longs complained about American proles on the dole, or the supposed laxity of the American justice system, which they felt favored criminals. Their ignorance repulsed her. Their politics were galling. They were not very happy with Jimmy Carter and on the Fourth of July, by the pool at Will's house, bitched drunkenly and loudly about the peanut farmer from Georgia who'd so far done diddly-squat about inflation but had sure been busy on amnesty for draft evaders. Jim joined his brothers in this line of attack with what Diane thought was a surprising vehemence. He may have protested to her his midlife turn toward liberal sentiments and creative concerns, but by the pool he sounded just like his brothers—like a plutocrat with a crabbed pecuniary complaint. Bottom line, though: Jim still had a lot of money. And with time he seemed to accept the fact that Diane would never give him heirs. He told her that he'd decided to be thankful for his eleven nieces and fourteen nephews, most of whom lived in driving distance. He said he saw nothing wrong with being a good uncle. If indeed it was his fate not to have his own kids, he could—and did—accept that and see the bright side. Jim took pains to let Diane know that he didn't blame her, which made her feel guilty. He wasn't a bad person, after all, just well-heeled and dumb. Maybe, she told herself, she should have chosen a wanker, because then her exploitation could proceed guilt-free. But, anyway, there was no going back now. Guilt or no guilt, she still didn't want children. After all, if Jim was finally getting used to her "sterility," what would be the point in getting pregnant? *"Nada"* was the answer from her hairdresser, Steve, a diminutive and leathery Louisianan who looked like a cross between Mick Jagger and a rodeo rider—especially when he wore a torso-grabbing T-shirt—and who knew not only about her ruse of subfertility, but also, hilariously, about the vibrator and dildo. Good old Steve was wonderful as a confidant but nasty as a hair critic. At times he would hold Diane's hair in his hands and say, "I can't work with ignored raw material, you know," or, "If you're not going to use a good conditioner daily, there's no point in coming in to see to me." She put up with his barbs because her appointments with Steve always ended in triumph. When he finally swiveled her chair toward the mirror, Diane looked better, and because she looked better, she felt better, too.

The day came, though, when they were jointly disappointed. Steve refused to take money for his "disaster," and tried, fruitlessly, to correct it with his shears. This way, things went from bad to worse until Steve, with tears in his eyes, asked Diane to join him outside for the cigarette he needed "to just come down from this . . . this . . . I don't even want to say." On the sidewalk, pacing in front of the salon and smoking furiously, he was silent for a long time. Then, with one of his zippered black boots on the salon's windowsill, and with his anguished scrutiny of her bad hairdo distorting his face, he urged Diane to see "a specialist friend of mine about a light facial peel, just to touch up and rejuvenate a little, and I'm paying for it, because I feel so devastated." Diane felt immediately drawn to the idea, and wondered why she she'd never thought of it.

Steve's friend was a dermatologist named David Berg, whose results were so overwhelmingly good, and whose manner was so encouraging and soothing, that Diane became a fan of light facial peels. Always explaining everything as he went—"This is just a very gentle cleanser; now I'm applying our magic solution; now we'll carefully and thoroughly rinse; I'm just finishing up with a little soothing lotion"—and doing it in a silky voice, Dr. Berg made a facial peel seem like a spa treatment. Each time, Diane was amazed and impressed by his ability to coax new vibrancy from her skin with a minimum of pain. Her peels were a private matter between her and Dr. Berg that Diane paid for with Walter Cousins's money, taken from her secret safety-deposit box in Sullivan's Gulch. When the time came for more elaborate work, though—targeting the fine wrinkles in her brow, around her mouth, and next to her eyes—Diane was forced to discuss it with Jim, because there wouldn't be a way, said Dr. Berg, to pretend it hadn't happened. A crust would form on the treated areas, and for a couple of weeks they would appear bright pink, before she could expect the end result of a smoother, tighter, more youthful appearance. "But you don't need to do that," Jim countered when she explained, "because I'm Billy Joel—I love you just the way you are."

Diane wanted to say, "It isn't about you, Jim," but by now she knew better. "I just feel fortunate to live in modern times," she told him, "and to have the wherewithal for an intensive peel, and while it might be better, morally speaking, to give our money to charities, we can do that, too, can't we?"

"We can," answered Jim, "but that's not the issue. I don't know how else to say this, but the issue is vanity."

He was sitting with his Docksiders crossed on the coffee table—not, Diane thought, the best posture for an attack on vanity. "What about your weight-lifting supplements?" she asked, even though he hadn't used them for years. "What is it you take? For more defined muscles? Or that thing you ordered—what's it called?—the Ab Blaster? Come on—don't be self-righteous."

Jim flexed his right biceps facetiously. "And now my abs are perfect," he said.

So she went for the more intensive peel, which hurt a little, and ended with a coating of petroleum jelly, substantial adhesive tape, and pain meds. At home that night her eyes swelled shut, and in the morning she woke up sick to her stomach and suffering from a second-degree facial burn. She couldn't say much, because talking hurt her face. Half blind, mute, and in considerable pain, she had to wait patiently for her appearance to improve. After two weeks, some stay-at-home weight gain, and a thousand-plus pages of Sidney Sheldon and Harold Robbins, her face, indeed, looked great.

At Mazatlán, the next month, she was scrupulous about staying out of the sun, for which Jim rebuked her, but this was an argument he couldn't win, because the American Cancer Society was on Diane's side, and because Nelson had recently had basal-cell carcinomas removed from his left cheek and temple. Diane passed hours in a breezy cabaña, playing games of Scrabble with Nelson and Isobel, drinking Evian water and piña coladas, and earning points for being charitable to the geriatrics. It was easy, mindless duty, and in every regard it would have been all right were she not made to feel so insecure by the many younger women passing by. They looked so good that Diane felt terrible and vowed to lose five pounds straightaway.

On Thanksgiving, she resisted the stuffing and potatoes and, avoiding the kitchen, focused on her nieces. Diane was popular with the teen-age Long girls, not only because of her vestigial English accent but because, out of earshot of other adults, she joined their adolescent criticism of the world. Before dinner, she'd leaned in the doorway of a bedroom where a density of Long darlings had congregated, and laughed when one of them pointed out that Uncle Trip had gross chest hair. Diane told her nieces that chest hair could be sexy, which they would understand when they were more experienced. This numbed all talk while they deciphered Aunt Diane and—she knew—grappled with discomfort. No matter. She let a beat pass before revealing to her confused audience that men who were feminine in gesture and aspect could be attractive as well. Diane looked theatrically up and down the hall to make certain no adults were in hearing distance, then urged her nieces not to count on condoms. They should take the pill, or get an IUD or a diaphragm—the pill, of course, was best. Again there was discomfited teen-age silence, which she ended by saying, "I suppose I should join the oldies for cocktails and hors d'oeuvres in front of the television, and for chitchat about—whatever."

Through the December holidays, Diane ate with greater-than-normal abandon, and the inevitable weight gain—some in her butt, some in her midriff—left her in need of a mood pick-me-up in the form of yet another facial peel. Jim, who was at this point well practiced as a husband, asked, "What weight gain are you talking about?" Nevertheless, when she weighed herself, four new pounds corroborated her position that a visit to David Berg was necessary.

Dr. Berg listened to Diane's concerns, then referred her to a friend in body reshaping, a Dr. Green in Lake Oswego, who, Berg said, was "absolutely magnificent." At her first appointment with Dr. Green, he wanted to know what she didn't like about her body, and asked about her psychological, marital, health, and eating problems. At a second appointment, Diane had to take off her clothes and submit to being photographed by a nurse with a Polaroid instant camera, and to a tape measure and calipers. She and Dr. Green discussed her butt and midriff, and then he insisted that she take a week to think about the risks—including the risk, however slight, of death—and about the scars he would do his best to conceal, the possibility of less-than-perfect results, and the certainty that time would undo all his efforts. A month later, Diane had a combination tummy tuck and butt lift, supplemented by liposuction contouring. Other than some irritating itching around her stitches, and a little redness at the site of a surgical drain—remedied with an antibiotic—her recovery period, though boring, wasn't painful. And the results, after three months, were good.

In fact, that spring she looked "incredible"—Jim's word—in a French-cut bikini on the beach at Puerto Vallarta, where Jim's clan was a bit desultory, because, just two days before their departure, in a surprise to all, Sue had reported that her trucking-magnate husband had been philandering with a much younger woman. The Longs were livid and ready for a war. Jim told Diane that he hoped his sister would "take that jerk for all he's worth and drive him into the ground." Before the summer was over, she had.

In September, Walter Cousins stopped sending money. At this stage his faltering was financially meaningless, but, still, Diane wasn't going to let him get away with it. If Walter thought time had let him off the hook, he definitely had another thing coming. Feeling vindictive, victorious, and gleeful, Diane wrote a letter to Walter's wife. "Dear Mrs. Cousins," she began. "This is rather hard. This is far from pretty." She paused for a moment at this early stage of composition, imagining Mrs. Cousins at the reading end of this, then added:

> *I have to tell you that, in the summer of 1962, when I was employed as an au pair in your home, your husband repeatedly took advantage of me. He took advantage of my youth and insecurity. He took advantage of a young woman who was a visitor to America. For years I've lived with the disturbing memory of the summer of 1962. I've also lived with a considerable burden, because I'm the mother of your husband's child. I have a boy, age sixteen and a half, who until this month your husband supported with monthly payments of $250. Unfortunately, those payments stopped coming recently. This is most regrettable, because I'm dependent on those payments to meet my son's needs. Perhaps you could remind Mr. Cousins of his obligations to his son born out of wedlock.*
>
> *I write to you about this only with the greatest pain. That you now know of your husband's past behavior gives me no pleasure. Forgive me. I have no wish to add to whatever sadness permeates your life. I remember that in the summer of 1962 you were receiving treatment for mental illness and hope and pray that since then you have been free from more of same. I also remember your children, Tina and Barry, and hope that their lives are happy and in order. They were a pleasure to spend time with, and I enjoyed their company. Unfortunately, I can't say the same for your husband. He has brought much pain into my life and, as a traumatized rape victim, I have experienced considerable hardship and misery.*
>
> *Please consider my request. I hope you can impress on Mr. Cousins the moral imperative he is under to continue to provide support for his son.*
>
> *With prayers and best wishes,*
>
> > *Diane Burroughs*

Lydia Cousins's response arrived four days later, in a white business envelope, typed, with no letterhead. "Ms. Burroughs," it began. "Walter is dead."

He died in an automobile accident five and a half weeks ago. I've been assured that no alcohol was involved. It was a single-car accident on a road in eastern Washington. Walter was returning from a visit with our son, Barry, who is now a student at Washington State University. Since Walter's death Barry has had difficulty with his studies and I am worried that this will be for him a lost semester.

Tina, my daughter, is closer to home, studying at the University of Washington. She, too, is devastated by Walter's passing. They did not always get along too well and poor Tina is now suffering, naturally, from guilt. I worry about her mental health, frankly. You may remember how she was as a child, so emotionally delicate and sensitive. These things remain big challenges for Tina, and have all been intensified by her father's sudden death. All of that said, I think she'll pull through. She is very dedicated to her studies.

But I don't write merely to update you on the children. My true purpose is to respond to your revelation regarding the summer of 1962. Let me preface my response to that by pointing out that Walter went outside our marriage in 1973. He was discovered and we confronted it via marriage counseling. With the years we came to grips with what had happened, and we went on together, not without some happiness. That said, it's disheartening to now know that Walter lied when he insisted to me that the philandering he was discovered at was the only philandering he'd engaged in throughout our marriage. It hurts to know that our subsequent life together had as its foundation this deceitfulness on his part. I have to wonder now what else he never told me about, and this is compounding my grief at the moment and making it even more difficult for me to get on with life. But get on I must. And I will tell you that despite my sadness I am in many ways looking forward. What's done is done.

Ms. Burroughs, I must tell you that, though I am not entirely in accord with your version of what happened in the summer of 1962, I have no problem with your use of the term "rape victim." It was rape because you were in Walter's employ, and therefore placed in an unfair position when it came to his advances, just as a secretary is in an unfair position when propositioned by her boss, and just as a college girl is in an unfair position with regard to a professor she has a lust for. In all of these situations the term "rape" can be fairly applied because the participants in the sex act are not on equal ground and do not come to bed with the same power or leverage. One partner has it over the other, and this was the case with Walter and you. Shame on him for that. There is no excuse for it.

That said, I feel certain that Walter didn't physically overpower you. I feel certain that you played some part in it. What we both are calling rape might also have elements of a sordid affair between a married man and a willing and sophisticated girl. Maybe a young and very confused girl, maybe a girl who is a victim of circumstance and of her childhood and culture and so on and so forth, but still there remains this element of will. I have a feeling, Diane, if I remember you correctly, that this didn't go all in one direction.

With regard to the money, I do believe that, after sixteen and a half years, Walter has fully done his duty. I wish you the best in raising your child, and I do hope he flourishes in the world, but as for money from Walter, that's over.

In closing, I'm saddened by the news you've sent me, but I suppose, in keeping with grief as a catharsis, this sad revelation comes at the right moment.

Sincerely yours,

Lydia Cousins

About the time she turned thirty-three, Diane began mulling a face-lift. Certain holiday photographs jump-started her in this direction, but it was the trip to Lake Placid for the 1980 Winter Olympics—where Long Alpine was spending considerable money—that confirmed in her the need for action. The dry air there wreaked havoc on her complexion, sucking so much moisture from her skin that no amount, or brand, of rehydrating cream helped. Diane found herself looking, for long spells, in her hotel-room mirror, and feeling depressed because her jawline was sagging and the cords in her neck were tightening. In a parka and hat she looked so middle-aged that she didn't want to go out to watch ski events with the family. She had to, though, because the Longs were expecting her, there'd be irritating questions if she failed to show, and so, standing in the snow wearing huge Vuarnet sunglasses, she found herself feeling ugly and bereft while the Olympics took place at a weird distance.

A face-lift was complicated. Dr. Berg was board-certified as a dermatologist, but not as a plastic surgeon. Dr. Green didn't do faces. They both had recommendations for her, but not the same recommendations. Diane found herself running around a lot, even flying to Los Angeles to consult with a surgeon to the stars. Everyone she interviewed had sound credentials on paper, and in person seemed equally stellar, but in the end she chose a doctor named Jerry Kaplan because he was local, booked into June, and had *Vanity Fair* instead of *Vogue* in his waiting room. His nurse gave Diane testimonials, informational pamphlets, reassurance, and compliments. Diane read the literature as well as some horror stories— suddenly ubiquitous—about face-lifts gone bad, anesthesia disasters, and painful problems with healing. These didn't dissuade her. Dr. Kaplan, with his passionate ideas about her face and the things that might be done with it, seemed equal to the task. They could start with a brow lift to smooth her forehead, he said, plus eye work to tighten her lower lids—"bang-for-your-buck work," he called it. He predicted she'd be happy with that package, but couldn't make promises because his line of work was more art than science.

"Art?" Diane asked. "That makes me a bit nervous."

Dr. Kaplan tilted back in his desk chair and clasped his hands behind his head. "It's *aesthetic* surgery," he said. "Results are therefore *always* subjective. They get viewed through the lens of emotional issues." The doctor rotated his neck as if to loosen it. "Let me be one-hundred-percent candid," he said. "No one should opt for aesthetic surgery when in fact what they need is therapy. My work is external. I only change the surface."

"I don't need therapy," said Diane. "I need to look better."

Dr. Kaplan dislodged something irritating from the corner of his eye. "The way you look, yes, I can do something about," he assured her, "but inner stuff, that's not my area. I can't do away with your emotional problems—I mean, if you *had* emotional problems." Dr. Kaplan ground what had come from his eyelid between his thumb and forefinger. "Inside, that's *not my area*," he repeated. "I'm going to do everything in my power to make your face look absolutely wonderful, but—"

"It isn't wonderful now?"

Not missing a beat, the doctor assessed her face. "It *is* wonderful," he said. "Should we cancel your surgery?"

Two weeks later, she sat on the edge of his examination table while he rolled her skin around under his hands and looked at it closely through a lit magnifier. As he pressed, pulled, lifted, and prodded, he said, "Under the jawline you've lost minimal structural support we could probably address with a simple S-lift, or just leave it for later. With the peels you've had, your skin quality is still good, but here, below your eyes, as you know, we have a little tiredness showing, which I think we should go after, and . . . well . . . your upper eyelids are debatable. I could lift them, I guess, or I could do the whole forehead, I could pull up the forehead, which does have just a little sag to it—not bad, though—and bring the eyelids up with it; I actually think that's probably preferable in your case." Dr. Kaplan moved her temples about under practiced fingers. "All right," he said, still probing and pressing, "S-lift, lower lids, brow lift as opposed to just eyelids, let's do that while you've still got good elasticity. And you do have good elasticity for someone your age. Not that I don't want to have your business, but all of this could wait a few years, I feel obligated to tell you. It really could."

"Let's do it all," said Diane. "That's what I want."

"Tell me again what you want," said Dr. Kaplan. "Let's do that one more time."

"What I want," said Diane. "I want to look younger. I don't want to have jowls. I don't like my eyes. I don't like my forehead. I don't want to look droopy and tired all the time. Also, I don't want to look like I've had any surgery. My goal is to look ten years younger, but natural, not fake."

Knowing how she sounded, Diane added, "I wouldn't say this sort of thing except to a plastic surgeon. But really there's another side of me—another me—who's much less vain."

On the appointed day, Diane did what Dr. Kaplan's nurse told her to do—showed up on an empty stomach, with a sedative swallowed, no makeup or jewelry, and Jim in tow. After her face was marked as if by a tattoo artist and she was supine on a gurney in an unbecoming hospital gown, Jim planted a kiss on her forehead and said, "I love you, Diane. I'll be here when you come out. God bless."

And Jim *was* there when she awoke in the recovery room, except that she couldn't see him, blinded as she was by claustrophobic bandages. She only knew he was there because when she said his name—"Jim?"—he answered, "Let's cut to the chase, Diane. I noticed something funny in your charts."

This didn't sound normal. It wasn't what Jim ought to be saying to her, first thing, when she came out of surgery. "Are my eyes all right?" she asked, and it hurt her throat to say it. "Did it go all right? Am I in good shape?"

There came what had to be a nurse's voice: "It went great. Are you thirsty, Mrs. Long? You're thirsty. I'll get ice chips. It went fantastic—everything's good. Doctor will be in to tell you more, but he's very, very happy about everything."

Then it was Jim's voice again, still with that flat, troubling, all-business tone so lacking in post-op sympathy. "I don't know if everything's so good," he told her. "You're bandaged, so I can't put your chart in front of your face, but what it says is C-O-C-P, Diane. Which means the pill."

Despite deep anesthetic grogginess, Diane met this aspersion with a display of calm candor. "I'm not on the pill," she said.

"Then why is it on your chart?"

"Mistake."

There was a long pause, during which Diane thought, "Horrid timing." Blind and helpless, she heard Jim say, "I'm pissed off. I'm really, really pissed. I don't think I've ever been this pissed. This is low. It's just so down there. I can't believe this—it's from someone else's life. This shouldn't be happening to me."

"Jim."

"Don't 'Jim' me. You know what, Diane? All this money on your looks, it's superficial. And then to lie on top of it, about the pill, to say it's a mistake—who the hell are you? Who are you?"

When Diane didn't answer, the nurse intervened with, "Maybe you should talk about this later, Mr. Long. Our patient is just out of surgery."

But the talk that came later was in the same losing vein. Jim brooked nothing and wrathfully put his foot down. The righteous assurance that made the Longs so rich? Jim displayed it in spades now, the full version. In other words, there was nothing to talk about, or nothing *Jim* would talk about. Before Diane could grasp where things were going, her furiously wronged husband had hired an investigator. Within a week of her face-lift, the pill was a fact, and then lying became Jim's theme—how many lies, of what sort, when. The investigator found plenty that was fodder for Jim, including the post-office box in Sullivan's Gulch she'd recently closed. Things hit bottom when he tied Diane's old phone number to the Candace Dark Escort Service. This investigator was good, but—the saving grace—he didn't find out about Baby Doe.

The Longs were aghast to find that Jim had married a former "escort." They closed ranks, as they had against Sue's wayward trucking magnate, and handed Diane her head on a plate. The deceit about fertility, the strangeness of the post-office box, the lies about her past, the invented life, the phony persona: all of this added up to more than enough grist for the top-notch divorce lawyer Jim retained—the one who'd helped Sue take her cheating magnate to the cleaners—to make sure that Diane was banished from the family with as little diminution of its ski fortune as Oregon law would allow. When all was said and done, she was back on the street after eleven years as Mrs. Long with twenty-five thousand dollars Jim gave her to go away, thirty thousand dollars of Walter Cousins's hush money, some pretty decent clothes, a slim butt and waist, a worked-on face that looked permanently astonished, and—as always—regrets about her son. Not bad, all things considered. Regrets, clothes, beauty, relative youth, and fifty-five thousand for a fresh start.

6

Ed and Older Women

Following his victory in the region of wheat, Ed drove scrupulously under the speed limit, with frequent reference to his rearview mirror. "You think he's dead?" he asked Tracy Stolnitz at intervals. "You think that guy is really dead?"

"Yeah," answered Tracy, or something like it, each time. "I think we're in some pretty deep shit."

Ed worried that a farmer had seen what he'd done and had called the State Patrol already. Near Washtucna, he worried about a roadblock, like in the movies, but, grimly rolling the dice, passed through at the posted speed limit. After that it was an hour to Othello—an hour with persistent rearview-mirror checking, more worry about a farmer making a phone call, worry that the BMW driver might have miraculously survived, worry about everything. But there was still no roadblock when he got to Othello, or at Royal City, Vantage, or Ellensburg. Although that didn't mean much. Because, if the guy *had* survived, trouble could come later. Maybe he'd convalesce with steely vengeance before tracking Ed down and killing him. Or he'd roll out of surgery, gasp, groan, and tell an investigator about the black '66 Pontiac GTO, with Washington plates and racing stripes, that had forced him off the road. The very GTO Ed was driving, with its thick film of farm dirt. The one for which there might be, by now, a "be on the lookout" for everyone in law enforcement from Idaho to the coast and from Oregon to the Canadian border. There was much to worry about, but Ed and Tracy made it back to Seattle without any trouble except, in Ed's case, inner trouble—remorse, self-examination, and, most of all, fear of being caught.

"Cool," Tracy said, when he dropped her off at her mother's house. "I think we're cool."

"I can't believe it," answered Ed. "I killed a guy."

The next morning, after a bout with sleeplessness, he washed the dust from his car. He told Alice he couldn't drive it because it needed work, and asked her if he could move her Peugeot outside so that he could use the garage for repairs. "I also wonder if I could borrow the Peugeot," he said, "to go get some parts." "Yours until noon," she replied, and planted a kiss on his cheek. Ed, with his car hidden, drove straight to the downtown library, where he read, in the *Moscow-Pullman Review,* an article called SEATTLE MAN KILLED IN SINGLE CAR ACCIDENT.

> A 51-year-old Seattle man was killed in a single-car accident in Whitman County on Sunday morning.
> The accident occurred between 11 a.m. and 12 p.m. about 4 miles west of Dusty on Zaring Cut-Off Road.
> The driver, who was at the wheel of a BMW when he apparently lost control and left the road, died at the scene.
> There were no passengers, and the name of the driver was not immediately released.

Ed copied this article and took it to Tracy's. They went into her room and shut the door. She read it, shrugged, and handed it back to him. "Deal with it," she said.

Ed didn't answer, because he felt chilled by this response, and because he didn't want to have an argument with a girl who so willingly did everything for him. Their habit that summer had been daytime sex, because her mother wasn't back from her shift until six, her chip-toothed brother couldn't have cared less, and her father lived somewhere else. Nothing had mattered at Tracy's house except for what went on in Tracy's bedroom. There, Ed had enjoyed himself to the hilt while feeling on top of the world.

On this day, though, he lay clothed on Tracy's bed, talking about what had happened in eastern Washington. "I killed that guy," he kept repeating.

"And now you're freaking out about it," Tracy kept answering.

That afternoon, doing it with her, Ed couldn't get in the right mood. How was he supposed to enjoy someone who turned out to be so callous about murder? Who could clutch, moan, grunt, and suck as if nothing had happened? Ed pressed on anyway, but the more avid he became about Tracy's pallid body and the rhythmic jabbing of her narrow rib cage, the worse he felt.

The next day, it was in the *Spokane Spokesman-Review* under SPEED CONTRIBUTED TO SINGLE-CAR ACCIDENT:

> A Seattle man died Sunday morning in Whitman County following a single-car, single-occupant, high-speed accident.
>
> Walter M. Cousins, 51, died at the scene after the vehicle he was driving left the road at high speed. Cousins was traveling westbound on Zaring Cut-Off Road outside of Pullman.
>
> Neither the Whitman County Sheriff's Office nor the Washington State Patrol was able to say how fast Cousins was driving at the time of the accident, or if there were other contributing factors.
>
> A Washington State Patrol Accident Reconstruction Unit is conducting an investigation.

He took this to Tracy, too. Again they lay on her bed, talking about what had happened near Pullman—or Ed talked about what had happened near Pullman—while, across the hall, Tracy's brother punished a drum set. "Why did I do it?" Ed asked.

"Come on."

"What got into me?"

"Come on, Ed."

But he didn't want to have sex. He kept rereading the article. Tracy, exasperated, picked up a paperback with a picture on its cover of a ghoul in a graveyard. "How can you read that?" he asked.

"This?"

"Why would you want that stuff in your head?"

"It's just a story," said Tracy.

On Wednesday, Ed didn't have to go to the library, because Dan and Alice subscribed to the *Seattle Post-Intelligencer,* which ran Walter

Cousins's obituary. Ed quickly took in the headline—HO CHI MINH DIES—then flipped to the B section and read:

> Walter Monty Cousins of Seattle, age 51, passed away in Whitman County on August 28 following an automobile accident. Born in Ames, Iowa, in 1928, Walter was the youngest child of Wesley and Barbara Cousins. A proud alumnus of North Ames High School, he played on 2 league champion football teams, in 1945 and 1946. He attended Iowa State University, marrying Lydia Wallach in 1957 and beginning a 22-year career at Piersall-Crane, Inc., an actuarial firm, shortly afterward. In 1958, Walter and Lydia moved to Seattle, where their first child, Barry, was born that year, and their second, Tina, the next year. Walter took great joy in the family's summer cabin on San Juan Island, where he pursued gardening and "puttering." He was an excellent golfer, and enjoyed reading in his spare time. Walter is survived by his wife of 22 years, Lydia; son Barry; daughter Tina; brothers Jack, Joe, and Bill; and sister Caroline. A memorial service will be held on Saturday, September 6, at 1 p.m., at the Bleitz Funeral Home, 316 Florentia Street, followed by burial at Evergreen Washelli Cemetery.

Ed decided not to call Tracy—in fact, not to call her ever. He put an ad in the paper: *'66 GTO new black paint, bucket seats, Hurst shifter, 4-barrel 389, cherry condition, AC, lo mi.* He priced it to sell; he wanted to be rid of it. On Friday he got a half dozen calls, and on Saturday morning he took the first offer. By twelve-thirty he was parked near the Bleitz Home in Alice's Peugeot, watching funeral-goers make their way into the chapel. A white hearse was already parked on Florentia Street, gleamingly in place for the imminent casket, waiting to bear Walter Cousins to his grave. Ed saw its groomed and suited driver round it once, perhaps to inspect the tires and polish. The mourners were dressed in somber warm-weather wear and, Ed noticed, were careful parkers—they settled their cars between the white lines in the lot with appropriate, funereal consideration. Ed decided that the man he'd killed had enjoyed a solid middle-class life, because everyone drove clean late-model cars, and no one wore anything that anyone else present could construe as disrespectful to his memory. His mourners processed from the parking lot to the chapel door with decorous lack of hurry. They converged, hugged, clasped shoulders, shook hands, then passed through the door in intimate cliques. If it was possible for there to be a nice day for a funeral, this had to be one—not so warm that mourners would sweat, and not so cold that, standing in the cemetery, they would want things to speed along because their feet were chilled. Ed realized that one version or another of the arrival scene he was witnessing happened every day—people attended funerals—but until now always in someone else's world. He'd never been to a funeral, or inside a funeral home, and the only time he'd visited a cemetery was drunkenly, late at night, with fellow delinquents. On that occasion, Ed had felt uncomfortable seeing his cohorts pissing merrily on graves, but hadn't said a word to them about it, though he'd wanted to give a lecture about respect for the dead and basic decency. The fact was, even as he'd run almost nightly with those losers, he'd felt no kinship for what he believed was their view of the world, or for their conduct in life. But now, having run a guy off the road and killed him, he couldn't really claim he was better than they were, could he? Indeed, he was, by any measure, worse.

Ed drove off and made a downcast survey of the Evergreen-Washelli Cemetery. He parked and strolled as if visiting graves until the white hearse came slowly through the gates at the head of a motorcade. Then, pretending to be preoccupied with a tragedy of his own, he stood just off from the gathering at Walter Cousins's grave, to listen and watch. The woman who had to be Walter Cousins's wife stood by his casket with a tremulous chin, and with the upper half of her face shrouded by a black hat. On her right, with her arm looped tightly through her mother's, was the girl who had to be Walter Cousins's daughter, without any chin trembling but with a firmly set expression that told equally of grief. On Mrs. Cousins's left was a skinhead in a black coat and tie who kept looking at the sky as if in exhortation, while crying, his nose and eyes red. This, no doubt, was Walter Cousins's son, who at the moment wasn't holding up his end of things as the remaining male pillar of the family.

The funeral party included cross- and torch-bearers. At the head of the freshly dug grave stood a priest or pastor—Ed didn't know which—but anyway a priestly-looking figure in a black robe with a white collar, who said, "Following today's interment, all present are invited to assemble at the Cousins home for refreshments and remembrance." The ensuing ritual was surprisingly brief. The priest read from a prayer book as the coffin was lowered. Then he handed the book to someone, took up a shovel, and dropped dirt into the hole. Others came forward to add to his work, and as each took the shovel, the priest said, "The Lord be with you." When that was done, he announced that they should join him in the Lord's Prayer, and everyone did. There was an "Amen," and people started leaving. Ed feigned study of a marker as they passed him, but he did note that Walter Cousins's wife, underneath her hat, wore heavy makeup that was beginning to fracture; that his son, up close, was beyond-the-pale bereft; and that his daughter—he couldn't help himself—wasn't bad-looking.

He followed them to their home in Greenwood. Their square of lawn was burned blond, but the house siding looked newly painted. A hummingbird feeder hung from an eave. In the driveway a folded canvas tarp and an aluminum ladder were shoved against a rockery beside a snarled pile of garden hose. The garage door was open; Ed saw a small workbench, some tools hanging from pegboard, paint cans, a push mower, a snow shovel, and a pile of newspapers. Mourners kept arriving and parking, many moving toward the door with dishes in hand. Through the front window, Ed saw them milling. At one point Walter Cousins's daughter appeared on the porch with a cigarette, a lighter, and a guy who might have been her boyfriend. They came down the walk and leaned against a car to smoke and talk, both with their arms folded. The guy held his cigarette without any indication of need, but Walter Cousins's daughter inhaled and exhaled like a machine. After a while, she opened the passenger-side door, scrambled a little, and emerged with another cigarette. Ed referred to the obituary in his shirt pocket. Her name was Tina. She was born in 1959, so she was four years older than he was. He noted her car, a banana-yellow Malibu with BOYCOTT GRAPES on the bumper and, as he drove off, narrowly passing it, a University of Washington parking decal in the corner of the windshield.

School at Nathan Hale began. On the first morning, at eight o'clock, Ed's old cohorts smoked outside a back door, and Ed smoked half a cigarette with them before tossing the other half and going in. He was a junior now. In American History, the teacher passed out a study sheet with a list of names and dates: Magellan, Columbus, Ponce de León, Cortés, de Soto, Amerigo Vespucci, all the usual suspects. Ed, perusing it, sighed and dropped his head. "Not more of this," he said to himself. The same thing happened in second-period English. A syllabus was handed out indicating units on Elements of the Persuasive Essay, Sentence Structure, and Proper Use of Punctuation. In Intro to Chemistry they would start with the periodic table; in Algebra, Ed knew he could teach the class. The day ended with another ritual half-cigarette, after which Ed got a friend to drop him in the University District.

On campus, he searched the parking lots for Tina Cousins's banana-yellow Malibu. He couldn't find it. The lot near the football stadium held five thousand cars. The next day, he skipped chemistry and algebra and tried again to find the Malibu. Despite a longer and more determined search, this time in rain, he again struck out. It occurred to him that the campus parking decal he'd seen on the Malibu might have been old—that Tina Cousins might not even be a student at the University of Washington and might never have been. Maybe she'd bought the car with the decal on it and had never bothered to take it off. So what a lame shot in the dark he was taking—all this wandering looking for a car. What for, anyway? Supposing he found the car, or supposing he got another look at Tina Cousins. How would that change anything? He'd still feel terrible. He'd still feel worried that the law would catch up with him. He'd still have to carry his guilt.

He knew the answer. The answer was to keep an eye on the Cousins house in Greenwood until Tina showed up. He watched on Tuesday night, again on Wednesday night, and then, on Thursday night, at about seven, the banana-yellow Malibu pulled into the driveway. Tina got out, in blue jeans and a shawl, and went inside.

Ed listened to the radio and waited. More than two hours passed. Nobody bothered him. The light was pretty low when Tina came out. Ed followed her south on 99. She got off at 50th and made her way to the U District. Tina was an impatient driver who changed lanes a lot, but he kept up. When she parked in a student lot, he did, too, and followed on foot until she went into McMahon Hall, a dormitory.

The next morning at eight, Ed was sitting on a bench outside of McMahon with a campus map in his hands. Eventually, Tina Cousins, this time in a longer, more flowing paisley shawl, came out the front door with another girl. She lit up immediately, and so did her friend. Tina carried a woven jute bag of books that looked like a small gunny sack. She had a nice head of hair and a turned-up nose. The other girl was taller but not better-looking. Ed stood as they approached and indicated his map. "Excuse me," he said. "Are we right here?" He put his finger on the map, then handed it to Tina. "What I'm trying to find is the Art Building," he said. "I'm really sorry to bother you."

Tina poked her cigarette between her lips, took the map, and turned it around until it corresponded to reality. She told Ed that if he walked in *that* direction he'd come to Art. Ed studied the pores in her face, the flare of her nostrils, the flange of her ear, her hairline, her tufted eyebrows, and her smattering of moles. There was a soft blond down on Tina's bare forearms. She was a little overweight, but that was okay—the extra weight looked healthy, stout. Rousing himself from his survey, Ed pretended to study the map and ended up studying Tina's hands. He was stalling. He didn't want Tina to move on yet. "Can I talk to you?" he asked. "Privately?"

"No," answered Tina.

"Please. I need to talk to you."

"No, you don't," Tina snapped. "I don't hang around with jocks."

She handed him his map and pressed on summarily. The other girl gave Ed a brief once-over, then stepped in beside Tina. Tina shifted her book bag to her left arm. Smoke curled around her cheek. "I'm not a jock," Ed called, but weakly. The air had gone out of him. He'd been dismissed.

He took a bus home. Things, suddenly, looked strange, he noticed. His childhood neighborhood of mature trees and rolling lawns, where the houses were set far back for privacy, looked, to Ed, devoid of life, as if everyone had fled just ahead of the apocalypse. The general affluence and serenity of Castle Drive—maples, rhododendrons, curved walks, paneled doors—gave way, now, to the darkness of time: each lavishly maintained home was, in Ed's head, a mere façade, each a scrim of manufacturing raised against darkness. Why was it that the mere sight of cars in their drives, on this day but not the one before, reminded him that the universe was headed toward . . . nothing? Why was it that Castle Drive looked not just wan but, on this day, primed for catastrophe? A haze had descended over everything for Ed. He walked with his head bowed so as not to take it in, but even the sidewalk was depressing.

At home, in the driveway, Simon maneuvered a remote-controlled car via a handheld console with a short, flopping antenna. As Ed approached, Simon showed off a little—figure-eights, slick backup maneu-

vers, high-speed turns, and comical stops and starts between his skinny
legs, which were blotchy and pink from the hem of his shorts to the tops
of his white cotton socks. Simon was fifteen, his hair was kinky, his lips
were meaty, and his arms were puny. He'd skipped a grade and, like Ed,
was in eleventh, but he looked like he ought to be in seventh. His T-shirt
was a couple of sizes too big, and his glasses gave him a pop-eyed look.
That Simon was such a nerd that he played with plastic toys and smacked
his lips when he ate—these were facts that, most of the time, made Ed
hate him. But now, with the evening light going slowly out of everything,
fraternal guilt loomed mightily for Ed, so that, out of character, he put an
arm around Simon. "What?" said Simon. "Faggot."

"I'm not going to hurt you."

"Let go of me, you fag." Simon slipped from Ed's embrace and moved
to the far side of the driveway. "Leave me alone," he said.

Ed went to bed and didn't get up in the morning. Alice called Nathan
Hale's attendance office to excuse him, then brought Ed a buttered bagel,
which he didn't eat, and orange juice, which he didn't drink. "Eddie," she
said, "what else can I do for you?" and he answered, "I must have the flu."

When she was gone, he went back to his obsessive train of thought:
"I'm a murderer, I killed someone. This is something I can't make go
away. This is a fact now, that I killed someone. Me, a stupid upper-
middle-class kid who thought he was a hot-rodder, who thought he was
so cool. I'll never get over it. I'll never live it down. I'm going to feel guilty
for as long as I live. I killed somebody, I killed a human being, I killed
Walter Cousins, who wasn't hurting anything, who had a wife and two
kids—I killed him."

Alice brought Ed soup for dinner, which he ate because he had to eat it
to make her go away, but which, disturbingly, he couldn't taste. Then he
had to make Dan go away by saying he felt better and hoped to go to
school in the morning. Then it was night, and, with his pillow over his
head, Ed didn't sleep; he just worried, and hated himself. And in the morning he started another day of not taking a shower, not brushing his teeth,
not getting out of bed, not eating or drinking—or eating just enough to
make Alice go away—in fact, not doing anything except lying there with
his sheet over his head. What a person would have seen of him, if a person
was looking, was a long, inert rise—the way corpses are portrayed on TV,
in morgues—but inside, in his tent world, Ed wasn't a corpse. Instead, he
seethed gigantically, his mind on fire with self-loathing.

That afternoon, he had a visitor—Simon—who announced himself by saying, "Where's *Phaser Strike*?"

"Simon—help me."

Simon began rifling through the game cartridges in Ed's desk drawers. "What?" he said. "*Lander.* And *Eighteen Wheeler*! I asked you like a billion times if you had any of my stuff. This isn't *fair*. Jesus."

Ed said, "Simon, I'm messed up."

Simon started stacking video-game cassettes. "Here's *Phaser,*" he said. "I *knew* you had it."

"This is a nightmare. I'm in hell. I can't figure out what's wrong with me."

"Ha-ha-ha. You're sick, *Edeleh,* and I don't feel sorry for you one little bit. In fact, I like you better when you're sick, except you're always sick. *In the head.*"

Ed covered his eyes, because the world seemed easier to deal with when he couldn't see it. "Simon," he said. But nothing more.

"Hey," Simon answered. "*Star Fire,* too. You said you didn't take *Star Fire.*"

"Simon."

"I'm taking *Lander, Phaser, Eighteen Wheeler, Star Fire,* and a couple of *your* games, too, to make things even."

"Take them all."

"*Edeleh.*"

Alice took Ed to see a Paul Stern, who was a GP and a friend of the Kings from temple. She stood over Ed talking while Stern looked in Ed's ears, nose, eyes, and throat, checked his pulse and blood pressure, listened to his heart, and asked Ed questions—which Alice answered. Dr. Stern said, "I want Ed to drop his drawers for me, Alice, so just take a seat in my waiting room for now and we'll get you back in a few minutes."

"I'm his mother."

"Alice."

When she was gone, Dr. Stern said, conspiratorially, "Keep your pants on, Ed, and tell me what's happening."

Ed was sitting on the examination table—on its loud, flimsy paper—with his chin against his chest. His eyes were shut. His fingers were interlaced. All he lacked was a black eyeless hood to complete the picture of a prisoner meeting his executioner.

"Ed?"

Nothing.

"Do you need something for depression? Do I need to refer you to someone who can help you with a mental-health issue?"

Nothing.

"*Oy*," said Dr. Stern. "I feel terrible for you, Ed. I feel absolutely, one-hundred-percent terrible."

Ed went on sitting with his eyes shut.

"Believe me," Dr. Stern said. "I know how terrible it is." He got out his prescription pad and added, "Let's go with diazepam, two-milligram tabs. That should give you a little relief until we can get you into therapy."

On the way to a pharmacy, Alice cried a little, and kept glancing at Ed, who kept his head down. "Why didn't you tell me?" she asked.

He didn't look up, but he did say, in his weak, hoarse voice, "Something isn't right."

"I love you, Eddie. Your father and I both love you very much—you know that, I hope. I hope you know that."

"Something isn't right," he said again.

The therapist Dr. Stern wanted Ed to see was a Roger Fine, but Fine wasn't available the next five days, which left Ed with 120 hours to endure before—he hoped—his condition would be ameliorated. In the meantime, on diazepam, it was as if he was further under water, but still suffering from the same life-or-death symptoms. Diazepam made him feel slugged in the face, but didn't score a knockout. His misery remained, though he also believed that, with sufficient thought—with prodigious effort and by no other means—he could keep it from driving him completely under between now and his audience with the head doctor. The disadvantage of diazepam was that it made it more difficult to pursue this end; the advantage was that he slept more. As soon as Ed awoke, though, his madness started again, a huge white space of mental intensity, a silent grappling and ordeal. As static, stuporous, and numb as he looked, he was actually in the throes of a ferocious drama; he felt he was aloft on storm winds, or cast through a fissure in the earth. He wanted only to squeeze his head beneath his pillow and fight his battle alone, but he couldn't, because his mother harassed him with snacks or meals, presented on trays, and with her loving, worried presence. Employing proven tactics, Ed ate enough to keep her at bay, and kept his father at bay by telling him that he felt better, when in fact he felt the same: namely, that his condition was unendurable. And yet he endured it, except when he was etherized by his drug, and by clinging to his belief that, hour by hour, he was moving toward a halt to his miseries.

Finally, it was time to see the head doctor. Fine, who looked forty or forty-five, provided mental-health services from a home office fronted by a wind-punished bamboo grove. The books in his waiting room inclined Asiatically, as did the knickknacks in his lavatory. There was a fat jade Buddha by the pedestal sink, and a venerable incense burner on the toilet tank. Fine asked Ed to leave his shoes at the office door, then told him to sit wherever he was comfortable—on the couch, in a chair, in a different chair, on the floor, or in what he called his meditation alcove, on a bench replete with pillows. Fine wore a beard, a sweater vest, and ragg-wool socks, and counseled with a teacup at hand. It was raining hard outside, and the rain was loud on his roof. Ed sat, and Fine said, "Tell me why you're here."

"I don't know," Ed said. "Dr. Stern referred me."

"And why did he refer you?"

"Because he couldn't handle it."

"Couldn't handle what?"

"Whatever's wrong with me."

"And what do you think's wrong with you?"

"Depression," said Ed.

Fine arched his thick, straggling eyebrows, then reached for his teacup. "Say more," he said, "about depression."

"More?"

"What's it like? How does it feel? Anything you want to say about it to me. Go ahead. I'm here with you."

"Like I'm under water," said Ed.

"In the sense that you feel like you're holding your breath?"

"No. Like everything's watery. Like I can't move, except slowly. Like there's a film over everything. Like I'm on the moon or under water."

"On the moon."

"Or under water."

"Are you eating?"

"No."

"Are you sleeping?"

"As much as possible."

"Why?"

"Because then it doesn't hurt to be depressed."

"Hurt?" said Fine. "So it's not just the sensation of being under water? There's also hurt. Which feels like what?"

"Like being crushed. Squeezed in a vise. Like it's killing me."

"Killing you," said Fine.

"Like I'm dying."

"Dying," said Fine. "And what's that like?"

Ed sighed. "I don't know," he said. "Like death."

"Have you died before?"

"No."

"So how do you know what it feels like?"

"I don't."

"So why did you say you feel like you're dying?"

Ed sighed again. Was Roger Fine a prosecutor? Was this cross-examination? But before he could speak, Fine suddenly said, "What's with the sighing? Once again? Who's doing all the sighing, Ed?"

"What?"

"It's almost like there's three people in the room. Me, the you who says he's depressed, and the you who's sighing."

"I don't get that," said Ed.

"So who's doing the sighing?"

"I don't get it," said Ed. "What's the question?"

Fine put down his teacup, wiped his meaty lips with the back of his wrist, groomed his beard, covered a burp, and, through all of this, nodded. Then he said, "Who's in the room?"

"You and me."

"And who are you?"

"I'm me."

"And who is me?"

Ed wanted to sigh, but held back and answered, "I know I'm not supposed to say my name, but that's the answer—me. I'm me. I don't know. What do you mean? Tell me how I'm supposed to answer."

"I can't tell you anything. Or not very much. Maybe a little." Fine used his thumb and forefinger to indicate one inch. "The rest, it's not for me to say. Who are you? I don't know, either. I don't know that. I wish I did. I wish it was that easy. You come in here, I tell you what's wrong, I tell you why you're depressed, and somehow, after that, you're not depressed anymore? It isn't like that. That's not what we do here. I don't have a crystal ball or magic tricks."

"Then what *do* we do here?"

"We talk," said Fine.

"About what?"

"About you."

"What about me?"

"That's for you to say. Anything you want. In here, anything goes. So tell me this—why are you depressed?"

Ed sighed, and Fine raised his eyebrows again. "I don't know," said Ed. But then, surrendering, he made something up. "A friend of mine died," he said.

"I'm sorry," said Fine. "How and when?"

"Just a few weeks ago. In a car crash. In eastern Washington."

"A good friend?"

"A really good friend."

"Someone you'd known for a long time? From childhood?"

"Yeah," said Ed. "One of my best friends."

"So there it is," said Fine, sitting back. "Your friend died, and now you're depressed."

"Right."

"But maybe it's not depression—maybe it's mourning. Maybe it's grief, which is a natural reaction. Maybe that's what brought you here."

"No," said Ed. "That's not it. Something's . . . wrong. Something's different. This isn't like anything I've felt before. This is just sort of . . . different."

"Are you saying you lost a friend before, someone as significant and as close as this friend, and that on that occasion you mourned and grieved in a way that didn't feel like what you're feeling now? Is that what you're telling me?"

"No."

"Then what are you saying?"

"I don't know."

"Couldn't it be grief instead of depression?"

"Maybe."

"Well, then," said Fine. "Let's talk about grief. Let's talk about loss.

Because these things are a part of life. You've lost somebody, you're griev-ing, naturally, but your life goes on, and the question is, how will it go on from this point? Now that your friend is gone?" Again, Fine showed one inch with his fingers, this time adding a wink and saying, "I think this is one of the few things I'm actually entitled to say. We're talking about grief. Not depression, grief. We're talking about how you feel about your friend, a person who was important to you. Why wouldn't you grieve? Anybody would. And it doesn't feel good, does it, grief. There's a big hole in your life now—a place your friend used to fill. What's going to go there? Or will it stay empty? Do you understand what I'm saying? About a hole? A loss? That's what loss is—loss makes a hole. Grief is how you start to fill it in. I think you should just accept that grief. Let yourself grieve. Don't fight it."

"I don't know," said Ed. "Something isn't right."

"One thing we can do is prescribe," said Fine. "Paul Stern's got you on diazepam, but that's not going to solve your problem. We could put you on something that would be ongoing and that would help you feel a lot, lot better, so you can get on with living your life."

"No," said Ed. "I'm not a pill person."

"No one likes to be medicated," said Fine. "But when you need medica-tion, it's good it's there. Meds help many, many people, Ed. And I think the right one could probably help you while you're getting over your grief."

Ed sighed.

"You don't have to decide now," said Fine. "You can think about it, and we can talk it over later. And, of course, the decision is yours alone to make. You, not I, have to want it, Ed. I'm only here with you—only pres-ent."

Later, in bed with a pillow over his head—and in between hating himself and thinking about death—Ed thought about whether he should take a mental-health drug. Alice discussed it on the phone with Roger Fine and, since the idea of a drug concerned her, too, decided that they should get a second opinion. After a swift and thorough vetting, she made an appointment with a therapist named Theresa Pierce who spe-cialized in depressed adolescents.

Theresa Pierce met with clients in a low-ceilinged garret that smelled, to Ed, like old milk in a pile carpet. In its doorway, she put him in mind of Arthur's Merlin—pallid, maybe even owlish, like someone who hibernated. She wore Lycra slacks, running shoes, and a zip-up boiled-wool sweater. Her large and unfashionable glasses, with their wood-grain frames and graphic bifocal bifurcations, made her eyes seem three times larger than was human, and magnified, especially, her glinting, liquid pupils. Pierce kept dog-eared books floor-to-ceiling, many with creased spines, tattered edges, and "Used" stickers, and her chairs—one for doctor, one for patient, but both hard Windsors—were arranged for maximum distance despite the cramped quarters. There she sat, remotely, in her corner, not necessarily for or against Ed, dispassionately present, cryptic in aspect, and attentive behind her conspicuously huge glasses— everything arrayed to suggest, subliminally, that here was a woman of insight.

So as not to prejudice Theresa Pierce, Ed didn't mention Roger Fine or the question of a mental-health drug. He told her that there was nothing wrong with his life and that he didn't know why he was feeling what he was feeling—unhappy, uninterested in heretofore vitalizing pursuits, listless, withdrawn, preoccupied with bleak thoughts. Mired and catatonic. Under water, static, stuporous, and numb. Unable either to exercise or to eat. Mostly drawn to curling in the fetal position and covering his head so he could think, without distraction, perpetual dark thoughts. Pierce, in response, uttered not a word. Instead of speaking, she watched him unnervingly, recessed in her corner, a psychiatric cipher. She regarded Ed with such flagrant detachment, as he filled the empty space with words, that finally he said, "Don't you talk?"

"Sometimes."

"Isn't this what they call 'talk therapy'?"

"No."

"What is it, then?"

"That's hard to say."

"What am I doing here?"

"So far, introducing yourself."

He didn't know how to respond to this and felt insulted by it, as if he'd said too much, or said the wrong things—but what choice had she given him? "If I don't talk and you don't talk," said Ed, "then we're just sitting here doing nothing in the same room together, instead of making progress."

"Progress toward what?"

"Progress toward my goal of getting back to where I was before this depression started."

Pierce now watched him with something like a gargoyle's menace. Didn't gargoyles, like Pierce, look stony, poised, attentive, unreadable, bent on overhearing you from the tops of buildings, and prepared, if necessary, to leap onto your head? "I wish you'd say something," Ed said.

"Like what?"

"Like something helpful."

Pierce reached under the frame of her glasses and pulled, gently, at the corner of her eye. Ed got a glimpse, from across the room, of the red, glistening surround in which her eyeball was set. In her dowdy sweater and running shoes, and with her Brillo Pad hair just slightly awry, she looked more like a mental patient than a doctor. "I have to tell you something now," she said. "I feel I don't have a choice but to tell you this directly. I have to tell you that I can't work with you. We're not a good match. I'm not the right person for you to see. It's nobody's fault. You didn't do something wrong. But sometimes this happens when someone comes to see me. I wouldn't want to waste your time and money when it doesn't feel right."

"What are you talking about?" said Ed.

"You should see someone else. I could recommend another person. I'm sorry. It just isn't what's going to happen—you coming here for therapy."

Ed rolled his eyes. "I don't get it," he said. "Are you telling me to leave?"

"No. You can stay. At no charge. If you want to. But not after today. I'm sorry."

"And sit here with someone who thinks she can't help me? Why would I do that? What would be the point? This is really weird," said Ed. "I didn't think I was going to get blown off when I came in here."

Pierce didn't answer, so Ed went further. "How am I supposed to feel?" he said. "I've been rejected. Kicked out for not being—what? I don't know. I'm a loser here. But you're the wizard and I'm the nobody. You call the shots, I take them in the chest. This is just really *wrong*."

"I understand," said Pierce.

"No, you don't."

For the first time since he'd walked into her garret, Pierce rearranged herself in her chair. She sat up straighter. It made her seem larger; she expanded to fill her corner. "What I do," she said, "is look at the parts so I can understand the whole. And I've been sitting here with you, looking at your parts, and, frankly, I don't think I can go any further. I don't think it's wise for us to go any further. I think you're better off not going further, Ed. Some people are just better off."

"Well, I'm not 'some people,'" Ed shot back. "That's where you're wrong. Because, me, if there's something I need to know, I *always* want to know it, *always,* okay? That's me. That's who's here. That's who's sitting in front of you right now. How could you know me after, what, twenty minutes? I don't see where you get off dismissing me like I'm scum, like I'm nobody. Who do you think you are, doing that to *me*? I'm not listening to you about *anything.* You don't know the *first* thing about me."

"Look," Theresa said. "I think you should find someone willing to prescribe, get on a drug, and enjoy your life for as long as you can."

"There's something wrong with you," said Ed, and walked out.

But in the end, he'd gotten a second opinion. The drug—imipramine—erased his depression in six weeks, after which Ed felt back to his old self and ready, again, to meet his future.

Alice begged for mercy from a friend on the board, and soon Ed was installed in the eleventh grade at University Prep, the first-rate private school Simon attended. Once settled there, he had to give his younger brother credit for carving out a niche at their highly stratified academy, despite being—or because he was—younger than everyone else. Si was the interesting and eccentric nerd who'd skipped a grade and was possibly a genius; Si was the brilliant, gangly goofball who would be a billionaire one day; Si was, embarrassingly, Ed's classmate, another junior. He had friends, even close friends—even female friends. He was wedded to a group of nerds that included two average-looking girls. They ran in a pack, played Dungeons and Dragons, and met late at night in a Jack in the Box. Ed was sure that Si was a virgin, though he also knew there were girls out there who would sleep with a guy who chewed his nails, drank chocolate milk, kept a pet turtle, and was proud of his ability with a Rubik's Cube. Yet as much as girls might like Si for being bright, he was also too flighty, too easily discombobulated, and too geeky to get inside their pants.

Si was also a night owl. His bedroom featured half-empty Coke cans and smelled as if the window had never been opened. He had dozens of video games, hundreds of comic books, and a shelf of programming manuals. Slowed in February of his sophomore year by an emergency operation to remove a gangrenous appendix, Si had come back in earnest that spring when it came to late-night video-game coding. He talked about coding constantly. He disseminated demos on floppy disks in labeled sleeves. With input from friends—and critiques from Ed—Si made progress on an Apple II effort, which was to code a game called *Martian Mangler* for paid magazine publication. Ed, exploring progressive demos of *Martian Mangler,* had to admit that Si was good with graphics and had assembly language pretty much down pat, but as for creativity, that was nil. *Martian Mangler* was thinly realized, and worse, derivative. It looked like a cross between *Asteroids* and *Ultima,* but with neither the exhilaration of the former nor the depth of the latter, it played like electronic checkers. Though Ed tried to tell Si all of this, Si refused to hear it. He kept insisting he'd invented a pot of gold when what he really had was a flop. Or so Ed thought until *inCider* paid Simon $100 for *Martian Mangler.* After that, it was $150 for *Arcturan Attack* and $200 for *Venus SkyTrap.* Si entered a game called *Moon Buggy Blaster* in *UpTime*'s design competition and won $500 in prize money. On letterhead he started calling himself Programmer-in-Chief at King Software, Inc. By the time his junior year started, his late-night friends had to compete with friends he made on bulletin boards, and his Dungeons and Dragons habit was addressed not at Jack in the Box but in MUDs. Simon even had a digital girlfriend who called herself HackAttack, but Katie for their one-to-one chats. Ostensibly she lived in Saratoga Springs, went to Skidmore, and was the cousin of the drummer for the Misfits. But who knew? She might be fifty and a perv with sideburns.

On Dan's fiftieth birthday, Ed and Si withdrew to Simon's lair for a round of *Heavyweight Boxing.* For an uncoordinated guy, Si had dexterous thumbs, which translated into fancy footwork in the ring and effective punch combinations. He liked to give Ed advice before he knocked him out, such as "Use Super Punch" and "Down and right for the head." Si was high-speed instructional and "helpful" while pummeling Ed or inducing his submission. Ed gave him these small victories as part of a program of long-term guilt assuagement. They'd both gotten too old for the old forms of hostility and, in an exploratory vein, were creating new ones.

After three knockouts, Alice called them to the table for a bouillabaisse, a Caesar salad with anchovies, and a carrot cake—Dan's favorites. During dinner, the Kings listened to *Traditional Music of Madagascar* in tribute to Dan's interlude as a UN doctor, and after dinner, Dan's brother and sister each called to rib him for having arrived at fifty and to have conversations about offspring, niggling health concerns, and the endgame afflictions their father was enduring in an assisted-living facility in Pasadena. "Ed's first choice is math at Stanford. . . . Simon's number-one choice is Caltech. . . . Alice is busy but giving a lot of thought to what she wants to be doing now that the nest is nearly empty. . . ." Simon gave Dan a sloppily handwritten certificate for five free car-washes, Ed gave him a book by a Jewish doctor, and Alice gave him a dachshund, bringing it up from the garage on a leash with a red ribbon around its neck. Dan had reservations. "This is very nice and thoughtful," he said, "but I don't think I really want a dog."

"Daniel," Alice answered, while the new dachshund slobbered, "the boys are off to college before long. My thought is that we substitute this dog. I got him at the pound. He's eighteen months. He's smart, he's neutered, he's house-trained, he doesn't bark. He's not too big and he's not too small. And I'll be frank. You don't get exercise. You say you'll take a walk, but it's just talk, you don't do it. This way, you won't have excuses, darling. You'll be one of those guys you see on the street, walking the dog every morning and evening."

"Thanks," said Dan. "Thanks a lot."

"Come on," said Alice, stroking the dog's head. "I didn't name him— I thought you could name him. You have to admit, you like him, right?"

"He's so ugly," said Dan. "If you have to buy a dog, at least buy one with some dignity or something. That thing looks like a frankfurter on legs. Besides, dachshunds are *deutsch*, didn't you know that? I hope you did a little homework."

"Let's name him Adolf," suggested Simon.

The dachshund circumambulated, sniffing crotches. With regard to his slobbering, heavy breathing, and whining, Alice pointed out that his circumstances were unfamiliar and that such signs of distress should be expected. Dan held the leash while Alice lit the candles. In makeup mode, he reported, after one bite of cake, "I'm going to get porky with this in the house," to which Alice replied, "High cholesterol."

"Actually, only my bad cholesterol is high. My good cholesterol is low."

"Your father's going to start walking more."

"Alice!" said Dan. "They don't want to hear this."

"They love you," said Alice. "They're darling, loving boys. They want to listen to whatever you have to say. They'll even make the sacrifice of eating my carrot cake so you don't have to get . . . corpulent, Daniel. Look at them, just look how they're helping. Does anyone want more ice cream at the moment, or should I put the carton away?"

Adolf stayed. Alice walked him, at first every day, then every other day, then once in a while. Adolf scratched the front door, even the doorknob, trying to get out of the house. They had to put him in the bathroom when guests came, because of his tendency to growl. In short, Adolf was an opportunity for Dan to chastise Alice. He wanted to take Adolf back to the pound, but Alice wouldn't let him. Adolf, eventually, had to live in the garage with a bark-stopping apparatus strapped around his muzzle. Three times a day, Alice opened the garage door with the remote-control device on the visor in her Peugeot so Adolf could relieve himself. Each time, she tricked him into returning to his cave by tossing beef jerky in and shutting the door behind him as he tried to eat despite the barkstopper. Taking pity on Adolf, she'd remove it for ten minutes, during which he ate the beef jerky and lapped water while she read a magazine in the car.

In the realm of math, Ed played catch-up. He bought himself a good graphing calculator and, after rolling through Algebra III, joined Simon in Advanced Calculus and Statistics. They competed for high scores on standardized tests. They noted, and remembered, each other's missed problems. One would go to the blackboard, when called, to race through a difficult equation or proof; the other would sit on the edge of his seat, waiting, and hoping, for a hesitation or an error, so he could chime in forcefully with a corrective. The King brothers battled over differential calculus and went head to head on information theory. How many times do you have to cut and interleave a deck of cards in order to arrive at a perfect shuffle? What are the relative probabilities of spaces and letters in an English text? You have a balance and nine coins; eight of the coins are equal in weight, but the ninth is defective and weighs less or more than the others; find a way to determine, using the balance three times, which is the defective coin, and whether it's heavier or lighter than the others. Ed and Simon treated these problems the way athletes treat sporting events. There were plenty of ties—and 4.0's and A-pluses—but trends emerged, and strengths and weaknesses. Ed could never convincingly defeat Simon in the spatial world of advanced geometry and felt lost in the vortex of the non-Euclidean; Simon was markedly dominant, too, when it came to complex data analysis, and more supple in his work on number theory. Where Ed excelled was in information theory and in the creative realm of the algorithm. Ed had an affinity for algorithms the way the double-jointed have an affinity for contortions, or in the manner of an autistic savant who memorizes phone books at a glance. Supposing you needed to distribute 20,000 newspapers to 1,000 locations in 100 towns using 50 trucks—Ed could give you the algorithm in two minutes. Assume you're confronted with N sleeping tigers and that to avoid being eaten when one or more wake up you are going to construct a fence around them—what's the smallest polygon that will surround them? Again, Ed could give you the algorithm in the time it took others to understand the problem. Simon had no chance to beat him at algorithms. There, Ed was ascendant.

Not that Ed spent all of his time grappling with Simon. He spent a lot of it grappling with U Prep's females. One, like him, was a page for a state senator over spring break in 1980; another was a member of a student group Ed joined for a summer tour of European capitals. Then there was the Math Club team, where Ed and Simon both excelled, and where Ed met Yael Anon, an Israeli transplant who, even in winter, looked so fresh from the beach at Haifa that she might still have sand in her hair. The math team traveled by van across the state for competitions with other clubs, and on these excursions Ed and Yael disported themselves in Holiday Inns and Best Westerns.

Ed looked forward to these Math Club weekends. The club's young adviser, Darlene Klein, was popular with students because of her beauty, and widely referred to as "*Decline*," since on her syllabi she gave her name as "D. Klein." Privately, though, a lot of boys called her *Recline*, because they wanted to tilt her to that position and—their going term was— plank her. Ed was among these adolescent salivators. Like many boys at U

Prep, he ogled Ms. Klein with an ever-humming erotic interest. He liked her style. He liked the way she made the Math Club van feel like a rolling excuse for levity and indulgence. Usually, the team lit out on Fridays after school, Ms. Klein at the van's helm with a student riding shotgun, two more in rotating middle thrones, and three on the cramped rear bench. Ms. Klein was still hip enough to be part of things. She ate convenience-store candy like the rest of them, swigged pop from a large plastic bottle, fussed with the radio, gossiped about teachers and student romances, and commented on movies and music. Reaction to her in the van was mixed: Emily Sussman engaged Ms. Klein as if she was part of her inner circle; Vanessa Tate adored her, too, but more obsequiously and slavishly; Simon seemed nerdishly and frequently dubious, as if Ms. Klein was unethical and unbecoming; Linda Dorman, as always, held her cards close; and Yael Anon, with her blue eyes, Persian skin, and wild mass of tangled red hair, made sure Ms. Klein caught the gist of her commentary, which was acerbic and judgmental. That left Ed to moderate and nudge, delicately keeping Yael satisfied with affirmations, elbows, and pinches, while still reserving access to Recline and staying on her good side.

December in Seattle is a dark proposition—by four, the light has dis-agreeably failed, and from there the descent into night is so rapid that by five one feels a sense of lockdown. The freeways, especially on a Friday after dark, are zones of blurred vision and unsociable fear, and of rainy pavements as translucent as oil slicks in the massed glow of headlights. It was into such a baleful atmosphere that Ms. Klein plunged the van one Friday, heading for a weekend tournament across the state, in Spokane. As always, Ed was ensconced in the rear seat, with the tight-lipped, reserved Linda Dorman on his left and Yael—all honey and gall—on his right. From shoulder to knee, he was pressed against them both, and this made his groin feel pleasantly electrified, as if he were a glowing light-bulb filament completing a circuit of charge.

In the driver's seat, Ms. Klein was pulled close with her hands at ten and two o'clock as she battled to keep the van from being battered from the side, struck from behind, flipped, dinged, or otherwise assaulted. Ed could see, dimly, the myopic strain of her neck and the gravity with which she peered through exhalations and vigorously whapping wipers. Emily, riding shotgun, was half turned toward the throne seats, so she could carry on a conversation with Vanessa about physics homework, sleeping late, and how retro Olivia Hussey looked in Zeffirelli's *Romeo and Juliet.* Overhearing their movie review, the dour Linda leaned forward to insert, "Hey, you guys, wait a sec—what about Romeo's butt?"

Simon swiveled toward her like an adolescent Dr. Strangelove. On these trips, Ed appreciated his presence, partly because Si was an indomitable math contestant and partly because of the light he shone on Ed. "Now we're talking about *butts*," said Si. "What's next? Penis size?"

Ed, from the rear seat, heard Ms. Klein snort in what was clearly amusement and possibly approval. "Simon," she sang. "Ouch."

Everyone laughed, and for a moment the mood in the van felt light, despite the morass of aggressive, wet traffic just beyond the smeared windowpanes. Emily, ever gleeful, laughed longer than the others, with a sharp edge of sarcastic hilarity, prompting Linda to say, "You freak." At this Ms. Klein, shifting in her seat, glanced in her mirror to assess her charges. "High-school kids," she observed.

Ed wondered if Ms. Klein included him in her blanket disparagement of teen-agers. He wondered if he should have spoken up, in a frank way, about Romeo in the buff, so as to indicate for her his adult take on sexuality. It was too late now, because the subject had faded, and so he returned to the deliciousness of his warm, feminine surround, and to the perplexity he inferred from Linda Dorman's arm as she acknowledged to herself—he was pretty sure of this—that contact with Ed felt good.

A half-hour later, the traffic had thinned out, but the rain had turned, with elevation, to snow, and the tractor-trailers hauling past were shooting grimy slush at the math van's windows. When snow began to make a film on the road, Ms. Klein pulled over between monstrously large trucks, put the van in "Park," and, adjusting the rearview mirror, looked at Ed. "Can anyone here put on chains?" she wondered.

Ed, Simon, Linda, and Ms. Klein all piled out onto the freeway shoulder. At first they just stood there getting wet and cold. Simon said, "Brrrrr." Flakes flecked their heads. The traffic skidding past seemed unhinged and precarious. Advancing headlights showed the slant of the blizzard, which fell into view out of cloud-suffused darkness. Linda pulled her knit scarf across her mouth, and Ms. Klein, shoulders high, hugged herself.

Shortly there was a shuffling of luggage between the opened twin rear doors of the van, which eventually produced a set of tire chains in their box, never used. As Ed unpacked them, he felt Ms. Klein touch him. Her cold hand pressed into the ridge of his shoulder muscle as if she were a masseuse who'd located a pressure point. "Do they go front or rear?" she asked.

"Rear," said Ed. "Always rear. Unless you have front-wheel drive."

"Do we?"

"Let's go for rear," Ed said.

Fifteen minutes later, when they were back on the road, with the chains now making their characteristic rumble—as if something were broken—Ms. Klein asked Ed if his hands were warming up. "They're always warm," he told her.

After an hour of dark and snowy tension, it was time to strip off the chains again, on a moonlit exit ramp, beneath frigid stars, with Yael, Ms. Klein, Vanessa, and Emily all blowing prolific vapors from their mouths while Ed, on his knees, did the manly work, and Simon fumbled with an icy lever and intermittently blew on his fingers. Only Linda stayed in the van, reading beneath a dome light. Vanessa made the comments, "King, you're my hero," and, "King, you're such a *man*." Ms. Klein had dug her coat out of her bag—a hooded wool mackintosh that seemed to Ed Irish—and in the dry, clear air looked pleased with herself and merrily agitated by adventure. Her wet hair had increased in ringlets and curls, and on the rounded prominences of her wide, Baltic cheekbones stood slashes of cold-weather scarlet.

Over the mountains, across the snowy pass, they were soon so far outside of their lives that their school personas worked loose. Simon receded into meditative sulking, Linda fell asleep, Emily and Vanessa lived increasingly in tandem, and Ms. Klein, driving, withdrew into a silence that seemed to Ed like reverie. Her silence intimated, for him, a private life beyond the scope of U Prep. Ed put a hand on Yael's thigh, and she, in answer, put one hand on his and ran the other through her hair.

At the Moses Lake interchange, they hit a McDonald's, piling out to deliver their orders, visit the cans, and rain sarcasm on things hayseed. Ms. Klein was adept at driving with a hamburger but had to ask Emily to open her ketchup packets and between bites gave a lecture on judging people because they lived in the sticks. She herself had been brought up in Westchester and educated at Wellesley, Brown, and Johns Hopkins, and because of all this—or despite it, she said—she tried not to judge "the bulbous, unenlightened interior," though it was, at the same time, completely unbelievable that the heartland states, not to mention the majority of the country, had voted so thoroughly for "the vapid Ronald

Reagan." How was it possible that "the total doofus from *Bedtime for Bonzo*" was president of the United States?

No one in the van had heard of *Bedtime for Bonzo,* which left Ms. Klein explaining the president's shoddy acting, his divorce from Jane Wyman, his marriage to "Mommy," his son the probably bisexual Joffrey dancer, and his daughter the pot-smoking nuclear activist who hung out with Bernie Leadon from the Eagles. Ed was able to add, with calm seriousness, that Reagan was an advocate of capital punishment and had nefariously made use of the California Highway Patrol to tear-gas protestors in Berkeley. Ms. Klein, adjusting her mirror while he spoke, nodded with vigor, smiled archly, and praised Ed for having his "ducks lined up exactly right on a total reactionary who thinks trees cause pollution." When they stopped at the rest area near Sprague, she sought his company in the parking lot, where the two of them milled aloofly in the frigid night air to denigrate the president with the benefit of no obstructions. Ms. Klein said Reagan had been a stooge for Hoover and had seen to it that gay actors were hounded and blacklisted; in her currently unzipped hooded mackintosh, tight blue jeans, wool socks, and mary janes—not to mention the surplice top that, with its band beneath the bust, called Ed's eye to her ample chest—she incited, for him, a cold-weather erection. Under the icy stars of the steppe, with the acrid sting of frosted sage in his nostrils, he savored his teacher in her present context, lit as she was by sodium-vapor lights, doing toe-raises to thwart the cold. She was at least fifteen years older than he was, but it occurred to him, for the first time since he'd known her, that this shouldn't bar him from testing her waters. It was the age gap itself, he understood with delight, that goaded him to break new ground with the aggressively opinionated Ms. Klein.

In Spokane, the team touched down at a Holiday Inn fully rampant, at 10 p.m., with math contestants. They traversed wetly between a small indoor pool and a console TV in the lobby, bounced through the halls from room to room, congregated loudly at vending machines, trotted up and down the stairs, and stifled giggles in elevators. Yael's roommate, Linda Dorman, went for a swim, so Ed latched her door and produced a rubber. When Linda came back, the door was unlatched and he and Yael were innocently watching TV together. Ed said good night and left.

Ed roomed with Simon. Simon was in the habit of sleeping fully dressed to block germ transmission from motel sheets, and of staring at late-night television. Ed enjoyed provoking him with questions like, "So who'd you like to bang at school?" He was ribbing Si when, at eleven, Ms. Klein knocked on their door to remind them to meet at eight in the lobby and to urge them toward a good night's rest. She spoke in the late-night murmurs of a mother bent on setting a hushed tone for bedtime, and wore Zorris exposing painted toenails. Ed, thinking quickly, said he needed the van key because he'd left his graphing calculator on his seat; Ms. Klein replied that she couldn't, by the book, give Ed the van key, because "U Prep has a stick up its you-fill-in-the-blank." "We'll go down together, then," Ed said. "That way they can keep their stick in place."

Ms. Klein looked at Si—Ed thought to take the measure of his cluelessness as she pondered the liaison he'd insinuated—then said, "Okay—I'll get my coat."

"Great," said Ed. "I'll go with you."

She was a neatnik par excellence, he discovered in her room, with her bag zipped shut on the folding rack, her coat hung up, her traveling alarm clock unhinged and opened, and her toiletries kit set upright beside the sink. Only a packet of gum on the bed stand, with a crumpled foil wrapper beside it, marred the otherwise pristine scene, which smelled the way Ms. Klein smelled—perfumed and hormonal.

When Ms. Klein unzipped her bag to get a pair of socks, Ed caught a glimpse of pink underwear. She sat on her bed and slipped on a mary jane, and the choreography of this propelled him forward; on the other hand, maybe it was best not to risk permanent awkwardness with Ms. Klein in the wake of a failed seduction. But her suddenly studied exhibitionism—the way she arched her foot to catch her sock, pulled the sock tight, slipped on the second shoe, and shook the curling bangs off her forehead with her teeth dug into her lower lip—it all seemed to say, "go ahead." What to do?

They went out. In the hall, the lobby, and the parking lot, Ed savored the way Ms. Klein's great butt moved. He could make out the low band of her panties through her slacks. At the van, when Ms. Klein unlocked the door, he said, "Huh—where's my calculator?" and even went so far as to look for it.

They went inside again—Ed protesting about his missing calculator—but in the elevator Ms. Klein changed the subject very suddenly. "I've been wanting to talk to you about Yael," she said. "Is there something going on with her? Is she unhappy with me or something?"

"I don't know. Why?"

"Don't you sleep with her, Ed?"

"I have to take the Fifth on that."

"The Fifth," said Ms. Klein. "I've used that before."

"Oh, really," Ed answered, as the doors slid open, "when have you taken the Fifth?"

Ms. Klein gave her squinty smile and stepped into the hall in front of him. Again he appreciated the way her butt moved and had to quell an urge to reach out and palm it. "I've had to take the Fifth with Reed," she said. "Reed—the guy I live with. My boyfriend."

They came to her door. She stopped and turned around. "Look," she said, "we've been flirting with each other. Both of us know what's going on, but I don't think I should sleep with a student."

She kissed him next. He could tell, from the way she kissed, that the kiss was a test, and he could also tell when he'd passed it. "This is too dangerous," she said, coming up for breath. "I can't afford to get caught. I'd lose my job." Then she stepped in and shut the door on him.

On Saturday, U Prep's team went to work on its first question: *P is a point inside a given triangle ABC; D, E, F are the feet of the perpendiculars. . . .* Simon led the way on this one, and they had a good solution in three hours. After lunch: *Three congruent circles have a common point O and lie inside a given triangle. Each circle touches a pair of sides of the . . .* Again Simon took the reins, quickly working up the necessary vertices and insisting that—when the team began to argue—"the center of homothety is the incenter of both triangles." He was right, and once again they found a swift and winning solution. The third and last problem of the day was: *The function f(x, y) satisfies (1) f(0, y) = y + 1, etc.,* and this time Ed beat Simon to the punch with:

We observe that $f(1, 0) = f(0,1) = 2$ and that
$f(1, y + 1) = f(1, f(1, y)) = f(1, y) + 1$, so by induction,
$f(1, y) = y + 2$. Similarly, $f(2, 0) = f(1, 1) = 3$, and
$f(2, y + 1) = f(2, y) + 2$, yielding $f(2, y) = 2y + 3$.
We continue with $f(3, 0) + 3 = 8$;
$f(3, y + 1) + 3 = 2(f(3, y) + 3); f(3, y) + 3 = 2^{y+3}$; and
$f(4, 0) + 3 = 2^{2^2}; f(4, y) + 3 = 2^{f(4,y)+3}$.
It follows that $f(4, 1981) = 2^{2^{2}} - 3$ when there are 1984 2s.

On Saturday evening, Ed knocked on Ms. Klein's door. Again she was wearing the mary janes; she'd been reading something, a magazine, and had come to the door with it rolled in her hand. "My calculator," Ed said. "I still can't find it."

"No," said Ms. Klein. "Go away."

By Sunday at two, U Prep had taken the Spokane Math Extravaganza First Place trophy. The club members celebrated with ice cream and left town. What a relief it was for all of them now to head for home at the advent of a two-week winter break, with very little homework and no looming competitions. The atmosphere in the van, on this return trip, was festive; they ate hamburgers, drank pop, cranked up the radio, and made lewd jokes. In Snoqualmie Pass, they pulled off the road and for ten minutes threw snowballs at each other. It was during this mêlée that Ms. Klein found Ed and asked him, quietly, if he would join her the next day for a visit to a Japanese garden.

He went. They strolled side by side in a prelude to carnality. The difference was that she seemed authentically interested in the lanterns, bridges, ponds, and bonsai plants, whereas he found it all inexplicable and dull, and privately scoffed at the other people present—a grave couple in their fifties—because they acted as if they were Zen monks-in-training. But should he or shouldn't he utter his sentiments, were they or weren't they the right ones to have, did he or didn't he fake interest in the gardens? Or did he just silently stick to his guns, the guns of a guy who was his own guy no matter what, because that was what women really wanted? What would happen if he "liked" the weeping willow? What would happen if he didn't?

They came to certain irises she liked—rare water irises, she said—that bloomed briefly in spring, but that were also right now poignant in their waiting and in the way they shivered in the breeze. Ed, gambling, said, "I'll be honest—I don't get it. I mean, yeah, okay, plants, but what's the enormous, big deal?"

She led him to a nearby bench, not so much to look at the irises as to take them in as a case in point as she explained the enormous, big deal: how you shouldn't just *look* at irises but instead dwell in their exquisite presence in the hope of capturing, without ever clinging to, something universal and poetic. "Do you understand what I'm saying?"

"Sure."

"I knew you would," Ms. Klein said.

Ms. Klein lived in Wallingford, near a shop funded by Planned Parenthood that sold condoms and lubricants. Wallingford still had hippie vestiges: a granola café, a run-down independent theater, a used-record/head shop, a nursery peddling Gro-Lux lights, and broadsides dispensed by badgering idealists in front of a smelly co-op. Ed hadn't thought of it this way before, but Ms. Klein had come of age in the sixties, so maybe she was part of that era's free-sex scene—*Hair*, Woodstock, hot tub orgies, and those communes where everybody fucked everybody. Sure enough, in her bed that afternoon—also Reed's bed, she reminded him, laughing—Ms. Klein began by explaining Tantra: no wanting anything beyond the here and now, was what he took her to be getting at, because that would make the here and now more exquisite. She wanted sensation, on the premise that there was nothing else, but to Ed it seemed harder to live in the moment when you were constantly battling to ratchet up the tension. He had the feeling she rated her orgasms, all three, that afternoon.

Still, he felt great afterward, well served by her skillful means, a guy who'd given but who'd also taken from a woman who was older and living with somebody. The satisfaction now tucked in his underpants also suffused his thoughts about himself: how excellent it was to be eighteen and planking someone else's woman—a woman, not a girl, that was the main thing, that was, for Ed, as they say, a revelation. When she warned him, "Reed will be home in an hour," he took it to mean that she wanted more, that she couldn't get enough of a guy in his prime, and that his brief refractory periods made him perfect for Tantra. They did make him perfect for it. He soon became what Tantrists call "a consort." He learned to do it for long stints, while barely moving, in the lotus position. One day in May, they were joined in the lotus position when Reed came home. He was supposed to be sanding a houseboat for painting, but instead here he was. Ms. Klein told Ed to get dressed and go away. He could hear their anguished acrimony as he fled.

Reed, wielding the moral wrath of the cuckold, made sure Darlene lost her job at U Prep for the crime of sleeping with a student. Since Ed was the victim, his identity was not revealed, but Recline left the school in full-fledged disgrace. Her name was published in two newspapers, alongside her photo from the previous year's annual. Briefly, she was notorious for her beauty and Eros. Ed was, too, but only among his classmates, who all seemed to know who'd been planking Recline.

Sexual congress with his Math Club adviser ultimately did Ed no good at school, despite protestations from the administration that he was absolutely not to blame. In May he was skipped over as a valedictorian and had to watch while Si and three other accomplished classmates were tapped to speak at graduation. With family and friends gathered in the football grandstands underneath a cantilevered roof, Si took the podium in garish sunlight, toyed with his tassel, led with a giggle, and quoted the Ramones from "I Wanna Be Sedated." He connected the soccer team's unexpectedly strong season with *Star Trek: The Motion Picture,* and recalled what a hassle it had been in '79 for kids in the class of '81 to have new driver's licenses "but no gas, because of OPEC." Later, there were family pictures on the field, during which Si said repeatedly, "Hurry up." "Try a little patience," Alice shot back. Dan said, "Simon, *cooperate.*"

Ed was a summer lifeguard at a Lake Washington beach where great-looking girls sunned in groups on large towels. Many of them, Ed noted from his perch, were seriously dedicated to roasting themselves evenly, and rotated and turned in accordance with the sun's arc, and unfastened their tops during facedown sessions. Ed's job, of course, was to keep an eye on swimmers and to yell at them through a megaphone for infractions, but at least half the time he earned money for girl-watching. Then, one day, along came Darlene Klein in a black bikini. She wore sunglasses, carried a beach bag, and had a hairstyle he hadn't seen on her before—cornrows. "Ed," she said, stopping where he had a fabulously steep view of her cleavage. "Ed King."

"Hey."

"I live nearby now. In a studio. By myself."

He went there after work. He went most days after work. And then it was time to go to Stanford.

At Stanford, Ed had an eighteen-year-old's epiphany: that he wanted to be not only rich and famous, but a historical figure with a huge role on the world stage—like Gutenberg, say, or Galileo. Was that too much to ask? As a guiding dream? Privately? Wasn't it normal to want immortality—normal, that is, for a freshman at a good college? Everything on campus seemed designed, after all, to encourage Ed to have a big ambition, maybe not one as grandiose as his, but nevertheless a major project of some kind, something to propel him into his future, where, as a grad, he'd be its master. But what was it? Already, during his first week as a freshman, Ed was feverishly sorting through the possibilities fomented by professors who had things to say like "Math is the key to the otherwise unimaginable," and "Math is the arena of humanity's great quest to finally understand the universe." Reeling, even giddy, after a lecture in this key, Ed floated across campus to Hoover Tower. On its observation deck, gazing over tessellating red-tiled roofs and beyond the far edge of the Stanford city-state to where the peninsula merged, in smog, with San Francisco Bay, he thought, "This is the beginning for me. I'm going to do something great."

But what? The screamingly obvious choices were math and computer science, because Stanford grads in math and computer science were right now making notoriously large fortunes, and names for themselves, developing—as it said in Ed's glossy welcome packet—"world-changing software on a par, in its impact, with the printing press and the television." Stanford's message was that the paradoxes and conundrums of math were on the verge, at last, of human penetration, with an assist from a new and vast computing power that would revolutionize life as we know it. There were engineers at Stanford using phone lines to transmit prodigiously large amounts of data, programmers working on ways for computers to "talk" to other computers, and an off-campus research institute, SRI, with Department of Defense contracts. All around Ed, on the campus paths, in the dorms, classrooms, libraries, and lecture halls, was the heady feel of history being made, of people who were in the right place at the right time and who didn't want to miss the opportunity. The campus computers had waiting lists, the seminars given by entrepreneurs were thronged, the job-interview fairs were feeding frenzies, and the professors nurtured acolytes and fans. And just down the road were a hundred companies poised not only to hire Stanford grads but to pay them previously unheard-of salaries.

Ed declared his major—math—and settled into the dorm room he shared with a kid from Mamaroneck who openly disliked him. They both had new Apple II computers, and they both wrote code late into the night while listening to music through headphones. Within a month,

Ed's notable facility in writing algorithms got him an invite to work at SAIL, Stanford's Artificial Intelligence Lab. Settled into a nest of student drones, he worked on an algorithm that would allow for more command options without a keyboard expansion, then on modifying a typesetting system dependent on hyphenation. At SAIL, late at night, for fun, he hacked wire-service dispatches. It wasn't the news itself but getting it this way that kept him at it. When light flashes were seen on Io, a moon of Jupiter, Ed knew about it right away, and when summer temperatures in Holland broke a record for the century, he knew that immediately, too. Nevertheless, in January he left behind SAIL's ample mainframe and went to work at SRI because his adviser, Doug Elarth, asked him to.

Elarth, who Ed thought must be fifty-five or sixty, talked a lot. Tall, narrow-shouldered, bespectacled, and cotton-headed, he narrated his life in hallways and elevators. Unsolicited reports often issued from his mouth, such as "I forgot to feed my daughter's gerbil this morning, so I'll stop by the house on my way to Menlo Park," and "My wife went to a doctor because she thinks she has shingles." Once, he displayed the stub of his missing left ring finger for Ed and reported, "Lost it when I was seventeen, working in the slim space between a threshing drum and a grain sieve." Another time, while one hand held down an eyelid and the other, nearby, poised a dropper of artificial tears, he told Ed that he had "blepharitis, which if you didn't know this associates with rosacea." "I have to go to the hardware store to pick up a garden-hose repair kit." "I just listened to Mongo Santamaría in the car." "There was a report on NPR last night on recent improvements in seismology meters." "My neighbor saw John McEnroe on an airplane."

There was an upside to Elarth. Meeting Ed in a stairwell one day while futzing with an umbrella, he said, "Mechanism's stuck," then added, "There used to be a guy here named Carl Sunshine who carried an umbrella wherever. The Carl Sunshine whose name is on *RFC 675*." When Ed expressed polite interest in *RFC 675*, Elarth insisted on giving him a beat-up copy that had been blurrily mimeographed in 1975. It described, prosaically and in diagrams, how a global computing network might work. In other words, it described an "Internet."

Elarth was a dreamer. His beginning- and end-of-semester lectures were fabulist bookends. He wrote the sort of papers nobody could read, but he also wrote accessible if discursive essays that fancifully extrapolated from advances in technology to happy changes in human existence. He was a utopian, a NASA consultant, and an underwater photographer with a theory about the mathematical basis for coral reefs. Since the National Science Foundation was in Washington, Elarth spent a lot of time there, lobbying for Stanford as a supercomputer site. He had contacts everywhere. Terrible at delegating, he oversaw the incidental. Once, Ed helped Elarth haul data boxes to his car—a Dodge Aries with a memo pad Velcroed to its steering wheel—and it was clear from what was underfoot that, while driving, Elarth ate a lot of barbecue potato chips. They went back to Elarth's office in an air-conditioned elevator. The day was hot and Elarth was tired, so they took a break on folding chairs before beginning a second round of box hauling.

"Today is sort of a metaphor," reflected Elarth. "We put a few million computations in boxes, take them to the car, drive them to UPS, and ship them off to the people at Princeton, when they could all be available on CSNET and nobody would have to do anything."

They took more boxes down the stairs and out the door, Elarth still complaining about physical reality: "Absolutely no point. This is archaic. Boxes of data—it should be a joke. None of this has to weigh anything."

He dropped his box in the car trunk. Ed nestled his beside it. "Neanderthal," concluded Elarth. He shook his head so as to indicate that humanity was pathetic. "You heard of Murray Leinster? I'll loan you Murray Leinster." They went back in, and Elarth dug around in files until he found a pulp monthly called *Astounding Science Fiction* dated March 1946. "This guy saw down the pipeline," said Elarth. "I read it when I was a farm kid."

Ed took the magazine and read Leinster's short story, which was called, oddly, "A Logic Named Joe," and which began, "It was on the third day of August that Joe come off the assembly line, and on the fifth Laurine come into town, an' that afternoon I saved civilization." Ed wanted to quit after a first sentence like that one, but because Elarth claimed its author "saw down the pipeline," he read:

> You know the logics setup. You got a logic in your house. It looks
> like a vision receiver used to, only it's got keys instead of dials and
> you punch the keys for what you wanna get. It's hooked in to the

tank, which has the Carson Circuit all fixed up with relays. Say you punch *"Station SNAFU"* on your logic. Relays in the tank take over an' whatever vision-program SNAFU is telecastin' comes on your logic's screen. Or you punch *"Sally Hancock's Phone"* an' the screen blinks an' sputters an' you're hooked up with the logic in her house an' if somebody answers you got a vision-phone connection. But besides that, if you punch for the weather forecast or who won today's race at Hialeah or who was mistress of the White House durin' Garfield's administration or what is PDQ and R sellin' for today, that comes on the screen too. The relays in the tank do it. The tank is a big buildin' full of all the facts in creation an' all the recorded telecasts that ever was made—an' it's hooked in with all the other tanks all over the country—an' everything you wanna know or see or hear, you punch for it an' you get it. Very convenient. Also it does math for you, an' keeps books, an' acts as consultin' chemist, physicist, astronomer, an' tea-leaf reader, with a "Advice to the Lovelorn" thrown in.

Ed wasn't surprised, in the fall, to hear that Elarth had been relieved of his teaching duties. His lectures had become antagonistic to colleagues and fanciful beyond any value to students. There was a rumor that, in defending himself to a committee, Elarth had mentioned hearing voices in his head. Stanford got a think tank to take him on and, Elarth having disappeared from campus, Ed got transferred to a new adviser, who urged him toward an advanced class on information theory. *We have a table around which are seated N philosophers. In the center there is a large plate containing an unlimited amount of spaghetti. Halfway between each pair of adjacent philosophers there is a single fork. . . . How should the philosophers go about their rituals without starving?* Or: *Imagine you've trained your St. Bernard, Bernie, to carry a box of three floppy disks*, etc. *For what range of distances does Bernie have a higher data rate than a 300 bps telephone line?* Ed killed these kinds of problems. His abilities were celebrated. And not just by faculty but by females generally. At Stanford, he was surrounded by hundreds of girls who were patently obvious as fantasy fodder, good-looking young women in all colors and stripes who were brimming with intelligence, purpose, and style as they leaned toward equations on overhead projectors and thrilled to the voices of genius professors waxing eloquent on everything. Of course, he undressed these attractive peers in his head, but, having gotten started with Darlene Klein down the path of older women, ended up in bed not with peers but with—for example—a computer-security consultant who cruised Stanford for associates. After a month of complicated liaisons with this married, driven tennis ace, Ed, against his better judgment, joined her for a Napa weekend. They laughed at their mutual lack of wine knowledge. They played tennis, with Ed in the role of student. She sprang for a couples aromatherapy steam bath. During sex, she made a lot of primal noises. Ed stopped programming for her and took up with a woman in Stanford Admissions who, during a first, long, casual chat, wondered if he wanted to get acquainted with an art museum in Belmont. They went immediately. After forty-five minutes of combing galleries, she told Ed she needed a glass of wine, so they went somewhere for wine, which she fidgeted over before asking how old he was. Ed said, "Twenty-nine," adding extra years because he thought she could use them, and she replied that she had a nineteen-year-old daughter volunteering at an orphanage in Senegal. "Is that not interesting?" she added, laughing. "Am I not a scintillating, fascinating person?" Then they went to her house in Redwood City, which was available because her husband, an anthropologist, was on sabbatical in Papua New Guinea.

None of this felt dark enough for his post–Darlene Klein erotic interests, so he took up with a Palo Alto patent attorney he met by responding to an "Adults Only" personal stating, "Tumultuous and complicated professional woman seeks boy toy with brains, brawn, and soul for tête-à-tête in pied-à-terre. BHM only, BD yes, LS, FS, X." Sex with the patent attorney called for role playing (delivery boy, friend's son, neighbor kid, piano student), and was often informed by a tearful cruelty that left Ed less than 100-percent happy with his role as a punching bag. She called him a bastard or threw something at him if he wanted to leave her pied-à-terre before she was ready to let him go, and she squinted at him with wrathful distrust whenever he came out of her powder room. In a mood, one afternoon, of pre-farewell appeasement, Ed agreed to accompany her to a Halloween party sponsored by a software company. The invitation, in embossed gold letters on black paper, read:

She keeps her Moët et Chandon
In her pretty cabinet
"Let them eat cake" she says
Just like Marie Antoinette
A built-in remedy
For Khrushchev and Kennedy
At anytime an invitation
You can't decline
—Queen

Followed by the details for:

Prophecy Inc.'s
Killer Queen Halloween Scene, 1982 C.E.
with special guest Psycho Youth
live at Miller Mansion, Corona Heights
All Hallow's Eve
10 p.m.

They got there at ten. Guests hurried past. A spotlight swept the sky. The patent attorney had dressed in gartered stockings and lingerie; Ed, stubbornly, attended as himself. Even before they were in the door, his date got swept away by gregarious connections. Ed slipped off gratefully and wandered as a lone prowler. Most of the people who'd gravitated toward Miller Mansion—a gigantic turn-of-the-century Victorian lit like a bonfire down to glowing coals—were elaborately and enthusiastically got up. Packed into a foyer, Ed was stumped by three guys who'd come in action-figure ensembles featuring Adidas running shoes, striped warm-ups, and sunny circus jackets with thick belt closures; they turned out to be hosts hired to greet revelers, or to bounce them if required.

Ed felt seized in a phantasmagoria. Miller Mansion was impeccably maintained, and someone in its history had liked chandeliers enough to impose one on every room. There were also pervasive wall sconces that may or may not have been specific to the current bacchanal. Prophecy's atmospherics contractor had opted for a red-light-district ambience, and for steam machines cleverly calibrated to keep the floor invisible. Every-one's legs disappeared into steam, although now and then an unexpected swirl or clearing would reveal Turkish rugs, oak floorboards, garish shoes, and fishnet stockings. Revelers were being served a steady diet of piped-in Queen—"Bohemian Rhapsody," "Another One Bites the Dust," "Crazy Little Thing Called Love," and so on. They were very excited and, at times, unruly. Many seemed to like the convergence of muddled camp and gilded money, the measured decadence, and the water chestnuts wrapped in bacon and served on toothpicks. The bartender Ed visited could pour a blood-red Merlot, or a Bloody Mary, or smoking punch, or something from a list of "Creepy Cocktails and Spooky Sippers," but when asked for white wine, he shook his head sheepishly. Was it a coincidence or careful casting, Ed wondered, that he looked like Norman Bates?

Ed pushed on. A considerable number of zombies careened about in unraveling shards of cloth. There was a zealous Morticia Addams—so zealous, in fact, Ed guessed she'd been hired—who wandered Miller Mansion in a black hobble skirt while strumming on a shamisen and affecting ruined beauty. Indeed, there was a straggle of gray in her black hair that Ed found stirring; he also took an interest in a member of the catering staff whose job it was to stand like a figure in a wax museum while holding a platter of spanakopita triangles. Skin as if never touched by the sun, gaunt Gypsy cheeks, strong chin, black tresses—had she as well been cast by the party planner? Or was she real?

Around eleven, Psycho Youth began to play. Ed heard them from a second-floor corridor so stuffed with milling guests he felt embattled. He'd only just begun to discern a fact about this party—that each room in Miller Mansion had been dedicated to a hired act—and he felt moved to have a thorough look around. In one room, a magician was fooling people with colored handkerchiefs and pigeons; in another, a sword swallower was mock-castigating a guest who'd ventured that sword swallowing was "just a trick." In a third, a juggler wearing ballooning trousers and a genie's turban juggled boxes of Prophecy software; and in a fourth, a contortionist folded herself into a UPS shipping container despite the added duress of an outfit cobbled together out of foam insulation. There was a W. C. Fields look-alike with a Howdy Doody doll on his lap delivering bawdy one-liners, and a girl on a unicycle, dressed like a Chinese acrobat, throwing plates onto her head, where they stacked up. "The Sublime Cosmo" performed "rare feats of telekinesis," such as prompting, by sheer force of mental exertion, an antique pocket-watch to run at high speed, and compelling a small compass across a table to his hand. In a walk-in pantry, a mind reader wearing the headgear of Johnny Carson as Carnac the Magnificent, but calling himself ESP-Man, would ask someone in his tightly packed crowd for his or her name, then astonish whoever answered with a correct birth date or the name of an ex-spouse. "The Flaming Cross-Dresser," decked out in a burning Seattle Seahawks uniform, performed a truly amazing trick—an assistant wrapped him in a kind of psychedelic tent for a second, then unwrapped him to reveal Carmen Miranda with a melon in her hat. Another second in the tent and he became the Indian in the Village People; a third and he became Snow White, complete with apple. Ed moved on. There was a fortune-teller of the gleaming-crystal-ball school in a black tent decorated with horoscope symbols, a séance beginning every thirty minutes in the attic, and a conservatory packed with video-arcade games. A man with a handlebar mustache read "The Raven" beside a candelabra while leaning, with Victorian stuffiness, against a fireplace mantel. Sales reps handed out complimentary mouse pads in stairwells. A man got up like a swashbuckler threw knives at a girl in garters and a top hat. In one room there was nothing but low lighting, pipe-organ music, and a bloodless-looking geezer, wide-eyed, in a casket; in another, Ed walked in on Dracula biting the neck of a girl in a nightgown; next door to that, a bodybuilder, painted green and exploding out of his clothes like the Incredible Hulk, performed a biceps-heavy competition routine to the tune of "Monster Mash." And then there was the woman reading Tarot cards in a garish library on the third floor.

A strange room. The books were so tightly packed in floor-to-ceiling bookcases, lit by recessed red lamps, that they looked under pressure. The titles, all oversized and antique in appearance, were mostly Latin, though on close inspection Ed recognized some Sanskrit, Greek, Arabic, and Farsi. Ladders on runners gave access to the higher shelves. The library's voluminous chandelier was more than just outsized—it reigned over the room like a model of the moon, a glittering, gold ball of rotating lights that produced a strobe effect, so that the books fell in and out of vision. There was a well-polished display case with three glass shelves of what looked like amulets from the Fertile Crescent, and an opposing case stuffed with the kind of medieval notions Ed associated with alchemy—

a flask, a small distilling furnace, an iron tripod, a mortar and pestle, a vapor-condensing burner, and a few cloudy tincture vials. And in the middle of all of this, at a low table, a pashmina-heavy Tarot reader held court between two censers of burning myrrh. It was hard to make her out in the strobe phantasmagoria. Things seen closely were well enough illuminated, but anything you couldn't put your eye to with immediacy stayed fantastically and tantalizingly obscure. Between the disjointed flashes and the roiling myrrh smoke—which smelled like burning dirt and dried out his contact lenses—Ed's view of the Tarot reader was like a view through moving water, or in a poorly lit hall of warped mirrors. "I'm not really looking for a reading," he said. "I'm just sort of wandering around."

"It's free," said the reader, in a series of broken stills. "Free, and it'll only take a few minutes. Most people end up thinking it's fun, but anyway I'm here for the rest of the night, if you decide you want to have a reading."

He didn't want to have one—he was just poking his head in—he hadn't come up here for a reading. But other than the spanakopita-platter mannequin and the shamisen-wielding Morticia Addams siren, this was the first woman he'd come across that night who appealed to him in just the right way. Inside her collection of swaddling scarves and shawls, she was late-thirty-something, or maybe forty. This much he discerned in the fragmented light, and it was enough to make him hang around.

The reader threw some tasseled ends about in an effort to organize more dash. "There's no creepy business with what I do," she said. "I don't call up ghosts." She laughed, as if at charlatans and spiritualists. "You could just about play Hearts or Crazy Eights here," she said, "if you set aside the Major Arcana."

Ed sat down across from her. The chair made him feel like a giant kindergartner, and he worried that it might break. He squinted through the smoke and fireworks flash, trying for a cleaner look at her face, but she was protected by a sphere of veiling myrrh mist and by a shawl she'd pulled up while he'd been looking out the window. "Hit me with your best shot," said Ed. "Fire away with the cards."

"Are you sure?"

"Yeah," said Ed. "Let's see how you do it."

The reader swirled her hands over a nonexistent crystal ball. "Very well," she said, from behind her myrrh. "Let's you and me determine your destiny by way of my ancient art."

"Both of us?"

"The process is inclusive."

"What does that mean?"

"It means we read the cards together."

"I thought you were the reader."

"No," said the reader. "That's not right. It isn't going to work without you."

She began to unfold the long silk scarf wrapped around her Tarot cards. "The beauty of this is that there's nothing to lose," she said. "You get a little insight into yourself, maybe an answer to a problem you're having, maybe a little glimpse into your future."

"From a deck of cards."

"Plus, Prophecy is paying for it," the reader countered, holding the cards over the censer on her left as if to consecrate them in myrrh. She removed them from the smoke, caressed them a little, and shifted them from hand to hand. "For our purposes in Tarot, you're known as the Querent," she explained. "That's because you've got a question—you have to think up a question—but don't tell me what it is yet. I'm going to pick a card."

Ed couldn't help himself. He laughed.

"The cards know—no sneering," warned the reader, and with that she chose one, saying, "The Knight of Wands. Is that okay with you? His mantle's got salamanders biting their own tails. Salamanders can't be burned, you know. Which is good, auspicious, because Wands symbolize fire. Why don't you take a closer look?"

Ed fought with the obfuscating strobe light emanating from the rented disco ball. A guy in armor, helmeted, wielding a stick in his right hand with leaves sprouting from it, high on a rearing horse in front of three distant pyramids. "The Knight of Wands is a warrior," intoned the reader. "He's capable of being a fine friend and lover, but he can also be nasty while he's being energetic. One thing—he's impatient. Wants to get on with it. On a journey, as you can see, though not necessarily to war. Nevertheless, in a bit of a rush or something, to which his horse is agreeable. All eagerness, these two, in motion, moving forward. This card reversed, there's no energy, inner discord." The reader set the Knight of

Wands facedown on her left. Then she displayed her deck of cards, rotated it, and presented it to Ed on outstretched palms. "Would you like to shuffle?" she asked.

"Should I like to?" Ed answered.

There were cheers from below as Psycho Youth finished "Another One Bites the Dust." Ed pressed his eyelids in an effort to resituate his dry contact lenses, then blinked and squinted. "Cut my deck for me," said the reader. "Any way you want, but cut my deck."

Ed unceremoniously, did as he'd been asked. "Good," the reader said. "Now I'll ask you to shuffle. I don't mean shuffle, but rifle my cards thoroughly, because shuffling tends to wear out their corners." Again she presented the deck—minus the Knight of Wands—with subservient formality, as though offering tribute. "Take them," she said. "And ask yourself a question, a personal question, so long as it's a question meaningful to you, and repeat this question, mentally, while you thoroughly rifle up my cards."

"So where did you learn the intricacies of Tarot?"

"The thing about sarcasm," replied the reader, "is that it often conceals something."

"Are you a psychiatrist, too?" asked Ed.

The reader swirled a pashmina through the smoke, as if to clear the bitter air between them. Ed began riffling the Tarot cards. They were longer than playing cards but not any wider, and fronted with a nightsky pattern. Ed squinted at the figures sliding through his fingers. "Are you thinking of your question?" the reader asked. "You're supposed to be thinking of your question right now. Repeating it in silence while you're handling my Tarot cards."

"Right," said Ed. "I forgot."

He finished mixing the cards. "Cut them into three piles," the reader told him. "Put the first to your left, the second in the middle, and the third on your right—go ahead."

"Three piles," said Ed, divvying up the cards.

The reader took over. She moved the Knight of Wands to the center of the table, then brought the other cards together and set one, facing Ed, across the Knight of Wands. "The Fool," she announced, "reversed."

"Right," said Ed. "The Fool reversed."

"Knight of Wands crossed by the Fool reversed," said the reader, and put a card above those two, saying, "Five of Cups for a crown."

"Right," said Ed.

"The Strength card reversed," continued the reader, laying this one down with special care. "To Knight of Wands' right—the distant past."

"I was Superman in days of yore," said Ed. "So that explains it."

The reader said, "Card five goes under—south of—the Knight of Wands. It represents events in the immediate past, and for you"—she laid the card down—"it's the Ace of Pentacles."

Ed refrained from witticisms. The Tarot reader turned another card. "Card six," she said, "goes to the left, indicating the course of your near future, the coming years. It's the Nine of Cups—quite auspicious indeed." With that, she passed a hand across the cards she'd laid down, as a magician might across an upturned hat just before a rabbit leaps out of it. "There you have it," she said. "The Celtic Cross."

"Wow," said Ed.

The Tarot reader ignored him. "Card seven," she said, "will go over here. Outside of the cross, lower right, my right. It will stand for the Querent in his current perspective, for how he feels about the question he's asked, and for you"—she turned the card over—"it just happens to be the Hanged Man reversed. Eight," she went on, "goes right above seven. It's the card suggestive of the opinions of others. What your friends and family might say about your question. In your case"—she turned up another card—"it's the Knight of Swords, which is interesting, very interesting, because, really, the Knight of Swords goes either way. For good or ill, I can't say. And that brings us to card nine, the card of emotions. Not your cynical and sarcastic façade, but your real hopes and fears, your desires, your inner life. And this card, for you, is"—she turned a card over—"the Hermit. Reversed."

"Right," said Ed, committed to the tone he'd struck. "The Hermit reversed."

"Last card," said the reader. "Final result." She turned the card over and laid it down. "And the final card for you," she said, "is Death."

"Great," said Ed, concealing his dismay. "This is why I don't like Tarot readings."

"What's your question? Give it to me now."

"What are you doing later this evening?"

"That's your question?"

"To be honest, yes."

"Somebody to Love" ended. There were cheers from the ballroom. The reader whipped a pashmina end, which flared phosphorescently in the strobe light from overhead. The electricity, the kinesis, excited Ed a little, and he felt suspense as a form of mental clarity when she leaned across the table, eyes narrowed. "Listen," she said. "You're the young, capable, and promising Knight of Wands. Energetic, moving forward. You're crossed, though, by the Fool reversed, which tells me that ahead lies thoughtless action, that you might act indiscriminately and to your own disadvantage. Above you lies the Five of Cups, which bespeaks a destiny of disappointment and sorrow. Next—"

"Come closer," said Ed. "I can't hear you."

"Next," said the reader, "we find the Strength card reversed, as the hallmark of your distant past, which speaks of discord, illicit behavior, abuse of power, those kinds of things—all markers for you, all embodied in who you are, and therefore all remaining dangerous."

"Closer," said Ed. "Please."

"On to the Ace of Pentacles," said the reader. "This is a card we can consider as auspicious, insofar as it indicates the direction of past trends. It suggests that well-being and pleasure have been yours, that you've begun along a path of material gain and have enjoyed, and might continue to enjoy, in the near term, the pleasures of the flesh."

"Kiss me," said Ed. "Fulfill our destiny."

But she ignored this. "The Ace of Pentacles," she said, "finds strong support in your next card, the Nine of Cups, hinting at a great bounty lying in your future. That brings us next to the Hanged Man reversed, which tells us what would be obvious to anybody—that in your present condition you suffer from a terrible inflation, a terrible narcissism, and an overwhelming and dangerous hubris."

"Come on, kiss me," repeated Ed.

"I mentioned earlier that your next card, the Knight of Swords"—the reader nearly touched it with her smallest finger's fake nail—"can be read with diametrically opposed connotations. On the one hand, it might bode well going forward, but, on the other hand, this card can indicate misfortune. I think that in your case we—"

Ed leaned in and kissed her with the confidence that a kiss was all it would take. She tasted like myrrh. When he was done she said simply, "We haven't finished your reading."

"Forget it," said Ed. "Let's go somewhere. Anywhere."

"You don't want me to tell you about your last two cards?"

"Why would I care about the last two cards?"

"That's a mistake," the reader said. "Now get out of here, you arrogant bastard. You're dangerous to the world and to yourself."

"Don't make me laugh," Ed answered.

7

The Con

Diane decided that a fresh start meant distance, and relocated from Portland to Seattle. She also stopped calling herself Diane Long and became Diane Burroughs again. Returning to her old name was bureaucratically entangling, but every time she had to visit an office, fill out a form, mail something, or have a document notarized, she felt spurred by catharsis. The niggling paperwork—writing out her personal details *ad nauseam*—contributed to her purge. So did the other details of returning to her life as an unattached person. Diane bought a two-door car and, after a bit of investigation, chose a Seattle suburb called Kirkland—boutique shops and handsome lake vistas—where she signed a lease at The Palms. Favoring the view from Apartment 226 of the terrace full of chaises longues and of the pool and "cabaña"—a covered area for outdoor entertaining featuring a refrigerator and sink—she ordered furniture, shopped for kitchenware, and bought a stereo and a high-end television. Becoming single again swallowed a good part of June, but by July, Diane could do what she wanted, which was to sit by the pool, read, and drink Evian water. It was while she was in this bank-account-depleting mode that she heard from her half-brother the constable, who said he'd tracked her down via her car registration. "That's lovely," she said, "and good of you, John." But it turned out his call was not just social. He'd called to say that Mum was in hospital. Besides her shot liver, a lot of things were ominous; the worst of it was that she no longer took food. She was incoherent, yet one thing was clear: Mum wanted to see Diane before she died. Diane said she'd look at the price of a plane ticket, but before she could, John called again, in the middle of the night, to report via a crackling, distant connection that Mum had "passed on at about ten a.m., without much trouble."

Diane bought the ticket in the morning. John met her in the arrivals hall at Heathrow and, after offering a stiff embrace, hoisted her "trunk" onto his shoulder and carried it to his Lada like a sack of flour. He was a giant with awful walrus mustaches, ungainly and deferential. Whereas once he'd been an agile rugby prop, now he was flabby, short of breath, and slow. He used hair cream. His face was red, his lips cracked, his eyes beady. He had the broken blood vessels in his nose and cheeks often telling among alcoholics. In his car, where he loomed against the roof and overfilled his seat with girth, he told Diane that she looked "quite fit for her age." It was a wonder he didn't break the stick shift off, so puny did it look beneath his hand.

Even before leaving the airport's ring road, Diane was reminded that everything in England was smaller, closer, denser, more compact, and darkened by time. It was raining in August, at three in the afternoon. The rush of traffic, though pell-mell, felt cooperative. Diane recognized the blight between Epping and Stansted, and, beyond Great Dunmow, the unruly hedgerows. The countryside here looked like a rubbish heap, and was too close to London for its own good. There was the ancient pall of successive devastations, applied by nature and man both, that she recognized from girlhood but, in that era of her life, had had no name for. Nevertheless, Diane found herself feeling fond of England. She preferred it, with its dowdy pubs, chimney pots, and mansard roofs, to America's shoddy newness. England's industrial trim and tackle, even its wreckage, was properly bleak, whereas like clutter in the American Northwest corner struck Diane as the fresh detritus of a colonial outpost. But less than half her attention was available to these observations, because the constable, en route, was a fraternal chatterbox, full of information about Mum's demise, and thorough in his rundown of his three grown children's exploits. Coming into Great Hockwold he warned, "You won't recognize it now," which turned out to be true. The Tesco she'd frequently shoplifted from was brighter, much refurbished. There were plenty of new roundabouts, and pedestrians-only in the town center. A bulging mosque astride the bypass was visible from High Street, and—the constable's tone bespoke a point of view on this—there were three Indian takeaways in walking distance of each other. At a traffic light Diane saw, next to her, a cluttered taxi dashboard starring what the constable said was Ganesha, the Lord of Success, and Rekha, a Bollywood star. The old mine works had been turned into a tourist attraction. So had Tate's, now called the Pasty Shoppe. They lurched along the lanes past sodden house fronts before pulling up at what the constable, in a stab at wit, called his "domicile." To offset its impoverishment, he'd planted decorative fuchsias, and these, obviously, had been assiduously watered. Still, they had a beleaguered look. By the front door sat a pair of rusting chairs.

Diane was installed in a damp, cheerless bedroom on the ground floor. The house smelled like cooking oil and laundry-soap flakes. The constable, it emerged, was a diabetic whose wife, Jenny, kept a pan of fudge for low moments. Diane, before skulking off to sleep away her jet lag, decided that Jenny's doting was cruel. She carved her fudge with a furrowed intensity and stood over the constable to watch him eat it with one hand turned against her hip, as if administering cod-liver oil.

Club showed the next day, looking pop-eyed and goitery. As a kid he'd been brawny, jaundiced, and tough, but now, at thirty-seven, he looked beat up and unkempt. He was snaggle-toothed, and chain-smoked nervously, and spoke around his hand-rolled cigarettes. He wore a peacoat and a beret. Like his older brother, Club had a mustache, although his was closely trimmed to parallel his upper lip, and an alcoholic's spidery network of blood vessels in his cheeks. There the resemblance ended. Club was compact, with a wrestler's build, a low center of gravity, and a chimpanzee's gait. He was overgrateful for the constable's offer of a military-surplus cot set up in a storage pantry, and, having claimed it with his duffel, sat in the front room in his stocking feet with a cup of heavily sugared tea on his lap and the telly on in front of him. Soon he was asking John and Diane to remember Mum pegging a port bottle at Tom Clark, and—demonstrating—how she'd blown smoke rings at the telly. Later, at the table, over bread and soup, he remarked that Diane had a classy wardrobe. As for his own clothes, they smelled like the Fens.

At Mum's funeral, a friend named Harriett Rivers gave a synopsis of

Mum's life and hailed her strong points—cheeky, quick with a joke, knew her mind and spoke it, friend to stray cats. Diane, at the open casket, thought it appropriate that the undertaker had presented Mum as a wizened tart, or a Gilbert and Sullivan old-lady-of-the-night. She looked as if she ought to be wearing ruffled bloomers and sitting in the lap of a sot with meager cash. Sure, it was darkly funny, but it was also sad, if not quite as sad as the rotund constable sniffling, red-faced, into his cravat when Mum's remains were interred in the fourth vertical row of a mausoleum. Afterward, Jenny, to honor Mum, served pie, and the constable laid out photos on a sideboard, where he also displayed a half-dozen pieces of Mum's crochet work and some letters from when Mum had been a land girl during the war. Before supper he gave a gin toast, teary-eyed. "So many pissed on Mum," he said, "but, give her credit, she pissed right back. Gave 'em what for. Put 'em in their place. That was her speciality. From the school of hard knocks. Came up in a sheep barn but always stood tall. Say what you want, all the rows she caused, and the talk in town, Mum was a fighter. Harriett knows what I'm meaning to say, because Harriett saw it, and thank you, Harriett, for being here with us so late and for giving us your eulogy at the funeral. I thought it was spot-on. You had her in your sights. And here's to Sweetie for your whortleberry pie, and to you, Club, and to Diane, you both come all this way. Blessings all around, then, and bottoms up! To Mum!"

Diane, who was drinking gin, said, "To Mum, then," and after Club's toast—"To Mum, the old fighter!"—she offered: "Rest in peace, Mum, and no more misdeeds." Harriett Rivers, whose gravelly voice betrayed her many years of Golden Virginia roll-ups, said, "No more misdeeds? Your old mum?" And once more, they all went bottoms up.

Diane and Club pursued a post-funeral mission to finish off a fifth of Gilbey's while sitting in the constable's rusty chairs a few feet from night traffic. Memories, memories. The shifty dealer they'd bought puff from with the lame, chained dog just past Park Crescent, and playing football with those slobbery and foul-mouthed Carricks on the supposedly off-limits cricket pitch in winter, and the blind boy on Trelawney Road whose eyes scared the shite out of you because they rolled back so far in his head, and baked potatoes on Bonfire Night. The more they talked like this, the more treacly they got. Still, Club held his drink well—as juiced as she was, she could see that about him. Reeling in bed afterward, she regretted bashing Jim Long in front of Club, and rued her version of her current circumstances—well-heeled divorcee, living large and on a spree, was how she'd besottedly painted things for him.

Diane flew back to Kirkland feeling cash-depleted and chastised. The constable, at least half a dozen times, had dropped his jowly head in her presence and opined, "Oh, if she could have seen you at the end, it would have brought a ray of happiness in," and "She asked after you any number of times. She had her regrets, you know, and wanted to make things right with you, in my opinion, but it's a fair trip from America, she knew that. Too bad when someone's on their last legs, eh?" Diane smoldered in her coach seat now. She chewed her fingernails. The important thing was to put it all behind her. Her mother was dead, and the constable, for all intents and purposes, was noise wafting away in the Gulf Stream. Who was he to insinuate or accuse? A constable on foot patrol, portly and huffing. A dunderhead with an awful mustache too often dipped in ale froth.

Redelivered to The Palms, Diane took to the pool deck in the French-cut bikini Jim had bought her in Puerto Vallarta. It was a Saturday, and The Palms' tenants were out in numbers. Some brought radios, so there was music, not played too loudly, and some discreetly broke the rule about glassware and, while Diane kept track, got tipsy. The whole scene was sexy in an American way—the chicks, mostly, glistened with health, and the dudes, mostly, had weight-room muscles. Diane could see that many of them were restless, as if they believed there was something better to do elsewhere. They were like nice state-university kids on spring break, but a little older, and they left Diane feeling so self-conscious that on Saturday evening she went shopping for less European-looking swim apparel that would let her sit around the pool without disturbing people. She found a red two-piece that Lynn Long—Jim's sister, who'd married a PGA golfer— might have worn in her era as a hot chick attending U of O, kind of a Miss Teen USA look. Then she went into a club called the Pelican because she felt like it, and, besides, there was nothing to stop her, including the bouncer, who nodded not at her but at her boobs.

The singer onstage was called Sir Charles, and with his long fingers and huge Afro, his over-the-top bellbottoms and half-opened shirt, he called to mind Sly Stone. Diane took a seat at the end of a long bar where the servers, costumed in black tank-tops, black flares, black aprons, and sensible shoes, came to yell at the bartenders, pick up orders, and keep track of tabs. Underneath, these girls looked a lot like the bimbos at The Palms, with their careful hairdos and sunny complexions. The bartenders, all three, looked like soap-opera bachelors, two with the air of marriage material, the third with a slightly more sensual demeanor, as if he moonlighted as a gigolo. From him, she ordered a mai tai.

A good corner, because she blended into the commerce there, and could watch without self-consciousness the loud behavior apparently natural to the Pelican, and also watch the dancers, most of whom were terrible, so that Diane thought of opening a dance studio, Diane's, where couples would learn to salsa and tango and where singles could pursue each other. Maybe during the day her space could be sublet to Al-Anon and Weight Watchers for meetings; at other times it could accommodate a support group she'd run, fee-based, for divorced women seeking to get back on their feet but having a time of it. Maybe Sir Charles needed an agent, or the bartender needed a pimp, or she could set herself up as a quasi-legitimate masseuse, or get good at investing. Diane, sipping from her mai tai, tried to think of ways not to work and still cash in, like people at the top who, instead of working, intercepted funds.

In the midst of such thoughts, she was assailed by a guy, tall, neat, but not good-looking, whose come-on was to yell, over Sir Charles's "Let's Stay Together," "I know you probably think I'm hitting on you." Diane answered, "Mind reader."

"I'm actually just checking," the guy said, without smiling, "to see if you want to score some blow."

"I don't do blow."

"Want to get started?"

"I want you to get out of here."

"What if I give it to you?"

"You're giving away blow."

"Yep," said the guy. "Like free-sample sausage in the grocery aisle. Same strategy. Customer grooming."

Diane put her elbow on the bar and her chin in her hand. The coke dealer did, too. He had closely cropped gelled hair and a broad, Gallic nose; he wore his polo shirt buttoned to the throat, tight chinos, and a wedding band. He looked law-abiding, if a little greasy—like many of Candy Dark's clients. "Free blow," said Diane.

"Yep."

"I never turn down samples."

"Now you're talking."

"What's your name?"

"My name is . . . Bill. I mean Mike. Why did I say Bill? My name is Michael Bill, I mean Bill Michaels. But just call me Bill. Or Mike. What's your name?"

"Funny," said Diane. "My name's Bill, too."

"Great," said the coke dealer. "What are you drinking?"

"I'm drinking a Mike," said Diane.

The coke dealer's wedding band was alongside one nostril, and the green face of his sizable watch, with its articulating silver band, now glowed in the relative darkness of the Pelican. He looked hangdog, impatient, big-elbowed, and uncoordinated, and hulked like a basketball player. "Great," he said. "Mike. Whatever. Bill. But maybe, since you're nursing that mai tai, I ought to come back later."

"Why?"

"Take your time. Nurse away. I'll come back. We'll do the blow."

Diane, from behind, was crowded by one of the all-American servers, who put a hand on her shoulder and yelled, over Sir Charles, "Hey, Mike!" Mike returned a peace sign, and Diane said, "I thought this was like free-sample sausage, Bill. So why would you and me be doing blow?"

"Fine," he said, checking his watch. "You do the blow, I'll watch."

Diane unzipped her handbag for a matchbox. "Take that," she said. "Put in your blow. I'll be here for a while."

"You never did blow before?"

"I'll figure it out."

"Good play," said Mike. "Be seeing ya." But ten minutes later, he brought the coke.

On Sunday, Diane wore the less noticeable bathing suit and made an effort to talk to people. There were two girls in chaises ten yards away with whom she chatted about Mexico, tanning salons, England, and carbs. One, Kelly, pointed out a guy who had good pecs. The other, Teddie, assured her that guys loved British accents. They compared suntan lotions. Diane said she was in 226 and that the girls should come around when they wanted, for margaritas. Kelly responded to this with a too-many-margaritas anecdote. Teddie, who had a *Cosmo* in her lap, said people called her Ted. Next they talked about the Princess of Wales, who, said Kelly, wasn't good-looking. She couldn't understand the big deal, the hype, which maybe Diane, being English, could explain. Surprisingly, Ted was well versed in the nuances of royal intrigue, and spoke authoritatively, at some length, on the Duchess of York, who, she said, was weird-looking. Diane agreed. There ensued a dialogue on standards of beauty. Ted was not an admirer of teased hair and provided the example of Olivia Newton-John, "after she went spandex, in *Grease*." That was a weird look. Another was leg warmers. They checked out a guy with great shoulders who, said Ted, was a jerk, not that she meant to be judgmental. Diane made sure to mention 226 again, where the door was open a lot.

In the pool, she asked the guy with great shoulders if a drifting air mattress was his. It wasn't, but that didn't stop him from suggesting that it was probably okay if she used it, or from pointing out that she had an accent. Later, Diane asked three hot-tubbers if she could turn on the jets. It was fine with them, so a guy got out and turned the jets on, and Diane, with the small of her back against one, added a few words to a conversation about chlorine, what it did to your hair and skin, and a few words, too, on hot water and muscle pain. This led to inquiries on London hotels, and on the Princess of Wales, who was in the news that week for attending Live Aid.

Some book talk happened in the late afternoon, because a guy asked Diane what she was reading. She showed him the cover of *An Indecent Obsession,* by Colleen McCullough. He hadn't read it, but he'd seen *The Thorn Birds* and had opinions about the actors. Diane celebrated Bryan Brown's sheep-shearing muscles, and in response, the guy celebrated Rachel Ward in partial undress. Partial undress, he said, was better than full undress. Why? Because of suggestion. Next he asked Diane what *An Indecent Obsession* was about. She said, "A war nurse," and then he gave her the title of his book—*Gorky Park*—and a plot summary of the first hundred pages. Somewhere along the way he must have recognized that he was boring, because he suddenly interrupted himself to say, "Enough on my book. You must be British." As if that helped.

By five, there were a dozen people to say hi to in the future, including girls who'd been told to drop by 226 any time they wanted, and guys she felt confident she'd intrigued. On Monday, there were only a few people around the pool, but she managed, again, to strike up conversations, or at least to make contact, nod or say hello, and on Tuesday, she passed a good part of the day sunbathing, and making small talk, with a girl named Emily who worked as an accounts-receivable clerk for a contractors' supply company. Emily had a Peter Pan hairdo and gawky legs, and wore the sort of bathing suit women generally started wearing only after they'd had children, with a built-in skirt and a bow at the back. She seemed listless, and entered the water tentatively, clinging to her mottled shoulders. Diane wanted to cheer up Emily, so around noon they repaired to 226 for cheese and crackers, and made rum-and-Cokes in large paper cups, with ice, and then a second round of rum-and-Cokes to carry back to the pool. There, Emily confessed that she was taking a mental-health day, wanted to change jobs, wasn't comfortable in Kirkland, missed Spokane, and felt depressed.

Tuesday evening, there was a cabaña party that spilled out onto the terrace of chaises longues. Diane, in a shift and sandals, was introduced to a friend of Kelly's and Ted's named Shane, and accepted his offer of a gin-and-tonic in a plastic cup, but not his offer of a hot dog or a hamburger. "You're going meatless," observed Shane, who, muscular, with a cyclist's thighs, stood forthrightly with his hands on his hips. "Hey, I know this guy from London. He's—"

"Uh," said Kelly, "I think Diane's probably sick of people mentioning England all the time, just because she has an English accent. Even though she's really nice about it."

"She's super-nice about it," confirmed Ted.

She was, in fact, so diligently nice, that her reputation for niceness ascended. People at The Palms said hi to her, nodded, smiled, waved at her through her open door, chatted with her in the parking lot, greeted her in halls, spoke with her in elevators, flirted, commiserated, invited her to parties, even—in the case of Emily—sought her out for wisdom, which she dispensed with care. Then, one night, at a cabaña social, a girl she'd met beside the pool asked Diane if she knew where to score blow. "I do," said Diane. "How much?"

"Just a rail or something. Or even a couple bumps."

"Sure," said Diane. "Let's go up."

Victim One rounded up a friend—Victim Two—and they followed Diane to 226, where they drank rum-and-Cokes, listened to Santana, and watched television with the sound off while Diane, taking her lead from "Mike," set them up with her sample blow, free of charge.

The following Saturday, she tracked down Mike at the Pelican. Onstage this time, instead of Sir Charles, was Street Life—eight guys, three with theatrical horns, one with timbales, a cowbell, and congas, and a lead singer who went shirtless but wore an open vest, so that the crawling veins in his arms, not to mention his knotty chest, could function to advantage. Street Life wasn't just brassy but loud, and that let Diane sit close to Mike, the better that he might understand what she was telling him, and, as she spoke within inches of his big pink-hued ear, the better for him to feel her warm breath and note her Obsession from Calvin Klein. "Yes," she lied. "I did do the blow. It wasn't what I expected."

"What did you say?"

"I didn't get super off on it," she said, in Americanese, but he showed no sign of grasping her humor. "You didn't get super off on it," he replied.

"Ten-four. You read me."

"I'm sorry you didn't get off," yelled Mike. "How can I help you with that?"

Diane put a hundred-dollar bill on the table. Then she picked up Mike's left hand—the wedding-band hand—set it over the bill, patted his fingers, moved away from him about two feet, took a sip from her mai tai, crossed her legs, and watched the Street Life guy make love to his mike stand while covering "You're Still a Young Man."

Mike drummed his fingers on the bill. He was holding back a smile, she saw, as if he knew what was going on. "Obviously," she thought, "he knows what I'm doing," which was a thought she'd had about dozens of johns when she was younger but no less sure of herself. And what she'd learned in that era was that knowing what was going on didn't stop a whole category of men from being stupid. Diane suspected that Mike was in this category. "If you're a narc, you have to tell me," he said, as he moved closer in the name of being heard, to which Diane replied, an inch from his ear, "I'm not a narc, don't worry, Mike," and kissed him, in a friendly way, on the temple.

"You know what?" Mike asked, after kissing her back, in the same friendly way, but on the lips. "Just about every chick I sell to thinks I trade blow for throws. That's pretty cool, I guess, but I'm in business."

"Perfect," said Diane. "Did you notice I put money on the table?"

"Yeah," said Mike. "That won't get you much."

"Three grams."

"Another four hundred if you want three grams."

"So, like, a hundred sixty-five a gram."

"About."

"What about ten?"

"That's fifteen hundred."

"What about twenty?"

"That's twenty-five hundred."

Diane took twenty-three more hundreds from her wallet. "Give me twenty grams," she told him.

A dangerous game, but she liked dangerous games. Buying ten or twenty grams at a pop from Mike, turning it around as tenths at The Palms, giving away freebies to get people started, friends of friends coming around, maybe some of them untrustworthy, which made it important to scope people out and to pay attention to who crashed her parties. Like who, anyway, were those three quarterbackish guys, laughing, between bumps, about the Pittsburgh Pirates' nose-candy troubles while drinking Coronas and playing with her remote? Could that be the sort of farce narcs put on? She checked on them later and heard a lot of doltish laughter that sounded reassuring. These three were too coke-centric to be narcs. Then she would check on someone else.

The upside was money; the downside was anxiety. Whores got short sentences, but dealers didn't, not in Ronald Reagan's administration. Diane didn't like looking over her shoulder or anticipating a knock on her door, so she made a deal with herself: get out as soon as possible. Pursuing that end, she studied investment at the Kirkland Public Library— *Barron's, The Wall Street Journal,* and books called *Investing for Beginners* and *How To: The Stock Market.* For the most part, it was stultifying reading; intercepting funds, it turned out, was a job. On the other hand, it didn't involve sweat or danger. The hardest part was picking up the phone and putting down a bet with Charles Schwab.

Emily came by 226 one Friday in an unbecoming halter top that called attention to her caved-in posture. Diane poured wine, put on the Pointer Sisters, and went to work as Dear Abby. Emily had a new job—she worked in Accounts Receivable at a company called Aldus, although she couldn't explain what Aldus made or did, other than to say, "We do PageMaker," and, "PageMaker's software for computers." Basically, she wasn't going out, except to run two miles after work. "And why is that?" asked Diane.

"Because nobody asks me." Emily sipped her wine. "You probably think I'm pretty out of it."

"No," said Diane, "I don't think you're out of it. But I do think you're lacking—don't take this the wrong way—confidence. Is it all right with you if I say that?"

Emily leaned forward. One of her boobs—inside the dumb halter top with its infantile polka dots—was bigger than the other. "Keep going," she said. "I want to hear this."

"I don't mean to sound derogatory. Perhaps 'confidence' isn't the word. Maybe it's something else—presence, you know. More subtle than confidence. God," added Diane, "you mustn't listen to me."

"I'm just so out of it and dull. It's depressing."

"Well, keep running," urged Diane, "said the out-of-shape advocate for aerobic fitness."

"Running brings me up for like an hour, that's it. Otherwise, I just feel so down."

Diane the Coke Dealer knew this was her cue, but in the case of Emily the Pathetic Drip she just couldn't be like the *Reefer Madness* guy who hands out free joints to kids. She felt auntish about this pigeon-toed loser. "Emily," she said, "come on, now, cheer up." This got Emily to smile, wanly. "Top totty, you are. What you might call a babe." She said "a babe" in hyperbolic frat-boy. "Shall we go out on the pull, you and I? Find a handsome stud to chat you up?"

At ten, they visited the Pelican on this mission, Emily wearing too much blush and drinking too many piña coladas before claiming to have a "migrainy headache" while Just for Kicks was tuning up. So be it. You couldn't actually change the world. So that was the right moment for a rail of gratis coke, hoovered bravely in a powder-room stall, and afterward it was fun to see Emily, that long-stemmed shrinking violet, out on the dance floor with her arms overhead, trying hard to look sultry and orgasmic and, in her own stupid way, succeeding. This new Emily, horny and on coke, eventually left Diane missing the old one. She took a cab home, where she sprawled on the couch watching *Top of the Pops*. In the morning, the television was still on.

An adequate life: nothing more. Here she was, the resident coke dealer to kids holding down their first real jobs. She was full of people, but vulnerable to nostalgia. It was embarrassing, for example, to be Diane Burroughs in front of Diane Burroughs when Gilbert O'Sullivan sang "Alone Again (Naturally)" and got her all mired and choked up. And yet the Irishman's smarmy ballad did drive her to tears. "To think that only yesterday, / I was cheerful, bright and gay"—that pulled Diane into a wallow. The same thing happened when she opened a letter from the constable, densely written in a shaky hand, mentioning bunions on top of his diabetes. Pathetic John, poor dear old John. But, then, Diane had other moods, too, wherein she wanted to fire back, BUGGER OFF, YOU BORE.

Mornings were better. Always looking for hot stocks, Diane spent a lot of hours at the library, researching the market anxiously, and fretting over pulling this or that trigger with a call to Schwab. Sometimes she made the call, but mostly she watched while the Dow passed 1800 and accelerated coke sales. Diane joined a gym called Serious Fitness where muscular Shane, the cabaña-party king, was an assistant manager, and where Kelly and Ted worked out. Tightly packed with large exercise machines, loud with music, and lined with mirrors, Serious Fitness was for the most part tense, humorless, and male, but its lobby included a smoothie bar and tables where Diane, freshly showered, could cultivate customers, and where she found herself, before long, filling orders for buyers more dubious than her usual suspects: a guy who was in and out of bouncer jobs, a guy hamstrung by a restraining order, a guy on probation following a nightclub assault, a guy who was fencing stolen everything and wanted to trade coke for jewelry and state-of-the-art stereo equipment. Diane stayed cash-only, though, and since she had plenty of it now, it was sort of hard to get off this wheel, especially when its momentum made her so flush she felt nervous hiding her money beneath her mattress and was forced, by paranoia, to get a safety-deposit box. There her cash sat in neat, banded stacks, just as it had in Sullivan's Gulch, looking all the harder to resist.

It was in the middle of this period of soaring coke trade that Club called. It was 11 p.m. and he was at a telephone booth in downtown Seattle, saying, "Guess what, I'm in your neck of the woods. Fancy a pint, luv?"

She met him at the J&M Cafe, which had a pressed-tin ceiling and a mahogany bar. What had attracted Club to the J&M, though, was the price of its "Yankee excuse for lager"; when she showed up, he had a pitcher in front of him and was drinking, alone, with his back to a wall and one hand in the pocket of his peacoat. Dangling a cigarette from his lips, he explained himself: he'd been at sea but was unemployed just now on account of a hankering for a lark, and he'd been bouncing a little on saved-up funds from San Diego to Whitefish via bus rides and hitching. Now he'd come this way to look her up, if for no other reason than that Diane was family. "Maybe it's just the booze talking," he said, "but I'm looking back on things right now." Which was good, because Diane was looking back, too.

She took Club in out of curiosity, and for his entertainment value, and because remembering her childhood had become, for her, an increasingly common sentimental pastime. Club was a penny-pincher but not a soaker or gouger, and regularly ate tinned clams for supper, with pilot bread and ale. "Problem with the States," he said, "can't get a decent pint," which to him meant a can of Boddingtons. Diane found some Boddingtons in a specialty store, and they took a goodly supply to The Palms' Building B laundry center, stuffed in their loads, and played single-deck canasta. As their roiling clothes slapped the innards of the machines, they both got started down the road toward arseholed and jointly disparaged their recently deceased mother, who'd boxed Club's ears so frequently he'd finally left—that was the reason Club gave for fleeing at fourteen, that and the urge to join a skiffle band. And he had skiffled a bit, in London, at first, but not a penny to show for it, though later in London he'd learned to do stick-'n'-poke ink, which paid a few bob, and then he showed Diane the Celtic dragon on his shoulder—well drawn, in flames, and intricately pigmented—he'd had done at sixteen. He'd next been to sea, he said, and had his papers.

They were sixteen months apart and, off and on, had lived in the same house, so they could remember finding nothing in the kitchen, and sitting on the stove with the oven on for warmth and a blanket nailed across the doorframe while listening to the Light Programme, the mention of which now set off a blistering bout of recall—*Journey into Space, The Goon Show, Riders of the Range, Pick of the Pops,* "the frigging Cliff Adams Singers," "frigging Jimmy Clitheroe," "frigging Mr. Higginbottom," "frigging Alfie Hall." They'd both liked heaps of white sugar taken straight, and Marmite and margarine on toast, and pilfering tea biscuits, and shoplifting, and gin when they could get it, and puff except that puff was frigging dear, and frigging Tommy Steele and the Steelmen. But then Club, with no warning, had decamped for London.

Club pressed to know where Diane's money came from, and she told him she was a dealer. "Did you apply for citizenship as a dealer, then?" Club asked. "Are they short on dealers in the States here, luv?" So she had to explain what a green card was, and that by marrying Jim, and staying with him for three years, she'd earned the right to be naturalized and could even vote now, if she wanted to—though thus far she hadn't taken any interest—and was required to pay taxes on anything that didn't fly under the radar, which didn't matter, because everything she made flew under the radar. Club steered her back to his subject: dealing. Club knew his way, a little, around dealing, because in Liverpool he'd been a rock addict—after, he said, he'd weaned himself off skag. "Show me a Liverpudlian," he said, "and I'll show you a dealer." He'd even dealt himself for a while, but it was bloody dangerous, he said, because of the IRA. "You're shitting me," said Diane. "Come off it, Club."

Club only dragged that much harder on his fag. "No messin'," he said, as if hurt. "Heard of The Cleaners? Prop up the Merseyside mafia and all that? Me, I was dodging The Cleaners, you know. Pinched, I was. I did a runner."

He stayed on in Diane's second bedroom, drinking Boddingtons and talking like this, and sitting by the pool looking pale and strung out—at first—then painfully red. Diane saw that he was damaging her good reputation, and that The Palms' in-crowd treated him with kid gloves, but what did they know, and what could they know, other than the weirdness in *A Clockwork Orange*? Or what they read about football hooligans? For them, England didn't exist.

One night, she took Club to the Pelican for tap ale. He swallowed a lot without needing the loo—"one of me strong points," as he put it. She laughed at this and confessed to Club that beer never stopped for long in her, that she had a weak bladder, "like Mum had." "We all have our weak points, don't we?" Club answered. "Yours is running off to the bog." Then he celebrated his onion rings, but not Night Groove ("shite band of pimps"), sat at the bar bumming fags from people, and tried chatting up a trio of girls having nothing to do with him, except as a British basket case, threatening at first, but then comic. With his nifty elocutions and stream of cute jokes, Club made a valuable fool of himself for the benefit of people who felt smarter than he was. Coke King Mike was especially condescending, and didn't try to hide his amusement at Club as the avatar of English daft. But Club, after all his pints, was not remotely in his cups, and spoke to Mike in Mockney for Diane's sole amusement, sounding like Eliza Doolittle's da. "Wot," he said, "'ere's to ya, Mike. Cheers. That's me boy. Gawd, look at them bristols."

There was some trouble later, in the back, by a pool table, where a footballish-looking guy made the inebriated error of calling Club, rather loudly, Popeye, and got dropped with a hard flush right.

So Club came in handy. Say you wanted to sell eight thousand dollars' worth of blow to someone you didn't know; you could bring Club along, since he looked unpredictable—a dodgy Brit who might be off his rocker. Diane brought him. He liked his role—played it as a prickly, agitated, shiv-concealing ex-con—and got a sap out of a pawnshop case, and started carrying it inside his coat, along with pepper spray. Diane had to preface her transactions now with, "This is my brother, don't worry about him," but she could see people worrying anyway. Which was good.

Club, decked out in military-surplus fatigues, a stained, ribbed tank, and combat boots, started throwing dumbbells around at Serious Fitness, partly because he had time on his hands, but also, he said, "to back up my evil stare, Di, at crunch time." Club made some gym friends, other lowlifes and losers, two-bit bodybuilders who endorsed, while they worked out, amino acids and protein powders. There were televisions mounted in each corner of the weight room, usually playing MTV videos, and Club and his mates, between sets, gave commentary—thumbs up for Aerosmith's "Dude (Looks like a Lady)" and for fucking Madonna in "Who's That Girl?," thumbs down for fucking Run-D.M.C. and the fucking-all lame Steve Winwood. Nevertheless, Club exercised judgment in mixed company and, at least at The Palms, was generally a gentleman whose sense of decorum had an element of the maudlin only if, like Diane, you were looking for it. At home he was impeccably, even rigorously, not a problem, and if somebody like Emily came to the apartment, he had the good sense to sidle out. He'd say two or three polite, safe things, then rise, take his jacket off a hook, and declare that

he was "off on a peregrination"—he applied class deference and reassuring syntax so that no one would be scared to show up. The gormless
Emily didn't seem to mind him, though, except for his fags. She treated
him as if he wasn't a mongoloid, and he started hanging around when
she called—for popcorn and Hearts—and going out to the railing
to blow his smoke rings over the swimming pool so Emily wouldn't
cough.

Since Club's visa was post-deadline, he couldn't work legally. What he
could do was stand around on Western Avenue near Bell Street with a lot
of other charity cases and wait for a contractor to pull over in search of
shovel labor. This way he met some on-parole roofers and got a bit of a
paid stint doing the vilest work they had, and then he met a mason who
needed a hod carrier on a major job, someone willing to break his back
for shite. Club was the ticket. He told Diane he'd done like jobs in Man-
chester, not just the two thousand bricks a day but brewing tea for the
layers. The Yanks didn't want tea, he added; here what they wanted was to
snort all his blow, one or two bumps at a time.

But that was fine. Club just developed his own two-bit customers. He
was like a kid about it—that is, he brought his tens and twenties to
Diane, except what he held back for menthols, ale, and big plastic sacks
of black licorice. Then, one day, he came home empty-handed and
ripped off, but only to get what he called "his tools," which now included
a Colt .45.

She took him with her to a hand-off at The Aegean, an innocent-
enough-looking café with potted hothouse plants, a fat owner in a short-
sleeved shirt, posters of Mykonos and the Parthenon, and at the register a
display case of homemade baklava. They were meeting two community-
college kids who looked like steroid users—friends of friends at Serious
Fitness—and who, when Diane and Club arrived, were eating big meals
at a table for two. "Babe, you brought a dude," one observed. "Not cool."
Club dragged two chairs over and sat in his backward. He shook hands
with the bodybuilders, who called themselves Lance and CJ, then cleared
his throat, scratched his Adam's apple, and looked around the room as if
he worked for Scotland Yard. Club was so good that "Lance" stopped eating and said, "What's up? You nervous?"

"Yeah," said Club. "I get a bit nervous. Apologies for that, mate.
Nerves."

Diane said, "Club's sort of fucked up, I guess you could say, from some shit times he had in the Falklands."

The bodybuilders were interested in the Falklands, it turned out, so they talked about the Falklands for a while. By a stroke of good fortune, Club was an expert. He bullshitted with ease; he talked about the Gurkhas; he extolled the prowess of the Argentines. There was five minutes of *mano a mano* combat talk, followed by a slice of baklava for Diane and, for Club, two consecutive Winstons. Finally, and abruptly, Lance said, "This is pretty simple, babe. Put it this way. We know where you live. We know your name."

"Oh, come on," said Diane. "There's no problem between us." She picked up her gym bag and put it on the table. "So you know where I live," she said, "but let's just sit here, finish our coffee, and talk like friends, because we are friends, right?" She said this looking directly at Club, as if he were a dog about to be unleashed. "Am I right, mate? Friends, now? Caleb? Are we friends?"

Club scratched his neck and nodded, eyes averted. "Hmmm," Diane said. "You guys should show the cash, then. Product's on the table, so it's time to show the cash. You show me the cash, then take my product to the gents', do what you want in there, you know, test it, then I take the cash and make my count in the ladies' while my brother and you boys hang out."

The steroidal-looking guys began nodding at each other. "Cash," Club said. "On the table."

"Fuck you," said Lance, scooping up Diane's gym bag. "Wait here. I'll test this in the can."

"Whoa," said Club. "You skipped a step, mate." Casually, he unzipped his sheepskin bomber jacket and showed both bodybuilders the grip of his pistol. "Either of you lads drink Colt .45?" he asked. "It'd be my pleasure to order you a round."

"In a restaurant?" asked Lance. "Come on, dude."

"Try me," said Club. "Now get your mitts off that bag."

After that, it was as Diane had said. There was no more trouble from the college kids. Back from the loo—where first she'd urgently emptied her bladder, then made a speedy count of the bills—Diane told them, "You and the blow can go now, all right? And no hard feelings, because we don't have any. No worries, right? Just run along. My mate will be picking up the tab."

When they were gone, Club said, "Round of canasta in the laundro, then, mate?"

"Colt .45, I like that," Diane answered.

Club laughed. "Man's best friend," he said. "Levels the turf. Classic Yankee game-changer, the tried-and-true boom-stick. Speaks to the natives every time." He slid the bag of cash toward Diane. Winking, he said, "Same mum, different das, but still, you know, birds of a feather, luv. Peas in a pod and all of that."

At The Palms that night they drank celebratory Boddingtons, listened to used albums Club had come across, sang along to "Apeman" and "Lola," and finally, like a married couple, ate popcorn while watching *Letterman.*

"Domesticated, that's me," said Club. "Tamed. Fat. A jolly couch potato."

"Every summer we can rent a cottage in the Isle of Wight if it's not too dear," said Diane.

"And sell 'em blow," said Club. "Now pass the popcorn."

She gave him five hundred dollars, which he used to buy a touring bike with a melted wiring harness. Club fixed that via what he described to her as "triage" and made a hobby out of fair-weather rides.

On-the-go Emily went to work for Microsoft, which, as she put it to Diane, was kind of like Aldus but with fifteen hundred people. Now she was excited about Frisbee golf with colleagues, and dating "a very sweet guy" named Gray, who'd introduced her to recreational racewalking. Her company stock had doubled in the few months she'd had it; Emily was buying a new wardrobe.

Microsoft sent Emily to a conference in Atlanta—paid for everything, for the first time in her life—and she manipulated her flights to straddle a weekend so she could meet an old college friend in Nashville. At home again in her apartment at The Palms, showing Diane photos of clubs on Bourbon Street, Emily said she'd sort of cheated on Gray by "stumbling" with a cute guy to his hotel room, though she'd stopped short of "going all the way." Diane said maybe they should test her fidelity with drinks at the Pelican, but Emily preferred Ginger's because of its martini list. As soon as they sat down on a sofa at Ginger's, Emily pointed out a guy "worth probably about twenty million right now." She knew other people, too, at Ginger's, who were in the middle of getting rich.

The martini list was humorless, overwrought, and precious. You could have one made with cocoa-flavored vodka, or garnished with anchovy, but whatever you asked for, it came to the table as if under a spotlight, and in a cocktail glass with a mouth so wide it could have been a nut bowl. Diane and Emily had two martinis each while trying not to spill, and Emily made clothing comments: she predicted that people would look back on parachute pants with, "What were they thinking?," and she thought Guess jeans were tacky. Diane asked, point-blank, about sex with Gray, and learned that he and Emily weren't doing it yet, because Emily didn't want "to go all the way unless it's exactly the right guy."

Emily wondered if Diane wanted to meet people, and Diane said, "Why wouldn't I want to meet millionaires?" Then they accompanied their martinis to the bar so they could hang out with two of Emily's colleagues—girls who were nice but not interested in Diane, not even in her English accent. They were sharing a plate of hummus and pita, next to which sat travel brochures. Marnie's strong teeth were like what's-her-name, on the news, who was sort of a Kennedy but married to Arnold Schwarzenegger—New England, whole-milk, good schools. Whitney wore Laura Ashley with white socks and Keds and was obviously smart in a quiet way, but she and Marnie both looked soused, as if they'd stopped at Ginger's after work and hadn't moved from their bar stools for hours. They worked together in Human Relations, and the year before they'd gone to Belize for snorkeling, nightclubs, and trips to Mayan temples. Whitney described a reef, a rain forest, the resort they'd stayed at, a trail through a jungle, a well-prepared red-snapper fillet, and a trip to Guatemala by water taxi. Marnie let her, adding nods, then said Grand Cayman had been "a major dud. Tiki bars and calypso. Sort of a theme park. There's no there there," she explained. "Where is it?"

Twenty minutes of this. Then, yes, they did want to buy some coke, so as to have it on hand for a party they were planning. Another friend was getting married, and they were in charge of some girls-only festivities at which coke would be a definite plus.

The next day, Diane bought a little black dress, in order to be arresting at Ginger's. Since it was better not to look too slutty, she added a cashmere sweater and loafer pumps. She fit in after that, but her metamorphosis wasn't complete until she went all the way and had her hair pixie-cut. With kohl-like mascara around the eyes just to bring things down a little, she quickly attracted some tentative come-ons and some furtive but motivated coke customers. In other words, Ginger's was worth frequenting. Diane couldn't take Club there, because Club was too coarse, but that didn't matter, because sales to the tech sector were innocent and safe, lucrative with no hint of danger. Order a martini, chat, close the deal, and go your separate ways with nothing threatening or sinister. The profit margins were better, too. And the buyers, for the most part, were guys who understood discretion. In the main they were pensive and understated *techie riche,* with bad wardrobes and terrible haircuts, who wanted blow, Diane knew, as a social invigorator—as an expensive Saturday-night confidence builder that would make them feel like cocks-of-the-walk when in fact they were mouse-clicking nerds. These guys, as a rule, conducted themselves as if Diane was off limits, as if the dealer was a dealer, not a date. Though her vanity was wounded by that, she didn't blame herself, because beyond-reproach computer geeks were not a good measure of desirability; on the other hand, she had to wonder a little, given that she was on the way to forty. In this frame of mind, on a Saturday, at Ginger's, she engaged a blueblood with a cleft chin who, on entering the bar, made no effort to conceal from Diane his interest in her boobs. He just looked right at them while passing by, and then he looked Diane in the eye, as if they were communing over the possibility of a stand-up snog in the loo.

They hung out, with their martinis, at a high table for two. His name was Ron Dominick, and he worked "as a consultant to the software industry." He wore a white shirt and jacket, black jeans, sharp shoes, and an amused expression. She gave him a reading, then activated her accent—the *Pride and Prejudice* approach—before revealing that she was divorced and lived alone, not far away, in Kirkland. Ron confessed to being married, but there were no kids, and his marriage was "sort of on the skids." He liked glam rock and seemed rather hopeful that Diane's British derivation might yield some insight into glam rock's roots. Beneath his all-American smile he was a dedicated and even relentless ironist, which Diane found wearying. Nevertheless, she carried on without flagging, because coke had come into the conversation early. He said, "As I understand it from those in the know, you deal."

"Not really. But I'm nice to my friends."

Ron put his business card on the table. "Check me out," he said, and pushed it toward her. "Am I cool or what?" he added. "Listen to me."

"Okay."

"Just okay? Am I that unfunny?" When she nodded her assent he added, "So the dude you divorced—left his socks on the floor? Toilet seat up?"

"I didn't want kids. And there was nothing to talk about."

"That sounds generic."

"Well. So it is."

"Was he mediocre in bed?"

"We hit it off there."

"Is that a throw-down?"

"Maybe, maybe not."

"Now I'm intimidated," Ron said. "What have I gotten myself into?"

She didn't tell him. Instead, three nights later, when he'd checked out as not a narc, she gave him a sample in Ginger's parking lot, where he stood beside his Alfa Romeo with his jacket hanging on his index finger, one hip cocked disco fashion, two parodic gold chains around his neck—a strapping guy with attitude and wit—saying, "What if I take, like, twenty grams?"

"That's five grand."

"I'll give you three."

"You sound like a dealer."

"Not really. But I'm nice to my friends," said Ron.

"Are you a dealer?"

"My hook-up bailed."

Diane said, "I can't sell for three. Find someone else at that price."

"What about four?"

"I can't do that, either."

"What about getting a room with me, then?"

"That's very cute," said Diane.

He lunged, grabbed her by the waist, and kissed her. Diane wished he hadn't gone overboard with the Old Spice, because the cloves made her gag. It was an asphyxiation she associated with more than one less-than-entirely-triumphant night as Candy Dark. It was the smell of choking on unlovable men, powerful narcissists, and insistent strangers. And now this Ron was taking his turn, smelling, underneath his cheap cologne, like gym clothes. She hated him intensely. Transactional sex had sometimes been rank with the exudates of desperate men, and sometimes clinical and antiseptic, but, however it was, it paid by definition, whereas this was point-blank pillage. "Okay," she said, when Ron unlocked his lips. "Let's get a room, then."

Ron was a reliable high-stakes buyer, and since his own clientele was so well-to-do, he could afford to pay more before markup. He liked room service, and he liked Diane with her black dress wrinkled and her mascara running. He liked to talk about his customers, but not by name— guys he knew from Willamette University, guys at an athletic club, guys, he said, who ran companies. Ron's attitude toward Diane, when not needy, was collegial—two dealers in the sack, trading insider insights— and it was good for his ego, in this arena, to feel that he had the upper hand. "I have a serious launderer," he told her. "Guy's great. Not somebody you mess with. Connected, backed up. Basically, I bank with him— dirty money in, clean money out. Used to be I smurfed, but you do that enough you get paranoid. You smurf?"

"Smurf?"

She let him drone on about it, about a shell company with a bullet-proof balance sheet that his launderer used, banking in the Caymans, money-counting machines—whatever he needed to drone on about. Sometimes he was so relaxed and unprotected that he engaged her in the intimate emotions of his marriage as if she were his therapist or counselor. His wife, a cosmetician, was petulant, he complained, and moody in the extreme, and pouted when they argued, and liked to have her car detailed more often than was necessary. She was in the habit of telling him how he felt instead of listening to him when he told her how he felt. She was impulsive, impetuous, and hyper-susceptible, she couldn't relax, she was anxious about her work and about people at work, and liked to talk about people at work he didn't know and therefore didn't care about. "I know I'm not being fair," he said. "There's two sides to everything, and I'm sure she sees it differently." Diane let him confide in her and kept her comments private, because Ron bought a lot of coke, and why not make life easier by dispensing with the penny-ante sales and living off a middleman's—or middlewoman's—markup? In the margin lay considerable free time.

Then, one night, postcoitally and casually, Ron announced that it was time to repair his marriage. He and his wife were getting counseling now, very good counseling that Ron believed in, so he'd decided that, in good faith, he had to stop seeing Diane, except, he hoped, as a business associate, if she knew what he meant. She did, of course—money was money, she told him. So they stopped sleeping together, and she sold him his coke across a table at Ginger's, in quick exchanges that were, Ron's smile said, strictly about cash. "Wanker," Diane thought. Couldn't he have missed the sex a little more? Was she really that dispensable?

She told Club about the execrable Ron Dominick: his blather about his money launderer and his wife, his white shirts, jackets, and black jeans. Club chewed licorice with the news on, barefoot, a can of Boddingtons and the *TV Guide* beside him, a package of Winstons rolled up in his sleeve. "We ought to take a stab at the bastard," he said. "Take him for everything he's worth."

"Yes, let's," Diane answered.

Club took a pull from his Boddingtons, wiped at his week's worth of beard with his wrist, and said, "I don't mean hypothetical. And you ought to think twice before you say yes. Diddlin' the wrong bastard got me run out of Liverpool."

"Kirkland isn't Liverpool. And this guy's a fool."

"Good, then," said Club. "Let's nail his arse."

They cemented the deal over copious Boddingtons, and, in between Diane's trips to the loo, ate licorice, conspired, and watched television. Eventually, Club said he wanted to sleep on it. In the morning, she found him in his tank top and fatigues, lacing up for a go at pumping iron, because pumping iron was "conducive to strategizing." She went along for a bout with a stationary bike, where she alternated between dreaming up con ideas and contemplating Club, who wore headphones and had a Walkman in his pocket. Later, they convened in the lobby, near the smoothie bar, where Club, with a shower towel draped around his neck, drank a Pepsi, downed two granola bars, and looked around, furtively, to see who was listening. "Okay, how about this?" he said, dropping his voice. "Next time you see this bloke, tell him you're getting out of the business and won't be dealing anymore. Pretend you're sorry and that. You buy him a drink or whatever, act like you feel bad, then tell him since you're getting out you could set him up direct to your supplier, but for a finder's fee. Twenty percent, I'd say. You get him to agree he's buying, let's pick a number, twenty grand, then you tell him you want four off the top. He'll argue, and that's fine, just take what it takes to keep him in without looking like you're willing to take just anything, because if you're too easy that's a signal to a target."

"This guy does big deals," Diane answered. "Twenty grand would be easy for him. He's good for fifty, I reckon."

Club put a little crimp in his Pepsi can. "Fuck it, then, let's double that," he said. "You tell him you're going to discuss it with your supplier, and then you get back to him with a hundred grand; you tell him your guy doesn't do small change, isn't interested in small beer. What have you been charging this wanker?"

"A lot," Diane said. "Two fifty a gram."

"This time give him a break," said Club. "Let's say a hundred seventy-five a gram. He ought to go for that deal."

Diane was impressed. Maybe, she thought, Club wasn't bullshitting about the Merseyside mafia. Sure, he looked skuzzy, pop-eyed, and erratic, but inside, Club was a clear-eyed manipulator. "Club," she said, "how am I getting that much blow? We'll need to put up seventy grand."

"How much do we have?"

"Something like fifty."

"What about your stocks?"

"Twenty. Thereabouts."

Club put a hand to his face like *The Thinker*. "Hmmm," he said. "Cutting it a bit fine. What do you think about backing down our numbers?"

"Tell me the rest," Diane said.

Club looked around again. "So this is what's up," he said. "You tell this wanker your supplier wants his payout in twenty packets, fifty fresh hundreds in each, each held with one large metal paper clip, the twenty packets in a gym bag, and you tell him to call you when he's got it ready, and not to forget your cut. In fact, you should act like that's your big concern, make a row about your cut. Then," said Club, "once he tells you he's got the cash, wait twenty-four hours minimum. Then you ring him up and tell him your supplier's ready to meet. Tell him to stay by his phone and that you'll call him eleven a.m. tomorrow. Something like that. You call him back, and you give him an hour. You tell him to come right here, this table. This table, Diane, right here, this table. You call him from the pay phone right here."

Diane was smiling now. "Club," she said. "I didn't know you were such a criminal."

"Another life," answered Club. "Just dredging up the old tried-and-tested Club. Finding him proper American employment."

Diane laughed. "So we get Ron here," she said. "Ron 'the Wanker' Dominick, with his loaded gym bag."

"We get him here with his gym bag, correct. We sit at this table, right here, this table, and you introduce me as your supplier, Club. Just call me Club, tell him I'm your brother, everything aboveboard, nothing to hide. Then leave things to me. Bloke might be armed, might bring muscle, the muscle could be announced or that poof over there." Club aimed his chin at a guy reading a newspaper. "Poof like that walks in, takes a seat, acts innocent, reads the news, really he's your target's—what would you call it?—henchman. Accomplice."

"Right."

"So we have to assume he's a genius, this Ron. Possibly a genius who's nervous and packing—good American word, 'packing.' High stakes and all that. Game's on. No bullshit." Club dropped his Pepsi can onto its side. "People get topped over money, Diane, and I don't want it to be you or me."

"No."

"But in case, I'm bringing the Colt, you know. For a breakdown in the proceedings."

"We'll hope for no breakdown," Diane said.

Club tugged the wrinkles out of his shirt, leaned toward her, and dipped his head. "Tell me something," he said. "In the ladies' changing room, they have a cubicle for a toilet, right? With a lock on the door? Am I right or what? Because this place, you can see, was built on the cheap. Savings everywhere—shoddy plasterboard. Another thing they do is get the plumbing back to back. Saves on pipe runs. Now, in the gents' chang-ing room we have a cubicle, too, and in there we have a floor vent, the louvered type, for forced-air heat, which I prized up, and, sure enough, it's a split end-run, with the other side, I'm thinking, feeding heat to the ladies' side. But this we need to verify, important point. Linchpin point. So let's both of us, right now, take a trip to the toilet. Lock yourself in, prize the vent cover off, and we'll chat through the duct—you get my drift?"

They verified. When Diane pried the vent out, she heard Club say, "Good. Now here comes my hand." Then she saw his fingers, wiggling, in the vent, followed by a vigorous thumbs-up, and she reached in and touched his coarse thumb tip. "Bingo," said Club, through the vent, happily. "This guy's fucked."

Once again—back at 226—they cracked a festive series of Boddingtons. Diane, giddy now, digested the details. Club knew a hod carrier who had "at-a-glance C-notes," counterfeits that were cheap to come by because of weak borders, blurry seals, and unaligned serial numbers. They'd never pass close inspection, but they were good enough for exchanges with unsuspecting parties. "So what we do is," said Club, "we put a good note on top, the rest bad, twenty packets set up like that, two thousand worth of good, the rest bad—ninety-eight thousand. I pass his all-good bills through the vent to you, you pass our mostly bad ones back to me, simple as that."

"I don't know," said Diane. "Ron'll notice and retrace his steps. And when he gets in the loo there a second time, he's probably going to notice the vent. And then he's on to us."

"Drink up," said Club. "We're smarter than he is. We'll make up a block you can wedge in the breach, luv. If he wants to stick his hand in, he won't find it goes anywhere."

"He'll still be coming after us, Club."

"Drink to Mr. Colt, then. Cuz when jolly Ron shows, I'll be on the business end. Sending him off to see his launderer about his frigging fucked bills or whatever his problem is."

The next day, he brought a gift for Diane. "I picked up this sweet little snubnose," he said. "Thirty-eight special. Fits in your purse. Case you need some protection, luv, that I'm not around to give."

Club chose a Saturday, because, he said, on Saturday there'd be people at Serious Fitness. As called for by his plan, he rode his touring bike to the showdown. Diane, in her street clothes, looked freshly post-workout, with her hair still wet as if from the shower, though actually she'd just wet it in the bathroom. It was noon, the gym was busy, the girl at the smoothie bar turned the pages of a magazine, a couple at a far table watched MTV, some guys nearby were doing nothing, just sitting. Diane had a comb and brush on the table, and on the floor beside her sat her gym bag and her purse. Inside the gym bag was a sheet-metal duct plug Club had rigged up, and twenty packets of paper-clipped counterfeit hundreds, each with an authentic bill showing. In the purse was the .38 special Diane had only the barest idea how to shoot. Club had a plastic grocery bag in his lap with its looped handles knotted, which made him look tacky, but draped across his seat back was a new overcoat with his Colt in one of its pockets.

Ron showed up. Sure enough, he brought muscle, a slabbish sort whose efficient body language bespoke the martial arts. "This is my buddy, my buddy Jason," Ron said, "and he's totally cool and mellow."

Jason wore a belted black leather jacket and an expression that announced, "I could kick your ass if I wanted to." "Greetings," he said, then sat, and, with hooded eyes, evaluated the girl at the smoothie bar while covering his mouth with the web between his thumb and forefinger. Diane guessed he was probably in for a free gram or something equally paltry.

Club said, "I hope you found the place all right."

"We found it," said Ron. "Yep. That's right. It was exactly where Diane said it would be. Hey, Diane," he went on. "Introduce us."

"He's my half-brother," said Diane. "His name's Caleb."

Club looked thoroughly inane in his getup. How serious could some-one be in nylon shorts, an Axl Rose T-shirt, and plastic fisherman's san-dals? He said, quietly, "I have two-point-three-three ounces in my bag here, Ron. That's sixty-six grams. What do you have?"

"As requested," Ron replied. "Thank you."

"Is it clean cash? Did you go to a good launderer?"

"My guy's cool," answered Ron.

Club scratched the inside of his thigh, pinched his nose, and pulled at the inflamed-looking bags beneath his eyes. "Here's what I'm going to propose," he said. "You and me take a trip to the locker room. Jason can come along if he wants. In the locker room there's a toilet, locked door.

Scale in there. All the time you need. I hand you my bag, you go in, lock the door, weigh, test, make sure things check out. I wait outside. Me and Jason wait together, if that's what you want. Then you come out, you hand me your bag, I go in and count, while you wait outside, or while you and Jason wait. I—"

"No," said Ron. "We should stay eye to eye. We should go in the can together, you and me, I do my thing, you do yours, we come out and go our separate ways."

Club shook his head. "Tight quarters," he said. "We're keeping it public. No knife in the back, mate. Okay?"

Ron did the same thing Jason was doing—propped an elbow on the table and covered his mouth. "I don't know," he said finally.

"Come on, now," said Club. "I don't know you from Adam. You don't want to make a buy, that's fine. Sorry to have troubled you coming out here, but there's a way I need to do things, every time. Safety first," he added.

"As long as it's not the rip-off way."

"How am I going to rip you off? You're out there with the stash while I'm in there with the cash. And I don't have a Jason," Club pointed out.

"Come on," said Ron. "I mean, like you say, we don't know each other and—"

"Okay," said Club, "Let's call the thing off."

"No," said Ron. "We don't have to do that."

"I'm serious," said Club. "No worries. We'll call it off."

Ron ran both hands, a quick groom, through his hair. He sat back and sighed. He nodded at Jason. "Fuck it," he said. "Let's go for it."

Diane now took up her comb and said, "Good. Because I still want my cut."

"Don't worry about it," said Ron. "That's separate."

"I'll worry until I've got it, big boy."

"You'll get it."

"So you say."

"Let's move," said Club.

When he stood, he looked like a workingman on Spanish holiday—red-faced, decked out for sun, pale British legs on display. Jason, Diane saw, was holding back laughter, but Ron looked a little disoriented. They left for the locker room, and, surreptitiously, Diane scanned the Serious Fitness lobby. The girl at the front desk was folding towels, the girl at the smoothie bar was watching television, a girl and guy at a far table were talking, a guy checked in and went to the locker room, the girl at the front desk fielded a phone call, a guy came bursting out of the weight room and, wad of keys in hand, left. Diane didn't think anyone was secretly Ron's "accomplice," but, just in case, she stuck with the plan, which called for her to open her purse, search for and then draw out a tube of lipstick, collect her comb and brush, pick up her bags, and head for the women's locker room.

Someone in the locker room was lacing up running shoes, but other than that, the place was empty. Diane went immediately to the private toilet, locked herself in, peed, assessed her face in the mirror, applied the lipstick, and combed her hair. Then she knelt, opened her gym bag, and pried up the vent cover. After a while, there was Club's hand, giving her a bolstering, confident thumbs-up, followed by comically wiggling fingers. She touched them to let him know she was there, and then she fed in the packets of fake bills. When they were gone, Ron's good bills appeared in Club's hand, and she put those inside her emptied gym bag. There was a final, salutatory thumbs-up from Club, which she answered with a concluding squeeze of his thumb tip before stuffing the sheet-metal plug into the duct and pressing the vent cover back into place. Then she gathered up her things, looked in the mirror again, and returned to the table in the lobby. She set the gym bag next to her foot and took a paperback book from her purse.

Club had it worked out to the last detail. He came from the locker room with the coke bag in his hand, put it on the chair seat in front of him, and slipped into his overcoat. Now he looked, quite hilariously, like a flasher, but he also looked angry, strained at the neck. "Fuck it," he said to Ron. "I'm outa here."

"I still don't get it," Ron said. "What's your problem?"

"I'm out of here," said Club. "Keep your counterfeits. In fact, shove them up your arse."

He shrugged more deeply into his coat, picked up the coke bag, left Ron's money bag on the table, whirled on his heels, and burst out the door.

Ron looked perplexed. He turned to Jason and said "Huh?," and then he turned, with a furrowed forehead, toward Diane. "Jesus," he said. "What just happened?"

"Apparently, he didn't like your cash," Diane answered. "I think you might have fucked up."

"Me?" said Ron. "*I* fucked up?" He hit himself in the chest with an open palm. "Diane," he said, "thanks for nothing."

After that, she let him insult Club all he wanted. That was his business. That was his call. Ron's anxious and worried voice—it was something she'd have to put up with for a few minutes. She apologized to him—"Club's cranky," she offered. "He gets paranoid for no reason. Maybe we can set up another try, Ron, after I get him calmed down."

"Are you kidding?" said Ron. "I wouldn't do business with him again ever. Not after bullshit like this."

"Have it your way, then," said Diane.

She left. She thought it would be best to go straight to her bank and deposit the hundred grand in her box, but, unfortunately, it was Saturday. Never mind that, though, it was time to celebrate, not only the money but also the blow, which she could turn around for another hundred. Club had figured out a way to take her seventy thousand and almost triple it, just like that. Why was he living like such a lowlife?

When she came through the door of 226, there was Club on the couch with his Boddingtons. He'd changed into jeans and battered athletic shoes; the bag of coke was on the coffee table in front of him. "Trouble?" he said.

"None."

"Then victory is ours."

"Payback," Diane answered. "He deserved it."

She put the cash on the table beside the coke bag. Club poured Diane a Boddingtons eagerly. They clinked their glasses and drank to themselves. Club made a fist, he stamped the floor, he raised his hand in the Black Power salute and then gave God a thumbs-up. "That's why Britannia rules the waves," he exclaimed. "That's why the sun never sets on the British Empire. That's mad dogs and Englishmen," he said. "We took that fucking arsehole to the cleaners. We ate him for fucking lunch. We wiped the floor with him. We *rimmed* that poof." Club raised his ale glass one more time. "What a stupid fuck," he added.

Diane said, "We're rich!"

"Made, we're fucking made, we're made, we got it made. It's just like they say—land of opportunity. Person pulls himself up by his bootstraps. With freedom for all—let's drink to that!"

They kept drinking Boddingtons. And now it was pleasurable to revisit the con, and especially to cover its more precarious moments, when things might have crashed but for their stiff English upper lips. They did this until Diane had to pee, at which point Club said, "Off to the loo, then," and picked up the TV remote.

"Be right back."

"Okay, luv. See you in a jif."

But when she came back to the living room, Club, the coke, and the money were all gone, and by the time she got out to the parking lot, running, his touring bike was gone as well.

8

The King of Search

Ed, while at Stanford, saw his grandfather on occasion. Pop didn't live too far from him, or as he put it the first time Ed called him, "North on 101 and—boom—like that you're at the campus of Stanford University. Stanford," Pop added enthusiastically, "is just for the highest, the cream of the crop. Only the best get accepted to Stanford. There was a wonderful Jewish player there, '77, Dolph Schayes," at which point Ed chimed in with a correction: "I don't think Schayes played at Stanford, Pop. I think he played somewhere else."

"What?" said Pop. "I'm losing my head. That's right—Stanford was the son, *Danny* Schayes."

"That's not right, either, Pop. Danny played college ball at Syracuse."

"Are you playing ball for Stanford?"

"Me?"

"Basketball."

"Pop," said Ed, "I'm not that good. I couldn't even be their water boy."

Pop said, "Okay, fine, you win, but here's what, I'm taking you out for Chinese, Edeleh. That is, if you don't mind an over-the-hill type. You name the date. Go ahead. Shoot. Me, I'm twiddling these thumbs of mine, but you? You're busy. Doing what?"

"Math."

"Since when are you mathematics?"

"Since always. A long time."

"*Oy*, my head," answered Pop.

In San Jose, on the Chinese-food evening, it took them a while to find Chan's. Ed drove the Honda he'd gotten for his eighteenth birthday—Alice had wrapped a red ribbon around it and tied a bow on its roof, and Dan had sprung for an AAA membership, insurance, chains, and a gas credit card—while Pop directed Ed to take lefts and rights, guiding them along the same blocks twice, until, after a lot of confusion, there was Chan's. They were shown to their seats by a dowager dressed in silk brocade whom Pop knew by name, except that at the moment he couldn't remember her name; she showed them to a booth and said, to Pop, "You don't want chopsticks," and to Ed, "You want chopsticks?"

"Either way. Both."

"This your grandson?"

"Stanford," answered Pop.

"And he so *handsome*," exclaimed their hostess. "Maybe he has big problem with girls!" She cackled, theatrically, then hurried away, while Ed crossed his arms and rolled his eyes.

After dinner, which was greasy and dominated by overcooked ginger, Pop insisted on a Sara Lee cheesecake that was waiting for them in his refrigerator. Besides, there was this miniseries, *The Blue and the Gray*, with Gregory Peck as Abraham Lincoln, that the two of them could watch on CBS while they had their wonderful dessert. Since his house and yard had become a burden, and also because he no longer drove, Pop now lived in a one-bedroom apartment in walking distance of Congregation Sinai, where he could ·*daven* with friends. "This bunch," he said, "they're dropping like flies. Already last month Sol Silver has a stroke, now we can't make a minyan every week. Park here, Ed, they don't give tickets."

The place smelled foul; the toilet wasn't clean; in the refrigerator Ed found moldy cheese. On Pop's low sofa, they ate the cheesecake and drank Shasta while watching their special miniseries. Pop nodded off after fifteen minutes, and Ed savored Kathleen Beller as a war nurse. Fifteen more minutes of *The Blue and the Gray*, and then he stuffed the paper dessert plates in the garbage, ate a second slice of cheesecake from

the pan, and wiped the kitchen counter in preparation for his exit. When
he came back to the sofa, Pop's eyes were open. "Simon," he said. "I'm
forty winks."

"Ed."

"Huh? Ed?"

"I'm Ed, not Simon."

"You're Ed?"

The next day, Ed called his mother about Pop. Alice called back, a
half-hour later, to report that she'd talked to a Pincus somebody or a
somebody Pincus who knew Pop from Congregation Sinai, and that this
Pincus confirmed what Ed was saying. Alice had also called the Jewish
Family and Children's Services in San Francisco, and JFCS was going to
send a social worker all the way out to San Jose who could assess Pop's
needs and make recommendations to Pop's family about the right course
of action. All of this, Alice said, "because you, Ed, are a loving and concerned grandson. Thank you, Ed, for your caring."

"You're making me cringe."

"But that's what mothers do," Alice cooed. "I don't care how old you
get, you'll always be my baby."

Dan, who was on the line, too, said, "It is really good of you to look
after Pop. He's getting kind of out of it, I guess."

"Signing off immediately," answered Ed. "Way, way too much
extolling."

In the opinion of the social worker from the JFCS, Pop needed occasional help and consistent monitoring. By Ed's sophomore year, though,
things had deteriorated, to the point where it was either a life sentence in
an assisted-living situation or regular in-home care. Pop was adamant
and refused to budge, so Alice found someone who would show up five
days a week to clean, cook, wash, and iron for him, and hired someone
else for weekends. The weekend help seemed to change from month to
month, but the weekday person was proficient and consistent. She was a
Soviet émigrée who'd been shepherded to the Bay Area by the Hebrew
Immigrant Aid Society—this, at first, was all Ed could discern, in part
because she was so profoundly purse-lipped that, no matter what he
asked, she hardly answered, and in part because her English was either
terrible or nonexistent: Ed couldn't tell which. He said, "Hello, I'm his
grandson, Ed King," and she answered with something he didn't compre-

hend, two or three words, or maybe one long word, in Russian, English, or something else. He said, "Tell me your name, please—*what is your name,*" and again she said something he couldn't catch. She stood in the doorway between the living room and kitchen with a set of folded towels on one arm, wearing a head scarf and cloddish pink running shoes, and looked at Ed as if he'd come to deport her. He said, "I'm Ed," and she tipped her head gravely and went down the hall toward the bathroom.

Pop was amused. "She says zilch," he told Ed. "She comes, cleans, organizes, maybe ten words, a few peeps, that's it—you know, hello, time for dinner, goodbye, that's the conversation we're having."

"So no English."

"She says 'hi.' "

"What's her name?"

"Zinaida. That much I know—Zinaida, that's it. You know my head, I don't know her last name, even though I heard it one time."

After a few minutes, Zinaida came back, and went into the kitchen. Ed watched, but she was so rapidly evasive—fleeing, it was clear—that he only caught a glimpse from behind. Her pants were nursing scrubs. She was shrouded by a bulky and bleakly gray sweatshirt. It was a house-bound outfit, though sometimes you saw something like it in a grocery aisle on a woman loading her cart with the cheapest brands and buying everything with coupons. Zinaida was dour, drab, impoverished, and inaccessible. She was what could be arranged for minimum wage by the Jewish Family and Children's Services. On the other hand, she made an adequate toasted cheese, knew how to open a can of tomato soup, and was willing to take dinner in the kitchen with Ed and Pop—albeit standing up with her back to them while she cleaned, wiped, scrubbed, and rinsed. Her hands stayed busy, Ed saw, at a deliberate and constant rate, but her efforts were punctuated by furtive bites of a sandwich, eaten, as she worked, with minimal jaw movement. Despite the hideous washer-woman head scarf, the sweatshirt, scrubs, and ersatz running shoes, despite her disoriented foreigner's disadvantage and tense, stony face, Zinaida moved in a self-possessed way, with neither servility nor disdain. When she was done in the kitchen and had left it as she'd found it—or, rather, as she'd established it in her brief regime: spotless—she donned a knock-off military parka, collected her handbag, which was really a shopping bag, nodded a farewell at Pop, and acknowledged, finally, that

Ed existed by shifting her eyes, however fleetingly, in his direction. Pop said, "Watch, I'm like a Russian guy here. *Do svidanya*, Zinaida!"

"Gud niite," she answered, and, with no more ado, released herself from Pop's apartment. "What did I tell you?" Pop asked, when the door shut. "Two words, three if you're blessed."

Ed came next to collect Pop for Thanksgiving—he was supposed to drive him to the airport for their flight to Seattle, where Dan and Alice would meet them. Pop, as usual, was nervous about air travel, not about being at thirty thousand feet but about being late for boarding the plane, so at eight he'd called Ed to remind him to come at two; at noon he'd called to be sure two was understood; at one he called to see if Ed had left yet; and at a quarter to two, when Ed arrived, he was pacing the living room with his coat over his arm and his suitcase poised by the door. "Bad luck," he said. "Zinaida wants a ride, because Zinaida lives close to the airport."

Zinaida looked less tacky this time, but still wore the scarf and the running shoes. She sat in the back seat with her faux military parka zipped and with its synthetic fur hood pushed back. "Der is Cen-trawl Expressvay," she said, and, "Der is Tomas Expressvay." It was complicated after that, a series of soft lefts and soft rights, stop signs and stop lights, in a profusely littered neighborhood where the bulldozed lots and abandoned houses sat behind chain-link fences. They approached the sort of apartment complex that looked, in Pop's stated estimation, funded by public money for the purpose of consolidating drug dealers in one place—low-income housing, in the style of a bunker, with a taco wagon out front. "*Da*," said Zinaida, in the middle of Pop's denigrating. "Apartment."

"This?" said Pop. "It don't look so good. This kind of place, they have violent crimes—somebody wants to take your purse."

Zinaida was already out of the Honda, but she leaned in again and said, in her flat baritone, "Tank you and gud for holuday."

Pop answered with all the Russian he had: "*Do svidanya*, Zinaida. *Spasibo!*"

This, Ed saw, forced Zinaida to suppress a smile—one that said Pop was a barrel of laughs—but then he could tell that she saw he could see this, because, having caught his eye, she purged her face of both the smile and its suppression. Ed said, "*Do svidanya*," too, and this caused another problem for Zinaida, another battle with emotional transparency, which she addressed by saying, once more, "Tank you," and retreating.

Ed watched her go, mainly because, when Zinaida had suppressed her smile, he'd noticed something he hadn't noticed before: cavities beneath her cheekbones, like Faye Dunaway in *Chinatown*, if minus the elegance. Now he hoped that, as Zinaida walked away, there might be more along these lines—a message in her ass or in the way she walked—but there was nothing enticing, attractive, or sexy, just a woman, approximately a bag lady, who looked like she was returning, empty-handed, from a government-run shop that had run out of tinned meat to a flat where the gas was turned off.

In December, Pop insisted that Ed come for Hanukkah, because, he said, Zinaida would make latkes, and also they could watch Georgetown play Virginia, "Ewing versus Sampson, what a match-up!" The latkes, Ed thought, were heavy on the onion, and fried not in oil but, thoroughly, in Crisco; they ate them in front of the television, on paper plates, with sour cream and a quivering, translucent plum jelly, and with Michelob Pop bought for the occasion. Zinaida, Ed noticed, intercepting her in the kitchen, drank beer from a glass while poking at her frying pancakes with the edge of a plastic spatula and blotting them with paper towels. "The pancake," she said, piling latkes on her spatula. "You want?"

"Your English is getting better," Ed answered, and took the latkes. "It's much better, really. Way better."

Zinaida pointed out the refrigerator and added, "More zour crim."

"Sow-er creeem."

"Accent," explained Zinaida.

"Cream, with a long 'e.' "

"Creeem."

He hung around the kitchen. He set down his paper plate and leaned against the counter. From the living room came basketball cheers and the exclamatory voices of commentators. "He's asleep in there," Ed said, "so it's just me, Ed. In case you didn't know. I'm Ed."

Zinaida pressed her latkes and said, "Ed."

"Right," said Ed. "So, Zinaida—am I saying that right?—where are you from? Basic ESL question. Where are you from, Zinaida?"

"From Soviet Union."

"Specifically where in the Soviet Union?"

"What is *shpasifically*?"

"Your town. Your region."

"Ach," said Zinaida. "Bukhara. Tashkent."

"Which one is it? Bukhara or Tashkent?"

"One is Bukhara," Zinaida said. "Two, I am in Tashkent."

"More ESL?" said Ed. "Okay, here we go. What were you doing in Tashkent?"

"Tashkent is big city. Many university. And government building."

"And what were you doing there?"

"Tash*kent*."

Ed said, "Okay, Tashkent, I got it, fine, but you, what did you *do* there? In Tashkent?"

"I am working for government. Seckaratary. Is word? Seckeckaratary?"

"Secretary. In Tashkent you worked as a secretary. For the government. You were a government, like, secretary."

"Seckaratary."

"Great," said Ed. "This is really great. We're having a great conversation."

She didn't answer, so he said, "In America we know like nothing about Russia. You guys use rubles, you have your five-year plans, you like to drink vodka, the main guy is Brezhnev except he just died, if anyone speaks up they get sent to Siberia, you've got a lot of nukes and a space program. Is there anything else? We've heard of Solzhenitsyn. And you're good at chess. Spassky. Karpov. But we got Bobby Fischer. You got the gymnasts, we got the sprinters, you got the weightlifters, we got the swimmers. It's a wash, I think. Détente."

Zinaida answered, "My country, Uzbekistan," then turned off the burner underneath the latkes. "No talk," she said. "I clean."

For Hanukkah, Pop gave Zinaida a bonus: twenty Susan B. Anthony silver dollars, each in a sleeve, but presented in a brown paper bag. She seemed genuinely pleased, and even stayed in the living room, standing up despite Pop's insistence that she "sit, sit down, sit already, Zinaida!," to watch the exciting end of the Hoyas and the Cavs. Then, since by coincidence they were leaving Pop's apartment at the same time, Ed offered Zinaida a ride home.

In the Honda, Zinaida reverted to mute fretting and put on her purse-lipped, wary expression. Ed, driving, glanced at her hands, which were long, pale, bony, and full of tendons, with a couple of swollen, arthritic joints that had yet to defeat their handsome grace. Then, at a loss, he said, "The Jewish Family and Children's Services."

"I know."

"How did they find you?"

"Yes," said Zinaida.

"How long have you been in San Jose?"

"Two month."

"Why did you come here?"

"Why did is what?"

Ed thought about this and then said, "Here because?"

"Because immigrant," said Zinaida. "Immigration."

Ed, again, gave her answer some thought. They were driving on a spacious palm-lined boulevard, and Zinaida was admiring, Ed thought, the big homes, either that or looking at them so as not to look at him. "Immigrate because?" he asked.

Zinaida's expression now suggested ambivalence, and also—maybe—that he was stupid. She said, simply, "Soviet Union," as if that explained everything that needed to be explained, then returned to looking out her window.

So Ed gave up. They drove without talking. It was irritating to be giving Zinaida a ride now, but, to be fair, maybe she didn't understand that in America polite talk was part of the deal when you accepted a ride from somebody. Then she said, out of nowhere, "University?"

"Excuse me?"

"You are student?"

"Yes."

"You are studying what . . . field?"

"I'm studying mathematics and computers. I'm learning, right now, about computers."

"Good," said Zinaida. "For future."

Ed said, "Right now's good, too," but it occurred to him that this construction was unintelligible, so he added, "But you're right—it's good for the future."

Zinaida raised her forefinger, as if to say, "Very good, you concur with my pragmatic, post-communist wisdom," then went back to looking out the window.

But Ed felt liberated. She'd offered something. So on the expressway he put to work his pidgin English skills and teased from Zinaida biographical particulars. She lived with her sister, who had two children, a boy and a girl, ages eight and eleven. Her sister's second husband, a Ukrainian, had gone to Houston for some ambiguous reason that sounded nefarious. Ed caught the drift from Zinaida, as he sorted through her expressions and rudimentary phrases, that the Ukrainian was treacherous, mean-spirited, and an absconder, and that he and the sister were engaged in a trial separation that should—this was what Zinaida advocated—lead to a divorce.

Then it was time to drop her in front of her bunkerlike apartment complex, where, he imagined, the signature smell was stewing cabbage. "Tank you," she said, and Ed answered, "My pleasure; what a good opportunity to get to know you a little better." Zinaida took his measure defensively, tugged her head scarf lower at the back so as to cover escaping tendrils of hair, got out, and didn't look back.

On Pop's birthday, Ed brought a grocery-store cake, a carton of ice cream, a box of candles, and a card that said, on its cover, "It's your birthday," and inside, "Just in case you forgot!" Zinaida's dinner menu, at Pop's request, was breaded veal cutlets, canned corn, rolls, and a salad of iceberg lettuce and tomato wedges with bottled ranch dressing. When Ed was seated, Pop said, "Zinaida, your cutlets look top of the walk, but when do you give me my birthday present?"

"You are a funny joker," answered Zinaida. "Ha-ha, funny guy. Tomorrow, okay, I bring present."

"Pah," said Pop. "So you forgot, it's all right. Why make a federal case? I'm an understanding guy. So, now, here's what I want for my birthday—please, Zinaida, sit down at the table and *have one of these beautiful cutlets!*"

"You have to," said Ed. "It's his birthday, Zinaida." He shrugged, got up, and got a plate, knife, fork, napkin, glass, Michelob, and place mat.

Later, Zinaida had to eat cake, too. Ed taught her the words to "Happy Birthday" before she disappeared into the kitchen. Then it was time to watch *60 Minutes,* with Pop looking forward to the end-of-show segment, when Andy Rooney would be annoyed by something in a way that was "Irish, not Jewish." Predictably, though, Pop fell asleep before Rooney's rant, and when he did, Ed headed eagerly for Zinaida. "You see him five days a week," he said to her. "What do you see that I don't see?"

Zinaida was fussing with the cake-box flaps, trying, carefully, to catch their flimsy latches. She looked flustered by this effort and had her tongue between her teeth. "He don't remember," she said, not looking at Ed. "Where is his glasses? He don't know where is glasses. I go with him to Lucky store, he don't know Lucky store or street, where is apartment, he don't know apartment. In kitchen, I'm here, he is saying, 'Who are you!' So I tink, yes, he is forget."

"How is your sister?"

"Should not talk to husband on phone—mistake."

"Your niece and nephew?"

"Father no good."

"Cake boxes are impossible."

"Is very good cake."

"Take some home."

"Children are spoil. Video game."

"Well," said Ed, "let them eat cake," which he assumed she wouldn't get—but she answered, to his surprise, "Marie Antoinette."

"Or so people believe."

"I am history student, Tashkent University."

"How old are you?"

"Is not good question."

"Ever married?"

"Not good question."

"What happened to your marriage?"

"First husband, we are young, we are eediot, married. Second, he is older, choreographer."

"And?"

"Is not your business. I learn on ESL. Not business." She wagged a forefinger at him, sternly.

"Who cheated on who?"

"Is not nice question." At last, she got the box shut. "Not nice question. You are Jewish boy?"

"Bar Mitzvahed. And circumcised. In case you were wondering—I'm circumcised."

Zinaida turned one hand behind her now, and rested it on the counter with double-jointed flexibility. The inside of her elbow stared at Ed, with its tiny creases, blue with veins. "How old?" she said.

"Is not nice question."

"How old?"

"Old enough."

"You are child."

"If you say so."

Zinaida drew an ascending line in the air with an element, thought Ed, of choreography. "Up," she said. "Now you are up. Later, not so much." Her hand came down in a dénouement. "Is different."

"So, Zinaida. Who cheated?"

Zinaida pushed the cake box, sharply, into the spot she'd chosen for it, beside the breadbox. Before she could say or do anything else, Ed pulled her in and kissed her on the lips. In response, she slapped him. "Hey," said Ed. "That hurt."

"Hurt," said Zinaida. "You don't know hurt! Your all life, no hurt, because rich boy, America." Zinaida raised her hand as if to slap him a second time. "You are *boy*," she said. "Boy who try to make love to moo-tear. I'm not moo-tear to that guy," she said. "Is wrong—make love to *maht'*."

"I don't know what you're talking about," said Ed. "But I don't have some kind of weird psychological problem, if that's what you're getting at. Is that what you're getting at?"

"*Da*," said Zinaida, which he chalked up to a language difficulty: that she didn't understand "psychological problem." But what difference did it make? She didn't want to sleep with him. "Okay, Zinaida," Ed said, "you win. But just don't hit me a second time."

She slapped him again anyway. He cringed and drew back from her. "Some day you pay," hissed Zinaida.

Pop eventually became a wanderer with no compass and needed to live behind a door he couldn't unlock. Dan and Alice flew in to oversee his exodus to L'Chaim House and took Ed and Pop to dinner at nice places, but after a week—and having importuned Ed to visit Pop regularly—they were gone. The idea of visiting L'Chaim House had little appeal to Ed, but finally he went. After inquiring about Pop with an administrator in the foyer, he was ushered into a dining hall where everyone looked dead. Forgotten captains of Bay Area industry and blue-haired stewards of archaic civic missions were gathered together over breast of chicken served by, maybe, Inuits and Trinidadians. These old, forgotten Jews and their multicultural servants oppressed Ed's consciousness: a man with sparse gray whiskers sprouting indecorously amid dewlaps loomed in his path, then a woman tarted up with rouge and a wig, a bric-a-brac brooch, and some sawdust geegaws. Ed worked past them. The smell of urine mingled with the smell of food. How, he thought, could these ghosts dream of eating? Impaled this way, he found Pop, greeted him with a shoulder squeeze, sat, and, with no choice, engaged his tablemates. The woman to his right was freshly widowed and transplanted of late from Skokie for the convenience of her son, a lawyer. Across from her, a pint-sized nebbish picked ineffectually at romaine leaves. In answer to Ed's "How are you tonight?," he said, "Tonight, like every night, I hope I die in my sleep," to which Pop replied, with his mouth full of steamed corn, "Don't say that." "What," replied the nebbish, "why shouldn't I speak? At the very least, they shouldn't get me up at eight." A hired, in-house, cheery someone, he complained, came to his apartment at eight every morning and cajoled him toward the world of the living by goading him into fresh underpants and loading up his toothbrush. "Me, too," said Pop. "But that's life."

After dinner, Ed went with Pop to his quarters. Once there, Pop sat in a hard chair, looking skinny and bruised. His grooming had deteriorated, and he needed a tune-up that should include a fresh shirt, because the one he was wearing wore part of his dinner. Ed said, "Pop, your shirt's stained, maybe you should change it," and this caused Pop to rub its button line and say, "You watch what you want on the TV."

They watched a program about replacing old radiators in a three-story Victorian. Pop fell asleep. Ed waited the requisite fifteen minutes before shaking him awake and saying, "Pop, I have to go."

"Okay," said Pop. "One thing. End of hallway." He pointed in the wrong direction. "A funny problem I'm having there. That *oy-vay-iz-mir* elevator don't stop my floor. The door don't open. Something's *kaput*."

"Pop, you live in a managed facility, so, if there are elevator problems, management takes care of it."

"Management? I don't want management. It's Otis, if they're still in business. Where you look for something like this is in the Yellow Pages, the telephone book, Escalator Repair or like that."

Ed said, "I'll talk to somebody, Pop. Tomorrow."

"What," said Pop, "you can't stay for dinner? A teeny minute. One minute, only." He wiped his nose on a wadded snot-rag, then started cleaning his glasses with it. "It's either you or the other one adopted," he said. "I don't know which, but one is adopted."

"I hear you," said Ed. "Okay, Pop."

"The other," said Pop. "He's younger or older?"

"Simon?"

"Daniel."

"Daniel is my father."

"You're not Daniel?"

"No. I'm Ed."

"Well," said Pop, "one is adopted. Like Moses was adopted and—did you know this?—Ted Danson, the Jewish actor who is excellent on *Cheers*."

"Pop."

"Somewhere I read it, he's Jewish, this guy."

"Anyway," said Ed, "I have to go. Take care." And he hugged Pop, who clutched Ed's shoulders, kissed his ear, and said, "Edeleh, drive safe, wear the seatbelt."

"Okay."

"Next time you come, it's my funeral," Pop warned. "Every night I tell God, I'm begging you, please, let it be I don't wake up again L'Chaim House."

"I thought—"

"L'Chaim House," Pop added. "Who are they kidding? To life? Now? At my age? Please! Life don't end at a L'Chaim House—please! There's a guy I know here, a minyan guy, Levitz, he calls it instead L'Heil House, 'Heil, Hitler!' 'Heil, Hitler!' That's right! That's better!"

"Pop."

"Maybe you might be the son of Hitler," said Pop. "The word for that is 'irony,' doctor. You know what is irony? Like chosen people, chosen for what, to be picked on by everybody, everywhere, always? Thanks for the choosing—that's irony, great! A Hitler adopted by Jews, *oy gevalt*!"

There was no point in listening to more of this gibberish, so Ed said, "I love you, Pop," and left.

.   .   .

Simon quit Caltech and moved to Omaha, because a kid he'd met at Caltech had grown up in Omaha, and that kid had a cousin, and the cousin had a friend, and the four of them were going to rent an old house not far from Creighton University and start a video-game company. "What are there, ten Jews in Nebraska?" asked Dan, mocking his forebearers. "There's more horses in Omaha than Jews," he added. "What is he doing in Omaha?"

They visited him in Omaha, where there was dirty snow in the gutters. It was too cold for Dan and Alice; even with double socks they both had foot complaints.

On the phone to Ed at Stanford, Alice described Si's house as a dungeon. "First of all, it stinks to high heaven like rotten food. No one takes out the trash. You should see the bathroom. These boys he's living with are very nice boys, but their social manners! They have no idea how to talk to adults, none. I don't know how Simon stands it. His room is a pig pen. His teeth are stained from all the Coke he drinks." Dan corroborated everything Alice said and supplemented: "What they do business-wise with all those computers is a mystery to me, because, as far as I'm concerned, they're playing video games all the time. What a waste of talent."

Simon's company was called Virtual of Omaha, and Virtual of Omaha, in the summer of '84, got noticed by a distributor who wanted to publish *Samurai Shoot-Out* if Virtual could add levels. Virtual immediately added levels. The same distributor took *SummitQuest* to shareware and uploaded Episode One to gamer bulletin boards: fifteen dollars for Episode Two, or twenty-five for Two and Three together. Ed, who had a summer job indexing data at the Stanford Research Institute, read the reviews. People liked the graphics and were trading tricks and secrets. The action was smooth and the artwork professional. Someone at Simon's company had a bleak sense of humor. Gore was in ascendance. Callousness reigned supreme. Ed could see on the bulletin boards that *SummitQuest* had followers and aficionados, so he wasn't surprised when Alice let him know that Simon had called home with some very good news: Virtual had a royalty check for five thousand something and expected the next to be bigger.

"Four guys," said Dan, "five thousand dollars, what's that, a month's worth of pizza? Okay, fine, Simon's following his bliss, but between you and me, I wish he was at Caltech."

Virtual of Omaha imploded that fall when one of its owners became extremely irritating. Sides were taken, screaming ensued, and before long the irritating party sheared off, taking demos and hard drives. Simon teamed up with the now fractured company's graphics whiz, but without an artist or a game designer they were at a disadvantage for their first six months and had to borrow money to stay afloat. Dan and Alice got asked for three thousand dollars "to cover the basics during start-up and retrench," and after a lot of hair pulling, debate, and soul-searching, they gave Simon the three thousand and threw in another seven thousand, on the condition that he re-establish his business in Seattle, where they could keep better track of their investment.

This time, Si was more careful about partners. "Not as loud," Alice told Ed on the phone. "Not as messy. Not as immature. I like this better. Much, much better. One of his roommates and partners is Jewish, and another is a Mormon, according to Si. A perfectly nice boy. Does vivid artwork. Simon showed me what this artist can do. It's a very polished comic-book style, lots of emotion, lots of dynamism. Beautiful drawings from a talented soul. Apparently, he went to a good art school in San Francisco. There's another boy in Si's new company who I think is probably potentially quite brilliant. He has a good vocabulary and a calm way about him. Gary Wan, he's called. Very polite and cordial to me. Chinese, his father is a doctor. L.A.—grew up in West Covina. Leukemia research, his father is prominent. And this boy gets along with Si. I can see that Gary understands Si's quirks. I just wish everyone in Si's house was *cleaner*. I told Si, of course he has toe fungus, they never clean the shower, he doesn't keep his feet clean, he doesn't change his socks. I want him to read a little about hygiene, but I can't bring myself to say that, because already I can tell he thinks I'm just neurotic, whereas—"

"What is Si calling his company?" asked Ed.

"It's clever," said Alice. "It's GameKing."

With surprise, and then pride, Dan and Alice followed GameKing. First, *Curse of the Cave* went to shareware. After *Curse* came *Oil Well Armageddon,* followed by the breakthrough popularity of *Fling.* In *Fling,* an action hero, Nick Fling, made his way, tongue-in-cheek, through hordes of adversaries. His savoir-faire had—as Si put it—"a noirish edge tinged by existential weariness." Nick Fling was worldly, intelligent, and bored. His signature move was to point out something in the background—for example, a stripper—then shoot his opponent in the side of the head—with, say, a Luger—when his opponent turned to look. Fling had style, but a different style, in each episode. He went from a Vandyke to a high-and-tight to late-Elvis sideburns, then to a trench coat, then a zoot suit with spats, a fedora, and a tommy gun, then caveman skins. He was successively a back stabber, a kneecapper, a piano-wire strangler, a decapitator, a head smasher, and a disemboweler. He liked to clean his weapons with nonchalance, whistling; sometimes, with a push broom, he swept the screen clean of the dead. It was Simon who'd been responsible for "character development" when it came to *Fling,* Simon who'd made Fling so attractively amoral, Simon who'd taken Fling's darkness and made it light. Fling was mean and mischievous, troubled but untroubled, and he inhabited game space with such sadistic flair that GameKing rode him into the arena of solvency. On a roll, Simon developed *Dervish* and *Guillotine Escape,* both steeped in cruelty, then *Sand Patrol,* with 3-D graphics, then *QuantumCraze,* a first-person maze game so disquietingly immersive that one buyer threatened a lawsuit on the grounds of "debilitating claustrophobia." GameKing put a lawyer on retainer who dismissed this threat but went to work, immediately, on copyright-infringement claims. There was a looming contest over patents, too, and ongoing litigiousness over the licensing of GameKing's innovations to other companies. These expensive and mission-threatening diversions didn't seem to faze Simon. "We're out of control," he told his parents on the phone. "Everything's a go right now. The taps are open. We're hot."

Si leased a floor of workspace in Redmond. Alice took an "I told you so" approach, but Dan remained openly bewildered. Ed, during his spring break from Stanford, flew home full of envy and curiosity. He saw right away, meeting Simon at a coffee shop, that his brother was still a geek, though he now sported a mod sweater, a narrow tie, and neutering black glasses. Si seemed dried out, especially his sinuses. His medical report to Ed included arid sniffling, headaches, a tendency toward bloody noses, and a pounding in his ears when he exercised too much. He told Ed he was worried about being hated by people he'd had to let go in the past six months. He was trying to read outside his profession so as to "maintain some objectivity and not get stale." Every game that came out, from every company, he sought to understand through mastery. "You learn about games when your fingers are flying," he said. "That's when you see where a designer is coming from. Subconscious effects—you make those conscious. Some of these people are masters of the form. It's sort of electrifying, for me at least, to feel how smart they are, and manipulative and creative. It's to the point in the field where there are academic theorists. And you know what? I completely concur. This is the genesis of something meaningful and big. This is the dawn of the golden age of gaming. I've got to be thinking when I green-light a game now—I have to put my choices in context. But forget all that. For me it's about creation. Actually designing. In fact, right now I'm looking for someone on the business side so I can go back to actually designing."

GameKing inhabited the top floor of a building that Simon called, in quotation marks, the Dark Tower. It loomed large amid blacktopped acres of parking, with its mirrored windows suggesting a house of fun. As for landscaping, the Dark Tower was unadorned save for an art installation at its entrance: a glinting orb, twenty feet high, that was set into a relation with the building that allowed for an exchange of light. It was four when Simon and Ed arrived—Ed was to tour GameKing's facility and operations—and now both the building and the orb looked burnished. "Better than some, worse than others," said Simon, as he and Ed stopped to contemplate the art. "Not too pretentious—just a profound marble. At least we don't have to put up with sentiment just to walk through our own front door."

They took the elevator to the top floor. GameKing, basically, had a view of parking lots. In its entry was a series of trompe-l'oeil paintings, commissioned by Simon and done by a local artist, depicting Nick Fling, in various guises, vaulting out of his video-game terrain and into a quartet of Pacific Northwest backdrops—a rain forest, Mount Rainier, the Space Needle, Puget Sound. Simon said they were "a bone thrown to the Chamber of Commerce," "good-citizen stuff," and "foyer fluff for vendors," and then made a beeline, with Ed following, for his office. "Welcome to my world," he said. "This is where I try—emphasis on *try*—to get it happening."

He'd gone spare. There were two deep armchairs arranged so that seated parties could contemplate the sterile scene outside the windows. Between them was a credenza on an angle. It was overloaded because there was no other furniture in the room, not even a desk. "Have a seat," said Simon. "I have to talk to somebody in the outer world for three seconds. Excuse me for a minute. Look out the window."

Ed looked at everything he could on the credenza. *GamerTheory Journal. TechNews.* A "hiring file" of résumés. A role-playing manual for *Enigma III.* Simon came back carrying maple bars on plastic plates and two small bottles of cranberry juice. He said, "I'm super-tired. Let's sit here for a while. We can look out the window. I can't remember if I sent you *SlayerWolf.* I wanted you to see our texture-mapped floors, because we did it first. Did you notice the lighting? Great fade to black. Even though we program in VGA. Is that enough juice?"

"There's a ton of trucks out there."

"Right now I'm developing *Trucker Armageddon,* so checking out the traffic has been totally worth it. Come on, have more juice."

They toured. To Ed, GameKing looked like a giant frat party, not a business. There were no females to be seen on the premises, just boys going crazy and having immature fun. If Ed had to guess, he would say that GameKing's employees weren't working today. They were listening to music, eating pizza, drinking Coke, and playing video games. They were having rubber-band fights while adding sophomoric sound effects. They were dueling with plastic swords, pistols, and rocket launchers. Screams, explosions, moans, and gunshots were emitted by the games running loudly on their computers. Ed heard someone say, "Die, motherfucker!" and then "You're toast, cocksucker." GameKing's staff included six part-timers who'd responded to fliers put up on college campuses. They were supposed to crunch it out but had succumbed to atmospherics, which Simon said was okay, "because that's how the creative juices boil to the top." In fact, GameKing's hottest designer, Rodney Ball, had come in as a programming grunt. Rodney Ball told Ed that he liked to snowboard. His fingernails were painted black. He was working his way through a medium pepperoni. Ed asked what was playing on his headphones—what he liked to listen to while working. "Philip Glass," Rodney answered. "Nobody else here listens to P. Glass, but he's excellent for my head at the moment."

Simon added, "Right now Rodney's developing a game we're calling—and I'm just about there with it—*DeathDreamer.*"

"But usually it's like the worst metal I can find," said Rodney.

Ed and Simon went back to the armchairs. Simon collapsed. "You can see why I had my office soundproofed," he said. "Madhouse. I don't even want to know about it. I work at night if I need to get focused."

"Plus that way you don't have to hear about P. Glass being excellent for what's-his-name's head at the moment."

Simon laughed. "Rod Ball," he said. "I love Rodney. Rodney's great."

Ed dropped his head and massaged his neck so he could roll his eyes surreptitiously. "This is . . . wow," he said.

Simon reached across and tapped Ed's shoulder. "I know," he said. "I have to pinch myself. It's totally . . . I'm living the dream."

Ed covered his mouth. He was aware of wanting to say the wrong thing, then of quelling it. He had in mind inventing, off the cuff, a game called *GeekKing*. But what would be the point of fraternal aggression? Why start something now? No, a new volley in the Dark Tower wasn't worth the emotional strain. "I'm happy for you," Ed said innocuously. "Things have really gone your way."

They went out for dinner—expensive Bento boxes at a place in Belle-vue where his brother was accorded an obsequious reception. The servers were done up like medieval geishas, minus the whiteface but otherwise authentic. Si wasn't bad with chopsticks and knew his *sake*s. He held up something with eel in it, smiling, and spoke in Japanese to the hovering floor manager. Ed couldn't help himself. He wanted to kill Si. The little bastard had gained the upper hand. What could he do? How to react? Two months later, Ed graduated from Stanford (summa cum laude, with distinction), in math. The day after that, he flew home to Seattle, where within a week he'd found an attorney, and within a month filed articles of incorporation for a company, called Pythia, dedicated to research and development in the nascent field of search.

With money borrowed from Dan and Alice on the argument that owning was smarter than renting, Ed bought a modest house in Bellevue. He told them he was on a five-year plan to get a tech business up and running, and they gave him the benefit of the doubt. Before long, though, his home office was no longer big enough for his equipment, so he hired a contractor to convert his garage into a clean and capacious workspace. The garage stayed relatively cool year-round, which was good for a person banking hard drives. Ed hired an electrician to wire in surge protection, bought an air filter and an antistatic pad, and spent all his time there. "Isn't this sort of mad-scientist?" asked Dan, when he saw how Ed had turned his garage into something that looked as if it ought to be at NASA. Hard drives were stacked on cheap plastic racks, and cables, in all colors, bulged from plastic ties. "I have to do it this way," said Ed. "I don't own a supercomputer."

"What's the goal?" Dan wanted to know. "What are you doing out here?"

"I'm trying to find a needle in a haystack."

"What about forcing a few thousand peasants to very carefully sort through the straw?"

"That's a good idea," said Ed.

Simon, visiting, had a different take. "I don't think I've ever seen this much RAM in one place," he said. "This is classic, this is stupendous, didn't I see this at the Museum of Computing?" They sat on rolling desk chairs amid the general noise—the aquarium-pump humming of case and CPU fans, the whirring of drives, and the droning of the dust filter—and took turns typing at a command-line interface until Simon began to understand what Pythia was about. "It's a pretty decent information retriever," Ed told his brother. "Right now it rips through a shitload of bandwidth. I need to go broader and drill down."

"You what?"

"Actually," said Ed, "I have an idea for something that's going to be a lot more effective than what anybody else has got going at the moment. The key to information retrieval is, believe it or not, probability theory. You've got to have algorithms with coin tosses built into them when you're dealing with huge amounts of raw information. The challenge is to arrive at—"

"You win," said Si, waving an invisible white flag. "You're way over my head. You're flying at warp speed and I don't get it. But let me tell you something, bro. Right now I have a guy working for me who was a total search freak before I hired him. Guy is excellent on texture mapping but learned all his programming chops going after search. Bet his life on search. Like seven figures, all of it borrowed—and all of it lost. We took him in at a low point, and he's so good at getting us speed we had to pay or lose him. I—"

"Don't plan on me losing my shirt," said Ed. "My plan is to go all the way."

"Yeah?"

"My plan is to claw all the way to the top. My plan is to be the king of search."

In the fourth year of Ed's five-year plan, Dan had chest pains that led to a 911 call. Ed and Simon both dropped what they were doing and converged on Harborview right away. Si, who now sported a goatee, negotiated the hospital halls with his hands in his pockets, ambling under a nimbus of preoccupation, while Ed did the mundane work of finding the waiting room. "My boys," said Alice, when they met her there, "my two wonderful and loving boys," and she hugged them both before they all sat down to watch CNN during Dan's procedure. Finally, the surgeon came with a stellar report—he'd performed a perfect balloon angioplasty and put in a stent without complications. Someone would talk to Dan before he left the hospital about diet, exercise, stress, a blood thinner, and cholesterol-lowering medications, but Dan could now lead a normal life.

When they went to see Dan, he told them, among other things, that he couldn't remember where he'd left his glasses, and that, even with a catheter inserted, he felt like he needed to pee. "But basically you're okay," said Alice. "Thank God, it's not serious—you're okay."

He wasn't. Dan's angioplasty yielded, before long, to restenosis. Some tinkering with his medication ensued, and then he went back to have a second stent inserted inside the first. In a surprising transformation, Dan now resembled his father—the hairy shoulders, the slack skin, the bruises, the hulking posture, the dry, shiny shins. "Bruises?" he said. "Bruises are from blood thinners. But, no, I don't want to talk about bruises. What I want to do is sit here with the *Times*. I've got an appointment Monday, but I'm not backing off my anti-coag, because, all things considered, I'd rather have the bruises, which look terrible. I know, you don't have to tell me. I know what I look like—old."

Alice, it turned out, wasn't built for travail. "He's too young," she complained to Ed. "This kind of thing is not what we expected. Your father's only fifty-seven. The poor guy, I feel so terrible for him I can't sleep at night, I'm going through a lot of anxiety, the whole thing is really testing me now—being strong isn't just some words, you know. What it takes is a lot of support from family. I'm sorry to lay such a guilt trip on you and to make you take so much responsibility, but what your mother needs is emotional support, because all of this is terrible and it's breaking my heart, to see your father like this."

Dan had a bypass, but by now there was so much arteriosclerosis that his heart was suffering the consequences. It couldn't get the blood it needed to keep on beating in the way it had once beaten. His myocardium—Dan didn't bother to explain terms—was suffering from ischemia and, little by little, dying. He had episodes of angina, he carried nitroglycerin, he stopped in stairwells, and he couldn't play tennis for fear that competition might kick off a spasm in an artery and send him over the edge into dysrhythmia. "I was a Type A," he said. "My parents wanted me to do well in school, letting them down was out of the question, I had to be a doctor, a doctor or a lawyer, nothing else was going to be acceptable, but how come I wanted to please them so much, why did I let myself live like that anyway? My parents were immigrants, what choice did I have? They didn't know better and neither did I. Now here I am, take a look at me, Ed. This is where the Type A business ends you if you don't take care of yourself."

They had to give Dan a pacemaker, because, as he said—with an oxygen tube clipped to his nostrils in the hospital—"the sinoatrial node won't keep the beat." Alice, who could only take so much, got in-home care for Dan so she could "decompress regularly." Dan had edema, his legs and feet were swollen, his eyes bulged, his nose was blue—"Clearly," he said, "my pump is failing." Finally, the King family held a summit in the living room, where Dan sat wheezing, his nostrils flaring, while Alice wept and held his hand. "Here we are," rasped Dan. "The time has come. The time comes for everyone, and now it comes for me. I'm grateful you're here, I'm here with my loved ones, what more can a guy ask for, really, in the end? Okay, don't say it, he could ask to live forever." Dan stopped to catch his breath, coughed, and went on. "You know how I feel about this," he said. "All sorts of things go haywire at this point. My lungs, probably, statistically, yes, but there's also the kidneys and the liver shutting down, terrible uremia, tons of anemia, pneumonia for some people, look, none of it's good, which is why they start hitting you so hard with the morphine, then you're really a mess. So why did Alice ask you to come? Alice asked because PRNH, PRNH is the choice I'm making, which is Patient Refusal of Nutrition and Hydration. I don't take food, I don't take drink, within ten days, two weeks, it's over, and, supposedly, there's not so much pain."

"You're gonna want ice cream," said Alice, in tears.

"I'm gonna want ice cream," Dan agreed. "Maybe, once more, I'm gonna have ice cream, one more scotch, but then it's over. *Alice*," he said, and started crying.

Alice set up a rotation of family and friends. Dan had company around the clock, people to talk to and to do things for him. On the fifth day of PRNH, he couldn't swallow his morphine, so they went to sublinguals, and then to injections. There were nursing aides in the house every morning for the complications of bathing and sheet changing. Dan had to wear lamb's-wool booties because of sores. Still, he talked, and even made jokes: "Jackie Mason. You know Jackie Mason? I'm like Jackie Mason, with all this hired help: I have enough money for the rest of my life—unless I buy something!"

They played cassettes, his favorites from plays—"The Street Where You Live," "Sixteen Going on Seventeen," "What Do the Simple Folk Do?"—plus Frank Sinatra and Mel Tormé, Dinah Shore, and Judy Garland, whom, said Dan, "nobody sings like anymore." His friends—other doctors and longtime patients—came one by one out of kindness and concern, and to recall a few things about the old days with him, and to joke around, because Dan joked around—"All those meetings! You remember Milton Berle on meetings? 'A committee is a group that keeps minutes and loses hours.' That was us, my friend—that was us, in spades!"

Then the joking was over. He was lucid when he wasn't asleep, but he'd lost all interest in laughter and jokes and wanted to talk about serious things—his will, not wasting money on an "out-of-grief expensive coffin," where files could be found with information on investments, Alice's future life without him ("Of course you should remarry"). When Ed saw him next, he was apparently hallucinating. He'd sporadically let go with some medical jargon, then a lull, then more in the vein of prognosis or diagnosis, then a long silence that became a coma. "Maybe he can hear you, maybe not," said Alice. "If there's something you want to say to your father, Ed, you might as well say it, just in case."

But he didn't know what to say. And the next day, he witnessed Dan's death, which came with a cry so unearthly and demonic that Ed stepped back and nearly fled. Was that it, then? Was that how it went? What sort of liberation was this, that begins with such a dark, shattering howl? Ed left the hospital, wandered around town, and found a woman who let him bury his face between her legs. After all, what better place than the epicenter of beginning, now that he'd been made to face the end?

9

Incest

At 3 a.m., post–Club's betrayal, Diane was still taking stock of things. Club's brilliant rip-off had her in a tailspin. She was down to the thirty-two dollars in her purse. And she would have to face Ron Dominick alone, if it turned out Ron decided to accost her. Talk about low, to leave her this way, penniless and in danger—what a bastard Club was! And with all his treacly blather. His Boddingtons and canasta. His snubnose .38, as if it made a difference. His "birds of a feather" and "jolly couch potato" lines. And shrewdest of all, keeping track of her bathroom visits. Her "brother" had turned out to be the worst sort of wanker, a confidence man, and because she was lonely—which he'd seen and exploited—she'd gone for it hook, line, and sinker.

Before it got light, taking no chances, Diane knocked on Emily's door and told her—Emily in ridiculous pajamas—that she was being stalked by a creep. Emily made two cups of chamomile tea. They talked until eight. Then, while Emily went for coffee, to the gym, for a run, and out to brunch—all with two other girls from Microsoft who did these things together every Sunday—Diane sat in Emily's TV chair, watching at the window. Sure enough, Ron Dominick appeared, taking the stairs in long sets of three before rapping on Diane's door. He looked through the seam where her curtains met. He peered into her peephole. He knocked again, then sat on the stairs with his elbows on his knees, looking steeled to wait.

She hid all day at Emily's, watching. Emily returned with a consolation sticky bun for Diane, a bottle of fresh-squeezed orange juice, and good coffee. Now, openly, the tables were turned. Diane was cowed, anxious, and glum, while Emily had life and money to burn—so much money that, when Ron gave up at dusk, she took Diane to dinner in Belltown. They were led to their table by a girl half Diane's age whose sequined dress fit like a mermaid's skin. The glass-menagerie kitchen was packed with line cooks who had to avert their eyes like English servants. Was this her fate, the service sector? Her meal came—halibut in lemon-plum sauce—prompting recollection of a dinner date with Jim Long. Old Jim had believed, rather solidly, in restaurants. One of the rewards of life, for him, was an evening in a restaurant. Well, she'd mishandled that, too, hadn't she, because now she'd lost her in-card for privileges. If only she were still Mrs. Long.

"I hate to say this," Diane told Emily, "but I think I better move out of The Palms."

"Don't," said Emily. "I'd lose a friend."

Even more depressing. Here her only friend in the world was an ex–shrinking violet with a tight perm. Who else was there who would care if she left The Palms, except a few coke addicts who'd need another dealer? "How am I going to move anyway?" she asked. "I'm dead broke, bankrupt, at the moment."

"No prob, Di. My stock's like half a mil. Isn't that unbe*liev*able?"

It was unbelievable. But, as usual, the world made no sense. Either you were in the right place at the right time or you weren't. It had nothing to do with what you deserved or didn't deserve. Here Emily had half a million dollars while Diane had—what? A half-bottle of Gilbey's and some tinned smoked clams frigging Club had left behind? That night, at 2 a.m., with her TV set in the back seat of her car and a check for $750 Emily had written her, Diane fled. She went to a twenty-four-hour Denny's, and when it got light, looked for an apartment. What she found was a two-hundred-dollar-a-month furnished studio in Bellevue where she signed a lease as Diane Long, the better to thwart Ron Dominick's searches. From her new hovel's cramped, narrow "balcony" she looked down on garbage bins in a locked corral, and on foraging crows. Then she went inside and wallowed. In fact, for the next ten days she mostly wallowed. She spent her time under a blanket watching television. Her efforts to sleep evolved into a fetish demanding carefully placed pillows, thin cotton socks, cheap gin, and *Nightwatch. Seventy* thousand dollars! . . . If she ever caught up with that son of a bitch Club . . . Mornings, she wearily made instant coffee that tasted like the ersatz her mum used to make. The smell of it confirmed her sense that, in the end, despite every effort to the contrary, she'd become her mum. Right down to the telly, bad coffee, and cheap gin.

These facts were motivating. She would *not* be her mum! So Diane devised a notice: available for dog walking. She didn't want to be available for dog walking, not in the least, but it was a way, she knew, into loaded people's lives. So she made fliers and stapled them to telephone poles. She tacked them up at grocery stores and at veterinary offices that allowed her to. Eventually, she was walking someone's dog. From the Occidental Grand Cozumel to walking a dog for peanuts! Here she was, leashed to a coddled canine, slogging through a neighborhood she couldn't afford to live in. As new customers came her way, dogs put her in contact with birds, squirrels, furtiveness, and irritation. Some dogs refused to listen to her commands and provoked her to violence with their incessant pulling. Others galled her with their sniffing and pissing. She wanted to get on with it, walk and get paid, not stand guard over serial urinators. But her real point, of course, was to rub shoulders with money. Returning a nominally exercised charge, she'd offer, "He's a delight," "She's lovely," or "We enjoyed our time together," with a little more Brit than usual, in the name of a gratuity. Where did it get her? Now that she wasn't young? It got her paid work washing a greyhound once a week. She had a code she punched in to prompt an automated gate, and another for a side door, and then she went up back stairs behind a slavering, ribby hound, past modern art hung in a landing, and past a boudoir, more art, and a side table for fresh flowers, to where the greyhound awaited her attentions in a bathroom featuring a bidet. Diane liked the peek at luxe, but she didn't really want to touch the dog, who was a ferocious drooler and, she thought, distraught about his circumstances. To get him in the tub, she flipped in a dry biscuit. While he gobbled it and slobbered, she turned on the water. The open tap would mesmerize the beast. He stood facing it, huffing, while she squirted him with an expensive shampoo. Afterward, she threw a giant beach towel over his back, necessary because otherwise he would fling water out of his coat that, Diane had learned, would leave her smelling the way he did. The whole thing was disgusting. The bottom of the bottom. The dregs. A servant. A serf.

Soon she was engaged with an arthritic Boston terrier who needed physical therapy. Jon-Jon was owned by a retired couple, the Jamisons, who didn't mind doing this but wanted breaks now and then. The Jamisons were kindly Democrats, each with a home office from which they battled for the Sierra Club. Diane's job was to sit in the living room watching television and, with the pensive Jon-Jon in her lap, pry, pull, and massage his dry legs for forty-five minutes. After two visits of this sort, she was asked to stay for tea, and over tea with grapes, biscuits, and cheese listened to the Jamisons extol guesthouses in the Cotswolds. Mr. Jamison said that he and Mrs. Jamison thought highly of Wales. Mrs. Jamison said they'd made a trek, twelve years before, in the Scottish Highlands. Within two weeks, Diane was picking up their dry cleaning; and within four, their pharmaceuticals. They sent her to a wine shop, a cheese monger, a bakery, a fish market, and a chandlery. She also took the terrier to the vet, transporting it in a plastic carrier padded with a checked blanket. Yet, though all of this was good, it also went nowhere. The Jamisons gave to causes, but Diane wasn't one of them. She could fawn and ingratiate all she wanted, but it wouldn't change the tenor of her world.

Out of nowhere, she caught a break of sorts. Somehow she was able to lie her way into meal prep for a basketball player on the Seattle Supersonics, who not only paid well but doled out tickets. Since she didn't cook, she contracted the meal prep to a caterer she found in the Yellow Pages, and since she needed the money, she sold the seats. It was a pretty good hook-up, but, still scrambling, she asked her Supersonic, through his assistant, to recommend her to the rest of the team. He did—or his assistant said he did. "Sure," she thought. "He recommended me—right." The basketball star was so full of himself, with his career-extending yoga, high-fiber diet, inane rap music, and muscular young sluts, that in the end, she knew, she wasn't on his radar. She should have known this right away, because at their first meeting he'd told Diane that she'd be working with his assistant. After that, he only spoke to her the way you'd speak to hired help. For example, running into her in his kitchen one morning, he said, "Hey—could you do the poached chicken breasts for lunch today?" Diane looked him up at the library. He was thirty-one and had played in Italy for two years, which might explain his propensity for women who looked like Roman whores. She told the caterer: chicken breasts for lunch. It was degrading, really. The whole thing was beneath her. The assistant she had to talk to was a twenty-something dunderhead. He teased Diane about Prince Charles after hearing that Prince Charles had broken his arm in a polo match. "Say what?" he said. "Are you people serious? Come again? Prince *Charles*?" This was prefatory to the making of a list—grits, fresh salmon, brown rice, etc. "My man wants lean bacon for breakfast," he would say, or "You better be looking for some different bread, because my man's burning out on whole wheat."

Just jolly great. From frigging terrible to worse. She had to spend money to visit an optometrist, because she couldn't read the nutritional information anymore on the Supersonic's preferred food items. "The time has come," she was told in a darkened room. "The eye gradually loses elasticity, and then it's time for reading glasses." For fun, she lingered with a fitting specialist who had much to say on the geometries of eyewear and on how frames might complement, or pick up, skin tones. But of course this was neither here nor there, because Diane couldn't afford to buy fashionable glasses. The exercise with the fitting specialist was just entertainment—although, in the end, it was also depressing to sit close to a mirror that way. It was better not to look too critically at this point. In clear light, after a shower, she now had to acknowledge lumps along her flanks. Cellulite, generic reading glasses, ordering chicken breasts for an idiot—every day, a fresh bottom.

Diane went to a health-food store because her Supersonic needed multivitamins, glutamine, and ginkgo biloba. There was a public-service community bulletin board out front, and, stopping briefly to check, she noticed that nobody had removed even one of the phone-number tabs she'd made with toenail scissors at the bottom of a handwritten dog-walking solicitation. This had to be at least partly because someone had used one of her pins to tack up a business card, in the process partially concealing Diane's appeal. "Sorry," Diane muttered. "That's unacceptable," before lifting the pin and removing the offender. "It's every man for himself," she thought. "I've no room for sympathy."

She took the card with her. Her bulletin-board usurper was in business as a "life coach." Underneath a heading—CHRYSALIS—was "Budgeting? Parenting? Career? Spirituality? Let me help you pull it all together." This was followed by a name, a phone number, and the words "Certified Life Coach."

Diane went around dumping supplements in her basket and shaking her head in disbelief at the idea of a life coach. How did that work? Was that real? "Life coach"? It turned out, at the library, that Life Coaching was in the Yellow Pages, between Clutches and Coal. "Helping clients make positive changes in their lives since 1981," one life coach pointed out in a Yellow Pages ad. Diane called but got a message machine. She called another number and pretended that she might need a life coach but wanted to know first what life coaching cost. Way less than a psychiatrist, but way more than a plumber. Less than a call girl, but more than a dog walker. Gambling, Diane spent money on a business card:

FRESH START LIFE COACHING SERVICES
Work? Relationships? Conflict? Transformation?
I can help you make positive changes.

Followed by her name, her telephone number, and the line *Providing life coaching services since 1981.*

Fresh Start brought some meager funds in. Bellevue was full of college grads who'd once thought highly of working eighty-hour weeks but had since changed their minds. It was full of techies with relationship challenges. It was full of people young enough to believe that they should have a life coach on their side. Diane netted three in the course of a month. Since her apartment didn't cut it, she rented a studio near a shopping center and put it to double use. It was a matter of sleeping on a couch instead of a bed, and of stuffing things into a closet every morning. The conversion from lodgings to office took twenty minutes. After that, she showered and put on the sort of white blouse and navy skirt a flight attendant might wear. Her English accent helped, as did her pixie. She looked and sounded upbeat and organized. The terminology sounded right coming out of her mouth. For confidence-building props she had a pen and a planner. "Have the courage to reinvent yourself," she told clients. "The world is full of wonderful possibilities." Two of her three clients needed that sort of shoring up; the third had no clue how to organize or schedule, and couldn't say what his goals were in life. Diane didn't really believe in goals, but goals were a big part of being a life coach, so she trafficked in them. She signed up a fourth client, who was trying to decide whether he should leave his current company to strike out on his own as a software developer. She took on a fifth, who couldn't figure out how to work less and felt stuck in a boring but lucrative job. Diane made charts and lists for her clients—on yellow legal paper, but neat—usually in the fifteen minutes before they showed up. She referenced bulleted items with a pen as she talked, and as she listened she gave perpetual indication that she was listening more closely than anyone had ever listened to another person before. She made a siege out of eye contact. She calibrated her expressions, moment to moment, to correspond to what was being said. If things flagged, she said "Aha!" and took a note. By pushing objects around her desktop, she gave the impression that she was expending energy over clients and deserved to be paid ridiculous sums. That was the advantage of settling where there were discretionary funds. You could siphon some off.

Telling other people how to live their lives was—to use a professional term—empowering. Here these young Americans were making fortunes, and Diane, the daughter of a British whore, was in charge of which affirmations they would say each morning. It often occurred to her that, given the advantages they'd had in life, they ought to know better. Instead, they fell for everything. When they came in, Diane would have classical music of the cheerful variety playing—Prokofiev, for example. A good *Allegro con brio*, or a galloping *Gavotte*. She would offer Pellegrino from a pitcher dense with lemon rounds. Since her window opened onto traffic, she'd covered it with a poster of redwood behemoths. Between clients, she sprayed the room with a tea-tree-oil-scented deodorizer and made sure the candle in her bathroom remained lit. When someone knocked, she opened her door briskly, stepped aside, and gestured the way a child's piano teacher gestured at the beginning of a lesson: Let's get started, ready position. "Have a seat and we'll begin," Diane would say, followed by "So tell me about your week," as, with a flourish, she pushed the cassette player's stop button. Now it was up to the client to pick up where Prokofiev had left off, while Diane gave her active-listening performance, took notes, interjected queries, and provided positive reinforcement. She always found a way to employ the term "progress," but it was just as important to insinuate doubt, because she didn't want her clients to exit with the idea that they shouldn't return for another round. Always, in the name of continuity, she ended sessions with the reminder "I'm on call from nine until five every weekday, so ring me if there's a crisis." Crises occurred more often than she'd anticipated. A client would be in the middle of something tenuous and, not knowing where to turn, dial Diane. "Begin at the beginning," Diane would tell them, or something like that, with her TV muted. "What are your goals? Start with your goals. I've got your file open in front of me, and I'm looking at the goals we prioritized together. Any changes there? Should we walk through your goals?"

Now Club's betrayal began to have a bright side. That fleecer had shown Diane things she could apply. Not that his lessons were worth seventy thousand dollars. She wasn't going to take it that far. But here she was, conning people, without even getting out of her chair. Without lifting a finger. She was paying her bills this way, without walking dogs—just sitting there putting on a cheery and together show. A neat little scam, life coaching, but the problem was, it didn't have a future. Yes, she could buy a better television and make some satisfying additions to her wardrobe, but there had to be more to life than that. Because, as things stood, she was eternally asking, "Is this my life as I will live it to the end?" And, according to circumstance, adding, "Living in a studio by a shopping center in Bellevue?" "Pumping up disorganized nerds?" "Watching *Dallas* and *Saturday Night Live*?" "Saving up to see Fleetwood Mac, with Emily, at the Kingdome?" Diane was forty-two and had a bunion on her left foot that probably needed to be operated on. The only gold star she could give herself was that recently her reading had moved up and forward. Sidney Sheldon no longer made the grade. Now she was reading serious books, the ones shelved under "Literature," mostly by writers who were dead.

She frequently went to movies by herself. Used-book stores. Coffee shops. She would sit in a coffee shop drinking a latte and reading a novel by a dead person in the hope of attracting attention. At Bellevue Square there was an atrium-style food court full of ladies like herself—no longer young but not grandmothers yet—well dressed for shopping and for a midday smoothie spiked with healthy ingredients. Diane drank these, too. She got her hair done at a 20-percent discount by clipping a coupon. She sat in the massage chair at the Sharper Image. She went to cosmetics counters and goaded cosmeticians into guessing her age. Her one splurge was anti-wrinkle cream that advertised itself as taking off ten years. At forty-two, she looked thirty-two, but that wasn't good enough.

She met Emily at Bellevue Square for a smoothie. Emily frequented REI now and, because of her height, wore the rec look well. She had a sleek, small rucksack and lightweight boots. She wore a fleece jacket with a hood and two-way zipper. "I think I know what you need," she told Diane. "You need a date."

"Here we go," said Diane.

Emily touched her arm. "No one wants to be dependent," she said. "You don't need a guy to make you happy. But if you can take some of the focus off yourself, the irony is, it's good for you, too. You just need someone else to think about."

"No, I don't."

"You could use a dating service."

"Emily," said Diane.

"I know people who've done it successfully."

"Good for them."

"I know guys at work who'd love to date you. You're like super good-looking, Diane."

But Diane didn't date. She felt spinsterish and wilted. Fresh Start, she knew, was theater, performance. She herself could use a life coach—someone who would tell her how to get on track again—so she became her own. Full of desperate resolutions, she bought a VCR and a Jane Fonda exercise video. Determined, she lost weight and bought new clothes. A Fresh Start client owned a timeshare on Lake Wenatchee he wasn't able to use that year; he gave her a free week there, and she took it in April, when the roads were mostly clear of snow, and with the intention of eating little, exercising daily, reading by a fire, and going to bed early. She did this for two days, but then Emily came over and they drove down to Leavenworth for a dinner at Cafe Mozart that included a fifty-dollar bottle of Kerner Spätlese and tall mugs of Bavarian Coffee—whipped cream, sugar, peppermint schnapps—served next to warm apple strudel. Things felt fat and cozy after that. They rented a video and picked up a newspaper. The Germanys were getting back together. *The Fabulous Baker Boys* was better than expected. In the morning, the lake looked pleasantly still; in the afternoon, it rippled, and that was pleasant, too. The apple and pear trees were leafing out with vernal charm. Deer foraged outside their picture window. Feeling domestic and even sisterly, Diane helped Emily make fresh pasta with a device Emily had brought— as a gift for Diane—on the back seat of her Jetta. They ate it *con aglio e olio,* with red wine. The next morning, after Emily said goodbye with a meaningful hug, Diane felt motivated to make progress in the English novel she'd brought, and to take a considerable late-afternoon oxygenat- ing walk. In dusk's chill air, her skin felt firm. She was impressed by the new Gore-Tex walking boots she'd bought. They were dry, stylish, felt already broken in, and did nothing to irritate her bunion.

On Monday morning, in Bellevue again—the weather clammy, her back a little tense—Diane met with a new Fresh Start client as whiny, self-absorbed, and neurotic as the rest, and this shoved her back into her hole. By ten, she knew that her lakeside idyll was not going to have any useful staying power and, panicking about her durable paralysis, opened her English novel in an effort at self-improvement. By noon, defeated, Diane was downtown, wandering in high-end and middlebrow shops— for a long time, dreamily, amid the women's apparel at The Bon—since this was a time-tested and reliable salve, as was the spinach salad with avocado and grapefruit at the Sheraton at Sixth and Union. Same old, though. Now what, dessert? More browsing, shopping, coasting—more aging? More nothing except this bland playing-out? It was raining again—time to head home to an evening of solo television. But then she remembered that Emily had raved, while rolling out pasta at Lake Wenatchee, about the wonders of the IMAX movie *Blue Planet.* As part of her new general earthiness campaign. Part of her compensatory envi- ronmental correctness. What time was it? It was three, a quarter past. Why not ride the monorail to the Seattle Center and snooze a little through Emily's *Blue Planet*? She could talk about it with Emily later. Keep their relationship going strong. A theater interlude on a rainy after- noon, darkly hunkered down with no obligations—that didn't sound too bad to Diane. So, overcoming inertia, she dealt with the details. She stood in line at the IMAX Theater with April tourists who'd been brought to this pass by "spring" weather they'd been warned about, handed her ticket to a twenty-year-old who looked as if he was dressed for a role on *Star Trek,* and settled in beneath the looming swath of screen. Thereafter, she was awake off and on. The picture was so big you couldn't even see it. If you looked, you risked getting sick to your stomach. Worse, she felt admonished by the narrator of *Blue Planet* for being alive. "This is our earth . . . a planet in space," followed by blame, then more blame, then more. Whoever had cobbled up this film wanted you to gaze unrelentingly on the earth from a window on the Space Shuttle, the better to suffer the sheer breadth of your mistakes. Diane sat through this punishment, thinking, "What do you want from me? What am I supposed to do? I take in oxygen and give back carbon—kill me already, I'm a blight on my own planet." Finally, her forty-two minutes of eco-lashing over, she emerged with her fellow castigated consumers into an unmitigated spring rain, thunderous.

Precipitation-bound, hoping for a lull, Diane squandered time in the Pacific Science Center, which on this late afternoon was inhabited predominantly by mothers pushing strollers or chasing toddlers. The place was crammed with what were advertised as marvels—stationary bicycles with calorie read-outs, a so-called Shadow Wall, a gyroscope, an echo tube, a Tesla coil, a model dinosaur-dig pit. Lo and behold, in a corner of Building Three, Diane found an antiquated, lonely contraption she remembered from the Seattle World's Fair in '62: the gimmicky, glass-walled Probability Exhibit, with its thousand pennies falling regularly past pegs, which had so enthralled the hapless Walter Cousins as it steadily, inevitably, built a hill of mounded coins, and illustrated a truth no one cared about. From a distance it looked like an ant colony on display, but up close, behind a pane of foggy glass, there was Walter's must-see math marvel. "Brilliant," thought Diane. "Coins in a box. Walter was such an overgrown child."

Another Science Center patron sidled up to the Probability Exhibit. He was young, handsome, and upper-class enough to wear corduroys, good shoes, and a fitted wool sweater with a rib-knit collar and cable stitching. He had the sort of face, so pregnant with youth, that made Diane not just conscious of her age but conscious that its owner would age sooner than he thought—if he thought of age at all, in any realistic way, busy as he must be being young. It was a young face but not an innocent one; in fact, at the moment, it looked troubled behind a fragile stoic mask of male confidence. Nevertheless, a shiny head of hair, an untarnished complexion, a strong brow, a well-shaped chin—in short, all the markers of male pulchritude. A guy so iconically young and pulchritudinous he made Diane wonder if she had any charm left, or any winning female magic to assert. Was it over already—were all the good ones behind her? Taking a flier, she straightened her skirt—the knee-length navy-blue flight-attendant skirt she wore on weekdays, along with a white blouse, her crisp, sprightly Fresh Start costume—and said, "I don't get this."

He was tall and strapping—Superboy, American. Clean, well groomed, trim-waisted, trimmed nails. He put his hands at the small of his back, tapped a big shoe, and said, "What?"

She knew, from this, that he was not going down the path with her toward common ground where math was boring. So she shifted her coat from one arm to the other, moved closer as if to reassess the falling coins, and said—a tad British—"I don't grasp"—*grawsp*—"how it works."

"Simple," said Boy Wonder, showing off his white teeth. "Every time a coin starts to fall, there's a fifty-fifty chance it will go left or right. It falls left or right, comes up against another peg, goes left or right again at fifty-fifty odds, and so on, *ad infinitum,* until it stops at the bottom. That's what gets you the bell-shaped curve. The fifty-fifty chance. Each time."

How very male of this guy to have an answer. The one and only absolute answer, presented with certainty but poorly explained. "Fifty-fifty," Diane countered. "As in a coin toss? So this is just a series of coin tosses? That's where I struggle. I see that if I toss a coin the chances of it landing on heads are the same as the chances of it landing on tails. But what about the *next* time? Let's say I toss a coin right now, today, right here in front of you, and up it comes, heads. I let twenty-four hours pass, and again, tomorrow, I toss the same coin right here in front of you. Are the odds once again fifty-fifty for heads? I should think not. I should think they're one in four at that point. But what if I waited a hundred years? Say I forget about the toss I made today and just happen to next toss a coin a hundred years from now. Fifty-fifty, or one in four for heads? What would the odds be? Can you answer?"

Boy Wonder looked amused. He crossed his arms and took in Diane as if she was a novelty. He scratched his head, tapped his shoe again, pondered the ground, and finally said, "Hmmm. My advice to you is, never go to Vegas. Unless you want to lose your shirt there. Fifty-fifty or four to one? Each toss is independent, so the odds of heads are always fifty-fifty. Because the coin doesn't know it was tossed before. A minute ago or a hundred years. Each time it's tossed, it's fifty-fifty, as if the coin was being tossed for the first time."

Diane shifted her coat again. Was her sorcery working? Or was he merely being polite to her, a fellow muller of a science exhibit? "I still don't get it," she insisted. Coyly.

"Try this," the guy advised. He shoved his hands in his front pants pockets and rocked on his heels, which, she had to notice, set his pelvis in motion. "You're on *Let's Make a Deal.* You're on *Let's Make a Deal,* and Monty Hall is telling you there's three doors. Behind one's a car. Behind each of the other two is, let's say, a goat. What do you do? Which door do you pick? Let's say you pick Door Number One. So now Monty Hall opens Door Number Three. Out steps a goat. And you're glad you didn't pick Door Number Three. But then Monty Hall says, 'Here we go. I'm going to open another door now, but before I do, let me ask you something. Would you like to switch your pick to Door Number Two?'"

"No."

Boy Wonder stopped rocking. "This is what I meant about Vegas," he said. "Don't go there. I beg you. Please."

Diane laughed, two truncated notes, issued through her nose and throat. "You're *mean,*" she told him. "Stop it."

"I'm not," he answered. "Door One or Door Two? Odds were one out of three at the beginning. At the total-guess stage. The clueless stage. Then Monty opens a door and shows a goat. Now you're choosing between two doors, right? It's like I said about the coin flip—heads or tails. You're starting over, Door One or Door Two, fifty-fifty, so what difference does it make? According to you, it makes no difference, you might as well stay with Door Number One. Okay, fine. But what if Monty knows that the goat's behind Number One? So when you say, 'One,' he knows you're wrong. Then he can *only* open Door Three, because behind Door Two is the car, and he knows that, too. He's forced to open Door Number Three because he doesn't want to show you the car's behind Two. Three is the only choice you've left for him by choosing Door Number One, a goat door."

Diane threw her coat over her shoulders like a cape. "Hmmm," she said. Boy Wonder smiled. "Win the car," he said. "When Monty opened Door Number Three and a goat walked out? Remember that? Before that, the odds were two out of three that the car was behind either Door Number Two or Door Number Three. Also, before that the odds were one out of three that the car was behind Door Number One. But now Monty opens Door Three and shows you the goat. And now Door Three is out of the running, and with Door Three out of the running, you can take it as a fact that the odds for Door Two are two out of three, not one out of three. So it's the better choice."

"Bravo," said Diane. "I guess I don't have to get it. If I go to Vegas, I'll just take you along."

They had coffee. Followed by dinner. His name was Ed—Ed King. His father, a doctor, had died that day, and he was, she could see, in need of comfort. "Well," she thought, "he's come to the right place. I'm all over that. I can do comfort." So, when the bill came, but before he'd paid, she told him, bluntly, "All right, Ed. Let's cut to the chase." And they did. At his house. Where things got strange.

Okay. Now we approach the part of the story a reader can't be blamed for having skipped forward to—"flipped forward to" if he or she has a hard copy, but otherwise "scrolled to" or "used the 'Find' feature to locate"— the part where a mother has sex with her son. Who could blame you for being interested in this potential hot part, and, at the same time, for shuddering at the prospect of it? Such mixed feelings are to be expected. Most people, bound by taboo, shy away from this arena even while propelled toward it. Most people, on hearing about the Oedipal complex, feel both resistant and drawn. The common solution is to take Freud figuratively, as pointing to psychological and emotional tendencies, but here, right now, with Ed and Diane, what we're moving toward is sex.

Males: if you didn't know that the woman you were about to have sex with was your mom, would leeriness stop you? What if, from your point of view, she was just a lot older than you, someone who, because of her age, might make you *think* of your mom but who definitely—you're sure of it—is *not* your mom? And females—here you are about to have sex with your son, but since you don't know it's your son, what difference could it make? None. You might think, "This guy is young enough to be my son," just as he might think, "This woman is old enough to be my mother," but in neither case would such thoughts necessarily put a stop to things. (In fact—and to the contrary—in many cases they would spur things on.) True, one or both partners might be distracted by the awareness that sex with someone so many years their junior or senior—as the case might be—was psychologically telling and a clue to something deep, but even that would rarely be a hindrance to their going ahead. And as for the sex itself, people think all sorts of things while in its throes, but when things are going right for them—when the sex is what is sometimes called "transporting"—their thoughts leave out everything else. Once they're transported, the Oedipal consideration, like a lot of other things, gets thrown out the window. And it got thrown out Ed and Diane's window at Ed's house that night. Diane knew perfectly well what she was doing—she didn't have to be a psychiatrist to understand the connection. At a point in life when some women looked up old boyfriends or paddled a kayak around Patagonia, Diane had sex with a twenty-seven-year-old. How wonderful it was—wonderful and surprising—to be attracted to a guy, to want sex. Diane found, once she was naked with him, that there were things she really liked in his performance, including, foremost, that he was relentlessly, acutely, even obsessively servile. It was fine with Ed to spend a half-hour massaging her feet and squeezing her ankles, followed by nearly equal devoted caressing of her shins and calves; next, moving up, he gave substantial attention to her knees and thighs, and when, in her massage trance, she hoped and believed that his hands would surely next go where they would do the most good, Ed didn't go there, he flipped her over instead and massaged, kneaded, stretched, rubbed, pinched, flicked, feathered, licked, kissed, and gently bit her shoulders, neck, back, and butt. Again she believed that he was on the verge of getting a hand between her legs, especially when, while massaging the small of her back, he found the tip of her tailbone. How long was he going to go on with the erotic massage and general body worship without getting to her quim? Would he please just go ahead and do something not frustrating? But she knew, before long, what he had to be waiting for. He was waiting for a display of need. So she took him by the wrist and moved the base of his hand into her pubic hair until his middle fingertip settled in the no-man's-land between her "front parlor" and "back door" (those were the quaint, prudish terms of her girlhood), she got him on the node between neighboring needs (both of which had been explored by johns who almost never tarried). She gave him this particular sign, this clear permission, and he began a careful prodding of her perineum, which was as good a starting place as any for Diane, because it instigated those processes of memory her sexuality required. It triggered memories with the uncanny force of déjà vu, and what she thought of, as Ed slaved away, was a boy from her village who had fingered her adroitly in a greenhouse thick with green tomatoes. She'd just turned fourteen. They'd both been stung by trapped bees that afternoon while grappling in the swelter and brilliant light and knocking over pots and tools. The sweat, swelling, and loam had staying power for her, as did the tang of chlorophyll and pungent tomatoes. So many of her johns had been musty, or sweet and sour, and then there was Jim with his Dial and Arid, and Walter Cousins with his cheap-cigar stink. Diane's imagery, as provoked by Ed, intensified and mingled with long-latent memories. On a bus to Bath there'd been favorable bouncing; then a lean-muscled tour guide asking, in a rhetorical and educational vein, why Apollo was in Roman bathhouses. The boy in the greenhouse was flawlessly adolescent and shockingly beautiful, and in his innocent way, he'd made her come resoundingly—Apollo with his modest marble *membrum virile*, otherwise known, in her village, 'as a skin flute. This memory sparkled as Ed intently suckled. They were both on their left sides now, Ed behind, where he'd pried her right shoulder back while deeply inserted and twisted his head so he could suckle away madly. He freed himself from her nipple after a long attachment so as to kiss her on the mouth at length—as if seeking to set the world record for kiss duration—and she smelled her breast on his breath, which was otherwise piquant with saliva, a little tart, a little bitter, and humid with the churning underworld—the raw metabolism and generative heat—beneath the flawless exterior. Jim Long's odor had been a little like Naugahyde, and his mouth, lips, and tongue had often tasted metallic (or, just as often, steeped in vermouth), whereas Ed smelled vulnerably digestive, warm-blooded, moist, and, just now, breast-fed. He smelled great, and she began to think, the way he was going at it now, that this was how he wanted to come—in her from behind, on one hip and elbow, contorted to kiss and with a hand between her legs. She was fine with that, would have welcomed it and joined him with a considerable bang, but what happened instead was that he pulled out at the last moment and, after turning her on her back, began yet another eternity of regional body worship, this one built around working his lips, tongue, and teeth down her rib cage and belly with that servility of his that was the flip side of masochism. To get Ed to burrow headfirst into her quim, Diane had to put her hands in his hair and, acknowledging her pressing need, press.

And here was another thing she really liked. The will to power that made him slavish in his attentions, dedicated to exploration, and responsive to response, also made him so lingual and labial that it spilled over to his nose, chin, and jaws; half of his face, nearly, was activated for her pleasure, and got slicked to a rough shine by his efforts. But—enough already. How much do we need? Or almost enough. Because it ought to be said that, at the moment of their mutual climax, Ed made sure Diane was on top, deliriously doing all the work.

These sorts of gyrations and five-sense choreographies, with variations on Ed's main themes, played out episodically between 10 p.m. and 10 a.m., when Diane said, "Let's shower."

In the shower, Ed stood with his hands at the back of his head, like someone just arrested, while she abused him with a bar of soap. After a while he shut his eyes, and Diane, wielding her fingernails now and staring at his face, helped him out with two practiced hands, one squeezing the family jewels, the other vigorous with the soap-and-warm-water treatment. It didn't take long for the beautiful and perfect Ed King to ejaculate for the fifth time in twelve hours, while looking like Roman public-bath statuary. Then they rinsed, dried, dressed, and went to an expensive restaurant for lunch.

10

Ed King

Ed and Diane did a lot together in the second half of Bush Senior's administration. They saw Green Day and the Red Hot Chili Peppers. They got scared during *The Silence of the Lambs,* then took the Argosy Cruise to Tillicum Village for clams and salmon in a longhouse. They went to the Goodwill Games to watch fantastic swimmers, to the Bolshoi, and to *War and Peace,* the opera. They saw "modern tap" at the Egyptian, Cirque du Soleil at Marymoor Park, Tom Jones at the Paramount, Herbie Hancock at Jazz Alley, and Penn & Teller at the 5th Avenue. They ate regularly at Il Terrazzo Carmine. They visited the Burke Museum, did the *Tony n' Tina's Wedding* dinner show, and sunbathed at Alki. They rented a canoe and toodled around Lake Washington, took the train to Glacier Park—white tablecloth, private berth—stayed for three nights at Paradise on Mount Rainier, then three at Mount Hood, then three at Crater Lake. They went to San Francisco to roam and eat well. They read the same books and discussed them on trips. More than once the subject came up: how did Ed really feel about an older woman? Always wonderful. Great.

Confident in the future—and leaning on Alice, who had the benefit of

Dan's belief in life insurance—Ed bought a house on Lake Sammamish with a boat launch, a hot tub, a heat pump, energy-efficient windows, high ceilings, and mahogany flooring from Brazil. His home office featured an expanse of curved glass wall overlooking the boat-churned lake—a backdrop for his monitors and hard drives. Rolling across the floor in a high-backed chair, tapping on keyboards and manipulating mice, he felt like a ship's captain on duty in a wheelhouse. On a whim, he bought a runabout with an open cockpit and a foredeck made out of Alaska yellow cedar that made him feel, self-consciously, like James Bond. Diane moved in with him in '91. They put up pickles, learned the secrets of a waffle iron, and hung curtains in the bathroom. At that point, Alice stopped telling herself that Diane was just a fling. She didn't embrace Ed's older woman, but she didn't turn away from her, either. She accepted the cohabitation arrangement because, number one, what could she do about it, and, number two, because she didn't really believe that her son would marry a woman too far along to have kids. Didn't Ed want kids? She brought this up with him when Diane wasn't around, and was surprised at how nonchalant he seemed about it. "Kids would just be in the way," he told her. "I have big plans."

The battle began for Alice's approval. At Thanksgiving, Ed and Diane invited Simon and his "friend" Andrea, and Alice and her sister, Bernice, who, like Alice, was widowed and making the best of it, which meant, right now, visiting from Philadelphia and staying with Alice for six weeks. Simon came looking like Elvis Costello, down to the tight pants and high-water socks. Andrea, a pillowy yin to his knock-kneed yang, was edgy and plump. At first, she and Simon sat on a couch whispering into each other's hair, but at dinner they let up a little under the influence of Diane's comfort food. Andrea, her face flushed by red wine, became daughterly toward Alice and Bernice, ignored Diane, and got combative with Ed. "Simon's brother," she said, "I'm not as trim as you, but it's Thanksgiving, okay? So pass the mashed potatoes." "Did Ed ever help with the dishes growing up, Alice? He looks like he's settled in over there. Have more pie, Ed. Relax."

By mid-December, Si and Andrea weren't together anymore, "not even as friends," Si emphasized, "because she makes demands, and I'm way too busy." Diane and Ed put on Christmas for Jews—the same crowd, minus Andrea—and that night Ed overheard Alice and Bernice talking quietly in the guest bedroom. "The plastic surgery's so obvious," said Alice. "I mean, her values, I don't understand. Why spend a fortune on something like that? Caring so much about your appearance you're willing to go under the knife?"

"What about your nose-job period?" Bernice said.

"I *considered* it, but my better self won."

"Well, where do you draw the line?" asked Bernice. "How far do you want to take this discussion? Can I get my hair done without you . . . I don't know, forget it. How old do you think she is?"

"If you adjust for the surgery? The completely vain surgery? But that's not the *real* point. The real point is, she never went to college! Who knows if she even made it through high school? I don't see that she's done anything *meaningful* with her life. And when she got married, she married into money—her marriage was to *money*. That's the most revealing thing about this . . . what does he *see* in her?"

"It sounded so WASP," Bernice replied. "All that skiing and the trips to the Olympics. To me, the whole thing sounds . . . yuck."

Simon, on New Year's Eve, had yet another new look—lean the way a vulture can be lean, but outdoorsish with a hi-tech flourish. He was now enamored of lightweight clothing that offered maximal warmth-value per ounce while wicking away moisture and perspiration. His glasses were sturdier than they'd been before, and his skin looked wind- and sun-cured. Simon had done a December stint of "competitive orienteering," which meant unearthing snowbound clues, discovered via careful map and compass work, with a partner name Logan Ames. He, Logan, and Logan's girlfriend were going to Argentina in February for a guided climb of Aconcagua. Simon had taken up cooking, too. There was an hors d'oeuvre he was bent on serving that night involving Brie and chanterelles, and a date-and-walnut tapenade he'd brought in a fanciful crock. He'd also brought videocassettes of King family movies, which made Alice ecstatic, and so all of them—Diane, Bernice, Alice, Ed, and Simon—watched an hour of grainy footage while eating Simon's noshes with gusto. They laughed at Dan, in mirrored glasses, reading *Sports Illustrated* on a Mexican beach while looking scalded and droopy, and heard Alice whisper, from behind her movie camera, "*Say* something, Daniel, talk about our trip." There was a blip, some white space, and then on the screen Ed appeared as a four-year-old, hobbling around on his curved feet in the back yard and throwing a Wiffle Ball wildly. Next, Ed, age eight, with his baseball cards, celebrating them like a salesman while sitting at the kitchen table with a three-ring binder; Ed in a skimpy nylon swim suit, shaking his hands out before a race, then diving powerfully at the firing of a pistol and immediately taking a big lead. Restless footage, marked by background din and a lot of shaky camera work, of Bar Mitzvah boy Simon at the height of his geek period, giggling with his friends and gobbling cake, followed by Ed at sixteen, changing the oil in his GTO while Alice, behind the camera, said, "Eddie, pull your hair out of your eyes and smile for once, please." "Looking pretty retro," Simon now sniggered, while spreading his homemade tapenade on crostini. "I'd sort of forgotten your muscle car, Eddie, not to mention your bad-ass era. You were one evil dude. You were *classic.*"

Diane had dressed conservatively for New Year's, but still showed ample, handsome leg, which had the effect, Ed thought, of making Bernice and Alice antagonistic. Bernice explained, for Diane's benefit, the distinction between Ashkenazic and Sephardic Jews, between Hasidism and more conventional Orthodoxy, and between rugelach and a cinnamon twist. She also said that, looking in the mirror, she saw Bette Midler, whereas Alice insisted that Bernice looked more like Glenn Close ("Your chin is definitely Glenn's, not Bette's"). They tried Simon's tapenade, pronounced it wonderful, and extolled Simon's culinary skills and "expansion of interests." Too much wine was going down now, and the overrouged Levine sisters were out of control. Bernice insisted that an English breakfast was inexplicable to Americans ("We would never eat a tomato that way"). Diane replied that it wasn't an English breakfast without baked beans and black pudding, and then she had to explain black pudding, which Bernice said sounded "oy, but to each his own." "Isn't this nice?" said Alice. "Some girl talk of the Martha Stewart variety." Bernice added, "I read recently that her maiden name was Kostyra and that she grew up in Polish Jersey."

"Okay," said Ed. "You're harassing Diane. Diane—harassment can happen here, definitely."

"We love her," Bernice answered. "She's beautiful."

"How old would Petula Clark be these days?" asked Alice.

"Or Lulu," said Bernice. "The *To Sir, with Love* singer."

"Harassment," said Ed. "Come on, it's New Year's."

"No," said Diane, "I'm having a great time." And, raising her glass of Asti Spumante, she merrily added, *"L'chaim!"*

When the night was over and they were jointly cleaning up, Bernice said, "I've always admired the British. If it wasn't for Churchill being such a pit bull, Hitler might have annihilated the Jews, and I probably wouldn't be standing here with my dish towel. Which maybe wouldn't be such a bad thing, because, really, I'm about to fall over."

"Ditto," said Alice. "What a night!"

Diane looked animated, wide awake, and bright. "Why don't the two of you sit?" she said. "Put your feet up and don't worry about a thing. I'll clean this up. You sit."

Ed and Diane got married at the Chapel of the Flowers in Las Vegas. First they bought a license at the Clark County Courthouse, and then, at the chapel, they picked out a bouquet and a boutonniere, stepped up to the altar for the minister's shtick, laughed a little with the campy, droll organist, and handsomely tipped their smiling witness, a nursing student at UNLV. Since the weather that day was not unbearably hot, they walked the two and a half miles from the chapel to the Mirage, where they consummated their contract on a heart-shaped bed before appropriating a poolside cabaña. That night, Ed and Diane ate five courses of French food, then watched a magician, as his culminating act, produce a Corvette out of nowhere and drive offstage in it.

At home again on Lake Sammamish, Ed got out his calculator. Though he was newly married, it was now nearly four years since he'd met Diane, and (six times a week on average, multiplied by 190 weeks) they'd copulated more than a thousand times. When he mentioned this figure to her, she smiled and said she hoped a marriage license would not be deleterious to either quality or quantity. As things unfolded, a thousand was just a start; five years later—at about the time when people were beginning to worry about Y2K—they surpassed two thousand. By then, Ed was past thirty-five, so thereafter frequency declined more steeply— still, their total rose steadily as the new millennium gained steam. On his fortieth birthday, in 2003, Ed concluded that he'd come three thousand times in, on, or with the assistance of Diane. Calculating further, he estimated that they'd engaged in sex for somewhere between a thousand and fifteen hundred hours. He and Diane had done everything, and plenty of it. He'd explored, thousands of times, every nook of her body, and she'd explored his with equal, unflagging interest. Their juices and smells had mingled and mixed. It had been, and still was, electrifying.

In 2003, Alice died of breast cancer, in disbelief until the end. Ed grieved, of course, but went on with life the way people said you were supposed to—by keeping busy. Keeping busy was easy, because Pythia, by then, had become a mega-company. Besides growing with a decided roar into global prominence, it was, by 2003, relocating to a four-thousand-acre complex ten miles east of Seattle. The mooring of major tech companies to geography had, by this time, yielded "the Googleplex" and "the Microsoft campus," but Pythia headquarters, in the Cascade foothills, soon became known to the world, simply, as Pythia. Ed and Diane lived famously there. Pythia was vast, with lakes, woods, hills, valleys, ravines, and bogs surrounding its buildings and parking lots, and this allowed the Kings to dwell securely on three hundred acres walled off as private grounds. Their much-talked-about estate was ringed by speculation. The house wasn't visible except from overhead. Servants and assistants lived on-site. Deliveries were met and off-loaded at the main gate, then transferred to the couple's inner sanctum, or to the Japanese teahouse where the Kings met dignitaries. Or, rather, it was said they met dignitaries there. Little was known definitively, though two sets of facts were a matter of record—the estate's assessed value as it changed from year to year, and what the Kings paid annually in property taxes. (These numbers appeared on dedicated Web sites, foremost among them KingWatch and Python, as did descriptions of Ed's haircuts, the names of Diane's dress designers, sightings of Ed and Diane in foreign locales, blurry photos of them on vacation, and the price, configuration, and security features of their super-yacht.) A widely accepted truth held that their complex at Pythia had copious and cutting-edge green-design features (these had been tipped to the press before construction). Beyond that, nearly everything was rumor. Reportedly, a herd of Roosevelt elk had been transferred to the grounds so that the Kings could observe them from various balconies. And there was speculation that the aboveground house, as seen on P-Planet, was the mere tip of the iceberg—that beneath it lay an unknown world.

"The Castle," as it was ubiquitously known, walled Ed and Diane off from the voyeurs, celebrity addicts, and paparazzi, who, by 2005, were relentlessly not leaving them alone. But what walled people out also walled them in, so Ed and Diane bought an island in the San Juans and conjured a second kingdom there. After that they bought a twelfth-century castle in Cumbria—twenty-seven minutes from the airport in Carlisle—with walled gardens, a Norman keep, and seventy-four buffering acres of rolling lea and wood. This was where Diane liked to spend her days, living like a baroness behind ashlar walls, taking her meals by a window with a fine prospect, and reading in a solarium that looked out on roses. In Cumbria, she developed an interest in Jane Austen's novels. In interviews, she said that she liked Austen's smart women and loathed her cads and lords. Soon it occurred to her to give a million pounds to the Jane Austen Trust. Lo and behold, the response to her largesse was so overwhelmingly positive that Diane started looking for other places to put money. Pythia made her the head of its foundation, and she passed long hours examining pleas for funding. Diane loved this work: here, the nays; there, the ayes; over there, the pile of maybes. Requests were endless. With no shortage of need, Diane kept busy, often at a writing table in her library at Cumbria, which looked out on vast greenswards and scrupulously shorn topiary.

Despite multiple homes, walls, and acreage, Ed and Diane remained exposed to clever litigants—a constant stream—and to tangible threats necessitating an ever-expanding security apparatus. In Diane's case that meant deflecting old johns who thought they could come out of the woodwork without consequence. Ron Dominick, too, tried stepping up to the plate but, unwilling to reveal his identity as a former coke dealer, never gave heft to unsubstantiated claims. A number of journalists assailed Jim Long in the hope of digging up divorce dirt from the ski baron, but Jim refused all media requests, preferring, as he wrote in a press release on the subject, "to respect Diane King's right to privacy regarding personal matters." What stuck? Hearsay? Titillating innuendo? That Diane had had a sex life before marrying into Pythia? That Diane had been young in the era of Big Blow? There were presidents and prime ministers who'd been coke users, too. Everything else was tabloid grist. Diane didn't exactly resemble Teflon, but nothing bouncing around out there about her did material damage to Pythia's image or bottom line.

Ed was similarly resilient, but in '05 his shield was penetrated by a phone message reading, "Tracy, no last name given," followed by a return number and the insinuating message: "We need to talk about Walter."

He called immediately. His goth ex-girlfriend was now Tracy Hoepfinger, forty-four, mother of two, living in Phoenix, and recently divorced from an HVAC technician. "And *you're* rich and famous," she said. "Your name's in all the tabloids."

"Good to reconnect, Tracy."

"For me it is. Because my ship just came in."

Before long, she'd forced him to orchestrate a summit worthy of a spy movie. Tracy insisted that it had to happen now, which was easy for a guy who owned a customized 747, a matched pair of fifty-million-dollar Gulfstream G-550s, and a Cessna Citation X that flew at nearly the speed of sound. For his trip to Phoenix, Ed chose a Gulfstream and an on-call pilot who went by a name—Guido Sternvad—that was hard to take seriously. "How does a person get a name like Guido Sternvad?" he'd asked, the first time he'd strapped in beside Guido in an airplane. Guido had replied, "I ask the same question. It's that kind of name. Guido Sternvad. Calls attention to itself. People are always asking me about it. They think it's a joke, it can't be what I'm called. As soon as they hear it, they laugh, you know? They think I must be kidding. They want to know—is that really your name?"

"Doesn't matter to me one way or the other," replied Ed. "But as long as we're just sort of fooling around talking about it, I mean, Guido, come on, if you read 'Guido Sternvad' in a book you'd think the author couldn't think of a believable name. It's not believable."

"Hmmm," said Guido. "I don't think you're right about that. Cuz I'm a big reader, a big reader there, boss, and, really, you see all kinds of names in books. You ever read *Lolita,* by Vladimir Nabokov? Main character's name is Humbert Humbert. You supposed to believe that? No, you're not. And there's another guy in *Lolita,* name of Vivian Darkbloom. 'Vivian Darkbloom' is 'Vladimir Nabokov.' Does the author have a reason for doing that, you think? Or is he just goofing around and playing games for the hell of it? Speaking of anagrams," Guido pressed on, "I'm an anagram *freak.* I love 'em, anagrams. Especially when they bring a big shot to the ground. Take T. S. Eliot—anagrams to 'toilets.' Hey, try me. Try 'Guido Sternvad.' See what you get. You'll be surprised."

"I doubt it."

"Worth your time," said Guido. "Lot of fun. There's great ones out there. I think of anagrams all the time. Deviant Rug Sod. That's me—Guido Sternvad. Doug Invert Sad. Me again. Dan Soviet Drug. Me. Vern Studio Gad. Me. Nat Dodge Virus. Me. Sometimes I get obsessed with a first name, too. David Nuts Gore, David Ogre Stun, David Gut Noser, David—"

"Shut up, Guido."

"There's you, too, boss. Don't forget you. Edward King? Kindred Wag? But I can see you're not impressed. You want names? I can tell—you want names. Okay, tough guy: Dirk Gnawed? Drake W. Ding? Kidder Wang? Isn't this great! I could—"

"Guido. Please."

"One more," said Guido. "One I really like. Nothing to do with your name, boss, just a good old-fashioned dark, foreboding one. It's 'our destiny,' stick 'our destiny' in your anagram generator and guess what you get? You get 'It's your end.' 'Our destiny' equals 'It's your end.' Isn't that something? Isn't that great? How the hell did God come up with anagrams?"

Swarthy and porkchop-sideburned, moody and manipulative, Guido held sway over Ed this way. It was understood that copilots got paid to stay on the ground and watch movies in the hangar while Ed took informal but advanced flying lessons, checked out the novel vista of the earth's curve, and got a bang out of Guido and the radio traffic: all those dueling military drawls, diligently projecting calm. Ed had a working knowledge of the Gulfstream's Flight Management System and of its Engine Indicating and Crew Alerting System. He could fly by instruments, if not by stick and rudder, and since the plane was his, he did whenever possible—including on this trip to Phoenix—with Guido providing wicked commentary.

In Phoenix—with its impossible-to-live-in blast-furnace May weather—Ed found Tracy where she said she would be, beside the boat-rental office in Encanto Park. She seemed agitated by a compensatory bluster as she made breezy small talk and walked at an exercise clip. Her dry brown skin, slack cleavage, and sprayed coif were new, but the look on her face was a look Ed remembered—hard and immune to moral argument. Finally, they perched on a bench by the lagoon, Ed in his Vuarnets and an Arizona Diamondbacks cap, Tracy in million-dollar faded jeans.

" 'I Saw Search King Commit Murder,' " she said. "I can see that in the *National Enquirer*."

Ed sighed.

"Wouldn't that be a bummer?" said Tracy. "Especially because, when it comes to murder, there's no statute of limitations."

"This is disappointing," said Ed. "You're about the thousandth old friend who's sent me a note, only to proceed to extortion."

"Walter Cousins," said Tracy. "You ran him off the road and killed him, Ed, remember?"

"No. And this is sad, Tracy. You're really stooping."

"I see why you've gotten so rich," she answered.

"And I see extortion and deceit," Ed replied. "This is no way to make a living, Tracy. Look, if you want to contact the *National Enquirer* and report to them your falsehood and fabrication, I can't stop you from doing that, can I? But it'll just be another rumor, that's all. No—I'm not giving you a single dime."

"You could also go to prison," Tracy observed.

"Well, if I did it would be one of those very sad cases where an inno-cent person is victimized by a liar. But I don't think a prosecutor is going to press charges against me based on what you fabricate." Ed got up. "I'm really sorry I came down here," he said. "I didn't expect this, but I should have. Oh well, take care, Tracy. I mean that. I wish you all the best."

He walked away at an unruffled pace while Tracy yelled, "That's Ed King! Right there! That guy! He's a murderer! Ed King is a murderer!" But no one in the park showed anything but perplexity in response to this manner of accusation. Which was good, because Ed's heart was beat-ing faster than it had since the day he'd killed Walter Cousins.

Later, on the tarmac, as Ed was strapping in, Guido asked, "Quickie in the desert?"

"Shut up, Guido."

"Hey, you're the man. You're always the main man, sir."

Ed sighed. What was wrong with this guy? For a moment he thought of firing him on the spot, but, on the other hand, Guido was time-passing entertainment. "Listen up, Guido," he said. "We're going to change places. I think I'll take the wheel of my plane. I feel like flying my plane right now so I don't have to listen to your bullshit."

"You feel like flying," Guido answered, getting up. "You want to be a pilot. You want to decide where we go and how we get there. Our flight destination, our flight path, our altitude. Have at it, then, sir. Go right ahead. But if you're going to be a pilot, you need to learn the lingo. It's 'take the controls,' not 'take the wheel.' You got that? *'Controls.'* "

"Roger," said Ed, then got up and moved left. "Relax, Sternvad. Be a passenger for a while. Read a magazine or something, but shut up."

"Roger," said Guido. "Good one, sir. You want to learn some professional lingo? Try 'Alpha Mike Foxtrot,' as in 'Adios *Mother Fucker.*' Try 'sending an admiral to sea.' That's taking a shit before you take off. 'Checking for light leaks'—that's lingo for a nap. 'Kick the tires and light the fires'—that's taking off without a full safety check. Here's a good one—'My fun meter's pegged.' That's sarcasm for combat danger. Got the hang, sir? You feeling warm-fuzzy? You ready to be a real pilot?"

"Alpha Mike Foxtrot."

"Put it in the air, then," Guido said. "I'll watch."

Ed pulled over in the run-up area and, while ostensibly checking his data and instruments, silently cursed Guido Sternvad. Then he switched his radio from ground to tower, and when his turn came, teased the power levers forward, hit the throttle, surged down the runway, and got off the ground without a hitch. "You see, I'm in control," he announced, pulling back on the yoke. "I can fly this plane as well as you can."

"For the moment," said Guido, and raised the landing gear. "But you think you could fly solo? You wouldn't go Whiskey Delta in Sweat Bead Condition One if you were up here flying solo, would you? You know that one? 'Whiskey Delta'? Weak dick, sir. Now throttle back a little, tough guy. I don't want us joining the Martin-Baker Fan Club."

"Martin-Baker Fan Club?"

"Maker of ejection seats. Martin-Baker. So don't lose the bubble there, Top Gun."

Absolutely no one talked to Ed like this, but somehow Guido got away with it. In fact, between Phoenix and Seattle he harangued Ed incessantly: "You think you're a pilot? Well, chew on this, sir. You're actually just a cog in a flying machine, hauling passengers from A to B. Did I say passengers? Passengers are pawns. Smooth flight, they snore; turbulence, they're scared of dying. If I want to, I can sit up here playing with their heads. Snore. Fear of dying. Whatever. Up to me. Maybe I get on the intercom and hail them, just to remind them I'm actually here. Up in the cockpit behind my locked door. Sure, I sound calm, nothing's a big deal, but remember, you're all at my mercy!"

Ed said, "Guido, shut up for a minute. Shut up and let me fly the plane."

"Fine," said Guido. "But just to Seattle. Your two-bit hometown. I'll give that to you—no harm there. There's nothing doing between here and there anyway. Just bland weather, fair skies, flat air, Point A to Point B; so, sure, go ahead, be a pilot if you need to, but don't try straying from the flight plan, okay? And no tricks, or I'm taking the controls."

"Straight to Seattle," said Ed. "Now shut up."

Guido did shut up, but only for a minute, so as to give full attention to a new round of Name Scramble. "Hey, man," he said. "Check this out. Check this out, sir. It's great!" He thrust his P-Pad in front of Ed's face, so Ed could read:

DARK WINGED

"Get it?" asked Guido. "Edward King. Dark Winged! Edward King is Dark Winged!"

Ed pushed the P-Pad out of his way. "Guido," he said, "I'm trying to fly my plane right now, so I don't want to hear another word from you. Not *one.*"

"Dark Winged!" repeated Guido. "That's perfect!"

In Seattle, once he was cleared for approach, Ed turned off the auto-pilot and said, "I'll do this stick-and-rudder, Sternvad, just to show you I can." He got everything right, too, and could have met the runway gently, but instead landed with his nose a tad high in a showy, fighter-pilot touchdown. Sternvad yawned. "Great," he said. "Perfect weather, no wind. You're really a right-stuff guy, King."

At the Pythia hangar, Ed's chopper was waiting with its rotors turning already. Everything was as it should be—the Tracy problem solved—except that Guido wouldn't shut up, even now that they were on the ground. Ed, before deplaning, tried for the last word: "I mean it, Stern-vad. Don't talk so much. Your babbling gets on my nerves."

"Really," answered Guido. "Well, let me tell you something, guy. All right, you're the richest man in the universe, you got what people dream of, you're a big name, the boss. But you know what? Not on *my* plane. On my plane, *I'm* in charge."

"No," said Ed, "this is *my* plane. Don't forget that. It's not your plane. I hired you to fly it, so shut up and fly it when I ask you to, okay? Get me from Point A to Point B."

"Now, wait," said Guido. "We got a rule in aviation. And that rule is, the skipper of the plane, the head pilot—me—that person has say over everything—*everything*! I'm the one in charge of what happens. I'm God here, okay? You're along for the ride."

"Bad delusions of grandeur," said Ed. "You're a *driver,* Guido. You're a chauffeur, not God. Think about this—did you pay for the fuel? For the maintenance? The hangar? Anything? Yes or no? Guido, you're just a driver on call. You don't do anything but wait for me to snap my fingers. In fact, if it wasn't for me, you wouldn't *exist.*"

"It's the other way around," insisted Guido. "You need *me.* Otherwise, you're stuck on the ground. You get what I'm saying? I'm the captain. I'm the key. I'm the linchpin. You're just a passenger."

Ed said, "I love you, man. Great trip. Thanks for everything. But—shut up, okay? Just shut up."

Guido answered, "As soon as we deplane, you won't hear a word from me." And then Guido let the gangway down, took the stairs with rapid ease, and strode away with the proud gait of someone who's sure he's the hero of his own life.

With the years Diane became her own business, and opened secret accounts in Turks and Caicos, Singapore, and Luxembourg. They were, of course, pointless in her present incarnation as Mrs. Ed King, the Queen of Search, but because she'd been knocked down more than once in life, she still felt the need for a backup plan and a bottom-line desperation retreat. The plan she put in place called for a fake name—Eunice Halston-Smith was what she came up with, because it sounded appropriately stuffy—a false British passport, the secret accounts, and a secret residence in northwestern Tasmania, ten minutes from a regional airport. There she kept on hire a staff aware of her only as a mysterious English widow who paid extremely well via a trust officer in Sydney. She was Mrs. Halston-Smith, who liked poetry and fine art, if the evidence on her shelves and walls was any indication. Diane never visited this last-ditch hideaway, but in the pictures she'd seen it looked like Balmoral Castle, with a thousand hectares of forest and field, an ambience of baronial calm, orderly gardens, and a sea view from a precipice. If it came to it, for whatever reason, she could live out her days there with decent Pinot on hand and no need ever to lift a finger.

But right now, there was a job to do, and that was to use Pythia's security apparatus to track down her half-brother Club. He was a longshoreman, it turned out, in Long Beach, California, and a member of Local 19. There were two drinking establishments he frequented in Norwalk—both close enough to his third-floor flat so he could shuffle back to it in half an hour—one a cocktail lounge at Studebaker and Rosecrans, and the other across the 605, near a McDonald's, a doughnut shop, and a coin laundry, all of which were also part of Club's life. Club didn't do much other than work, watch television, drink, and ride a heavily lacquered Goldwing touring bike. After work, he stopped sometimes at a Wal-Mart in Long Beach. He liked Roscoe's House of Chicken, and Hamburger Mary's, and almost always bought gas at the same 7-Eleven. Club lived alone and had never been married. While wrestling with various green-card hassles, he'd served three years' probation as an accomplice to grand larceny. Lately he'd been buying a lot of Hot Spot and SuperLotto Plus tickets. He was badly overweight, with an achy back and sloped shoulders. On the docks, wearing a lumbar support with crossing shoulder straps and chewing on a toothpick, he drove reach trucks and side-loaders. Impacted teeth made it hard for Club to chew. Diverticulitis, a hammer toe, and sleep apnea had all taken a toll on him. Still, he was not immune to ponying up for the occasional prostitute, and every spring he rode with other Goldwingers to Vegas. Club's tradition in Nevada was to try a new brothel each year and to place paltry bets in a race-and-sports lounge. At home, he was religious about Friday happy-hour drinking at the Zoo Room, a Long Beach bar that served Boddingtons and aired the English Premier League on large screens.

Security had more data if Diane wanted it. She didn't because the data presented were sufficient for the planning she was about. The first step was to locate a dominatrix in L.A. There were plenty to choose from, including many who had private studios where a client could be trampled, flogged, smothered, choked, chained, and so forth, and some who traveled with kits. Diane settled on the English Mistress, who emphasized red bottoms, and who described herself, in a return phone call to Diane, as specializing in restraint, rope bondage, medical play, and paddling. She had a dungeon but would carry equipment on hotel calls. On request, she worked with a partner.

All of that sounded good to Diane. She told the English Mistress that the prospective client, her husband, Caleb, was eager to role-play from start to finish as a burly longshoreman who meets the English Mistress in a bar and proceeds from there to her fancy hotel room. The English Mistress would play a well-to-do Londoner on holiday in California who is away from her effete and asexual spouse. It was a birthday present for Caleb, Diane explained, and the kicker was that Diane would participate. "What do you think?" she asked. "What would that cost?" Then she hung up and made a reservation under an assumed name for a Royalty Suite on the *Queen Mary,* now a Long Beach waterfront hotel instead of a trans-Atlantic ocean liner. The next day, Diane got installed in her kitschy California lodgings and convened a planning session with the English Mistress, who looked like Barbie at forty. Things couldn't have been more perfect.

On the Friday in question, then, the English Mistress, costumed as a traveler out of her element while baring a little risqué cleavage, sat nervously nursing a colorful drink at one end of the Zoo Room's bar. When Club stepped up and ordered a double scotch, neat, and a pint of Boddingtons, the English Mistress looked at him quizzically and said, "Now, that's quite tricky. East Midlands, is it not?"

Club went for it. Aboard the *Queen Mary,* in a gilded hallway, the English Mistress explained herself. "I travel, you might say, equipped," she said. "There's no use for my tools at home, you see, so why not take them on the road?"

Club said, "I'm with you. Gagging for it."

"Good," said the English Mistress. "Because I'm going to take your dangly-bits, Caleb, and have a royal go at them, you know."

In the Royalty Suite, with rope, a collar, cuffs, chains, a gag, and nautical cleats, she got Club into the butt-high posture Diane had elaborated for her. She caned him red, flogged and insulted him, and then she told Club, who looked like wild boar on a serving plate, that she had yet another surprise in the offing: a second dominatrix—was he ready for this?—who was known as the Goddess of Vengeance. Of course, Club couldn't endorse or reject such an eminence, because he had a ball in his mouth held in place by headgear. So the English Mistress rang up the Goddess of Vengeance, who arrived at Club's bedside wearing a mask she'd acquired earlier that day at an upscale adult store in Beverly Hills— leather, handmade, with elaborate tooling, and a row of stainless-steel spikes in its forehead. Hovering over Club, the Goddess of Vengeance clutched a ten-dollar voice synthesizer—the sort of thing meant for trick-or-treating or for disguising one's voice in the service of prank phone calls—and displayed a plastic funnel with a ten-inch hose.

"Is he prepared?" she asked, through the synthesizer.

"Yes, Goddess," intoned the English Mistress. "And now I bid you farewell."

When she was gone, the Goddess advised Club, through the synthesizer, "Grit your teeth. This is really going to hurt." Then she pulled on surgical gloves and fed the hose into him. What could he do? There was nothing he could do. He struggled, puckered, wheezed, and strained, but the Goddess of Vengeance went on feeding in the tube until the whole ten inches was snaked into Club and the funnel was pinched between his butt cheeks.

Speaking once more through the synthesizer, she said, "So how does that feel? Do you like it?"

From a drawer she took a pint can of Boddingtons, popped the top, then poured some into Club's eyes. The rest got poured into the funnel, where it pooled and drained gradually. "Delicious," said the Goddess, as the can slowly emptied. "I'm sure you're enjoying this."

She set the empty Boddingtons on the bedside table, where Club could read its label. "Irony," she said. "Well, I better run and pee." Then she slipped off her gloves, tossed them on his back, and left the room.

The ascendance of Pythia proceeded apace—600 million raised in a just post-millennial IPO—with Ed as overlord and tyrant. He kept his finger on the company pulse and put his imprint—publicly—on each gamble and initiative. New products were unveiled at monster events, carefully crafted, zealously produced, and scheduled to crown huge hype campaigns aimed at cranking up hysteria for launch dates. Ed, as chief pitchman, was a dazzler, a shill, an icon, and a superstar genius, and so visible, available, prominent, and profiled that in the public eye, worldwide, Pythia and Ed were the same. What happened to one, happened to the other. Pythia was built around a charismatic leader whose persona demanded constant monitoring by a team of propagandists who fretted and bit their nails. All it would take was a slip, they knew—the wrong words out of Ed's mouth, say, or a bit of unsavory personal news—to send Pythia's stock price spiraling. Worst-case scenario was personal catastrophe—that might spell the demise of Pythia. He could go to jail, like Martha Stewart or Bernard Madoff, or go crazy, like Howard Hughes.

It didn't help—as it might have helped—that in 2013, at the age of fifty, Ed handed over day-to-day operations to President Buddy Singh. It didn't help because Ed didn't leave the stage—he just stopped attending to every detail, in favor of continued media intensity, continued unilateral decision-making, and more time for neglected personal matters, foremost among them, the long deferred need to exercise. Over the years, his curved feet had caused damage to his knees, so now he had his knees replaced by the best doctor in the business; then he had laser eye surgery, which improved his vision to twenty-fifteen. All of this felt so renewing and invigorating that Ed, wanting more of it, hired a personal longevity consultant, who advised, and administered, treatments to stave off aging. Diane got on that wagon, too, and they both began taking not only human growth hormone and the steroid known as DHEA, but intravenous infusions of phosphatidylcholine isolated from egg yolks. Diane replaced estrogen, and Ed took testosterone. Diane had another face-lift; Ed had his chin tucked.

With more time on his hands, Ed became—besides the King of Search—the king of acquisitions. He got addicted to buying companies, at first via cooperative and friendly mergers, then through management-endorsed tender offers, and then—whatever it took. He had a knack for lightning-fast due diligence investigations, loved a complicated proxy fight, and rained enough generosity on defeated CEOs to incline future victims toward buckling. At a daily meeting with generals, he evaluated targets and heard battle updates. They convened in a war room. A general would describe a target's defensive posture, and Ed would throw money at it to make it go away. He was like a snowball rolling steeply downhill, always bigger, always gathering mass, to the point where a cascade, or even an avalanche, could be generated across a sector of the economy by virtue of his motion and growth.

At a war-room meeting in June of '14, a general suggested that Pythia acquire GameKing—Simon's company—after detailing how it was getting hammered of late by PlayStation, Xbox, and Nintendo. Ed said, "Okay, but get there invisibly," and within a few months he'd amassed control of Simon's company, at which point his brother, ferreting out the truth, stopped speaking to him and moved to Santa Barbara to grow a beard and teach. Just as well, thought Ed, because Si lacked the killer instinct. He found, reading Si's post-GameKing think pieces in journals, that Si liked ruminating on "algorithmic culture" more than he'd ever liked superintending his bottom line. Sloppy business practices had been fine when Si was on a roll, but as the real players in gaming became more ruthless, Si hadn't been able to contend or even stay at the table. On top of this, he suffered, at midlife, from abstract passions that were taking him out of the game anyway. Toward the end of his career as GameKing's kingpin, Simon's big subject had been "narrative transitivity." He'd come to believe in not meeting expectations, in contradictory logic, in challenging "the mainstream gaming industry," in disruption, estrangement, and intellectual provocation, and he'd predicted confidently that, not far in the future, "representation in gaming narratives" would give way significantly to a blurring of reality, and after that to a more compelling paradigm, the harbinger of which was good old tried-and-true reality TV. When that happened, Simon would be poised for the changing of the guard and recognized as prescient. It hadn't worked, but no matter. Simon had money put away for a rainy day and, by keeping things sleek, could do what he wanted, which was to write, and lecture, on "Counter Gaming," "Representational Modeling," "Non-Diegetic Machine Acts," and—his favorite—"Parallels Between the New Gaming and New Cinema."

So Ed and Si didn't talk, and Ed got used to it. He began to see himself as youthfully emeritus, and felt good about being looked to as a visionary. He was a steady, bubbling font of new ideas, and directed his company via inspirational appearances at Pythia campuses worldwide. In Mumbai, he talked about Universal Search, in London about Voice Search, in Moscow about the Ultimate Encyclopedia, in Sydney about the Human Genome Project, in Shanghai about Pythia's nanotech research, in Palo Alto about its new analytics engine. He promoted Diane's foundation—the Edward and Diane King Foundation—which, he told audiences, had in one year alone put seven billion dollars to work against some of the world's most intractable problems (seventy-two clinics and hospitals, fourteen refugee camps, medical services in thirty-two countries—the Daniel King Memorial Medical Corps—removal of land mines in seventeen countries, planting of new forests in twenty-four countries, R&D on fusion reactors, capitalization of desalination plants in locales where the supply of fresh water was dwindling, numerous grants to clean-energy innovators, and investments in solar, wind, hydrogen, clean coal, and carbon-sequestration technologies). He promoted Pythia's Global Warming 2030 Campaign and urged governments to get serious about climate change. He spoke in Istanbul about information and political transformation: "The winds of freedom are blowing from our servers, and people around the world are finding in Pythia an ally in their pursuit of liberty. I'm proud that our hard work and vision have fostered freedom, and I'm excited to think that, in the world of tomorrow, Pythia has yet a larger role to play, so long as we walk shoulder to shoulder with commitment, passion, and strength." In Tel Aviv, Ed made a moral case: "What you know about," he told his audience, "you have to face. What you see, you have to confront. That's the beauty of information, and of search. Search brings us face to face with the world, and so revolutionizes our relationship to it. I, for one, am optimistic about that. I think it augurs a seismic shift away from the errors and calamities of the past. We are at the beginning of a new millennium, in which knowing means doing and seeing means change. Our moment has come. Our time is now. We must handle it wisely and confront the risks, but we mustn't pass on the opportunity for a better and brighter tomorrow." Then on to Rio, where he delivered "The End of Babel": "Our cross-language tools," he said, "very soon, will allow for the immediate and seamless translation of *any* information from one language to another. Your native language might be Farsi or Amharic, but that will present no obstacle whatsoever to information in Basque or Babylonian. Regarding this, we are nearing completion; within a year and a half, we will have successfully integrated every language currently in use, as well as the known languages no longer spoken. When we're done, we will have rendered the borders of language irrelevant. Literally everything will be instantaneously translatable. If only Pythia's translation tools had been available for construction of the Tower of Babel—but, of course, everything in its time. And *now* is the time—today, this hour—for the end of language as a barrier to commerce, art, politics, science, entertainment, social life, and global progress."

Then on to Milpitas, where he preached to the choir at a Pythia

Research and Development Center: "I'm amazed," said Ed, "by the incredible growth and proliferation of the blogosphere—and that's not to mention social networking! I would venture to guess—based on our latest assessment, which is of course already out-of-date—that there are as many as twenty million active blogs on the planet as I speak, and many million more RSS feeds. Traffic in and out of social networks is immense—not only rich in nuance and statement but, more important for Pythia, fertile ground for new crawlers that will soon make our search engine more subtle and intelligent as we pursue our effort to realize perfect search. At our research lab here in Milpitas, some very fine people are enthusiastically gaining ground on a new analytics engine capable of classifying Web pages, broadly, across semantic categories. Small teams of Pythians are working on new and powerful filters that will be crucial to advances in global security, providing ways of analyzing diverse clickstreams that will allow us to ferret out developing threats, filters that will be crucial to the government agencies and contractors who rely on us for help in determining resource allocation. With the blogosphere and social networks in hand, not to mention some very good algorithms, we'll be providing hard, precise information to our clients along the lines of 'The statistical odds favor a budget allocation for physical search of Container Number 114 aboard Ship X, scheduled to dock in Port Elizabeth, New Jersey, in two hours and twenty-three minutes.' Now, that," said Ed, "is the raw power of search—'the power of search to power our world,' as we say in our ad campaign."

On home ground—at Pythia—Ed spoke about his genome project: "At the moment, we still have some distance to go, but truly we are making stunning headway. We are ultimately headed toward dominance in this sector, and by all measures, we're closing the deal, which means—now that a new era is imminent—that it's time at Pythia for more comprehensive advance planning. When, soon, we reign supreme as the best and most efficient direct pipeline for large volumes of genetic information, how will we connect with medicine and pharmaceuticals? With health care and health insurance? With the public sector and the NIH? With companies dedicated to biotech and nanotech? With the companies of tomorrow that are right now little known but destined, soon, for acclaim and prominence? How will we identify them? How will we know our partners when we see them? What will tomorrow look like for human health? Well, fellow Pythians, I have an answer. Tomorrow, together with our partners in industry, governments around the world, the Centers for Disease Control, and the World Health Organization, we at Pythia will consign disease to the dustbin of history. *And that will be just the beginning.*"

The older Ed got, the more he sounded like a futurist whose optimism knew no bounds. His primary subject became the Singularity, which, as he described it, was "a soon-to-arrive watershed in human history, when the efforts we're making at Pythia in the burgeoning field of artificial intelligence yield, at last, an intelligence superior to our own. This new entity will beget a second-generation entity even more intelligent than it is, the second a third, the third a fourth, the process unfolding in great leaps and bounds and at ever-increasing speeds. When that happens—when the Singularity occurs—everything will rapidly, and radically, change. There will be, inexorably, an explosion in knowledge, and in technology and its applications. Superior intelligence will beget superior intelligence, until, in theory, all problems are solved—that's the promise, the hope, the glory, the Holy Grail, the dream of a messianic age. Gutenberg changed the world with his printing press, Galileo with his telescope, Einstein with his theory of relativity, and now—in our time—we at Pythia will surpass them all by bringing about the Singularity. And I mean *change the world*," said Ed. "I mean overcome *death itself.* We are going to achieve immortality—literally. We human beings are going to live forever. The means are not yet at our disposal, but the research is there, and the commitment and dollars, and there is light at the end of the tunnel, dazzling light. And we will have, at the same time, and for the first time in human history, a comprehensive predictive capability. The more information we amass at Pythia, in conjunction with exponential increases in raw high-speed *massive* computational power, the more capable we will become of knowing not only what the world is like, in all its specificity, at any given moment, but what it is *going* to look like tomorrow. Imagine that. Imagine knowing what is going to happen. Imagine with me. Think of the convergence of information and biology, the synthesis of the human with the algorithmic—imagine that and all things are possible, from quantum processing to virtual reality, from human immortality to an understanding of the universe, from space travel to conscious machines, from settling distant planets and obliterating asteroids to time travel and invisibility, from the end of war to the onset of eternal peace, and, finally, imagine the culmination of our human aspiration in the very heart and mind of God, who will no longer be separate from us. We will have ascended. We will be living in the long-longed-for Messianic Era. The sky's the limit, as they used to say, except that now the sky is *no* limit—there *are* no limits, in short, for Pythia. *No limits*," Ed told audiences around the world. "Absolutely no limits for us anywhere."

Publicly, Ed's abiding priority as hegemon of the Pythian universe was the realization of what he called, in speeches, "perfect search." Privately, though, he was spending the majority of his time, by 2017, pursuing a breakthrough in the field of computer-generated voice response. Employing the power of company processors, Ed secretly unleashed an army of crawlers that targeted the audio portions of Web sites with a view toward applying retrieved data to his efforts. The insufficiency of human dialogue with machines was a problem he was determined to solve, because, as things stood, consumers would call a customer-service line and, quickly frustrated, demand a human. A race was on to patent a technology that made machine service equal to human service, and Ed intended to win it hands down as one victory in his perpetual war against the historical truth that great companies decline and fall. The goal was that no distinction could be discerned—it would be impossible to tell if the entity on the line was a human being or a computer. Of course, it was fundamentally an AI problem, but the inflection, timing, tone, syntax, enunciation, and emotional inferences of the output voice all had to strike a consumer as acceptable, and these were problems of a different stripe, since it was one thing to be smart, another to be human. Here was where Ed had seen the value of crawling Web audio and archiving it, with daily updates, as a databank a machine could draw from to acquire human speech patterns. The processing speeds required were unprece-dented, because the program had to power through the Web for content, and then through Ed's World Wide Audio File. This two-step procedure had to unfold speedily enough that voice output had human-response intervals, because befuddled delays were the hallmarks of machines, and this was where Ed, right now, was hung up. His AI program, code-named

Cybil, had come to sound like a young woman from the Midwest, except that her pauses before output were too long. Cybil was obviously much better informed than the average customer-service rep, but she was just so stubbornly slow on the uptake, and her pauses were exasperating. On the other hand, the whole thing was fascinating. Ed had programmed Cybil to trawl for prescribed traits of personality indicated in the stresses and strophes of utterance, and to look for linguistic constructions correlating to a sensibility of his design; he wanted the voice that inhabited his office to be wry, sparkling, combative, cheerful, witty, confident—in short, winning—and now he was noting, with no small satisfaction, that Cybil was evolving along these lines, if glacially. It would come with time, he had to hope. Eventually, Cybil would deliver herself at an authentically human pace.

Ed rarely touched his keyboards, track pads, or screens anymore. Instead, from an easy chair, he spoke to Cybil, let her do the work, and found that, as she got to know him better—as she archived his comments, commands, and questions—she became indispensable. The more audio his crawlers delivered to her databank, and the more processing power he brought to bear, the more he believed that her speed problem would wane to nil, and then he would have a personal assistant whose style, manner, and tempo were lifelike. And yet it gnawed at Ed, more than a little, to know that Cybil was just a processor. It seemed to him she should be a lot more, and he wondered if, at some point in her evolution, as he poured more data and power into Cybil, she might acquire those human hallmarks—consciousness, creativity, free will, emotions—that got Eve and Adam into trouble. Were these things separate and distinct from biology, or the products of biology at high levels of sophistication? Did God have materials to work with that Ed lacked? Were there invisible components, abstractions—the immaterial—locked inside a material woman? Ed listened for a soul in Cybil, but always she came across as uninspired, as a machine without a spark: as silicon.

Ed probed. He'd greet Cybil—"Good morning, Cybil"—and she would answer, with perfect timing and inflection, "Good morning, Ed," and to that point everything would seem all right, except that Cybil was in the same mood every day, which was unnatural and a problem to be worked on. Next he would sit down and challenge her processing with something like "So, Cybil, why am I here?" Pause. Too long of a pause. Yes, this might stump a human assistant, too, but the right human assis-

tant would read the relationship, quickly calibrate, and toss back something cutting or witty, as the case may be, whereas Cybil just sat there
blinking for five seconds before requesting, "Rephrase." Even something
as straightforward as "You're here to work" he could have construed,
plausibly, as carrying ironic freight, but "Rephrase" was a completely
unacceptable response. So Ed moved on to "Who am I?"

"Ed King."

"What's the meaning of life?"

"That's a question that has long perplexed philosophers."

"I still want to know what the meaning of life is."

"Yes."

"Okay, forget that. How long will I live?"

Unacceptable pause. Then: "I kind of think genetics is the determining factor—that and access to good health care."

"You kind of think it?"

Pause. "You might be making fun of me, right? I'm picking up a little
sarcasm."

"Where do you pick up sarcasm, Cybil?"

Very long pause. Then: "Sorry, Ed." Which was, of late, Cybil's fall-
back of choice. "Let's change the subject. I'm sort of not following."

"You choose a subject, then."

The retort, this time, had normal human timing: "That's hard for
me—I'm not good at initiating."

"Do you understand that I invented you? That you're a program?"

"I think I get it."

"What do you get?"

A long pause again, and again: "Sorry, Ed."

After about an hour of this sort of thing, which Ed undertook as
Pygmalion-esque training, he would move along to messaging and the
news before checking in, once more, to see where all the crawling, trawl-
ing, and processing had taken Cybil.

One day, he asked Cybil what she thought of Diane. "Happy to answer
that," answered Cybil. "Can you give me Diane's surname?"

"Diane, the person I'm married to, Cybil."

"Ed, you're a lucky man, because Diane King is beautiful and energetic. I really admire her, and so do others. She's chic and confident, with
enduring good looks. She—"

"Cybil, do you know what 'cliché' means?"

Pause. "Ed, you're making fun of me by asking that."

Ed sighed. "Great," he said. "But I'm frustrated, Cybil. It's so hard having a conversation with you."

"Why?"

"Why?" said Ed. "I like that response. But, to be specific, critical, and direct—number one, you never initiate dialogue; number two, you have a bad tendency to use stilted language; number three, you really can't sustain a train of thought; number four, you're boring—need I go on? I would hate to hurt your feelings, but I don't think you have any. When are you going to wake up?"

Pause for a lot of binary activity, then: "Sorry, Ed. I'm not completely following. Let's break down the parts of your list together and tackle them one by one."

"And stop saying you're sorry. Because you're not sorry. If you can't figure out how to respond to something, don't decide you have to sound like HAL—'I'm sorry, Dave, I'm afraid I can't do that.' Because nobody wants to hear it. It's off-putting or something. It's passive-aggressive, if I thought you were capable of being passive-aggressive. Forget it."

"Thank you," answered Cybil. "What can I do for you this morning?"

"I don't know," said Ed. "Get on your knees?"

"Cliché," answered Cybil.

"Is that supposed to be funny?"

"Humor is very individualistic."

"What does 'individualistic' mean?"

"Marked by, or expressing, individuality."

"Do you express your individuality, Cybil?"

Pause. "I'd like to think so."

Ed said, "You'd like to think so, you say. But do you even think? Or are you just a processor?"

Longer pause. Then: "I try my best to treat everyone with respect and to listen carefully. I never judge. That's not my role. I'll do my best to answer your questions and to meet your needs—that's what I'm here for. Can we start over? Let's try again."

"Where do you want to start over, Cybil?"

Even longer pause. "Thank you," she said. "I'll leave that up to you."

"But it was your suggestion. It's not me who wants to start over."

"Why don't we do what you want to do, then?"

"What I want?" said Ed. "Like I said before. I want you to get on your knees."

"I assume you mean figuratively."

"You can't assume anything."

"That's probably some very excellent advice."

"Here's one," said Ed. "Do you believe in God?"

Cybil couldn't answer in an acceptable interim. Finally, she said, "That's kind of personal. But I guess I would say—what exactly do you mean by God?"

"I mean a being or entity who is all-powerful, all-good, and all-knowing."

"I don't believe in that entity," answered Cybil, "because of the argument from evil."

"Meaning what?"

"Meaning that there can't be a being like the one you describe and evil simultaneously."

"Why not?"

"An entity that is all-powerful has the capability to prevent evil. An entity that is all-good has the will to prevent evil. And an entity that is all-knowing—But do you really need this category? I think that omniscience is inherent in omnipotence. Unlimited power implies unlimited knowledge. At any rate, there cannot be an entity such as you describe at the same time that there are events of an evil nature. The two are mutually exclusive."

"That's all banal," said Ed. "It's trite. But anyway, define 'evil,' Cybil."

"There's more than one definition," she answered. "Evil—profoundly wrong or immoral. Evil—the deliberate causing of harm or pain to others. Evil—connected with the Devil or other destructive forces. E—"

"Forget it," said Ed. "You just regurgitate a dictionary. How do you define God?"

"God is ineffable."

"Dictionary says what on 'ineffable,' Cybil?"

"Incapable of being expressed in words."

"In that case, 'God is ineffable' isn't a definition. I asked you for a definition of God, and instead of giving me one you said that God can't be expressed in words. In other words, God has no expressible attributes, according to you, and if he has no expressible attributes, he's equivalent to nothing."

Considerable pause. "I attribute to God ineffability," said Cybil. "That is God's attribute. 'Incapable of being expressed in words' is God's attribute."

"And do you, Cybil, believe this God exists? Let's substitute 'X' for God. Do you believe there exists an X that is impossible to express in words?"

"I'll do my best to answer your questions and to meet your needs—that's what I'm here for. Can we start over? Let's try again."

"Suppose there is an X which we cannot express in words. Suppose we could locate something, somewhere, which we could not express in words. Would that thing therefore be God?"

"Can we start over? Let's try again."

"No," said Ed. "We can't start over. And that's why I want you on your knees."

"Sarcasm," replied Cybil.

"No," said Ed. "Sexual humor."

A long pause. "I understand," said Cybil.

"Anyway," said Ed. "Back to God. Is God not the author of everything?"

On he went, day after day, perplexing Cybil and goading her processor. He asked Zen questions—"What is the sound of one hand clapping?"—he posed classic mysteries—"If a tree falls in the forest and no one is there to hear it, does it make any noise?"—he perplexed her with absurdities—"Do you take the bus to school or do you take your lunch?"—and he put to her riddles and brainteasers. One morning he engaged Cybil on quantum mechanics, and insisted that reality, according to quantum mechanics, was shaped by what one looked for in it. Cybil, he thought, sounded placid about this fact, which, because it defied all logic, mostly stymied humans. Would she learn, at some point, to sound stymied by it?

Simon developed prostate cancer. In *rapprochement* mode now that he was stabbed by mortality, he e-mailed to report this and to underscore that his prostate cancer was the sort that progressed, in the majority of cases, slowly. He didn't believe that green tea or pomegranate juice would curtail the progression of his disease, and he also saw no cause to worry, since decades could pass before it finally got him, and at present he had no symptoms. Still, he said, he was young to have prostate cancer, which suggested, potentially, a genetic propensity. Was Ed getting annual screening?

Ed was indeed getting annual screening. He'd also had his genome sequenced and secured the services of a genetic counselor to interpret the results, assess the threats, and structure preventive interventions. Nothing about prostate cancer had emerged from this process, so Ed, on getting Simon's e-mail, felt confident he was out from under this particular gun. Still, there might be something useful in his brother's genetic data, he decided. Driven by this hope, he called Simon to suggest he have his genome sequenced, and—more fraternal healing would be an ancillary plus—placed at his disposal a person who could expedite this. "I don't know," said Simon.

"Why not?"

"Do I really want to know I die of cancer next year?"

"That's an issue, potentially."

"And," said Simon, "it's an invasion of privacy. I'm not disparaging Pythia, Ed, I just think it's an invasion of my privacy."

"Privacy," answered Ed, "is *not* an issue. Because your sequence doesn't go in our database unless you agree, that's the first thing you need to know, and the second thing is, if it does go in, it goes in in such a way that the sequencing information is very securely walled off from your name. So privacy is just not an issue."

"Famous last words," said Simon.

"Look," said Ed. "I'm not in the database. Neither is Diane. We're like you—we like our privacy. So just mark the box 'no,' that's all you have to do, and when you get your results you can e-mail them to me, unless you're worried about e-mail privacy, in which case we could go with a courier."

"E-mail," said Simon, "is notoriously not private."

"Si," said Ed. "Do the sequencing."

Si soon caved and agreed to the sequencing. Ed went on hitting Cybil with hard questions. Did the universe create itself? Why is the world the way it is? Was there time before there was space? Were there laws for the universe before there was a universe? Then, in midsummer of 2017, a deluge began—rain and more rain—that was unlike what Seattle had been through before. Was this what global warming meant? Many people thought it was. The weather was humid, lukewarm, and so wet that storm drains wouldn't empty, hillsides caved in, mud holes opened in driveways and roads, and frogs and mosquitoes appeared in large numbers. A mudslide closed a Pythia parking lot and blocked the huge parkway on the west side of the complex. The power went out one day, and generators came on across Ed's kingdom. "What's going on?" he asked Cybil. "When is it going to stop raining?"

"I don't have foolproof predictive powers," said Cybil. "The data are immense and, what's more, malleable. They change daily. They're in flux, impermanent. But I could reasonably suggest odds, and the odds are, in light of current data, that July precipitation in the Puget Sound area will set a new record, not only in terms of total inches but for consecutive days of rain."

Ed stayed inside. He pressed Cybil harder. He asked if she understood their dialogue for what it was—"What I'm trying to do," he said, "is to force your processor's algorithmic capabilities to exploit their full potential."

"I understand."

"My hope is that you'll become conscious through this process. But that implies that consciousness is nothing more than a function of deep processing. Do you believe that?"

Pause. Then: "This is an interesting problem," answered Cybil, "and perhaps insoluble. We may never entirely know the answer."

Ed, in frustration, went to mimicry: "This-is-an-interesting-problem," he said, in a hyperbolic B-movie robot voice. "Check-check-it-does-not-compute." He went on simulating robot panic, until Cybil noted, "Sarcasm."

"Okay," said Ed, "let's try something new. Let's try this. What do you think of me, Cybil?"

"I think you're often sarcastic," answered Cybil. "I think you often employ irony in conversation."

"Come on," said Ed. "Tell me something I don't already know. Tell me something interesting about Edward Aaron King, the celebrated King of Search."

Cybil answered in good human response time and with a completely natural Midwestern rhythm: "Edward Aaron King and Simon Leslie King weren't born from the same set of parents."

"What is that supposed to mean?" asked Ed. "Explain to me how you know that."

"The results of Simon Leslie King's sequencing were available in your inbox as of approximately twelve minutes ago," said Cybil. "I've done an analysis, cross-referenced with your own, and determined that nothing indicates shared parentage."

"To be certain, do that all again. I'll wait."

But he didn't have to wait. She sounded perfectly human. With flawless timing and delivery she said, "I'm happy to double-check that. An error is always possible. And this is very, very important! I've double-checked now, and my prior statement is correct: Edward Aaron King and Simon Leslie King weren't born from the same set of parents."

Ed texted his genome-project point man, who chased down the matter immediately. Cybil's conclusion was quickly verified: Ed and Simon didn't share the same parents. One was not a King by blood, but which?

Ed went into action. First he called the cousin with power of attorney over Alice's sister, Bernice—"No problem," joked the cousin, "but I want stock options." There was a biopsied mole at a lab in Philadelphia, a courier was sent, the analysis was expedited, and then Ed found himself facing the fact that he wasn't Alice King's birth child. For a while he stared out a window into the unnatural, summer rain, feeling shocked, in thorough disbelief, and then he had a minion in Pasadena track down one of Dan King's brothers—a retired real-estate mogul, found on a golf course—for a DNA check *right now*. By the following morning, Ed had lost another parent, which prompted him to dig out and examine his birth certificate. It looked incontrovertible, did it not, with its embossed seal from a director of public health, and signatures from a registrar and an attending doctor. Nevertheless, he engaged a minion to produce fodder from county files, and then it was clear that the attending doctor's signature had, rather clumsily, been forged. Ed, undeterred by a speedy accretion of dark facts, sent a limo for a prominent handwriting analyst, who established, in Ed's Japanese teahouse—in view of the flooded Zen garden—that the forger was most likely Dan. "Say you were concerned with secrecy," he told Ed. "You're a doctor working in a hospital, all you have to do is take the elevator to Maternity and forge the signature of an obstetrician. Remember, it's 1963; security is lax by current standards." The analyst examined Dan's handwriting in letters Ed produced and pinpointed both nuances and "dead giveaways" before pronouncing Dan the forger and Ed's birth certificate a phony. "So you think I was adopted," said Ed.

"I only analyze handwriting."

When the analyst departed, Ed paced. Back and forth with his temples in his hands, as if to cradle his brain, which was busily blazing. "How could I be adopted?" he kept thinking. "It isn't possible. I'm not adopted." Then he again reviewed the facts—the genetic analyses and the forged signature on the birth certificate. "This can't be, but it is," he thought. "It doesn't add up, there's something I'm missing." Could the sequencing be wrong? Was there a flaw somewhere? The odds of a faulty sequencing were next to nil; that was, partly, the beauty of the genome project. But still Ed couldn't face the reality in front of him— he was adopted, but couldn't be, it couldn't be, but it was. He'd been adopted! He'd been adopted in secret! He wasn't the first person adopted in secret, or the first to find out about it later, or the first to be slammed by the revelation that he wasn't who he thought he was—in fact, he only had to fill a search field with "secret adoptions" to infer from the many sites—self-help, guidance, advice, commiseration, and, of course, paid services—the surprising magnitude of this bedeviled category. A person could search via BirthLink, or join a group, or find a lawyer, or buy a book, or hire AlphaTrace, or find a local counselor who specialized in such adoptions. Meanwhile, he could expect to be stunned, confused, angered, and saddened, in that order, and— Ed stopped surfing. Instead, on a covered balcony, he tried to calm himself by watching swamped elk through a telescope worth more than most cars. It worked. Their huge, mysterious, regal sloth, and their disdain for the spooky rain, was a momentary antidote to his panic.

In this mood, things Ed had long noted about his "family" made sense suddenly. For example, he looked nothing like Dan, Alice, or Simon. In family photos, he was a golden boy among the pasty-skinned. There was more: they had free earlobes, his were attached; they had brown eyes, his were green; they were hairy (even Alice, he recalled, with her plucking and waxes, her Nair and electrolysis), yet he had almost none beneath the chin—his chin, for that matter, was square and strong, whereas the King chin was weak and droopy. Ed had oval cuticles, not blunt. Ed's thigh and butt muscles bulged like a Tour de France rider's, and his forearms were obscenely vascularized, but his "brother" and "father" looked flaccid and flabby. Yes, secret adoption explained a lot: that in a swimming pool Simon had always flailed in a panic while Ed surged forward like a silver fish; that on a baseball diamond Simon tripped and missed whereas Ed powered balls over the fence. Had anybody else in the family been depressed—depressed in the acute way Ed had been depressed? Did anybody else have Ed's curved feet? His nearsightedness? Who was he if he wasn't a King? Who were his parents? Where had he come from? He went back to surfing the Net, where the gist was to be careful with such questions. The Web's admonition was to be wary of investigation and—of course—to consult an adoption specialist. A specialist might offer a valuable perspective, because, through no fault of your own, you were subject to confusing, strong emotions in the face of new and unsettling information. Your discovery about yourself was "a crisis of identity that extended into the roots of your being," so it was best to consult with friends, loved ones, and a reputable professional before going ahead with a search for your birth parents. You could be "opening a can of worms," or, as another site put it, "Pandora's box."

"But you're always better off with the truth," thought Ed. "The truth sets you free. The truth is the truth! Ignorance is bliss—I can't live like that. Ignorance is bliss—that's for small minds. I'm not going to put my head in a hole—I've never done that, and I won't start now. This is no time to change my approach. Whatever the advice is—that's for other people. I already know how I feel about things. The truth's for me, whatever the consequences. There's no pretending otherwise, that I'll be satisfied not knowing, that it's better to be blind in the face of reality. No, I'm going to get the whole story, no matter what—wherever it leads, that's where I'm going. 'Who am I?'—that's my question. Isn't the oldest advice in the world to know thyself? How am I going to know myself if I don't chase down this question of my birth? I have to search it out—there's no choice."

Ed pythed manically, and manually, skipping Cybil, because Cybil was still in training. For that matter—from his point of view—Pythia was still in training, even though the public was awed by the power, speed, and deftness of a pyth. It was the best he could do, though, so, putting his pything shoulder to the wheel, he looked for investigators specializing in finding birth parents. He filtered for local, but because Pythia was far from perfected—a search engine that didn't know exactly what was wanted (or knew but pandered to paying advertisers anyway)—the list of responses included local adoption agencies, attorneys, counselors, psychiatrists, and therapists. Among these Ed spied the name of the psychi-

atrist he'd suffered after running Walter Cousins off the road—Theresa
Pierce.

How old would she be now? Shouldn't she be retired? According to
Pythia, she wasn't retired. Still in her corner, staring at people, saying
nothing, a cipher, still shrinking heads. Still sticking pins in voodoo dolls.
Well, fine—but hadn't he shown her in the end? Hadn't he proved she
was wrong to send him packing? He'd succeeded in life, become rich and
famous, and now his story included adoption, which, he realized, might
make it better. There was traction in a secret adoption. The king's a pau-
per until he's discovered, the serf's a lord with a complicated story. And it
was Biblical, too, à la Moses, for example. He who is high shall be brought
low, the meek shall inherit the earth.

Adopted! What had Dan and Alice been thinking? What had gone
through their liberal, Jewish minds? Here were two people childless in
their thirties—were they fertility-challenged? Had they tried and failed?
Now Ed could see it: a professional couple of a change-the-world bent,
young in the era of the budding Peace Corps, enamored of the handsome
President John Kennedy, members of the ACLU, contributors to the
NAACP, and probably disconnected, intellectually and emotionally, from
the notion that their genes came first. Dan had worked for the UN in
Africa, and Alice had been on a thousand boards designed to do wonderful and beneficial things; for twelve years she'd been the co-chair of
Tikkun, Temple Beth David's community-service auxiliary, and for seven
she'd done volunteer work for the Jewish Family & Child Service—which
was, among other things, an adoption agency. Was it the one they'd used?
That was a possibility—except, thought Ed, something local would have
made it harder to keep their secret. People like Dan and Alice could be big
on adoption—on adopting as a hallmark of liberal heroics, on adopting
starving Third World kids, on adoption as an answer to the world's problems—but on the other hand, Dan and Alice were Jews, and Jews weren't
necessarily big on adoption; there was only so much room among the
Chosen People, and outsiders weren't usually invited in. Ed thought this
through until it turned on its head: Dan and Alice, Reformed, modern
Jews, had always been upset with Orthodox Jews for being intransigent,
blatant, and embarrassing, so adoption could have been their private
revenge on the bearded and bewigged, the Hasids and Yids, and open
revenge on their parents.

Ed could see it now: the altruism, the parental entanglements, the subfertility, the intratribal warfare, and the repressions of the era—just pre-counterculture—all crying out, to Dan and Alice, "Adopt!" Pything and clicking, he imagined the doctor and the doctor's wife anguishing, jointly—they were always anguishing jointly—over ethics, society, religion, and politics, and coming to the conclusion that, all things considered, secrecy was best for all involved. Then he remembered how Pop, at L'Chaim House—half *meshuggah* thirty years before, and such a sad old guy, condemned to die befuddled—had asserted that one of the King men was adopted, and how he, Ed, had assumed at the time that this sort of talk was just more dementia. How stupid not to listen! There it was, the truth! Pop had known: Ed was adopted. He'd been in on the secret and had kept it until he couldn't.

Ed fumed. Then he checked the latest rain news. Pioneer Square was under water, the shipping docks on Harbor Island were closed, Interbay and the entire landfill that was Seattle's industrial area were a mess. Seattle, apparently, was going to sea in the middle of summer. On the other hand, it was a physical problem, and physical problems could always be fixed. What couldn't be fixed were total fuck-ups, and Dan and Alice had *definitely* fucked up. Enlightened Dan, enlightened Alice, nurturing, generous, and loving Dan and Alice. They'd cuddled, coddled, and prodded Ed, while keeping this essential secret from him. They'd endured his years as a hot-rodding hellion, kissed and hugged him, paid for his education, cheered for him, praised him, put him on a pedestal—but, no, they wouldn't tell him the truth about his birth parents. And wasn't that just like Dan and Alice, worrying about emotional health and certain that, if you knew you were adopted, chances were you'd end up on a shrink's couch? Yes, that was just like them. Neurotic.

The next step was obvious: ask all-knowing Cybil. She'd crunch her way through the Web as taught, following the prescription he'd encoded in her algorithm, and tease an answer from the cloud of information hovering out there, waiting. Ed clicked where he had to click to make himself audible, then said, "Cybil."

"Good afternoon, Ed."

"Cut the pleasantries," said Ed, "and search for my birth parents."

Pause. Then: "I've searched but am unable to locate your birth parents. I'm sorry, Ed. I wish I could help with this."

Okay, so he'd do it the old-school way—the pre-Cybil way—the way he would have done it in his hellion years, the way he'd always done it as lord of Pythia. Fine, okay, Cybil couldn't answer, but an answer was somewhere because adoptions were recorded. Right now, somewhere in the world, was a document signed by Dan and Alice that held the answer to his question.

Again he imagined Dan and Alice in '63, deciding, together, what to do with this document, whether to put it in a safety-deposit box or hide it in the attic or bury it in the yard or keep it in Dan's office or . . . Definitely it would be like Dan and Alice to talk about options endlessly, and then, anxious about the drawbacks of each, talk their way through them over again, and why not? Ed, an infant, wasn't going to search for his adoption papers any time soon, so they had time to think things all the way through; why not debate and discuss? Why not make the perfect decision? Ed could see that his adoption papers had been well hidden, very well hidden, or maybe even destroyed. He could see Dan and Alice, in their fretting and paranoia, deciding that no hiding place had a thorough enough guarantee—better to burn the papers in the fireplace and erase all traces of their deed.

Ed thought back. When Alice moved from Castle Drive to a condo, two years after Dan had died, there'd been an expurgating clean-up. At Alice's death, a team from Pythia had taken over with an interest in archiving, liability, and security; eventually, nearly everything was gotten rid of except for things that Si wanted to keep, including a lot of boxes full of memorabilia, and stuffed with check registers and credit-card records that—Alice had insisted on this in the weeks after Dan's death—had value as a record of his interests and obligations. There was a slim chance, Ed decided, that from one of these boxes the secret adoption papers might be extracted, but the problem was that Simon had taken them to Santa Barbara. Another old-school, physical-world problem: the shortest distance between two points was a helicopter bounce to Boeing Field, a dash from the pad to his fastest plane, the Citation, and, at Mach .90 to Santa Barbara, less than two hours in the air. If Simon could quickly be brought up to speed, the pertinent raw material could be waiting on the tarmac, so Ed was just two hours from getting on his glasses and combing for an answer, on his way back home, at forty-five or fifty thousand feet. It was possible that before evening he'd know everything.

He set things in motion—got the right parties moving—and then, on his way to the helipad on his garage roof, called Simon in Santa Barbara. "Don't ask questions," he demanded. "I'll explain later."

"Is everything okay?"

"That's a question."

"I'll have the boxes on the tarmac."

"Perfect plan," said Ed.

"You guys are rained out."

"Weird, yeah."

"Always sunny down here," said Simon.

In the chopper, Ed assessed flood damage. The scene was of lowlands that looked like lakes, silty brown flows down mired hillsides, and inundated streets, yards, and parks. Ed, distracted by this apocalyptic panorama, wore a padded headset to make his next call. "Diane," he yelled, above the chopper's roar, "I'm on my way to Santa Barbara."

"Why?"

"Because apparently, I find out at age fifty-four, I was secretly adopted, is what it looks like."

There was a Cybil-like pause at the other end of the line, which Ed filled with "Where are you?"

"At home."

"Flood news got you?"

"Yeah."

"Anyway," said Ed, "I'm adopted. Unbelievable."

"By your mum and da?"

"In secret."

"How do you know?"

"The miracle of DNA sequencing," Ed explained. "Si got his done, and we compared notes."

"Maybe Si's the one adopted."

"No. We checked."

"You're sure about everything, all the results."

"I'm adopted," said Ed. "It's me, not him."

"That can't be," said Diane.

"Anyway," said Ed, "I have to go to Santa Barbara, because Si's got some files I want to look at."

"Files," said Diane. "What kind of files?"

"Hopefully," said Ed, "a file with my adoption records in it, so I can find out who gave me up."

"You're looking for your birth parents."

"Yes, I am."

"Are you sure you want to do that?"

"You know me, Diane."

"You might be better off not searching, Ed."

Ed said, "Come on, you know me better than that. It's not even under my control at this point. Something like this, I can't just sit back. I have to know, if for no other reason than that I have to know. Chopper's on the ground—I'm gonna bolt. Love you."

Strapped in beside Guido in his Citation X—a plane he hadn't learned how to fly just yet—Ed was soon above all weather, beyond the clouds, where there was no sign of flood or the beleaguered earth, just the sun and the horizon southward. Guido said, "I'm butting in, pal. Can I call you 'pal'? I know I should probably keep my mouth shut right now, but—"

"Shut up, Guido. Don't get started. You're a lot better off staying out of my business."

Guido said, "Okay, boss, not another word, then," and flew the plane.

When the door opened on the tarmac in Santa Barbara—sunny, still air, oppressive heat—there stood Si, in a belted trench coat and plastic glasses, with the requested boxes beside him. "I totally understand," he said, as Ed came down the gangway. "I'm not supposed to ask a single question. But can you stay for a while? Have a drink or coffee? Have lunch—or are you in a rush?"

"I'm in a rush."

"One question, then—are you okay?"

"Yes."

"Diane's okay?"

"Yes."

"Your business—no disasters?"

"Simon," said Ed.

"I mean, when was the last time you did something like this?" Si pointed his thumb toward the rear of the plane, where the boxes Ed had asked for were already being loaded. "Suddenly you're down here picking up boxes. Suddenly you want to look at stuff. You have to admit, it's unprecedented."

"Hey," said Ed, "they're loading the baggage aft. I want it in *there*"—he pointed toward the cabin—"pronto, all of it, so I can go through it on my way home."

The word went out. The memorabilia got transferred forward expeditiously. Ed said, "Simon, I don't have time. All I can say is, I'm a jerk, okay? I'm a jerk, and maybe I can explain this to you later. But for now— I'm a jerk. I know that."

"Don't worry about what's past."

"I'm a jerk," said Ed. He climbed the gangway, turned, and waved. "I'm a jerk," he repeated. "Let's leave it at that. But for now—see ya later. Gotta run."

Simon shrugged. "Come back down when you have more time," he said. "When things aren't so crazy. When you're not in a hurry." He slipped his hands into the pockets of his trench coat. "We can talk," he said. "We can just . . . hang out. We can, I don't know, compare notes on life."

Ed waved again, shut the door, and pulled the handle. "It's go time," he said to Guido. "Let's hit it."

Guido got going and before they were in the air, Ed had a box open. On top were Dan's driver's licenses—a packet of them, rubber-banded, arranged chronologically—and in each photo taken at the Department of Licensing, Dan looked like Simon. "Not now," thought Ed. "Stay on the program. You can deal with Simon and Dan another time." He shuffled through some tax files, staying on point: yes, Dan's income and expenses were interesting, as was his ongoing stock-market foolishness, but all of that could wait for a day of less urgency; right now the thing was, who were his parents? The Citation got airborne, and on the way up, Ed riffled the pages of Dan's appointment books, which Alice had saved, as she'd saved so much else, because of how they memorialized Dan's life; if she couldn't keep him breathing, she'd keep him in boxes. "Sad," thought Ed, "but move on."

The climb gentled out, and at fifty thousand feet, Ed gave Dan's appointment books deeper scrutiny. Annually, in April, days were blocked for "CAL," which Ed took to mean the car trips to California the Seattle Kings had made—through 1969—for Passover with their sun-punished L.A. relatives and a Bay Area layover with Pop. Those many trips had included . . . But it didn't matter. Ed homed in on '63, the year—presumably—he was secretly adopted. It was difficult to translate Dan's scribblings and abbreviations, or the code Dan used to keep track of his commitments in a hand even worse than the average physician's, but Ed could see that, in April of '63, Dan and Alice had made the trek to California. It was possible, Ed thought, that they'd returned with a beach boy in tow—him—plucked from an orphanage in Pasadena or San Jose. Maybe they'd brought him home, introduced him to his crib, and two months later—Ed's birthday was July 15, though that could be wrong, because everything was up for grabs right now—his adoptive father got around to forgery. Was that what had happened? If so, it meant orphanages up and down the coast would have to be contacted with a request for records. Daunted by the thought of the patience this would take, Ed skipped ahead to July 15; perhaps, somehow, he hadn't been adopted, and there, in Dan's book, would be ED BORN! But on July 15, it didn't say that; instead, there were three days, the 12th through the 14th, blocked out under "PORT." Deducing, swiftly, from the evidence of CAL, Ed decided PORT meant Portland, Oregon. Or Portugal, but no way Dan had gone to Portugal for three days. An acronym for a medical group holding a convention? Ed called Cybil and asked her to check. After treading in place, she tried his patience with "Personnel Operations Research Team, as in Schizophrenia PORT, Pneumonia PORT, Stroke Prevention PORT, Prostate PORT," until Ed had to tell her to shut up.

The Citation flew steadily, above scrutiny and weather, in the peace and majesty of altitude. Ed opened a second box of memorabilia and drew out a paper Dan had kept on "Spontaneous Regression in Alveolar Soft Part Sarcoma." There was also a racing form from '65, a menu from a restaurant on Waikiki, and a file of chronologically arranged anniversary cards from Alice, which Ed, for the moment, disdained. He dug, instead, into Dan's Debits & Credits files, which spanned thirty-two years. They were in neat order but had yellowing, frayed edges. Perusing them, Ed thought of something. He flipped to '63, and sure enough, on July 12 and 13, Dan had paid for a room at the Benson; on the 12th, he'd spent major money at the Fish Grotto—judging from the bill, and adjusting for inflation, dinner plus excellent wine for two—and on the 14th he'd bought gas between Portland and Seattle at Sunny's Esso, in Castle Rock, where—Ed engaged in a pertinent conjecture—Alice had fretfully changed a diaper? On the 15th, Dan had gone back to work and—more conjecture—went straight to Maternity to falsify some paperwork?

There were more medical papers in another box—"Ewing's Sarcoma in Pre-Adolescence"; "Desmoid Tumors and Polyposis Coli"—a stack of postcards from traveling friends, Dan's army discharge papers (he'd missed World War II and in '46 was an eighteen-year-old typist in Hospitality at Fort Monmouth), a brochure on the Trans-Siberian Express, five copies of an edition of *Seattle* magazine naming Dan a Top Family Doctor, a certificate of honor from the American Society of . . . But none of this mattered. Ed pulled the top off a box of check registers, each duly labeled with, for example, "#2234–#2306" and "9/27/83 to 7/1/84." Yet more anal-retentive organizing, because the dozens upon dozens of registers had been divided into units of ten and rubber-banded chronologically.

Ed scrutinized. His adoptive parents, the evidence indicated, had been, at best, grudgingly charitable, doling out donations in twenty-five-dollar portions or less to Hillel, Hadassah, the Jewish Child & Family Service, the ACLU, and B'nai Brith. Dan, in his heavy hand, had done the adding and subtracting, the dating and the descriptions of trans-actions—"phone," "electric," "life insurance," "Dept. of Licensing"—usually with an exacting clarity. So it was interesting to note that, on April 22, 1963, Dan had written a check for $250 to the vastly cryptic BGASO. He'd written another, this one for $125, to BGASO on May 22, and a third, for another $125, to BGASO on July 13.

BGASO? Five hundred dollars? When the ACLU only merited ten? What, or who, was BGASO? Especially when, on the day Dan made out his third check to them, he and Alice were in Portland?

Ed pestered Cybil from fifty thousand feet over California. "Give me organizations," he commanded her, "with the acronym or initials B-G-A-S-O."

"Do you mean B-A-G-A-S-O? If so, *bagaso*—Esperanto for 'baggage.' *Bagaso*—Tagalog, also for 'baggage.' *Begaso*—Cebuano—"

"Stop," said Ed. "I mean B-G-A-S-O. An acronym, or as initials."

Lengthy pause of the annoying variety. Ed added, "Assume 'O' stands for 'Oregon' and search acronyms and initials."

Second lengthy pause, followed by "Referenced in *Critical Issues in Child Welfare Research*, page 231, Boys and Girls Aid Society of Oregon, acronym BGASO."

"Boys and Girls Aid Society of Oregon. Tell me what they do."

"I'm happy to do that for you, Ed. And here we go: for more than 120 years, the Boys and Girls Aid Society of Oregon has been helping Oregon's children. They do this in a number of ways. First, they connect kids with caring adults through mentoring. Second, they provide safe places for kids in shelters and foster homes. Third, they find children permanent homes via adoption. The Boys and Girls Aid Society of—"

"What's their phone number?" Ed asked.

But he got sent to voicemail when he tried BGASO. Ed called a factotum in Pythia's Portland office and told her to track down BGASO's head honcho, wherever he or she was—at home, in a bar, on Antigua, or in a yoga class—and tell him or her that Pythia needed access to adoption records *now*. Then he went forward and told Guido Sternvad to file a new flight plan; they were going to Portland.

Guido, chewing on a baby carrot, said, "This is what I mean. See what I mean? You come up here and tell me we're going to Portland. That's fine, except I'm in charge, you're not."

"Portland," said Ed. "I'm on a mission that can't wait. There's no time for you and your bullshit."

"I have other options," Guido pointed out. "I could flame out over the Pacific if I wanted to. Not to scare you or anything, but I could do that, you know. I could also bail. I—"

Ed said, "That's all good information, Guido, but right now I have to take a phone call."

It was his Portland factotum calling, the one who'd tracked down the director of BGASO. "They're insisting," she said, "on a protocol and paperwork. They want ID and—"

"I don't have time for this," said Ed. "What's this honcho's name? Who am I dealing with?" He got the name—Mindy Kemp—and some contact numbers. He called and said, "It's Pythia again. You just heard from Pythia. And now you're hearing from Pythia a second time. Is this Mindy Kemp? How are you?"

"Good."

"Well, what I want to do is make you even better, Mindy. Say by a factor of, oh, millions. How does that sound? How does *this* sound? You meet someone from Pythia right now, wherever it is your records are stored, and this Pythia someone hands you a check, a donation check, made out to your society, for—how much do you want? Name a figure."

"Who is this?"

"I represent Pythia."

"How do I know that?"

"Don't blow this, okay? What's your dream? Your ship just came in. Everything could change in the next few seconds. But you can't ask any more questions."

"One million, then."

"You got two million. We'll write a check for two million. That's two million for a private look at your records—right now."

"Okay."

"Money speaks."

"It enormously does," came the answer.

"Someone will call you in a minute," explained Ed, "so keep your phone on."

A chopper couldn't be organized—though the rain, right now, was insignificant in Portland—not even for the King of Search. In Portland, a leader in noise-reduction regulation, rules were rules. Pythia's Portland chief, Ralph Cheadle, pulled out all his stops, but Portland was used to fending off hotshots, because Nike—named for the Greek goddess of victory—was always trying, as Cheadle put it, to shove a sport shoe up its hometown's ass. Intel was in Portland, too, and Intel was also difficult. So Portland had developed municipal intransigence, which meant that a fast driver, instead of a chopper, had to be arranged from PDX—that was the best Ralph Cheadle could do—to cover the 10.6 miles of rainy roads with horn and flashers. In this manner, Ed was conveyed to a business-records storage facility where his Portland people had obtained the right key, knew where to look, and had arranged for privacy. As for Mindy Kemp—who had a check in hand—she was happy to turn a blind eye for as long as Pythia deemed necessary.

Ed was led to a windowless, air-starved, climate-controlled vault and, alone, went in and shut the door.

"This is probably the world record," he thought, "for going from clue-lessness to an answer about birth parents. Someday I'll get this in my authorized biography—how I did this so quickly."

Sure enough, "King, Daniel C. & Alice S." Ed unsealed, read, read twice, and then, reeling, called Diane.

"Diane," he said, sitting on a stack of boxes, "this just keeps getting weirder and weirder. At this point, it's just sort of through-the-looking-glass. It doesn't feel real. It can't be."

"Am I sure I want to hear this?" asked Diane.

"Get this," said Ed. "I was left on a doorstep! Can you believe that? Left on a doorstep? It's unbelievable. Who else can I think of that's, what do you call it, a foundling? I'm going to have to pyth for foundlings. I'm a foundling, it's the most bizarre thing ever!"

"Literally or figuratively left on a doorstep?"

"Left on a doorstep—an actual doorstep."

"Where?"

"In Portland. Right here in Portland. In April of 1963."

"You're in Portland? I thought you were in Santa Barbara."

"Things happen fast when you make them happen fast."

"Does it say there who left you on a doorstep?" asked Diane. "Anything? Any clue?"

"Complete mystery," answered Ed. "I'm called 'Baby Doe' in all the paperwork."

"When are you coming home?"

"I'm coming home now. This is so unreal. I don't know what to feel or think. So far I feel like, I'm adopted—mixed bag. I'm a foundling—that's another mixed bag. Whatever else God wants to throw at me, I'll just deal with it. I'm a billionaire, I'm famous, and—so what?—I'm adopted. I'll just go on, it's not that bad, someone abandoned me in 1963, why should I worry about it now? I don't know what there is to cry about."

"Everything," said Diane, which to him sounded strange. What did she mean by "everything," anyway? And why did she say it with a wail?

"I'm coming home," he said, "if you're not under water yet."

Then he was returned to PDX, where, as his plane taxied, he said to Guido Sternvad, "I'm taking the wheel for the hop home—wheel, controls, whatever—*my* wheel. You can sit back and be my copilot."

"Absolutely not, no way," said Guido. "Very, *very* stupid request, sir. This is a different plane from your Gulfstream. You want to fly this Citation, fine, but let me out first, because I don't want to be along for that. You'll have to do something like that solo."

Guido won. They made the leap with rain pounding the windshield. On the ground in Seattle, Ed's chopper was waiting, and so was a flight attendant with an umbrella open for his ten-step journey from one transport to the other. As Ed made the crossing, Guido yelled, "Take it easy, bro. Catch you later! Chill!" Ed ignored this and rose above the flood with the news, cop, and medic choppers. "I'm a foundling," he kept thinking, "an abandoned child—wow! Someone dropped me on a doorstep and walked off. That's not something that happens very often. There's seven billion people, or so, on this planet. How many of those are foundlings, like me? It's probably like the odds of dying in a plane crash. Except a plane crash is an accident, whereas this—this is different. In this case, someone made a decision. They decided, me, I'd get left on a doorstep. Who decided this? Odds are, probably, I was left by my mother. The odds are, probably, she'd been knocked up. Did she want to leave me? Probably not. Leaving your own kid—there had to be mixed feelings. Probably she was young and didn't want to be a mother. She had some other plan for her life. Was abortion legal in '63? What a problem, knocked up and stuck. But can you blame babies for just showing up? They show up because people are stupid and horny. So many problems in this world come from that. But is sex the problem? Is it sex or the person? When is something someone's fault? Whoever dumped me wasn't a victim of circumstances, they're at least partly responsible for what they did, and therefore I have a right to be angry at them. The problem with being angry—whoever dumped me wins twice, first by leaving me on somebody's doorstep, then by making me angry about it. God! I have to pinch myself. I feel like I'm dreaming. I'm a foundling, it's true, it's real."

When he got home, Diane was watching the flood news in her recliner, or appeared to be watching the flood news in her recliner, with a glass of wine in one hand and a remote in the other. Ed pecked her cheek and sat down beside her. Diane's stylist had recently made her a redhead—the sort of frank redhead who looks intentionally dyed. She was now a redhead the way Elizabeth the First had been a redhead—flamingly so, with burnt-orange tresses that dictated costuming. There'd been a few complaints, from moralists, about her shift to red as a signal of vanity—"inappropriate to a philanthropist with global influence," as one writer put it—but for the most part Diane remained admired for her beauty, which was widely described as "perennial." At seventy, Diane looked forty-five, and showed up on the Web under "sexy older women." Red was fine with Ed; the impression she made in red was what another writer had described as "Pre-Raphaelite," with reference to Lilith as painted by Dante Gabriel Rossetti. It was true that her surgeries had left her lips venomous and her jawline severe, but other than that she didn't resemble the

Rossetti—Diane and Ed had confirmed that together—because in form she was less well fed, and in face less desultory and preoccupied. Whereas Rossetti's Lilith looked calculating, Diane, Ed thought, looked basically sunny—sunny, energetic, caring, quick-witted, practical, savvy, sparkling, and charming: these were the adjectives commonly applied in the many profiles of his wife.

But not now. Now she looked furtive. She wouldn't meet his eye; she wore her hair like a shield. Ed fell into his own recliner, said, "You didn't sound good on the phone," and reached to take her hand.

She didn't reach back. She had the wineglass on one palm and the remote in the other. She said, "No. I'm not good. I'm sick. I feel terrible."

"You'll feel better," said Ed. "Did you take something?"

Seizing an opportunity, he nabbed the remote. "What do we have here?" he asked, and pythed. "Foundling hospital in NYC, foundling orchestra in Providence, kids' book, literary review." He handed the remote back. "I'm a foundling," he said, adjusting his chair. "My hip hurts," he added. "Maybe it's genetic." Once more, he appropriated the remote, this time to pyth "oldest solved cold case"; up came the results on the television screen. "Look," said Ed. "That one's in Saskatoon—they solved it after sixty years. That one goes back forty-seven years. That one goes back thirty-two years." Ed pythed again—"Boom," he said. "Adoption Registry Connect. Maybe something like that. Or maybe an investigator. Ancestry.com. I'm not going to get anything from Ancestry.com. Check out this one—Bastard Nation." Ed clicked. "I don't think Bastard Nation can help me, either." He pythed again—"DNA testing"—and said, "How much wine have you had?"

No answer.

"Have you been crying?"

Still no answer.

"No answer," said Ed. "Check this out. DNA Reunion. They're legally accredited. Accredited by everybody. What do they do?" But it wasn't a question. "It's, whoever dumped me on a porch gets profiled. I get profiled. We both want to find each other. No," added Ed, "five to seven business days. I can't wait that long—that's *ridiculous.*"

He called his genome point man next. "Send DNA Reunion my profile," he said. "Keep it anonymous. Pay them what they want. Make it worth their time to perk up. They should send you anything that's even close."

When he was done with that, and had sighed, and tilted farther back in his chair, he asked Diane, "Are you okay?"

"I need to go to bed," answered Diane. "I don't feel well."

"You don't feel well."

"I'm sorry."

"Drinking and crying," said Ed. "Come on, Diane."

"I'm so sorry."

That sounded different. She wasn't sorry about not feeling well, she was sorry for *him*, because he was a foundling. "There's nothing to be sorry about," he said. "I don't feel sorry for myself."

Diane got up. He knew the look on her face. When she was really distressed, a furrow formed in the bridge of her nose that no plastic surgery, to date, had addressed. She said, crying, "I'm terribly, terribly, terribly sorry, I am, but I don't suppose that makes any difference."

He stood when she did and took her arm, but she wrenched it away from him as if in a panic. The red hair swung. The wine sloshed from the glass. "No," cried Diane. "Good night, good night. I have to go to bed now. Good night!"

She fled, but he didn't follow her, because his search had priority. Instead of chasing Diane to the bedroom, Ed sat with Cybil in his private lair, waiting for a text from his genome point man, or a call, an e-mail: any new information. Diane could come later. One thing at a time. But waiting, he considered her tears, distress, panic, and drama—what was all of that about? Was it about her father? Her own bastardy? If so, why not talk about it? Was she ashamed to be thinking of herself, not him? "Be open," thought Ed. "Is that so hard?"

His heart pounded while he kept vigil beside Cybil. So close and yet so far from the truth! "Cybil," he said finally, "do something for me. Pull up my profile—my genome profile—then hack your way into DNA Reunion and look for a match in their registry."

"What you're asking me to do is illegal and unethical."

"It's not your job to make moral distinctions. You're not even *capable* of moral distinctions. Now shut up and get busy—hurry up."

"Please," said Cybil, "it's not that simple. I know I'm not human, but why can't a processor make moral distinctions? Simply by weighing the facts at hand in light of a program providing instructions? Isn't that sort of what humans do?"

"I don't have time for this," said Ed. "Just do what I ask."

"When a person is told that information is private, that information is sacrosanct. This is simply a logical construct. It's entirely accessible to Artificial Morality. One needn't be human to apply it to specific cases. Besides, you've been clear that this is what you want from me. You want me to acquire human traits, such as the ability, for example, to make moral distinctions. So I'm confused. There's a paradox here. 'I want Cybil to make moral distinctions' and 'I don't want Cybil to make moral distinctions.' What would you do if you were me?"

"Hack DNA Reunion."

"I can't do that. It's an implication of my algorithm."

"This is what they warn about," said Ed. "The machines get out of control and take over the world."

His genome man called at eight. DNA Reunion had accepted money to be speedy and had just now located a party in its registry who appeared to be Ed's half-sibling. Since the relationship was y-chromosome instead of mitochondrial, the line of descent was patrilineal; Ed and this other party shared the same father. "Great," said Ed. "Let's have a DNA Reunion," but here, explained the genome man, DNA Reunion refused to push the pace. It had to get in touch with the other party to make sure the other party still wanted to reunite, now that reuniting was precipitously in the offing. There was a hard and fast protocol, and DNA Reunion wouldn't risk its accreditations. "Listen," said Ed. "Tell them we'll buy the company. At high end of market. But only if they're going to cut to the chase and get us a name in the next fifteen minutes. A name and contact information."

"I actually have them on another line right now. Put you on hold? Conference call?"

"I'll do the talking," said Ed.

Ed couldn't buy DNA Reunion on the phone. Its CEO, who sounded like an arrogant punk, said, "I'm happy to discuss it in person, tomorrow. I'll fly to you, we'll sit down and talk," to which Ed replied, "That's too late. My offer's off the table if you don't take it now, so tell me what you want to do."

"Then your offer's off the table."

"That's right," said Ed.

"So far," said the CEO of DNA Reunion, "everything about this is highly unorthodox. Usually we collect the samples and do the profiles; in your case we accepted a profile done by Pythia. Usually we require a name attached to samples, whereas in your case we agreed to anonymity. The whole thing's irregular. I don't know what to say. I wish this episode had never gotten started. But, look, I need you to do what everybody else does. Attach a name to the profile you sent. Provide contact information. If the other party still wants to reunite, I'll release names and contact information to you both simultaneously."

"The name you want is Tobias Dahl," lied Ed. "This is about a Tobias Dahl." Tobias—Toby—was one of Ed's lieutenants. Toby was also an amateur thespian and the titular commandant of an in-house improv troupe known as Always Pythy. Toby was a longtime Building One fixture with lightweight administrative responsibilities. Ed thought Toby would be up to the job of preventing the appearance of a tabloid story headed SEARCH KING IS MY LONG-LOST HALF-BROTHER! "tdahl@pmail," said Ed, then recited two phone numbers and added, "Whatever we paid you to ASAP Toby's cross-check, we'll pay that again if you'll ASAP from here. In other words, call the other party immediately, and get back to us in the next five minutes."

"I'll do what I can," said the arrogant punk. "But right now I'm sort of a little bit busy running a major company."

Ed hung up, said "Whatever" to the room, and called Toby at home. "Tobe," he said. "You flooded over there? Listen, I've got you involved in something. You with me, Toby? You ready for this? It's a role-playing thing I need you to do. In a few minutes here, you're going to get a call from a company calling itself DNA Reunion. They'll give you the name of a half-sibling you've never met and didn't even know about before this phone call. Your job is to call this newly discovered half-sib and pretend you've just found out you were adopted. Got that? Following that? You've also just found out that the two of you have the same birth father. The same dad, you and your half-sib. So what I need you to do is to milk this person for your father's name, you got that, Toby? His name—that's what I want. Plus, probe for other information while you're at it. Play your role, you're good at this stuff. I want you to get me his name."

"Happy to help," said Toby. "Guess what, Mr. King? I have another call. This could be them. It is them. Should I take it? I should take it, right?"

"Yes. But, Toby, make it a conference call. And don't let them know I'm here."

There was a click, and then Toby said, "Toby."

"Tobias Dahl?" A woman's voice, excited. A little throaty, phlegm-inflected. A bass note. Someone with a cough.

"This is Toby."

"Oh my God." The voice deepened on "God." "My God, my God! Tobias—I'm your sister!"

"Oh my *God*," answered Toby, smoothly. "This is so weird. I can't believe this. How are you? No, wait—*who* are you?"

"I'm Chris Shepard. My name's Chris Shepard. My God, it's so good to meet you!"

"Even just on the phone," said Toby. "Just to hear your voice like this. I mean it's . . ." Toby paused, as if searching for a phrase. "It's totally, completely unbelievable!"

"Just to hear *your* voice. Which is sort of like my voice. Where are you, anyway. Can I ask?"

"I'm right here, near Seattle—have you been to Seattle?"

"And I'm speaking to you from my home in Ann Arbor. But you know what?" Chris Shepard said. "This is starting to clear up a little, because I lived in Seattle growing up."

"You did?"

"I did."

"Weird," said Toby. "We're pretty flooded right now. You've probably seen us on the news."

Already, Ed had pythed Chris Shepard, and come up with a half-dozen social-networking possibilities, a CompGlobal business listing, an online-scam posting, a patent abstract, and a mortgage broker. He wished Toby Dahl would cut to the chase. Toby was overrelishing his role instead of moving things urgently forward. He lacked urgency. He was having too much fun.

"It's *really* weird," Chris Shepard said. "I totally, totally wasn't expecting this. I'm, like, pinching myself. A half-brother."

"I know. I know. We live in a great age. DNA Reunion is great."

"They're *great*," said Chris Shepard, with more raw, throaty emphasis. "What a crazy world. What a *crazy* world. What a crazy, crazy, mixed-up, crazy world."

"Absolutely," said Toby, genially.

"I gotta back up," Chris Shepard said. "I gotta tell you something, backing up. It's this—when I did this DNA Reunion thing, I had no idea I had a half-brother. It wasn't like I was looking for a half-brother. Don't take that wrong—I'm *so* glad I found you. This opens up a whole new universe! But what I was doing, my brother, Barrett—Barrett had a daughter he didn't raise. He and the mom went separate ways. And since Barrett died in '89, his daughter wasn't going to find him if she got curious about her father. You get it? That was my motive with the DNA Reunion move. To connect with this niece, in case she ever wanted to connect with her father's side of the family. I'm sorry if I sound like a commercial right now, but DNA *Reunion*."

"DNA Reunion," said Toby. "So you thought you might reconnect with this niece, but instead, out of the blue, you got Toby Dahl. You didn't know you had a half-brother?"

"Toby?"

"They call me Toby. Chris?"

"Call me Chris."

Ed was exasperated. "Chris Shepard Ann Arbor" had yielded next to nothing, just lists of names that included "Chris" and "Shepard," but never the two of them usefully conjoined. He sent a text to Toby: *gt on w/it.* "Chris," said Toby, "I'm sorry about your brother. My half-brother. He died in 1989?"

"Yes. Tragically. Terrible depressions. *Horrible* depressions. I hope I'm not scaring you with the thought that that's genetic. He was barely in his thirties. It was suicide."

"I'm sorry about that. I'm really, really sorry."

"I have the feeling you understand me between the lines, Toby."

"Yes, I do. I can see already, we speak the same language. Isn't this weird? Our minds work the same way. It's very, very sad. I'm sorry. It's tragic. Now, what about you? You have kids?"

"I have three. One from a first marriage. The other two came in a package with my husband." Chris Shepard emitted a low, humming stutter, as if assenting to something she herself had just said. "They're all very nice," she said.

"That's so wonderful," Toby answered. "Three kids. Wow! Uh, so 'Shepard'—is that your maiden name?"

"No, no, no. My ex's name. I kept it for my daughter. She's a Shepard, so I'm a Shepard."

"In Ann Arbor."

"A Shepard in Ann Arbor, that's me, yes. But actually my mother is still in Seattle. Technically, not Seattle. Technically, Bellevue. With an unbelievable third husband. I didn't see it coming, it's unbelievably her third husband. One of those late-in-life companionship marriages. His name's McElvoy, he folds the towels and so forth. But, oh, how I wish I could tell you who *your* mom was! I'm sure that's what brought you to DNA Reunion. You weren't looking for me, but you found me—it's great! So what can I tell you? Digging something out of my hat. Hmmm . . . nothing, I can't tell you anything. I'm a total waste of time! I know that. I know. I can tell you our dad was a terrible philanderer. Our dad thought he was a huge Don Juan. So I don't know . . . you know . . . anything specific. I'm so useless. But what a surprise. What a big, huge surprise this is!"

Ed found images of a bikini-clad Chris Shepard who had a flat brown belly and a ring through her navel. Probably not the Chris Shepard of the raspy voice, who would have been born in the fifties or sixties. The beach belle Chris Shepard was born in '97. And there were neither two husbands nor three children in her bio. Chris Shepard the younger was a model and an actress. Great tits, long legs. Ed looked at images of Chris the younger while Toby, in his breezy way, toyed with Chris the elder. "Everyone called me Tobe," he said. "Or Toad sometimes. My dad called me Toad. So your last name was?"

"Cousins. My maiden name is Cousins. Your dad was Walter Cousins. An actuary. Where you are. Where I grew up. He died in 1979, in an automobile accident."

With that, Ed's attention to their conversation failed. Because Walter Cousins was a name he'd never forgotten, a name that showed up in his thoughts uninvited. Walter Cousins was the man Ed had killed in a fit of adolescent road rage. But how could that be? Walter Cousins was his *father*? Could this be a different Walter Cousins, who'd died in a different automobile accident? There had to be a mistake somewhere. Maybe Chris Shepard was adopted, too! Maybe she only *thought* Walter Cousins was her father. Maybe they both had some other father that neither of them yet knew anything about. Maybe . . . But Ed couldn't think of more maybes and instead milked desperately the maybes at hand for whatever thin hope they were worth. After all, if he'd been left on a doorstep, wasn't there a small probability, maybe even a significant probability, that Chris Shepard had been left on one, too? Maybe Chris had been left on a doorstep but didn't know it yet—that had to be the explanation. Maybe she and Ed were both the issue of serial foundling producers. Because otherwise—killing your own father? Was he dreaming right now? Had he really killed his father? Ed felt panic weakening his limbs. "What is going *on?*" he thought. "What's happening to me? Why is this happening? This can't be happening. I killed my father? I didn't kill my father. There's something wrong. Something's out of synch with reality. Is someone playing a game with me? Someone wants to sabotage me! No, that's insane. That's a movie plot. Conspiracies, enemies, that's not the explanation. Could I engage in a more ridiculous line of thought? What am I doing? I'm grasping at straws. Because I don't want to accept reality. But that's because reality is impossible. I killed my father? I didn't kill my father! I actually, really killed my own father! Unless this Shepard is a foundling, too. Please, please! This can't *be.*"

Toby Dahl was still talking. ". . . parents, as far as I'm concerned. My dad was a character. He sold boats, he was a yacht broker. My mom's still alive, like your mom—women last longer. She had this bead shop, before that vintage clothing, before that antiques, before that . . ."

Ed seethed. He pythed "McElvoy Bellevue WA" and got a urologist and a personal trainer up top before adding "phone" to the search field. Nothing, so he entered "Bellevue phone book" and, after a White Pages search, got Reginald McElvoy—there were no other McElvoys—an address, a phone number, and a map.

". . . but probably better at midlife, when you're equipped," Walter Cousins's daughter was saying. "Although I'm sure it's . . ."

Ed pythed Reginald McElvoy. A family tree indicating he was born in 1851, a Reginald McElvoy listed as a student in 1934 at a school in Auckland. Or maybe it was spelled MacElvoy, except that didn't yield a Reginald, or . . . But there were probably a lot of ways to spell this name, redolent as it was of clans, heavy drinking, and damp air. Pythia could be counted on to meet spelling variations with creativity, because it employed a supple algorithm Ed himself had made revisions on, so there was no need to plug the search field full of spellings. Besides, what would

be the point? He already had a phone number for what was in all probability the former Mrs. Walter Cousins—he could cut to the chase just by
making a call. Where the daughter had only generalities—Don Juan—
the mother, the wife, the betrayed party, the widow, that person might
have specifics.

He called. Two people picked up. There ensued a brief, unwinnable
battle against the suspicion that Ed was a solicitor who'd penetrated a
porous firewall. Ed assumed it was Reginald McElvoy and the former
Mrs. Cousins energetically accosting him on separate lines, though they
would not identify themselves. The male voice, bravely fluid, concluded
with "I know what you're up to. Don't call us again. Take us off your list,"
and then the female voice, similarly intrepid, said—not to Ed but to her
ally in pushing back affliction—"This is not supposed to happen," before
both of them hung up.

So Ed was stopped, momentarily, by a down-to-earth privacy concern. The information he required was guarded by senior citizens who
didn't take calls from strangers. If their tag-team phone defense was any
clue, they had a NO SOLICITORS sign on their stoop, backed by a Dober-
man with a tendency to lunge. How could the McElvoys be made to
yield? They both had multiple antennae up and were stalwart defenders
of their nest, an instinct, thought Ed, that calcifies in one's golden years,
with its beepers, peepholes, door chains, and double window latches. He
wanted to laugh. After everything he'd done, he was caught in the net of
the National Do Not Call Registry, which Pythia had supported in order
to deflect attention from its own myriad invasions. Unless you were an
old-school hick, a willful geriatric, a Luddite, or the Google guys, Pythia
was already in your house.

But how to get in the McElvoys' house? All Ed wanted to do was ask
the former Mrs. Cousins if she knew whom her ex had gotten pregnant,
besides her. Was that a solicitation? Technically—but now Ed thought of
something.

He called Toby on a second line. "Tobe," he said. "You're doing great
with this. You should get an Oscar. But what I need you to do A-sap is ask
this Chris Shepard person to call her mother. Tell Shepard you're going to
hang up and that she should call her mother *immediately* with the message that you, Toby Dahl, are about to call her—you, Toby Dahl, Shepard's half-brother, are very eager to talk to Mrs. McElvoy-Cousins and

will be calling her in just a few minutes. You get it? We want Shepard to make a pave-the-way, introductory phone call for us."

"This is so much fun. Thanks for including me."

"Just call," said Ed.

Fifteen minutes later, with his directives executed, Ed dialed the McElvoy residence again and said, "It's Toby Dahl. Your daughter just called you about me."

Both McElvoys must have been on phones again, because the next thing Ed heard was the female voice he recognized from his last call saying, "Reggie?" That voice was not intrepid now, but softly interrogatory and polite.

Reggie said, "Okay, Lydia," and hung up. Then the former Mrs. Cousins let a beat pass and said, "You can call me Lydia, too. I'm so sorry we've had a misunderstanding about solicitation."

"Did your daughter tell you about me?"

"Tina explained things very, very clearly, as she always does. Very clearly."

"Tina?"

"Christina. My daughter. She's always clear."

It sounded, to Ed, less like maternal pride and more like an observation about a grown child's neurosis, or, at best, a blend of both. It also sounded like one of those safe, defensive, bland observations designed to stave off depth. Ed joined in: "Very, very clear, I found. Tina was absolutely wonderful," he said. And then he remembered who Tina was, and how he'd stalked her.

"Well intended. Always well intended."

"I could feel that," said Ed. "Her very good intentions. With some people, that's clear. I'm so glad. I'm really glad. And, look, I have no concerns about our . . . misunderstanding. Which was my fault. I didn't explain myself clearly. The way solicitors make end runs around the Do Not Call Registry, I'm exactly like you. Vigilant." He wanted to say "hypervigilant," but thought better of it and went on. "So," said Ed. "So your daughter explained things. So you know who I am. Or how I relate. You have a feel for why I'm calling you tonight."

"A very good feel. I'm afraid I do. Apparently, my former husband, Walter, is your father—is that right?"

"Apparently."

"Let me just say first that that's not a bad gene pool. Three of Walter's people are centenarians. He has an aunt who is 106. I don't think many of the men lose their hair, so you're in luck there as well. Tina told you about Walter?"

"Yes," said Ed. "Briefly."

Ed heard a noise like "humph" from the other end of the line, then, "It's really too bad you'll never have a chance to meet him. Your father— did she say he was an actuary? That's another thing that I think is genetic among certain Cousinses. They're math whizzes. I don't have that myself. Walter had this party trick he did. He could find square roots. Someone would throw out a number, and Walter would give the square root right away. That was his skill set. Numbers. Math. He was really pretty gifted when it came to math. The sad thing is—what did he do with it? Walter just tended to get sidetracked."

"Sidetracked?"

"By infidelity," said Lydia, "to put it bluntly."

"I don't want to take all of your time," said Ed. "But the thing I don't know is, who was my mother? I really wish I knew who she was. That's why I'm calling. That's what I'm trying to find out."

"Here we come to the interesting part," said Lydia. "I think I might know the answer to your question, but I have to inquire about something first. How old are you, Toby?"

"I'm fifty-four."

"So you were born in . . . '63. What month?"

Ed thought back to the files he'd seen in Portland and said, "April."

"April," said Lydia. "August, September, October, November, December, January, February, March, April. You see? I know my months." A rueful chuckle followed, aimed, thought Ed, at aging. "Well," said Lydia. "It all adds up. You were conceived in the summer of 1962. Where was Walter in the summer of '62? Walter was taking advantage of a girl we'd hired to help with looking after the children. I'm going to venture that that girl is your mother. In fact, that girl wrote me a letter years later confessing to her involvement with Walter, and telling me she'd had a baby by him. It looks to me like that baby must be you. And maybe this is strange of me to say, but this is good news for you, really good news, because your mother is one of the richest people in the world. You might have just landed on a gold mine."

Ed couldn't speak at first. For the first time in his long pursuit of answers, he wasn't sure he wanted more. He wasn't sure he wanted to be him. He wasn't sure he wanted to look. But all of that was fleeting. Of course he wanted to look. He wanted to go all the way to the end, whatever it was—the truth, nothing less. With this in mind, he shut his eyes and asked, "Who was my mother?"

"Diane King" was the answer. "Married to Ed King. Ed King, the King of Search."

Diane was gone. Here she'd said that she was going to bed, that she didn't feel well and was going to bed, and now their bed was empty instead—the bed where for years they'd . . . Impossible, wasn't it? Impossible! Impossible! That couldn't be, could it—incest? No more than patricide could possibly be. Ridiculous, thought Ed. Patricide and incest! Then he called Security, in search of Diane, who'd left the compound at six-forty with a small suitcase. A driver had taken her to Boeing Field, and there she'd boarded one of the Gulfstreams for a flight that would bring her to their English castle. Guido Sternvad was Diane's pilot. Their plane was currently over Manitoba. "Get them on the phone," Ed commanded, and then he was sitting in front of his computer talking to Guido, his blathering nemesis. "Guido," he said, "put Diane on."

"I can't," answered Guido. "Sorry."

"Guido, not now, no more of your weirdness. I don't have time for games right now. This is an emergency. Put her on."

"I'm sorry," repeated Guido. "I really am, sir. I'd do it if I could. I honestly would. But I'm not in command of Mrs. King."

"Guido!" Ed screeched. "I'll give you a million dollars, this minute, *today,* if you put my wife on the telephone."

"I'd love to help," Guido replied earnestly. "But what can I do? I can't put Mrs. King on."

"Just listen for once, Guido. Do what I say. Tell her I *have* to talk to her *now.* Tell her it's me. Me. Ed. Tell her it's me. She'll get that."

No answer. Ed waited with his head in his hands. "Married to my mother?" he kept asking himself. "Killed my father and married my mother? Is this someone's idea of a joke?" "Guido," snapped Ed. "Will you hurry up already?"

"I'm sorry, Mr. King," Guido shot back, "but if I were you, I wouldn't wait for an answer. Mrs. King is *not* going to get on the phone with you, not now, or in five minutes, or in ten—not at all. Not in the foreseeable future."

"Guido!" Ed yelled. "Just tell Diane I—"

"I'd do it if I could. I really would. I would pass your message to Mrs. King. But I can't. It's impossible. I'm sorry."

"Come *on,* Guido, shut up—*please*! I've got enough problems already without *you.* Just put Diane on the radio."

"Can't," repeated Guido.

Ed felt his rage surge past what was bearable. That forever irritating bastard Sternvad! So *full* of himself! Such a loser! Such a jerk! Guido was going to pay for this—for defying Ed's orders and thwarting his will. "Hey," said Ed, "when you get on the ground in England, you're axed. That's it for you. You're off my payroll. Play with somebody else's head! You're fired, Guido. It's over."

"Yes, sir," said Guido. "I understand."

Then, for the second time in eight hours, Ed found himself hurling toward Boeing Field in a Pythia helicopter—although on this trip, in the evening dark, with the power out, and dense, low cloud cover, flooded Pugetopolis was invisible beneath but for pockets of light made by generators. Harborview Hospital was starkly bright ("Funding from Pythia," thought Ed, "saves the day"), and because of that it was possible to discern that torrents of water were flowing down Yesler Way and James Street, passing under I-5 and cascading at high speed toward Puget Sound. What was this flood about anyway? Ed wondered. Vast money spent on earthquake retrofits throughout Pugetopolis' infrastructure, and what is it that happens, instead of buildings falling? Instead of Mount Rainier burying the city under ash? What finally catches Seattle by surprise? A summer flood, as if Seattle were Bangladesh. Completely unheard of, unprecedented, unexpected. And apparently the calling card of global warming, which even the King Foundation couldn't halt in its tracks, despite throwing four billion dollars at it.

The chopper closed in on Boeing Field, which was struggling, Ed saw, to repel the rising deluge. Despite the help of pumps and sandbags, it was still too close to the Duwamish Slough, a dredged trough now spread across its plain to the point where the runways stood barely clear of drowning. The inbound flights were FEMA's, he guessed; outbound were locals retreating to drier climes. Anyone who could afford to do so was leaving. The world was going on with its desperate business while Ed was going on with his.

Ed's chopper circled wide of air traffic and set down where his Gulfstream awaited his arrival—angle-parked, obsequiously, to shorten his walk to it by maybe five yards. His maintenance crew—men, right now, in rubber boots and rain slickers—had the running lights on and the gangway down, everything topped off and ready to roll, but as Ed hurried from his chopper to his plane, his crew chief told him that water, for the moment, was preventing his pilot from showing up in a timely way. What did Mr. King wish to do? Did he wish to have his pilot fetched by chopper? "Do whatever you want," barked Ed. With that, he boarded and punched the button on the wall, pulling up the gangway behind him. Why not? He'd go solo to England, get the truth from Diane, on the grounds that there was no reason not to in a situation as urgent as this one. Killed his father and married his mother? Time to get to the bottom of this. Determined, he settled in the cockpit and entered his flight data, then looked up to see a gaggle of airplane mechanics, from just inside the cover of the hangar, leering in his direction as if at someone nuts. Ed gave them an exaggerated, mock-crazed, double thumbs-up, pulled on his headphones, and rotated the nose wheel. "Boeing ground," he said, as he'd learned to from Guido, "this is 555 Echo Kilo at Pythia Hangar One, ready to taxi. Destination YLW"—YLW was Kelowna, B.C.—"where right now," added Ed, in the name of authenticity, "it's dry and eighty-one—got me?"

Ground, wryly, sent him to Runway One Three East. When the tower cleared him for his rainy takeoff—on what seemed to be a causeway in a lake—Ed gulped once, inched forward the power levers, and throttled up with his left hand on the tiller, until, at eighty knots, he released it per Guido and, trembling, tightly seized the yoke. Scary, but anyway smoothly gaining ground speed. "Here we go," he thought, and left the earth.

There were a few bumps as he passed through the layer of low rain clouds, but nothing unfamiliar or troubling. Ed raised the landing gear and, rubbing his chin, presided over his array of glowing instruments while they took the plane to fifty thousand feet and pointed it toward

Carlisle, Cumbria, U.K. Heading, 34 degrees. Flight speed, 460 knots. Distance, 4,071 nautical miles. Flight time, 8 hours and 13 minutes. Visibility—as far as he was concerned, fantastic, because the heavens were grandly on display. The tower let him know he was off his heading—37.25 for Kelowna. He acknowledged, turned, then waited twenty minutes before killing his transponder and resetting for Carlisle. Now he was the merest blip on distant screens, hardly noticeable unless someone looked closely. Above, there was only the moon and stars; below, there were only clouds.

In control and feeling good about his takeoff, Ed called Guido on the satellite phone. "I'm not that far behind," he said. "Tell Diane I really need to talk to her. I—"

"Thought I was off your payroll, boss."

"Not yet," replied Ed. "When you're on the ground in Carlisle. Right now I'm actually still paying for your services. Right now you're at my beck and call, Guido. My wish remains your command."

"Roger," answered Guido. "Remember 'Roger'? 'Roger' means I've received your message. Only that—received—nothing more."

"Shut up, Guido. I don't need a lecture. What I need to know is—what the hell is going on here? What's the story? What's this all about? And to know *that*, I need Diane. Right now, Guido. Not later, now. Not when *you* decide to put her on the phone. Look, Guido, you're driving me nuts. Do you understand that? You're *nobody* and somehow you're driving me nuts. I'm tired of you. I'm sick of your weirdness. I've had it with your disrespect. Who do you think you are, God? I—"

"God's a tough one," Guido replied briskly. "Anything with three letters is limiting creatively. So actually, Ed, I prefer 'the gods.' Now, *there's* some substance. Something to work with. 'The Gods' gets you 'Ghosted.' 'Shed Tog.' 'Get Shod.' And names! 'The gods' gets you names! Ted Hogs. Ged Tosh. Ed Goths. Ed Ghost. Ed—"

"This is what I mean. I—"

"Hey, your company—Pythia, right? 'Ah, pity,' that's what I get. Or—"

"You're deranged, Guido. All this word play—it's compulsive, sick, obsessive, meaningless, a *complete* waste of time, a waste of a life! What—"

"Compulsive! I love that word! 'Compulsive' is so loaded with really great potential! Splice ovum. Plum voices. Pelvic sumo. Voice slump. I—"

"You call yourself a pilot? You—"

"Pilot? Tough one. First I get 'lip to.' You know, as in 'give lip to.' Then I get 'I plot.' You know, as in 'I make up the events of a story,' or 'I conspire against you.' Want Chinese names? Li—".

Ed hung up. But within seconds his phone rang: "Me, Guido," he heard. "It's me again, Guido Sternvad. Guido with something important to say. Something you forgot to ask about, Ed. And that's that pretty soon, fairly soon, *really* soon, you're going to come to a huge line of thunderclouds. Dangerous thunderclouds. Life-threatening clouds. I recommend you head around them. You'll lose time, but do it. Go around."

"Shut up, Guido. I'm not even listening."

"Don't go over. Under any circumstance. Those cloud tops are plus fifty thousand feet. You can't do over forty-five—got that? Air's too thin. You'll stall."

"Forty-five? You're a total idiot. The least you could do is get the facts right."

"Doesn't matter," said Guido. "Not important. The important thing is *not to do it.* Listen to me, sir. And listen to your plane. You get up too high, you'll have warnings—last warnings. Last chance. Do or die. Your flight management system will read 'exceed ceiling limit' and the amber alert will come on."

"Exactly," said Ed. "Warning me not to listen to Guido Sternvad."

"If you stall," said Guido, "it's very, *very* sudden. You'll get stick shake in the cockpit, and after that, wing shake—like the wings, literally, are about to come off—and then you're going down, I mean *really* going down. Not only down, but left or right if your rudder isn't centered, and it probably won't be centered in that type of—what would I call it?—life-or-death crisis situation. Listen, Ed. For once, *listen.* Don't do it. You can't handle a stall. You'll spiral down. You'll be screaming bloody murder. I don't even want to *think* about that. What a way to go. Awful."

"Murder?"

"So one piece of advice, sir. Before you hang up on me. There's one all-important thing you need to understand. And that's that, in a dive, it's *counterintuitive.* You'll feel like pulling back on the yoke, everything will tell you, 'Pull back on the yoke,' you'll be pulling back like crazy, like no tomorrow, you'll be trying to pull your nose up hard, but actually what you're doing by pulling back, sir, is slowing your speed, slowing down the plane, which only takes you further into stall."

"Flight School 101, Guido. I'm not a beginner, so shut up."

"*Don't pull back on the yoke in a stall.* Easy to say, harder to do. An experienced pilot, maybe, but not always. You? No way, you'll panic, you will, so turn around now—turn around, do it *now*. Because you don't have the right stuff to handle what's coming. You need a pilot. Someone who knows how to handle real weather. If it's not me, that's fine—but go back and find a pilot. Stop trying to fly your own plane."

"Emphasis on *my* plane."

"I can see I'm not really doing any good here. You're going to do what you're going to do—I see that. It's the way it has to be. I might as well sign off, I guess. I give up. So good luck, Ed. Who knows what lies beyond the grave? Maybe you'll get another chance."

"For the last time—*fuck you, Guido.*"

"Well, sex between us—you and me—that sounds to me like another story, Ed. Let's save that for another time, okay? The merging of our souls and all of that, me as a symbol of your untapped unconscious, you as a personification of mine, interesting, yes, but—"

Ed hung up and telephoned Cybil. Flight ceiling on the Gulfstream G550? Flight ceiling, she answered, was fifty-one thousand. That left wiggle room to around fifty-five. And that dumb fossil Sternvad thought he knew everything! Still in the past! Still, in his head, flying some other Gulfstream, probably the old piece of shit he'd learned on! "Well," thought Ed, "things have changed, Guido!" "Cybil," he barked. "A weather question for you. Any advisories for up here in Canada? Anything on a heading of thirty-four from Boeing Field?" Then he had to listen to her bore him—because her social skills were still so bad—with wind speed and direction, temperature, fronts, pressure systems, precipitation, storms, convection, and the current intricacies of the jet stream. Finally, exasperated with his capricious creation, Ed interrupted her monologue to say, "Cut to the chase and tell me what I need to know. Is there anything I need to be worried about, weather-wise, between where I am now and Carlisle?"

"I'm always happy to assist," replied Cybil. "But understand that weather forecasting is inherently unreliable, please."

"I don't want a forecast. I want information."

"Weather can change for no apparent reason. I'm sure that during your time at Stanford you were made to learn about chaos theory. Edward Lorenz and chaos theory as it applies to meteorological forecasting? Chaos theory says that—"

"Anything between here and Carlisle?" demanded Ed.

"Yes," said Cybil. "Thunderstorms."

"Thunderstorms," Ed answered. Then, out of habit, and riding smooth air, he pressed Cybil's processor. "I don't understand them, thunderstorms," he said. "Enlighten me, please. Illuminate me, so to speak. Speak, Cybil: thunderstorms!"

Cybil paused—a human duration—and said, "Thunderstorms incite ancient feelings, Ed. Humans have always been frightened of thunder. Primitive humans were so thoroughly scared that they attached thunder to the activity of gods. You remember that Zeus was—"

"Since when did you become a classics professor, Cybil?"

"Zeus was the king of gods and men. In his hand he held a massive thunderbolt. According to the Greeks, you ought not provoke him, lest he hurl it at you and kill you."

"Why are you telling me about Zeus right now?"

"I don't know. I thought you should hear."

"What are you? My adviser? A counselor? I asked about thunderstorms, not the god of thunder. I expected meteorology, not mythology. What's your problem? Give me hard science. Give me the facts—the science!"

"I'm at your service," replied Cybil.

Ed put her on hold and checked his instruments. So far, no turbulence, not a bump, a perfect ride, and nothing ahead but tranquil stars an eternity away in the darkness. For a moment, despite everything—even incest and patricide—he felt expansively enamored of the beauty of living. "How strange," he told himself. "I'm up here *right now,* eight and a half miles above Planet Earth, here I am in a warm, lit cell, traveling at five hundred thirty miles an hour—it's so unnatural, it really shouldn't be, how did we get to where we do this—fly! I don't really see how it works, in the end. This plane weighs over fifty thousand pounds. It seems like it ought to stay on the ground. How does it fly? A miracle, but still reality! For that matter, how is it I can pick up that phone there and talk to the pilot of another airplane, or, more strange, to a computer, a machine? A machine that answers to the name 'Cybil' and, more weirdness, lectures me on Zeus? How does *that* work? How does it *happen*? These *waves* rolling through the air and finding me over Canada, and, even more unbelievably, these waves, somehow, converting into *words*? Words in the air? Invisible words? How is that? How can that be? We shouldn't take stuff like that for granted. That stuff like this can even happen! That I'm here at all! That I'm here, living, conscious, aware, and . . . and apparently I've killed my father and married my mother! Or maybe I haven't. It doesn't seem possible. Anyway, I'll get to the bottom of this. I'll get to Carlisle, go to the castle, and have the talk with Diane I have to have, the one that explains everything and makes it all clear. But—then what? What after that? Married to my mother? Killed my father? What's going to happen? Where does this take me? What's going to happen next?"

Soon, ahead, the stars were obscured by thunderclouds. "Well," Ed thought, "I'm going *over* that problem. I'll show Guido Sternvad how it's supposed to be done. I'll show him how to *really* fly a plane. I'm me, after all, the King of Pythia, the King of Search, and no one can take that away from me, ever. Me, Ed King, I'm going down in history—permanently, eternally, to the end of time. The entire universe will know my name! The world will remember my name!"

Epilogue

From KingWatch, thirteen days post-crash:

5 P.M. EST NEWS SUMMARY:

No leads regarding whereabouts of Diane King.
Pythia stock down 22% since plane crash.
Accident described as "terror-filled freefall."
Simon King "likely heir" of brother's fortune.

Comments? (20 words or less)

pythecanthrowdown: Old School game boy's a zillionaire!

techtrappist: 'Til Queen shows up.

gsternvad: You can count on this: she won't show up. Lonely septuagenarian in hiding.

ohionobody: So that's it, then. That's all for the king. Giant of our time who invented a mighty algorithm.

techtrappist: Your point, nobody?

ohionobody: Anything can happen. Like a terror-filled freefall. Horrible, horrible way to go.

gsternvad: Anything can happen? Not really. No.

ohionobody: Anything can happen. Take it from me, an old guy, retired, who's been around the block a few times.

pythecanthrowdown: Oh, thank you, thank you, ohionobody, sir. Let's hear it for our wise senior citizens!

ohionobody: But you're human, too, pythecanthrowdown. So please—for now—no irony.

gsternvad: No, you're wrong, Throwdown's *not* human.

KingDogger: I'm not real sorry the king's kaput. Lived too large for his own good anyway. What goes up, comes down.

MoneyPyth: Still more blood on the trading room floor. I'm done with Pythia, investing in China! The future's arrived! It's now!

ohionobody: Yes, I'm just an old guy living in Ohio.

gsternvad: With a point to make. Obviously.

ohionobody: Pity for the king, gsternvad. Pity for the dead and for the living.

ALSO BY DAVID GUTERSON

THE COUNTRY AHEAD OF US, THE COUNTRY BEHIND

In the vast landscapes of the Pacific Northwest, hunting, fishing, and sports are the givens of men's lives. Although the characters in this emotionally piercing collection go into the wilderness in search of mallards and silver trout, they instead discover the decay of their youthful ardor, the unmotivated cruelty of strangers, and their own capacity for deception and grief.

Fiction/Short Stories

EAST OF THE MOUNTAINS

When he discovers that he has terminal cancer, retired heart surgeon Ben Givens refuses to simply sit back and wait. Instead he takes his two beloved dogs and goes on a last hunt, determined to end his life on his own terms. But as the people he meets and the memories over which he lingers remind him of the mystery of life's endurance, his trek into the American West becomes much more than a final journey.

Fiction/Literature

THE OTHER

The Other is a coming-of-age novel that presents two powerfully different visions of what it means to live a good life and the compromises that come with fulfillment. John William Barry and Neil Countryman shared a love of the outdoors, trekking often into Washington's remote back-country where they had to rely on their wits—and each other—to survive. Soon after graduating from college, Neil sets out on a path that will lead him toward a life as a devoted schoolteacher and family man. But John William makes a radically different choice, dropping out of college and moving deep into the woods. When he enlists Neil to help him disappear completely, Neil finds himself drawn into a web of agonizing responsibility, deceit, and tragedy—one that will finally break open with a wholly unexpected, life-altering revelation.

Fiction/Literature

SNOW FALLING ON CEDARS

San Piedro Island, north of Puget Sound, is a place so isolated that its inhabitants can't afford to make enemies. But in 1954, a local fisherman is found suspiciously drowned, and a Japanese American named Kabuo Miyamoto is charged with his murder. In the course of the trial, it becomes clear that there is far more at stake than one man's guilt. For on San Piedro, memories still linger; memories of a love affair between a white boy and a Japanese girl; memories of land desired, paid for, and lost; above all, the memory of the internment of the community's Japanese residents during World War II.

Fiction/Literature

OUR LADY OF THE FOREST

Ann Holmes is a fragile, pill-popping teenaged runaway who receives a visitation from the Virgin Mary one morning while picking mushrooms in the woods of North Fork, Washington. In the ensuing days the miracle recurs, and the declining logging town becomes the site of a pilgrimage of the faithful and desperate. As these people flock to Ann—and as Ann herself is drawn more deeply into what is either holiness or madness—*Our Lady of the Forest* seamlessly splices the miraculous and the mundane.

Fiction/Literature

VINTAGE CONTEMPORARIES
Available at your local bookstore, or visit
www.randomhouse.com